Clarity

Loretta Lost

ISBN-13: 978-1505560657
ISBN-10: 1505560659

Table of Contents

More important than the quest for certainty is the quest for clarity.

– Francois Gautier

Prologue

Clutching the wall for support, I slide down to collapse gracelessly on the stairs. *What's wrong with me?* I stare forward into the darkness that is my world, gripping the edge of the cold metal step beneath me. I am having trouble breathing. My chest is heaving with short, abrupt gasps; I think I might be crying, but there are no tears staining my cheeks. I have no idea where I am. The dark has never frightened me, but now, staring into the infinite expanse of nothingness... I can't help thinking about death. My mother's death. My own death. Placing a hand on my chest, I try to mentally force my pounding heart to settle down.

Breathe in. Breathe out. Come on, Helen. You're tough.

They all said it would take time. They said that I should give myself time to grieve and get past this. But as usual, I rushed in headfirst, thinking that I was stronger than everyone. I conquer such huge obstacles on a daily basis. What's one more? Of course, I was wrong. I'm always wrong, lately.

"Miss, are you okay?" asks a gentle male voice.

I lift my head at the sound, surprised that I hadn't heard this man approach. He sounds young and innocent—there is genuine concern in his tone. Of course, my tears would choose now to start spilling over. I completely lose all grip on my resolve as my body begins to shake with sobs. I gasp and clutch my knees, trying to fight against my misery.

Just breathe in. Breathe out. You can handle this. You can handle anything.

I feel a large, warm hand resting on my shoulder, and it's instantly comforting. Why is this stranger being so kind to me? It only makes me cry harder. I have been holding on for so long, and keeping this all inside. I just need to be weak for one moment. Just one moment. There is a secret organ gathering pain like a balloon within my chest, and it has been threatening to explode for the longest time. I just need a little cry to let some of the pressure out, to deflate it and keep it from destroying my insides with a near-nuclear detonation.

"What's wrong?" the young man asks. "Can I help you? Anything. Anything at all."

"I'm just..." My voice sounds pitiful and wretched. I take a deep breath and try to speak again. "I don't know where I am."

"You're blind?" he asks me.

I bite my lip and nod. I'm ashamed of the fact, and I generally try to navigate without using the collapsible white cane that rests tucked away within my backpack. It feels like a badge of disgrace, announcing my disability to the world. I don't like being treated differently. I don't like being considered abnormal.

"What's wrong?" he prods. "You look like someone died."

I try to resist, but another sob shakes my body. I am crying again. Just like that; just so easily. I don't have time to mentally insult myself, or try to give myself a pep talk to be strong before I feel the stranger's arms wrap around me.

"Shh," he says, holding me against his chest. "You're okay."

I dissolve against him, completely vulnerable and hopeless. I am not usually this needy, but in this moment, I need to fall apart. I need to accept how brokenhearted I am before I can even try to mend. Just one moment. All I need is this one moment, and I can get back to being me.

That's enough, Helen, says my ever-cautious inner voice. *Get it together. Stop. Stop now. Breathe!*

"Can I help you, honey?" he asks me again. "Anything I can do. Just say the word."

"I don't know where I am," I say again, in

a small voice.

"This is the engineering department," he tells me. "Are you an engineer?"

I release a burst of derisive laughter, and it cuts through my tears. "Do I look like an engineer? Gosh. I'm more lost than I thought."

He chuckles. "Let me help you," he says softly, as he caresses my hand in a soothing manner. He slips my backpack off my shoulders, as if taking the entire weight of the world away from me. "C'mon! I'll guide you wherever you need to go. You need to hold onto my elbow, right? Is that how it works?"

"Yes," I say, inspired by his infectious enthusiasm. "Thanks. My name is Helen, by the way."

"Helen," he repeats, testing it on his tongue. "Helen. What a pretty name. It suits you. You're such a pretty girl."

I smile and wipe my sleeve across my face to remove the moisture. "You're just trying to make me feel better," I accuse as I allow him to help me to my feet.

"Is it working?" he asks.

"Maybe a little," I answer. I'm lying; it's not working. But I do appreciate his efforts. I feel him take my hand and wrap it around his elbow. I am surprised by the size of the bicep that I am grasping. "Do all engineers hit the gym as much as you do?" I ask.

"Only the ones on a football scholarship," he says proudly.

I force another smile. "That's impressive. I'm a just a psychology major."

"Psych? Nice. Do you plan on being a doctor or something?" he asks.

"No. I'm going to be a writer," I tell him. "I just like to understand people. For some reason, I have a class in this building—but I never come here, so I'm not that familiar with the layout."

"It's kind of tricky," he tells me. "Even people with perfect eyesight get lost in this labyrinth. Here, I think I know where the psych class is. Let me take you there."

"Thanks," I tell him faintly. I grip the man's solid upper arm as he guides me off the stairs and through a pair of double doors. He walks at a comfortable pace as he leads me through the halls. Not so brisk that I have to powerwalk to keep up, and not so slow that I feel like a stupid child. I had been a little more than just physically lost, so it is reassuring to feel the strength and warmth radiating through the sleeve of his shirt.

My fingers tighten around his elbow as we make some twists and turns through the building. I am so relieved to be with a competent guide; as prideful as I can be, it does make things easier to be able to rely on someone.

After a few minutes of walking, the boy finally comes to a stop. "Here we are," he says.

I make a face in puzzlement. "I—I don't hear anything. It's so quiet. Are you sure we're in the right place?"

"Sure. It's just through this door."

Something in his voice gives me chills. My body shudders. I hear the door being unlocked, and there is only a deathly silence on the other side. *Run,* my inner voice tells me. *Run!* But it's too late.

Just as I'm turning away, a hand clamps over my mouth. I lift both of my hands to try to pry it off, but another hand fiercely clinches around my waist. The boy roughly drags me into the room. I try to scream, and violently push away with my legs, but I am held fast.

"Be quiet," he whispers. "No screaming, or I'll rip your tongue out. I'm going to release you, but keep your mouth shut, okay?"

I nod. The silence in the room is deafening. My skin is prickled by rising goose bumps, and my heart furiously pumps hot blood through my body. As soon as his hands release me, I swivel and smash my fist into his face. He roars in pain, and I fling my foot outward, letting my heel connect with his knee. Feeling his leg beginning to buckle and crumple, I quickly duck away from him and lunge for the door. Grasping the handle, I pull the door halfway open before I feel it being slammed shut. The boy grabs a fistful of my hair at the back of my head and uses it to smash my face against the door. I cry out at the sharp pain in my nose, and my lip splits open against my teeth. I taste a bitter, metallic liquid against my tongue. My head spins and I grow dizzy. I feel my body being hauled away from the door and thrown to the ground amid boxes and other debris. I struggle to raise myself onto my elbows to fight against my assailant, but there is suddenly a heavy, crushing weight on top of me.

A large hand clamps around my neck and squeezes. He is suffocating me.

"I can make you feel better, Helen," he says in a tender voice. "Shhh. Just relax. Relax and let me take care of you." I feel his hand reaching down to slip under my skirt. "Relax and spread your legs."

"Are you insane?" I hiss, clawing at the hand he's holding over my throat. He's too strong. Tears flood my eyes once again. "I thought you were nice."

"I guess you missed one too many psychology classes, huh?" he says with a laugh. He leans down and puts his lips very close to my ear. "Just don't worry, sweet thing. You can't see me, so I'm not even really here. Out of sight, out of mind."

"You monster!" I scream hoarsely, struggling against him. "How could you..."

He removes his hand from my neck and hits me across the face. My already bloody lip is swollen and pulsating. I am afraid for my life. Maybe I should stop fighting and let him do whatever he intends to do? My sister and father need me, and I can't die. It would destroy them. They've lost too much already. I can't seem to stop sobbing. I think of my mother. Maybe I should fight with the two-hundred-pound football player, and hope that he kills me so that I can be with her? My mind is a mess. I don't know what to do. I don't know where I am. I don't know if I'm going to survive this.

"Think about calm ocean breezes," the man on top of me says in a soothing voice. "Shhh. My sweet Helen. Think about soft waves of the ocean. Shhh. That's all we are. Soft waves of the ocean."

His sadistic banter chills me to the bone. Why is this happening to me? Why is this happening to me *now?* Why, at my lowest moment, has the universe found a way to drag me down even further—into an even deeper pit of despair? Is this some kind of sick joke? I must be dreaming. This can't really be happening.

But his thumb and forefinger continue to press down painfully on either side of my windpipe. I gasp for breath as he steals the life away from me. This is very real.

"Helen," he coos in a singsong voice as he moves on top of my body. "Helen, Helen, Helen. Such a pretty name, for such a pretty girl. My sweet, sweet Helen. The things I'm going to do to you."

I am not sure what this man looks like, but I imagine that if I could see him, I would be staring up into the face of pure evil. Perhaps I should be thankful that I will never have to behold something so hideous. *If I survive this*, I inwardly promise myself, *I will have to get stronger, somehow. I can never let something like this happen to me again.*

Chapter One

Three years later...

Something does not sound right.

My fingers pause, hovering above the keyboard of my braille typewriter. There is a suspicious vibration in the air this morning, like the incessant whirr of electricity. People always used to be surprised when I asked them to turn off the lights, considering that I am incapable of seeing even the faintest glow—but for me, it was deafening. The city was full of noisy lights that were powerless to brighten my shadow-soaked world, constantly teasing me with their insect-like buzzing. One of the main reasons I moved out here was for the peace and quiet; but at this moment, it is neither peaceful nor quiet. That bugs me.

I hear the sound of footsteps crunching in

the snow, almost a mile away.

Footsteps are not uncommon around here, but they do not usually belong to people. I prefer it that way; I have surrounded myself with acres of harmless, innocent forest, so that my only neighbors are squirrels and birds. They are far more polite than human neighbors, and never dare to bother me—not even to borrow condiments. The trees, of course, have no voices. Unlike in Narnia, they don't whisper my secrets to each other, and mock me when my back is turned. They have been kind, loyal friends—quite dissimilar to most of the people I have known. Anyone who has had the good fortune of spending time with the infinite silence of the trees, will acknowledge their wisdom.

Two distinct voices are approaching my residence.

This is strange and unsettling; there is a flutter of fear in my gut. The only voices that ever come all the way out here belong to the mailman, or occasionally, the repairman from town. I am not expecting any visitors. When I hid myself away in the wilderness all those years ago, I changed my name and did not tell my family or friends my address. I knew they would have come looking for me, not believing that I could manage on my own. They would have continued coddling me, and fussing over me like I was an invalid, and ultimately driven me insane. I have been happy with my solitude. I thought I had escaped the world of prying, controlling, and frustrating people, but these two voices sound self-important and righteous. They sound like the types to callously invade my serenity and toss my life back into chaos.

I am simply not in the mood for this. Pushing my typewriter aside, I rise to my feet and begin pacing in my small cabin. On the carpet, my own light footsteps are soundless and catlike. However, my ears are filled with the cacophony of men's boots smashing the thin layer of ice above the snow, again and again, in an offensive rhythm. I wish they would turn away and go back to their own homes! I wish they would magically turn into tiny chipmunks, scurrying along on their business. I like chipmunks. From what I understand, they are quite adorable. As the male voices approach, I can begin to make out their words—they already sound rude and detestable, and not nearly as charming as chattering chipmunks.

"I swear, Liam. If you made me come all the way out into the godforsaken boonies for nothing, I'm going to be pissed. I could have been relaxing at home with my girl this weekend."

"Come on, Owen! You wanted a special candidate, and she's the one. I'm sure of it."

"But what if she doesn't agree to join the study?" asked the one called Owen.

"Why wouldn't she agree?" countered the

man called Liam. "There are virtually zero health risks! Almost every blind person we've approached has been excited at the idea of being able to see again. There were a few hold-outs... but they were nutcases."

"Yeah, some of these patients with LCA can be real wackos," Owen said. "Being blind messes with their heads. Just don't get your hopes up."

My eyebrows knit together in a deep frown as I eavesdrop on this conversation. Doctors. Why did it have to be doctors? Could it not have been Jehovah's Witnesses or bible salesmen coming to knock on my door instead? Could it not have been girl scouts peddling cookies, or some disaster relief fund requesting donations? Anyone but doctors! Are there any people on the planet as two-faced as doctors? They pretend to care about you, acting sweet and condescending, and as soon as your back is turned, they reveal that they are only self-interested. I haven't had such a scowl on my face in a long time, and my muscles are already beginning to hurt. How did they find me? My name no longer matches the one on my records. LCA, or Leber's congenital amaurosis, is the disease I was born with, and it bothers me that these nosy physicians know about me and my medical history.

A knock finally sounds at the door. "Hello! I'm looking for Helen. Miss Helen

Winters?"

I am furious. That is *not* my name anymore. I consider remaining quiet and pretending that I am not home, but they could come back later. It might be better to send them away with a definitive negative response to whatever offensive query they have for me. They probably just want to poke around inside my eyes and use me as a guinea pig. My father worked for pharmaceutical companies for years, and I know all about the unpleasant nature of such experiments. I knew a few kids with my disease when I was younger. Many of their parents put them through dozens of stressful surgeries and failed research trials, to no avail. I was lucky that my parents saved me from all the heartache of hoping and being disappointed.

"Miss Winters?" asks the man again. "Are you home? Sorry to intrude on you like this, unannounced. My name is Dr. Liam Larson, and this is my partner Dr. Owen Philips. We are currently leading a team conducting some clinical trials with groundbreaking gene therapy…"

"Gene therapy?" I ask in surprise. I had not been planning to speak, but they caught me off-guard. My voice sounds strange and awkward; I have not used it in so long. I am a bit embarrassed that my throat feels like a rusty instrument.

"Yes. We're looking for candidates

14

between the ages of 23-26 to test a modification to an existing drug that has shown great promise. If you agree to join this study, there's a chance that we might be able to give you the ability to see. Would you like to open the door and let us tell you more about our research?"

My mind has begun racing as I stand frozen and rooted to the spot. I place my fingers against my lips to keep from making any strange noises. I don't want to betray how I feel by breathing too erratically, so I try to clear my head and settle my nerves. I have read about recent gene therapy research conducted for my disease, and it was extremely fascinating. Many people were able to regain their sight after the experiments, but there was no confirmation on whether it was permanent, or whether other problems would not arise. Still, I feel an incredible rush of excitement, and my imagination runs away with me. What if I tried? What if it worked, even for a few days? What if I could see all the things I have never seen?

I could see my sister, whom everyone declares to be stunningly beautiful. I could see my father, and finally know what he looks like when he releases that bellow of deep, booming laughter. I remember how prickly his beard used to feel when he would hug me, but my mother always said that she considered his beard handsome. How could something that feels so unpleasant actually be appealing to the eye? What does a beard even look like? Why was my sister always so obsessed with the color of her hair? Why did she struggle to dye it blonde, and then red, and then black? What do those words even mean? What does *blue* look like? I have heard that the sky is blue. I used to dream about supernaturally getting my vision back when I was a child; a fairy would come and grant me a wish, because I had been good, or she had heard me crying and taken pity. The first thing I would always do in these fantasies is run outside and look at the sky, and figure out what the heck *blue* means.

"I don't think she understands what you're saying, Liam," said the man named Owen. He cleared his throat. "Look, lady. We have a great opportunity for you! This gene therapy stuff? It's *astronomically* expensive. So, if you help us now, we'll help you. You can get your eyes fixed for *free*. You could wait a few years for the drug to be approved for general usage—it could be decades— but it will probably cost millions of dollars to get the treatment, and be inaccessible to most people. So, if you let us in, you can ask us questions and sign these papers. We'll be out of your hair in no time. If you're not interested, please tell us so we can leave."

I am not sure why this man seems so rude. Crossing my arms over my chest suspiciously, I am reminded of all the false promises and misleading statements that people have ever said to me. I am reminded of why I left the city in the first place. Dealing with men like this on a daily basis was far more headache than it was worth. Why should I bother? What if I spend months undergoing trials, only to find that it doesn't work for me? What if I never see even the tiniest glimmer of light, even after these doctors have convinced me to be optimistic and to even *believe* that it is highly likely? Why should I overthrow my quiet, tranquil existence for a potentially devastating letdown?

"I don't need your help," I say sharply through the door. I immediately regret the words as soon as they leave my mouth, but my pride is like a snowball being pushed down a hill. "Thanks for offering, but I'm perfectly happy being blind."

"See?" Owen says with annoyance. "I told you this was a waste of time."

The snow begins crunching again as he starts walking away, but I do not hear the second set of footsteps leave. I move closer to the door, and press my ear against the surface. I hear a quiet sigh.

"Please excuse my partner's bad manners," says Dr. Larson. "It's really cold out here and we've been driving for hours. Dr. Philips is just… grumpy."

A warmth and sense of comfort begins to spread through my chest at the sound of his voice. I open my mouth, tempted to apologize. I feel a

17

strong desire to open the door and invite him in for tea. I have not had a conversation with another human being in a long time. I occasionally talk to my publisher over the phone, but it is usually concise and strictly business. Chatting face-to-face could be nice. My imagination starts to run away again, but this time, I keep it in check. The muscles in my forehead have pulled taut in yet another frown. Experience has taught me how this goes; to be fooled by a kind voice and soft words. Buried memories of a haunting deception begin to push into my consciousness. It is always there, chewing at the edge of my mind. Long ago, I promised myself that I would be wary of strangers, and stop trusting my own flawed perceptions.

"How did you get my address?" I ask him angrily. "How did you get my medical records?"

"Your old specialist recommended your name for the trial. Do you remember Dr. Howard? I admit, it was difficult finding you—but I pulled a few strings, and saw that you had some prescriptions sent to this address a few years ago..."

For a moment, it escapes me. Then I remember and swallow in embarrassment. "My anti-depressants," I say, with silent fury. They had been prescribed to me when I suffered a small breakdown after my mother's death. That was absolutely no business of his! Also, unfortunately, the infernal things had not worked.

"Yes. Please, Miss Winters! This treatment could change your life."

I grit my teeth together angrily. "You should not be looking into people without their permission, Dr. Larson. I'm sure you could get in trouble for this."

"Maybe." He sighs again, and I can hear a soft noise, like he is scratching his head. "I only came all this way because Dr. Howard said that you were a really bright girl, and a lovely person. She said that if anyone would benefit from this research, it should be you. She also said you were a writer—she's read some of your books, and was amazed with how much more you've accomplished than most other people with your disease."

My books are my soft spot. I find it very difficult to be upset with people when they compliment my work. I pour so much of myself into those pages, that I cannot help being super sensitive to all acclaim and critique. I press my ear closer against the door as he continues.

"Heck!" exclaims Dr. Larson. "She even gave me one of your books, and it was spellbinding. I'm not a fiction-person usually, but I couldn't stop reading. You've accomplished so much more than most other people, period! People who haven't had to face the obstacles that you've had. You're an incredible girl, and you really deserve this more than anyone. Just have some faith in me, Miss Winters. I promise that I can help you."

I am a little annoyed with him, but my curiosity gets the best of me. "You read one of my books?" I ask him, putting my hand flat against the door. I find myself listening keenly for his answer.

"Yes," he responds. There is a pause. "*Blind Rage*. The revenge thriller. I loved it!"

His words manage to draw a small smile from me. "Thank you, Dr. Larson." My smile spreads through me quickly, and I finally understand what people mean when they describe *fuzzy* feelings in their stomach. It's silly, but the doctor has made my day. Now, if he would only go away before anything more can be said which might ruin my day, that would be ideal.

"You're a smart girl, Miss Winters," he says softly, through the barrier of my front door. "You must know that in 2008, for the first time, there were three research trials done where patients with your disease saw vast recoveries of their vision. My partner, Dr. Philips, is a jerk—but he's right. There's only one gene therapy drug approved for use anywhere in the world, so far. In Europe they recently started making..."

"Glybera," I finish for him. "I know."

"Yes," he responded. "And it's the most expensive drug in the world, costing $1.6 million for treatment. I anticipate that once this drug becomes approved and available, it will be in a similar ballpark."

"That's okay," I tell him, leaning my shoulder against the door. "I'm going to be a rich and famous author someday. I'll be able to afford it, eventually."

"But what about the *time,* Miss Winters?" he asked, his voice pleasing. "You could learn to drive a car! You could get married and have children, and see their faces. See them grow up. That's what everyone with LCA really wants most of all. You could stop hiding away from the world, and get back to society—you could be comfortable around people again. It's easier to communicate and form connections when you can see facial expressions…"

He should have stopped talking when he said he liked my book. This is making me upset. "Dr. Larson, if I wanted to form human connections, I would live in a location that facilitated more interaction. A city or town. Maybe I'd even stay in a nunnery or a brothel. But I am in none of those places. I am in the middle of *a forest. In the mountains.*"

"That's exactly the problem! This isolation simply isn't healthy for you, Miss Winters. You need to…"

"No!" I shout, pounding my fist against the door for emphasis. "Do *not* tell me what I need. I was perfectly fine before you came, and I will be perfectly fine after you leave. My life is wonderful, and I love my privacy. There are plenty of other deserving people my age, with my disease, who would be overjoyed to be selected. Go find them, and please get off my property, Dr. Larson."

He sighs again. This man sure does sigh a lot. "Okay," he responds, after a moment. "Sorry to bother you, Helen."

"That's not my name anymore," I whisper—so softly I hope he cannot hear me.

This time, I do hear his footsteps departing. They are not as loud as before, and I imagine he must be stepping in the tracks left by his partner in the snow. I wait until I can no longer hear his marching, and finally bow my head in misery at my own self-sabotaging ways. I am acutely aware of the fact that I just lost the opportunity of a lifetime. The opportunity to have my vision returned and be a completely normal person. All because I was too scared to open my door to a strange man.

I had been blissfully lost in my writing only a few minutes earlier, but after this unexpected turn of events, I am in no mood to continue. I consider reading instead. Once a month, I have a few books shipped to my little cabin, and I have accumulated quite the library. However, as I walk over to my bookshelves and caress the braille titles, I feel dissatisfied and disappointed. Reading with my fingers is natural and easy, having done it my whole life, but I have always been curious to see what text looks like. I have always wanted to read a book with my eyes. I have always imagined that the first book I would read, if I ever regained vision, should be one that I had written. But now, I'll never even see what my own books look like in print. I'll never see the images on the cover, which are "hauntingly beautiful," according to my publisher.

I stumble over to my bed, and curl up under the blankets. I think I will just lie here and call myself *stupid*, over and over again, for several hours before getting back to work.

Chapter Two

I can't seem to focus. My mind is wandering all over the place, and I can't get a handle on my thoughts. I can't sleep. I tried to rest and calm my fretful brain, but after anxiously rolling around in bed for what felt like hours, I can no longer stand the discomfort of this new information. The words are gnawing at my skin like a sudden rash that has covered me from head to toe; neither scratching furiously nor lying completely still does anything to easy my agony. *Gene therapy.* It sounds too good to be true, which means that it probably is. I'm not foolish, and I'm not going to fall for pretty words. Still, the itch has gotten under the protective layer of my skull, and I can't manage to get at it. It's burrowing deeper, and infecting me with promise. *There's a chance that we might be able to give you the ability to see.* Standing up, I begin pacing in my small cabin, moving back and forth across the creaking floorboards.

How dare that arrogant doctor come to my front door and tell me what's wrong with my life? I have carefully designed it this way. I am comfortable in my small, secluded little world. I already tried life in the big city, going to college, and socializing. I tried to be like everyone else, and ignore my disability; but *they* could not ignore it. They were all either too kind and condescending or too sadistic and brutal—there never was anything in between. Why would I want to subject myself to that again?

My cabin begins to feel unusually small. Within a few minutes, I have paced from one end to the other dozens of times. Every lap I complete seems to make the tiny enclosure shrink even further. Now that the doctors have left, it feels achingly desolate here. The once-comfortable silence is now ominous and depressing. I pause in my pacing, as an alarming thought makes my blood run cold.

Am I going to die here? All alone in the middle of nowhere?

Lifting a hand to touch my forehead, I exhale slowly. I'm only twenty-five, but from the way I live, you would think I was an old woman. I bought a hideous, small house in the backwoods of New Hampshire—where no sane person would want to reside. I told myself that this was what I wanted, but if I were to be achingly honest, I would admit that I do miss my family. I miss people. I miss their voices. I miss the simple, comforting sensation of a hug. I haven't had a hug in over three years.

And I just missed out on the opportunity of a lifetime, because I was too scared to open my door.

Suddenly overwhelmed with the realization of what I've lost, I move over to my desk and fall into my chair. My aim is slightly off, and my thigh collides painfully with the arm of the chair before I can find the cushion. I barely notice this injury as my hands begin to scramble over my desk, searching and rummaging for an item that I generally try to avoid using. Then my fingers brush against it; the cool metal surface of my cell phone. I clasp it victoriously in my hand, and rip it out of the wall socket, where it sits perpetually charging in case of an emergency.

Holding the phone close to my lips, my hand shakes slightly. I have been tempted to contact my family in the past, but I have never broken my vow of solitude. However, I don't think I have ever needed human contact as much as I do right now. I need to hear the voice of someone I love. I jab my thumb down on the large, circular button on my phone.

"Dial Carmen," I command. I wait for the cell phone to follow my instructions.

There is a beep of acquiescence. *"Calling Carmen! Please stand by."*

I take a deep breath. I press the phone against my ear as it begins to ring. I'm terrified that my sister will hate me. I abandoned her without a word. We had been so close, but I had needed to get away with an undeniable urgency. The ringing stops and a rustling noise is heard. I imagine that she might be pulling her phone out of a purse cluttered with random accoutrements. Finally, there is a voice on the other end of the line.

"Carmen Winters speaking! How may I help you?"

For a moment, I am too emotional to respond. A thousand fond memories come rushing back to me, without warning. Her tone is upbeat and perky, with a feminine cadence. There is just a touch of sophistication in her enunciation, so subtle that it might go unnoticed. I've missed her more than I can say.

"Helloooo?" she says again. "Is this some creepy-ass stalker? Because I'm not in the mood..."

"Carm," I say softly. My own voice comes out in a clumsy croak. "It's me."

There's a silence on the other end of the line. I hear her breathing become louder and more erratic. Finally, she releases a sound that is half-sob, half-laugh. "Hel—Helen..." A whimper filters through the line that is somewhere between a gasp and a sniffle. I recognize these sounds. She is trying desperately not to release a torrent of tears.

"Oh, Carm. Please don't cry," I beg her. "Please."

"I knew you'd call me," she says, and her voice breaks. "I knew it! I knew that I'd somehow get in touch with you again, before it was too late."

"Too late?" I ask with worry, my face immediately contorting into a frown. Is something wrong? Is she okay? Dozens of dangerous situations dance across my mind, and I temporarily forget my own issues.

There is another silence on the line.

"Helen... I'm getting married tomorrow."

Now I'm the one making a strange sobbing-laughing sound. "Oh my god! Carmen, really? Tomorrow? To Daniel?"

"No, no. Oh, Helen, you've been gone so long. Daniel and I broke up a few months after you disappeared. I was so depressed, and he just couldn't handle it..."

This news upsets me, and I bite down on my lip. Daniel was a decent guy, and I had liked him. "I'm so sorry, Carm."

"Well, you know. After mom's death— none of us were in good shape." Carmen laughs a little. "What guy wants to date a girl who's crying and moping all the time? And always going on and on about how much she misses her baby sister?

But I got past it. Shortly after that, I met Grayson, and he's an absolute angel—not to mention a total hunk. He's really been there for me."

"Are you sure about him, Carm?" I ask her with worry. She used to have a miserable track record with men. I know how she has a tendency to cling to anyone who shows her a bit of kindness. "You're not rushing things?"

"Honey, I'm *29!*" Carmen reminds me, putting emphasis on the number as if it is a critical turning point. "I feel like an old bat. Most of my friends have already gotten married."

"That's not what I asked," I tell her with a frown. "Is Grayson a good guy?"

"Heck, yes!" she says, almost a little too enthusiastically. "He's the one—I'm sure of it. It's going to be an amazing wedding! Daddy is paying for everything."

We haven't even been talking for a full minute, and I am already developing a headache. I am already beginning to remember why I left. I have always felt so inadequate compared to Carmen. She is so dazzling and vibrant, even in her lowest moments. When we were teenagers, and she temporarily experimented with being a blonde, she had decided it simply would not work for her because she appeared "too bubbly." I was confused about how a change of hair color could be so significant, but I never asked for clarification. Most of her fashion-obsessions and idiosyncrasies completely escaped me. Not just because I could not see, but because I could not bring myself to care.

"Helen," she says softly, and her voice is suddenly serious. "Please come to my wedding. Please come home."

I hesitate. There is an odd undertone of fear in her voice, which piques my curiosity and concern. Could something be wrong?

"Please, Hellie," she begs, using the old childhood nickname that had always irked me so much. "It's the most important day of my life, and I need you to be there, standing beside me. I need my baby sister. Will you come?"

I am acutely aware of the fact that she has not asked about me. She has not asked about my whereabouts or my health. Although it's on the tip of my tongue, I find myself unable to spill my own guts to tell her about my infuriating experience with the doctors. I had hoped she would offer a listening ear, but as usual, she is too focused on her own events. Of course, she would be; they are far more momentous and dramatic than anything that could ever happen to me.

"You should be my maid of honor," she tells me. "Please? Helen? I'll get you a bridesmaid dress. There's still time. Have you gained weight?"

I smile. It's the first question she has asked about me, and it is completely ridiculous. "How would I know?" I answer, reaching down to check how much fat I can pinch on the side of my stomach. It's not very much. "I don't own a scale—and even if I did, I couldn't read the numbers."

"Oh, I'm sure you're just as gorgeous as ever, sweetie! Will you come? Please say yes." She pauses, and her voice takes on a somber note. "Please..."

Hearing the wavering sound in her voice, I sense trouble. Scowling, I reach up to scratch my head in disorientation. "I—I don't know, Carm."

"I'll only have one wedding, Helen." Carmen sounds dejected and upset. "It's hard enough knowing that Mom can't be there... but you're still *alive*. Do I have to accept that I've lost my sister, too?"

This guilt trip is working very well. Even though I'm frowning, and trying to be strong and maintain my ground, I feel myself caving. "Fine," I mutter. "I'll try to make it, but..."

"Great! Thanks, Helen! I'll see you soon. Come home as soon as you can, because I'll need plenty of help getting ready."

The phone went dead.

I groan, clenching my fist around the little metal box. "I'm doing fine, by the way. Thanks for asking, Carmen. All that horrible shit that happened to me? Dropping of school? Oh, yeah. I've gotten over it, and I'm living a happy and well-adjusted life. I'm living life to the fullest,

31

really. I have tons of friends. Boys? Sure. There are plenty of men in my life. Most of them are chipmunks, but I wouldn't discriminate." Slamming the phone down on my desk, I roll my eyes and rise to my feet. I march over to my kitchenette and begin ripping cupboard doors open, rummaging around for a bottle that I had tucked away for a special occasion. Or a dismal one. When my fingers collide with the smooth, cool glass surface, I grab the neck of the bottle and yank it from the cupboard. I quickly find my corkscrew, and retire to my small bed to comfort myself with some good wine.

"Oh, you really enjoyed my latest book? Thanks for telling me, Carmen! It's so thoughtful of you to keep reading my work. I haven't been insecure at all. It's not even slightly difficult being a blind writer." I can't be bothered to get a glass, so once I remove the cork, I drink directly from the bottle. The rich, robust flavor of the liquid smothers my tongue, and I lean back against the wooden wall in satisfaction. "By the way, I'm making *tons* of money. That's why I bought a rundown cabin in the wilderness. Because of the hot location—I'm sure my property value is doubling, as we speak. Thanks for asking."

I know that it might not sound this way at the moment, but I love my sister. Everything about her is just so flawless that I can't help but be frustrated; her personality feels radiant—almost luminous. Even her name! *Carmen* makes me think of the legendary heroine in an opera. *Helen* just sounds like a boring scientist. That's why I tried to change my name and leave my old life behind me. But today, the past won't stop hunting me down. I take another swig from my bottle. "Of course I'll come to your wedding! Tomorrow? Sure, that's not inconvenient at all. Let me just get in my fancy car and have my chauffeur bring me over there. It's only two states away—not much of a trip or anything." I take another drink.

I'm in the middle of talking to myself, yammering on like a crazy person, when I hear the crunching of footsteps again. In my surprise, I nearly drop the wine bottle I'm cradling against myself. More visitors? A determined knock echoes against the wooden door of my cabin. I look up sharply, glaring in the direction of the sound. I remain motionless for a moment, staring into the dark expanse of my oblivion. It may be black, but my imagination has never failed to paint fantastic images in every direction I gaze. Even when my eyes are closed, my mind creates whimsical shapes and patterns, dancing and spinning in the empty darkness.

But in this moment, my imagination falters. There is only obscurity.

A stronger knock is heard on my door. "Miss Winters!" says a demanding male voice. "Open this door. We need to talk."

I hug the wine bottle closer against me. I recognize the irritating doctor's voice from earlier. I am not sure whether I should be relieved or upset that he returned. It is true that I had been clinging to a sliver of hope that I could get a second chance to accept his offer. But now that he is here, I am not sure how to tell him that I might like to try. I have spent so much time running away from people that it is difficult to accept help. Long ago, I promised myself that I would lock myself up and never open the door to anyone. If I were to turn the knob and crack the door open even a few inches, I know that all kinds of danger would pour through that crevice and surely ruin my life.

People can never seem to walk into my world without walking all over me.

They also leave their filthy, muddy footprints all over the floor, which I simply hate cleaning. I realize that most people hate housework, but it's actually very difficult to clean when you're blind. I would like to believe that I have more justification for hating cleaning than the average person.

He knocks again.

"Come on!" he shouts through the door. "I'm a doctor, Helen! You can trust me. I know that you want to be a part of this study. Who wouldn't? Let me in. Let me in so we can discuss this like adults."

Scooting my body into the corner of my

bed and the wall, I arrange my pillows around myself so I feel safe and protected. If this is a siege, then I'm willing to wait forever. I am not going to open that door. I take another large drink of my wine.

"What is wrong with you?" yells the doctor. "I won't let you miss out on this opportunity. My colleague gave up on you, but I haven't! Don't you understand how expensive this procedure is, and how valuable it could be? You could have a life, Helen! A real life!"

I frown deeply. *He sure is charming and polite,* I think to myself sarcastically.

"You could see the sunrise," he tells me. "You could see the sunset." He pauses. "Do you remember that scene near the end of *Blind Rage*, where the couple is standing and talking on the balcony in Greece, at sunset? You described such a breathtaking sky, and it just broke my heart to think that your readers were all getting to see the picture in their minds—but you, the writer, could not. Wouldn't you like to know what a sunset looks like? I could show you."

I squint a little, making a face of displeasure. He's using my books as a weapon against me. That is not fair. A sunset is the natural phenomenon that I most desire to see.

"The aurora borealis," he continues. "You've written about that, too. You have no idea what it looks like, Helen. These crazy, mystical lights dancing all over the northern sky. It's mind-blowing. Wouldn't you like to see that?"

I would. I would very much like to see that, and so much more. I clamp my lips together tightly to keep from responding and betraying my eagerness and apprehension. The conflicting emotions are giving me a headache. "Just go away," I whisper. I speak so softly that I am sure he cannot hear me. "Just go away."

"Helen, I can help you. For god's sake, woman! Have a little faith." He hesitates, speaking a little quieter. "I don't know what people have done to you in the past that have made you so guarded, but you need to trust me. I became a doctor so I could take care of people. If you let me, I'll take care of you."

His voice has a strange quality that gives me a tiny shiver. I feel the little hairs on my arms and the back of my neck standing up. It feels like my body is trying to tell me something; is it trying to encourage or warn me? Should I trust this man? I want to. I want to just throw caution to the wind and shout, *Yes! Yes! Fix me! Please make me normal.* However, a nagging negative feeling restrains me. I know that if I accept this offer, something terrible will happen. Something terrible always does.

"Okay, look." The man sighs. "You don't have to agree to participate in our study. But I was really excited to meet you. I came out all this way... and I would hate to leave without something to remember you by." He begins to fiddle with my door. The sound of rusty metal grating against rusty metal is heard.

My entire body tenses up. Is he trying to break into my cabin? I feel my heart rate quicken, and my hands clamp tightly around my wine bottle. The muscles in my thighs become so taut that they hurt. I shrink even further back into my corner, reminding myself to breathe. Finally, a dull thump is heard. The metal noises abruptly stop.

"I just slipped a copy of *Blind Rage* through the mail slot," says the doctor. "Do you think you could autograph the book and pass it back to me? It would mean a lot."

My face contorts in puzzlement. A small laugh escapes my throat. I place my wine bottle down on my nightstand and move over to the door. Stooping down to the ground, I feel around for the paperback novel. My hand connects with the soft, familiar pages. I smile. I can almost feel that it's my book, even before brushing my fingers over the raised lettering.

"Who should I make this out to?" I ask softly.

"To Liam," he responds.

I move over to my desk, and begin pulling out drawers in search of a pen. My hand finally touches a slender cylinder—I do not have much use for pens, so I am surprised that I even have one. I quickly scrawl a few words over the inside cover of the novel. I do not write often, but I have done this many times for book signings. My handwriting is probably not that attractive, but it's the best I can manage. Using my finger to guide my lines, I write a personalized inscription:

To Liam
Please leave me alone.
Winter Rose

With a sly smile, I move back over to the door. I feel around for the mail slot and lift the metal flap, sliding the book through the opening. "Here you go," I tell him. "A special autograph just for you."

"Thank you!" he says with enthusiasm, reaching to take the book from me.

His fingertips brush against mine, and I jerk my hand away hastily. I stumble backward and collide with my desk. Clutching the hand that he had barely grazed, I feel my fingers to see if they have been somehow burned or scalded. I hold my breath, pressing my stinging fingers against my stomach. It feels like they are on fire.

I have not touched another human being in

over three years. It's unsettling.

Having read the inscription, Liam laughs lightly. "Wow! Thanks, Winter—uh, I mean Helen! Sorry, I didn't mean to call you by your pseudonym."

"Act—actually," I say haltingly, as I try to ignore the odd sensation in my fingers, "that's my name now. I legally changed it to Winter Rose."

"Well, it is very pretty," he responds, "but I think Helen has a certain charm, too. Why did you change it?"

Pulling my lips into a grim line, I display distaste—even though he cannot see my expression through the door. "I just... I couldn't be Helen anymore. I didn't like her."

There is a silence. I begin to feel a bit stupid for saying something so personal.

Liam moves to sit outside my door, and I hear his back thump gently against the wood. When he speaks again, his words are soft and serious. "It would be a great help if you could assist me in my research study. I really think you're an excellent candidate."

I hesitate before responding. "What if it doesn't work out?"

"It will. I promise that it will be worth the risk," he assures me.

"Can you give me a little more information?" I ask him softly.

"Maybe if you let me in. It's fucking cold

out here."

I bite down on my lip as I consider this. Immediately, I feel self-conscious. "Uh, I'm not sure how tidy it is in here. I wasn't expecting visitors, and cleaning can be difficult."

"I don't care," he responds. "Heck, I'll tidy up for you! Just let me in, Winter. I promise you won't regret it."

I take a deep breath. Remembering how lost I felt before, when he walked away and I thought the opportunity was gone forever, I step forward boldly. I reach out and touch my doorknob, tracing the lock with my fingertip. "I'll let you in," I tell him, "but you have to do something for me in return."

"Sure!" he says instantly. "Whatever you need."

I smile deviously. My fingers turn the lock, and for the first time in three years, I open the door to a stranger.

Chapter Three

As the door swings open, I begin to have panicked second thoughts. I try to slam the wooden panel closed, but there is already a person in the way. He walks into my cabin, and I can sense him looking around and assessing everything.

"This is a sweet little setup," he says in surprise. "You're very organized."

I'm a little nervous, so I keep holding the door open, letting the cold air gust into the room. "This wasn't a good idea," I tell the doctor. "I changed my mind. You should go."

"Wow," he says softly. "You're drop-dead gorgeous."

I shift uncomfortably as I imagine his eyes roaming all over my body. I crinkle my nose up in a rebellious attempt to look unattractive. "Well, I wouldn't know. I have never looked into a mirror."

"For that reason alone, you should take my offer," he informs me. "When you gain the ability to see, the first thing I'm going to do after the operation is present you with a mirror. You should know what you're missing. This? What I'm looking at right now? It's on par with your sunsets."

"Ha. You're some kind of smooth talker, aren't you?" I ask with a grumble. Self-consciously, I reach up to touch my hair. The texture is bland and dry; not smooth and silky like my sister's hair. I am sure it looks as lackluster as it feels. I really don't take care of myself and all those superficial details quite as much as I should. "You don't have to butter me up with fake flattery," I assure the doctor. "Just give me the facts."

"Could you at least shut the door and give me a minute to warm up?" he asks me. There is a sound like he is rubbing his hands together and blowing on them. "It's colder than a banshee's nipple ring out there."

"Oh," I muse to myself. "I like that phrase. I'll have to use it in a book, sometime..."

"Helen, please? The door?"

With an exasperated sigh at his childishness, I shut the door with a dramatic flourish. "Is that better, tough guy? Does that make invading my privacy and ruining my workday a little more comfortable for you?"

"I still feel like my hands are going to fall off," he said, blowing on them frantically. "I was trying not to complain, but I think that's the coldest wind I've ever felt in my life."

"Aww," I say, making an exaggerated sound of sympathy. "Would you like a cup of tea to warm up?"

"Sure! That would be great," Liam says with enthusiasm.

I point to the other end of the cabin. "The kitchen's over there. Knock yourself out."

He seems to pause for a moment in surprise, taken aback by my words. "You really are a lovely little lady, aren't you?"

"What gave me away? My hospitality?" I ask sweetly. Gesturing around at the desolate location, my lips curve upward in a little grin of sarcasm. "It's obvious that I'm a huge people-person."

The sound of footsteps echoes in the cabin as he heads toward the small kitchen. "Good God, woman. Do you live on granola bars and protein shakes?"

"Yes," I say slowly, "and vitamins, of course. What more do I need?"

"Where do I begin?" he says, evidently appalled by the sight of my barren kitchen. "How about a good, balanced meal with fresh vegetables and meat? How about some fruit and dairy?"

I lift my shoulders in a shrug, pretending

not to care. "It's all too complicated. The things I buy have very distant expiry dates, so they're not likely to go bad. It's tricky enough for me to cook and clean, but leftovers are a pain in the ass. I can never figure out what plastic containers in the fridge contain what, and how long they've been sitting there. It gets annoying when you need to sniff everything and do taste tests... I would rather just be secure in the fact that everything is good to eat. Also, it makes garbage disposal a lot easier."

There is a silence, and I can feel him staring at me again. "No wonder you're so skinny. You don't enjoy food."

"Hey! I love food," I tell him with a frown. "I grew up eating delicious meals—I just can't be bothered to prepare them for myself. It's far too time-consuming and frustrating. I would prefer to spend my time punching away at my keyboard."

"Hmm," says the doctor. "I think that if you could see, your diet would improve vastly. Fruit and vegetables can be colorful and aesthetically appealing; you would *experience* your food a lot more."

"Why are you so judgmental?" I ask sharply. "I have a system. It's a good system. Look around! Everything works. I get my groceries delivered every two weeks, and I consume more than enough nutrients to keep me alive and functioning. Actually, I'm quite comfortable with this state of affairs. I write great stories that lots of people enjoy reading. I am a productive member of society." I put my hands on my hips. "Why are you trying so hard to fix me, when I'm not broken? You act like you're some white knight, coming in here to rescue the damsel in distress from her tower. I don't know if you noticed, but I don't need rescuing. I was just chilling here and enjoying a fine bottle of Cabernet Sauvignon, when you interrupted me!"

"I'm sorry," Liam says quietly.

Truthfully, this is a bit of a sore spot for me. I really do miss having wonderful home-cooked meals. When my mother died, things became difficult for us around the house back at home. Carmen and I were both terrible cooks, and we ended up going out for dinner with our father on most nights. But since I left home, it's been hopeless; I have been living on these bland and tasteless concoctions for the sake of efficiency. My occasional bottle of wine for celebration, or misery, is the most delicious thing I ever consume, these days. I won't allow myself to possess anything else, for it will almost surely go bad without my notice. Most of the time, I don't mind being so unsatisfied; I realize that culinary delights are a luxury, and I didn't move all the way out here for the high life. I just hate being forced to remember what I'm missing.

"You can't really enjoy living like this,

Helen?" the doctor asks. "I think I'd go crazy."

"Are you an ophthalmologist or a psychologist? Stop asking such personal questions," I grumble. "Who cares what I eat?"

"It's important," he tells me. "The whole body is connected. If we manage to give you vision, you'll still need a good diet to maintain your optical health."

I twist my face into a scowl. "So, are you going to give me information on the procedure you want to perform on me? Or are we going to stand around making pointless small talk? Are you going to keep complaining about the weather and my diet until I go crazy and scratch out my eyes so badly that you couldn't possibly fix them?"

He cleared his throat. "I have my documents right here in my bag. Let me read them to you."

I listen to the rustling of papers. "Are you wearing a man-purse?" I ask him curiously.

"What? No!" He seems wounded. "It's... like a briefcase. Why do you ask?"

"No reason. You just seem like the sort of person that would carry a man-purse," I say with a shrug, returning to my wine bottle. I sit on the edge of my bed and take another deep swig. It occurs to me that without the few ounces I had consumed earlier, in frustration at my self-centered sister, I might not have been bold enough to open the door. Dr. Liam Larson does not seem as awful as I first expected, and I am grateful to the liquid for emboldening me. I listen closely to the sound of him shuffling through papers. I am eagerly, yet anxiously awaiting more information on his research study, but I am determined to appear cool and aloof.

"You seemed to know a little about gene therapy when I mentioned it earlier," the doctor says. "How much of this data would you like me to go over? I don't want to bore you."

"Just give me everything," I say hungrily. "I would prefer to hear as much as possible about this treatment before diving in."

"Great," Liam says, clearing his throat. "Well, as I'm sure you know, LCA is caused by a mutation in the RPE65 gene. This causes blindness in patients with your disease, because your eyes can't produce a specific protein which allows you to use retinal, a form of vitamin A, to allow your photoreceptors to convert light into energy."

I nod to indicate that I'm following his lecture.

The doctor continues. "The treatment targets RPE65 by delivering genes directly into the retina. This is meant to sort-of *reprogram* the eye so that it can function," he explains. Liam pauses, shuffling through his papers. "I don't want to mislead you. Unfortunately, this treatment is still in its infancy. We're still in the middle of a trial-and-error process. Many people have experienced improved vision immediately after treatment, but some have experienced a rapid loss of the vision. It only works in the short term for some patients, while others have seen vast improvements for at least three years."

"I understand," I say softly. Being able to see, for even a few years, could be life-altering.

"A few years ago, researchers got really excited and thought this was like a magic cure, but it's not quite so simple. We're trying to improve the gene delivery technique, because it only targets a small portion of the retina at the moment. The old, damaged parts of the eye can poison the treated areas and cause them to revert back to their dysfunctional form." He pauses for a moment, brushing his fingers across the information in his binder. He clears his throat. "The reason I hunted you down is because I looked through some of your tests from when you were younger. There are different types of LCA, but your specific genetic mutation looks like it might respond well to our therapy."

Nodding thoughtfully, I run my finger around the rim of my wine bottle. I know that my disease is rather rare, and there are probably a limited number of potential candidates in my age group. It would make sense that he would choose me based on a recommendation. This allows me to grow a little less upset at his intrusion, and a little less suspicious; only a little.

"Helen, you should accept my offer," he tells me seriously. "I really do believe that these clinical trials are going to yield the best results we've ever seen. We're trying a different, dual approach this time to try to cause more complete healing of the entire eye."

"And what would you need from me?" I ask him.

"Well, we'll need to closely monitor the thickness of the outer nuclear layer of your photoreceptors. This means we'll be using coherence tomography to take serial measurements, quite often. A thinning of this layer indicates degeneration of the rods and cones, which we're trying to prevent." He exhales, and there is a sound like the closing of a binder. "Basically, the main issue we're facing is determining how to create a permanent, safe, and thorough solution. You should do this, Helen. If you agree to participate in these clinical trials... it could be amazing for you."

"Why me?" I asked him. "Why are you bothering to try and convince me? Aren't there others, closer to your hospital?"

"Well, as I told you, I'm friends with Dr. Leslie Howard. You're one of her favorite patients, and she actually gave me your book a while ago. When this study came up, I mentioned it to her, and she became insanely excited and began pushing me to find you and convince you to participate."

"Ah," I murmur. This does make sense. I had always gotten along quite well with Leslie. She was an old family friend, and I had even kept in touch with her sporadically after leaving home. Taking another sip of my wine, I quietly mull over this information.

The doctor clears his throat. "Can I make a confession?" Liam asks nervously.

"Sure," I tell him with a shrug.

"Meeting you... is wild. I feel like I'm in the presence of a celebrity."

Smiling a little, I scoff. "Don't be silly. Because of my books?"

"Yes. You're a little different than I imagined, but I did expect you to love your wine." The doctor laughs lightly. "Why are all writers such heavy drinkers?"

"I don't know. Why are all doctors such nosy pricks?" I retort with a growl.

He chuckles at this, and does not seem to be offended. "Did you know that you're really popular in the blind community? I always tell my patients about you to inspire them. There was a fascinating feature a few months ago..."

"I know, I know. That dumb magazine article on the top ten most successful and influential blind people of 2013. That was just a publicity stunt by my publisher. It's marketing. They're capitalizing on my disability to sell books.

Don't believe everything you read."

"You're right," he says. "I shouldn't believe anything without hard evidence. Journalists often get it wrong. And so do photographers; you're much, much prettier than the picture in the back of your book."

I raise my eyebrow. "At this point, I almost want to agree to your study just so you'll stop talking. Calling me pretty isn't going to further your case. Also, I don't really care if I'm pretty; what does that even *mean?* I have no concept of what an attractive person looks like, versus an unattractive one." I growl a little. "Are you taunting me? Trying to flaunt that you can see what I look like while I have no earthly idea? Or are you lying to manipulate me, because I'm actually hideous, and I have no way of knowing that?"

"I was just paying you a compliment," he says defensively. "Obviously, it's a subjective matter, but personally, I find you stunning."

"Yay," I say in a monotonous tone. I take a sip from my bottle again. "Well, I think I have an answer for you. On whether I'll participate in your study..."

"Wait!" he says quickly. "Don't you want to know more so you can make an informed decision?"

"You gave me plenty of information..."

"Just take a moment to really think about

it," he tells me. "I don't want you to miss out on this because you're being hasty and prideful. There might not be another study like this in the near future. And it's rare to find one in your age group..." Liam sounds like he's getting flustered.

"I'll do it," I tell him.

The doctor continues to panic. "Think about what this could—wait, what? You'll do it?"

"Yeah. But you'll have to do something for me in return, like you promised earlier." I take another sip slowly. "I need a ride somewhere."

"A ride? Sure, that's easy. Is that all?"

"I need a ride to New York," I inform him. "Tonight"

"New York?" he says in surprise. "Well— we were going to head back there anyway. But Dr. Philips and I have a room booked here for the weekend, and he's meeting family..."

"Tonight," I repeat, unwaveringly. "It's for my sister's wedding. I need to be there as soon as possible. If we could leave now, that would be best."

"But it's at least a six hour trip," he says weakly. "We've already been driving so much today. I'm exhausted..."

"There must be some reason you want me, specifically, for your study," I inform him. I'm bluffing a little, and overestimating my own importance. I'm also gambling on the fact that the doctor seems like a really nice guy. "If you take me to New York, I'll be your guinea pig. You can poke around at my eyes all you want."

He takes a moment to ponder my offer. He sighs. "Could I have some of that wine?"

"Oh. I've been drinking from the bottle..."

"That's fine," he says, crossing the room toward me and taking the bottle from my hands. He is not standing too close to me, but I can still feel his breath against my face. A subtle whiff of his cologne invades my senses.

I flinch and scoot away on my bed, pressing my back against the wall. My heart rate quickens, and I am suddenly very afraid. He seems nice, but one can never be too sure. My chest feels suddenly very full of a breath that I have been holding. I can hear gulping noises from his throat as he swallows a generous helping of my wine.

"Okay," he says finally, placing the wine bottle down on the desk. "I'll take you to New York. Let me just text Dr. Philips, and we'll get going."

I release my breath in relief. I am glad he did not notice my momentary anxiety attack. "Great," I say in a confident voice. "You're also going to help me pack."

Chapter Four

The doctor grunts as he drags my suitcase out of my cabin. "Do you really need all this stuff? It's like you shoved your entire life in here!"

"I like to be thorough and prepared," I tell him as I step over my threshold. The frosty air rushes at me, slapping me in the face and filling my lungs. The initial shock of the cold fades as I breathe in deeply, and I can't help basking in the refreshing sensation. The air inside my cabin tasted hot and stuffy, although I didn't notice this until I was immersed in an atmosphere of superior quality. The cool breeze swirling around me feels alive—it infects me, causing something to stir inside my bones. All of a sudden, I am feeling somewhat adventurous.

I adjust my backpack over my shoulder, as it contains the most important items: my Braille note taker, wallet, phone, and some other handy electronic devices. I figure that I can get some writing done from the back seat of the car while the doctors drive me to my destination. This doesn't have to be a completely wasted workday. I could still write a few thousand words—or possibly take a nap.

"You packed like you don't intend to return here," Liam observes as I turn the key in the lock to secure my front door. "I don't think you left anything of value behind."

"I like to keep the things I value very close to me," I respond, turning away from my cabin and taking a few steps in the direction of the road. Obviously, I haven't shoveled my driveway, and my winter boots crunch through the top layer of ice and sink deep into the snow. I'm bundled up warmly in a heavy coat and mittens, so the cold does not bother me. I turn to look back over my shoulder toward the cabin where I spent the last three years of my life. Of course, I see nothing. But as I try to envision what it might look like, I begin to feel an odd nostalgia for this contrived image in my mind. "Maybe I won't come back," I say suddenly. "There were many reasons I left home; if those reasons are no longer relevant, maybe I'll stay there with my family."

"What were the reasons?" he asks me.

I shake my head, with a small smile. "No. Nuh-uh. You're not going to extract my deepest, darkest secrets only a few hours after meeting me."

"Don't be so sure," he tells me. "We have a long car ride ahead of us, and I can be very persuasive. I am almost positive I can dig up all your skeletons."

"Pfft." I blow air through my lips in a sound of contempt. "You can dig all you like, but I buried those rotting corpses pretty well."

"Then I'll just have to dig a little deeper," he says gently. "I think I see Owen's car pulling up. Would you like me to help guide you to the street?" He places his elbow against my arm.

Jerking away from him, I frown. My neck flushes with heat, and my stomach churns with nausea. His touch was respectful and kind, meant only to offer me support and direction, but I'm not comfortable with this. I'm not comfortable with accepting help from a stranger unless there's some sort of bargain agreed upon beforehand. Unless I know what I owe him in return. We already have a bargain, and I am determined to never need anything more from him beyond this drive. "I can walk," I assure him. "I'll just follow the sound of your footsteps."

"Why are you so stubborn, Helen?" he asks me. "It won't kill you to accept my arm. I'm a doctor. I'm here to help you, not to hurt you."

"You are helping me," I say with forced cheerfulness. "You're carrying my suitcase and offering me a ride to New York. Isn't that enough for one day, Dr. Larson?"

"I just don't understand you," he says as he begins trudging toward his colleague's vehicle. "All the blind people I have met usually prefer a little more touch in their communication."

"Well, you hadn't met me," I say simply as I stroll behind him. "I don't like being touched. I don't like it when people use my disability as an excuse to fuss over me."

"That's not what I was doing!" he says defensively. He grumbles to himself, but continues moving toward the road. He walks in silence for a few seconds before speaking again. "I think I should warn you: road trips with Dr. Philips can get a little... crazy."

"Crazy?" I say with a mixture of concern and curiosity.

"Dr. Philips is usually very professional, but there's something about long drives that turns him into a teenage boy. I think he used to do road trips with his frat buddies to Daytona Beach for spring break. He's kind of... odd." Liam clears his throat. "Maybe he'll behave himself with you in the car."

"I'm sure it won't be that bad," I say with a smile.

"I hope not. We're a few steps away from the car now," Liam informs me.

There is an unlocking sound as Dr. Philips pops the trunk open, and a little *oompf* as Liam tosses my suitcase into the back of the car.

"Would you like me to help guide you into the backseat?" he asks.

I am worried that he is going to touch my arm again, and I step back. "No, thank you."

He sighs. "Look, Helen. I work with patients who have limited vision all the time. Almost every day, really. Touch helps them to connect and understand, the way someone might observe facial expressions..."

"Does it seem like I want to connect and understand?" I ask him.

"Not particularly," he responds with disappointment.

"Good." I would reach forward and touch the car, and fumble around for the door handle, but I know from experience that the handles are on different places on every car. It's frustrating, and I am almost guaranteed to look like an idiot while blindly groping the side of the car and getting my hands all dirty. I would rather behave like a bitch than seem like a moron. So, instead, I thrust my chin into the air. "I'm a writer. I like words. If I wanted to connect and understand, I'd listen to the words people say. That's all I really need. Are you going to open the car door for me, or not?"

"I thought you didn't need help," he says with a chuckle.

"I thought you were polite!" I reply curtly, crossing my arms under my breasts. "I don't need you to shove me into the car, but it's customary to open the door."

There is a sound as his hand pulls the latch and swings open the panel of metal and glass. "I really hope we can restore your vision, Helen," says the doctor. "Maybe once you can see how beautiful the world is, you'll be a little less bitter."

"I'm not bitter because I'm blind," I tell him as I take off my backpack and move into the vehicle. I feel around to get a sense of the layout of the car. "I've just encountered one too many assholes, and lost my faith in humanity."

"Then I'll just have to restore it," he tells me with determination, shutting the door and moving to the front seat.

"Hi," says the man in the driver's seat. His voice is not quite as deep as Liam's. "I'm Dr. Owen Philips. I don't have any faith in humanity either. I think I lost it when my buddy Liam convinced me to come out here for the weekend, and then randomly decides we're going back to the city without any warning."

"Sorry, Dr. Philips," I say with regret. "That's my fault."

"No, no. I blame Liam," says the other doctor. "He's got a fanboy crush on you, so he was easily manipulated into doing whatever you wanted."

"It wasn't like that," Liam protests as he settles into his seat and yanks out his seatbelt.

I hear the little *click* as it locks into place,

and I am reminded to fasten my own. I can't believe how long it's been since I was in a vehicle. I usually get everything delivered to me, so I can avoid people—I never go anywhere anymore.

"No, it was exactly like that," Owen says. His voice takes on a high-pitched tone of mimicry. "Oh, I can't believe I'm going to *meet* her! She's *such* a great author! I wonder if she'll sign my book?"

"Jesus, Owen. Stop it," Liam says with annoyance.

Owen laughs. "I bet it doesn't help that she's really pretty. Helen—can I call you Helen?" He does not wait for an answer before continuing. "I know you can't see, so I feel obliged to inform you that Dr. Larson is blushing furiously. He is red as a beet."

"I am not," Liam says seriously. "He's lying. If there's any redness in my cheeks, it's from the cold wind outside."

I can't keep a smile away from my face. His voice is so masculine and confident sounding that it is hard to imagine him displaying visual signs of embarrassment. "I'm sure you're not blushing, Dr. Larson."

"Enough with the formalities!" Owen says, as he puts the car into gear and slams his foot down on the gas. The car lurches forward, peeling away from my cabin. "We are going to have fun on this road trip. Helen, just forget that we're your doctors and treat us like your friends. Just feel comfortable to say what's on your mind. This is a safe and judgment-free zone. I'll get started!"

"Oh, no," Liam says with a sigh. "Please don't..."

"Right now, I'm upset," Owen tells us. "I'm upset because I was relaxing in our hotel room, and enjoying this movie I ordered on the TV, when *Liam* texted me that our vacation was over. He said I had to drive over here right away. And I was *really* enjoying the movie, if you know what I mean."

Liam groans loudly. "Dammit, Owen! That hotel room is on *my* credit card."

"It was just one movie, man."

"Yes, but—dammit! You charged porn to my credit card?" Liam asked angrily. "I didn't say you could do that."

"We're friends. I knew you'd help a brother out," Owen says. There is a sound, which I assume is him reaching over to clap Liam on the shoulder. "Besides, I'm sure it shows up as something discreet on the bill."

I lift my eyebrows. I should probably reach into my backpack and pull out my notetaker to begin working, but I am a little too surprised and entertained by the doctors in the front seats.

"Maybe you shouldn't talk about this sort of thing with Helen in the car," Liam says quietly to Owen.

"Why not? She doesn't mind! Do you mind, Helen?" Again, he doesn't wait for me to answer before continuing. "Since you so rudely interrupted my movie, Liam, and have no appreciation for the art of porn, I'm going to tell you all about it."

"No," Liam says. "Absolutely not. Here, let's just listen to the radio..." He presses a dial on the dashboard and begins sifting through stations.

There is another noise as Owen slams his hand down on the dashboard and turns off the radio. "Actually, this is *my* car, so we play by *my* rules. If you wanted to pick the topic of conversation or radio station, then we should have taken *your* car. But no, your car is new and shiny, and you wanted to keep it all locked up safe in your garage. Let's take Owen's crappy car, because who cares if we put more miles on it!"

Liam sighs again. "Owen, can you please try to act like a grown up..."

"What's more grown up than porn?" Owen asks innocently. He turns back to me, which I can tell from the direction of his voice. "Hey, Helen! Have you ever seen a good porno? Well, silly me—what a stupid question! Since you're blind, let me try to describe what porn looks like."

"Uh," I say awkwardly. "I really have no interest..."

"No, no. This is important. You need to know what you're missing out on! The skin pressed against skin, the bodily fluids slowly dripping down thighs..."

"Oh my god," I say in discomfort, sinking down into the backseat and clutching my head which is quickly beginning to ache. "I really don't want to hear this. I was actually hoping to get some writing done while we drive."

"Sure, sure. But maybe this could inspire you! Just let me tell you about the movie I was watching. I promise; it had a really great storyline."

Liam grunts with exasperation. "Not this again, Owen. Please, she really doesn't want to hear about..."

"Nonsense! She'll love it. So there's this housewife, and she's all alone at home. And then she notices the pool boy, who is cleaning their pool without his shirt on. His abs are glistening in the sun..."

I let out a large groan. "Please stop. That doesn't sound like a great storyline to me."

"No, no! You only *think* you know what's going to happen, but there's a twist! She asks the pool boy if he feels like pizza, and orders delivery. So then the two of them are making out while waiting for the pizza, and when they open the door to see the delivery boy—*he's* not wearing a shirt! So then the pool boy and the pizza delivery boy..."

"Please kill me now," I say miserably.

"Only if you kill me first," Liam responds.

"But if I kill you, then you won't be able to kill me!" I say frantically.

"We could try to do it at the same time, but it seems technically challenging," Liam says. "I guess we're just stuck with listening to Owen."

"Will you two stop interrupting me?" asks our driver. "Now where was I? Oh, yeah! The pizza delivery boy pulls out his pepperoni sausage..."

I should have brought earplugs. It's times like these that make me wish I was deaf instead of blind.

This is going to be a very long trip.

Chapter Five

Three hours later...

"...but my favorite was when the schoolgirl didn't complete her homework on time!" Owen was saying enthusiastically. "It was a great piece of filmmaking, because the professor had this dungeon..."

"Hey, buddy," Liam said, leaning forward. "Looks like there's a gas station at that exit up ahead. Didn't you say you were running low? How about we stop and fill up, and maybe grab a bite to eat?"

"But I'm in the middle of my story!" Owen protested. "Don't you want to hear what happens to the schoolgirl? Helen does! Don't you, Helen?"

"Get. Gas. Now." My voice has never been more deadly serious.

"Sheesh," Owen says sadly, signaling and pulling over to exit. "Fine, Helen; if you insist. I'm disappointed in you. Liam is a spoilsport, but I would have thought that since you're a writer, you would appreciate a good story."

"A good story?" I repeat incredulously. "Owen, nothing you've said in the past three hours has been anywhere *close* to a good story. Listening to you is making my ears hurt. I think they're melting—your words are like acid being poured into my ear canals."

"Hey! That's not nice," Owen says in a grumpy tone. It sounds like he might be pouting. "It's medically impossible to lose your hearing from listening to someone talk about the glorious art of pornography."

I grumble to myself unhappily. "It's possible if I buy a popsicle at the gas station, eat the popsicle, and then use the popsicle stick to gouge my own ears out so that I can tolerate the rest of this trip!" Sighing, I lean to press my head against the glass of the car window. It is cold, and I use it like an ice pack to soothe my aching ear and temple. I really do feel like if I need to listen to one more ridiculous tale of sexual depravity for no particular reason, I'm going to lose my mind. I really wouldn't care if they were *good* stories. "Seriously. I think I'm going deaf. It hurts."

"Well, that's a bad problem to have when you're in the car with two eye doctors!" Owen says cheerfully.

"Jesus, man," Liam says to his friend in dismay. "It's been hours. You need to stop talking. Just let me put on the radio... please. What's the point of us trying to mend her eyesight if you destroy her hearing by talking about bad porn?"

"Bad porn? Bad porn? Haven't you been listening!" Owen shouts. "I'm discussing the all-time classics of porn! Highly stylized, exotic foreign films! The vintage movies of yore! Indie sensations featuring young, starving artists; endearing and awkward *real* couples who were just trying to pay the rent!"

The vehicle comes to a stop, and I assume that he has pulled up to the gas station pump.

"Honestly," I tell the doctors. "Can someone look at my ears and tell me if they're bleeding?"

"Sorry, honey," Owen says as he unlocks his seatbelt. "We can't help you there. We're only ophthalmologists, and you need an otolaryngologist. We can recommend you to a few good ENT docs."

"Just buy me a popsicle," I command him with a frown.

"Oh!" he exclaims as he exits the car. I feel the vehicle shift with the loss of his weight. "That reminds me of a great porno. I'll tell you

67

about it once I get back!"

"Get me a popsicle, too," Liam says weakly. Once the door shuts, Liam turns in his seat to glance back at me. "I'm so sorry about this, Helen. I think he's doing it on purpose."

"You should have warned me more," I say with a fake grimace. Although I've been acting horrified, I actually find the whole situation quite hilarious—Dr. Owen Philips is somewhat adorable in a slightly pathetic way. I try very hard to keep myself from smiling at Liam to betray that I am enjoying the eccentric company. "I almost wish I'd spent thousands of dollars on a cab ride," I tell him teasingly. "At least I wouldn't be scarred for life."

"He means well," Liam assures me. "He's a good doctor, and a great friend. He's also really amazing to his girlfriend."

"Wow," I say in surprise. "How does someone like *that* get a girlfriend? Is she human?"

Liam chuckles. "Yes. Oddly enough. He treats her like a princess, but he still makes time to hang out with me."

"I can see that he cares about you," I say gently. "It's been a long time since I had a friend like that..."

"Why?" he asks.

"Can't say. It's one of my dark secrets," I explain cryptically.

"Damn. I wish Owen would stop babbling about porn so that I could actually talk to you for five minutes," Liam muttered. "You're such an interesting person."

"Me?" I ask in confusion. "I'm just your average hermit writer."

"Exactly," he says. I hear a smile in his voice. "I don't know too many of those. You're part of a very rare species."

I look down to hide my embarrassment. I can feel him staring at me; the tension is beginning to grow thick in our small quarters. He is sitting very close to me, even if we are separated by the back of his seat. When Owen was in the car with us, the atmosphere was light and funny. But now, it's dark and intense; it's laced with something I don't understand and don't want to discover. I try to think of something to say to take his focus away from me and my life. "It's just a job," I say dumbly.

He scoffs. "Just a job? Helen, I work with other doctors every day. We heal people, and it should be glamorous; we should feel like heroes. But in truth, it gets... mechanical. At some point, you start to question how important your work really is. I mean, you can heal a person's body... but that doesn't really heal the person. We aren't just bodies, you know? That's where your books come into play." He pauses, and I can feel him giving me an earnest look. "Books are medicine for the soul. They heal the eternal parts of a person."

"Liam," I say in surprise.

"You are a doctor of sorts, too," he tells me, "except for the fact that your work persists. If a person reads a good book—they become permanently changed. They can't even help it. They can't unlearn what they've learned. It will always be with them. Our bodies all crumble and fade, and we'll all eventually lose our eyesight near the end, along with many other basic bodily functions. But I like to think that even when we're gone, the soul retains some of that wisdom—some of that feeling. What I do is simple science, but what you do is... magic."

"Stop talking," I whisper. "Seriously, stop talking right now."

"Why?" he says, somewhat hurt at the interruption.

"Because I'm pretty sure that if you keep talking like this... I'll have to marry you, or something," I explain nervously. "So just zip it."

"You'll have to..." Liam is repeating what I said in confusion, when his car door opens.

"Okay!" Owen says. "I filled up the tank, and got popsicles. But Liam, you're going to have to take the wheel, so I can play games on my phone. It's very important. And if you don't want to drive, I'm unwrapping your popsicle and tossing it on the ground."

"Fine," Liam says, and there is the sound of crinkling plastic as he grabs the popsicle and gets out of the car.

I am very surprised that this mild level of blackmail is so effective. Liam really is a softie. I feel the car shift as Owen lunges into the seat in front of me. I flinch when a cold plastic item is pressed against my cheek.

"Your popsicle, as requested, milady!" Owen says happily.

Lifting my hand, I take the popsicle away from Owen. I smile as I begin to unwrap the item, so I can press the sweet concoction against my tongue. Just as I taste the frozen sugar-water, the driver's side door opens and a cold wind blasts into the car. I shiver. "Dammit. I should have thought of something warm, instead. I wish hot chocolate could be converted into a weapon for self-mutilation..."

"I also got us some potato chips," Owen tells us. "That should keep us going for the rest of the trip!"

"Couldn't you have gotten something more substantial?" Liam asks him. "Like maybe some sandwiches?"

"But you love potato chips!" Owen says to his friend in astonishment. "They're your guilty pleasure. You have some tucked away in your office at work, and all over your house... you can never get enough of potato chips. I thought you'd like them."

"I do," Liam says in dismay, "but you

could have tried to make me seem a little more mature in front of Helen. You could have avoided sharing *my* dirty secrets with the highly respected author that we *just* met."

"It's okay," I tell him gently. "I like potato chips too. I'm just surprised at how... casual you both seem."

"We work really hard all week," Owen says, with his mouth full of potato chips. "We need to let loose sometime and just be ourselves."

Liam starts up the car and begins to drive away from the gas station. I instantly feel safe. A wave of comfort washes over me. Sliding off my boots, I pull my legs up underneath my body and snuggle deeper into the soft fabric of the backseat. I remember the way it felt to be driven around by my father when I was younger. I remember being cozy and warm as I listened to the sound of my father's laughter, while staring out the glass window and imagining all the things I could not see. I remember my mother describing the landscapes; fields of cows relaxing lazily in the sun, majestic mountains covered in snow at their peaks, and bridges that stretched farther than the horizon out over the ocean. I remember deserts and double rainbows, waterfalls and fire-breathing dragons—well, my mother might have taken some liberties with the landscape. My sister and father would often join in with the fantastic storytelling, but I never minded the fiction too much.

I did become a writer, after all.

Liam's driving is so calm and solid compared to Owen's. I can't help thinking that I wish I could be driving with him forever. Even if we never get to my sister's wedding, it will have been worth it to me for the trip. I haven't had this much fun in years, and it's so nice to be around other human beings. These two doctors are so silly and nice, and I simply love road trips. Liam's words from earlier come back to me, unbidden, and I try to shut them out. For some reason, the doctor's words really did make me feel special and important. I had not realized that my work had caused such a great impact on anyone. I am suddenly stricken with the realization of what's happening.

Am I really doing this? Am I really in a car with two men I just met, heading back to New York? Am I really going to have a chance at getting my vision back? Could it be possible? Am I really going to see my family? For a few minutes, I get lost in thoughts of my mother and father. I remember how much they loved each other. I remember Carmen's boundless energy and enthusiasm, and how she could never miss an opportunity to insult or tease me. I remember when things were good.

"Tell us a story, Helen." My mother's voice filled my mind. *"You're such a great storyteller. One day, you're going to be an*

73

illustrious writer. Blind or not, you're going to take the world by storm. That's why I named you after Helen Keller. She never let anything stop her! Neither will you."

The memory is almost too bittersweet to bear. I realize that I have forgotten to lick my popsicle for several seconds, and the juice is dripping down onto my hand.

"Oh, that's right!" Owen said suddenly. "I was going to tell you two about the popsicle-porno!"

Liam and I groan.

"No, really, this one's great," Owen says. "You'll never guess where they put the popsicle."

"I really don't want to know," Liam says.

"Helen wants to know!" Owen protested. "You want to know, don't you Helen? Don't you want to hear about how that sweet, sweet popsicle got shoved up someone's..."

"Hey," I said softly, cutting him off before he can assault my eardrums again. "Can you guys both do me a favor?"

"Sure," Owen says, and he seems suddenly attentive. He seems to know that I need him to pause his joking around for a moment.

"Okay," I begin. "First of all, I don't really believe that either of you are capable of considering me a friend."

"Helen!" Liam says in angry surprise.

"Wait, listen," I urge him. "I'm a female,

and soon I'll be your patient—I also think I'm a few years younger than you guys, although you act like adolescents. I'm also disabled. All of this would allow most people to automatically consider me inferior in several ways; it would be hard for you to consider me an equal. I know how the minds of men work. However, if you are intent on continuing this charade and pretending to be my friend, could you please stop calling me Helen? I changed my name, and I don't like being called that."

The men seem to be sharing an uncomfortable look as they silently disagree with my statement. I can *hear* the way they are looking at each other, and hear them choosing not to argue with me.

"What do you want us to call you?" Owen asks.

"Winter," I tell him. "Please call me Winter."

"Oh! Like the name on your books," Owen muses. "Sure thing."

"I don't know if I can do that," Liam admits. "You feel more like a Helen to me."

"Please," I coax him. "It really bothers me."

"Why?" he asks again.

My lips curve upward into a smile, and I am almost certain he is peeking into the rearview mirror to examine my expression.

"That's another deep, dark secret," I tell him, trying to make light of my own psychosis. I return to gazing out the window, even though the act is futile. I wish Liam and Owen would tell me what's going on outside the car in the world around us. I wish I wasn't too embarrassed to ask. I try to imagine breathtaking landscapes to distract me from Owen's disturbing visuals, and I manage to transport myself away in my mind.

Chapter Six

"I'm getting too tired to drive," Liam says gruffly. "My eyes are closing. I'm sorry."

"No worries," I tell him. "I know you weren't planning on doing this tonight. Sorry for roping you into it."

"I decided to give you a ride because I wanted to. You should be at your sister's wedding," Liam says. His voice is laced with sleepiness as he turns to his friend. "Hey, Owen? Can you take over, man? I'm seriously fading fast here. Getting tunnel vision, and everything."

His question is answered by a loud snore.

"Dammit," Liam mutters.

"I wish I could take over," I say in disappointment. "I'm wide awake."

"Do you mind if I stop at a motel, Helen?"

I am a little annoyed that Liam won't even attempt to call me by the name I prefer. "I think I

77

made an error in judgment," I inform him.

"What do you mean?" he asks,

"From the sound of your voices, I would have guessed that you guys were no older than your early thirties..."

"We're actually both in our late twenties," Liam tells me. "I'm 28, and he's 29."

"But you get tired fast," I tease, "like old men."

Liam laughs lightly. "I know we seem childish and carefree," he says, "but we actually do have crazy hours. It's Friday night, so you can bet that we both haven't had a full night's sleep all week." He yawns loudly. "Okay, I can't even make it to a motel. I saw a sign for a rest stop a few miles back, and I'll pull over as soon as I see it. I think Owen has blankets in the trunk."

"A rest stop?" I ask nervously. "Is that safe?"

"It's safer than crashing and dying."

I ponder this for a moment, but as I'm worrying, I feel myself beginning to yawn. I must be getting old, too, for I could also use a nap. When Liam pulls over and parks the car, I am already dozing off. I hear the car door open and close as he moves to the trunk to gather blankets. He opens the door nearest to me and drapes a blanket over my legs.

"Feel free to lie down and get comfortable," he tells me.

"Would it be better for you to come and rest in the backseat?" I offer quietly.

"I don't want to make you uncomfortable," he says. "I'll be fine in the front." He shuts the door and moves back around the car to the driver's side. Once he gets into the car, he locks the doors and turns the heat up. "Wow, Owen is completely out," he observes as he tugs a blanket over his friend. "He doesn't seem to mind sleeping like this. I think I'm tired enough not to care."

I unbuckle my seatbelt and stretch my legs out on the seat. My feet collide with my backpack, and I reach out to lift it and place it on the ground to give myself more room. I begin to feel slightly guilty that I have so much space while the men are cramped in the front of the car. I assume that they are both far taller than me, and they must be very uncomfortable. I arrange the blanket over my legs, looking awkwardly in the direction of the tired doctors.

"Liam," I whisper, trying not to disturb Owen.

"I wish you could see this," he responds.

I hesitate. "See what?"

"The stars. We're still out in the country, so the light pollution from the cities isn't hiding them from view quite as much as I'm used to. They're just blanketing the entire sky, like snowflakes on asphalt. There's also a little sliver of moon; not big or bright enough to distract from the stars."

"What does it look like?" I ask him softly.

"The moon?" He pauses thoughtfully. "It's like... God's fingernail clipping."

This causes laughter to bubble up in my throat. I touch one of my fingernails to refresh my concept of the shape. I trace the gentle curvature and imagine the moon. "Thanks," I tell him softly, pulling the blanket snug around my neck. "I can see it clearly."

"Good. I'm going to have to turn off the car now," he tells me. "If I leave it running, the battery might die, and then we'd be in a pickle. If you get too cold, let me know."

Nodding, I try to get comfortable. My legs are feeling a little frozen, so I bring them closer to my body. I wrap my arms around my middle, hugging myself. Listening carefully, between the sounds of Owen's snoring, I hear Liam's teeth chattering. I suddenly feel awful for making him do this. I consider inviting him into the back seat again, and maybe moving close to him so that we can both keep warm. The idea makes me a bit nervous, but it's the least I can do since I got us into this mess. As my shoulders begin to tremble violently, I acknowledge that having some body heat near to mine does not sound so terrible at the moment.

"Liam," I whisper again. "Are you sure

you don't want to..." Halfway through my sentence, I realize he is asleep. I can hear the change in his breathing. I am saved from needing to ask an embarrassing question, and potentially getting into an even more embarrassing situation. As I drift off to sleep, I imagine countless snowflakes scattered over asphalt. It's an enchanting image, and I might use it in a book someday. I can also picture the glowing fingernail of God, scratching the sky fondly, the way one might caress a sleeping pet.

Chapter Seven

I must have dozed off for a few hours, when a piercing noise startles me awake. For a moment, I'm not sure where I am, or why there's hard plastic digging into my back and making my spine ache. I try to move, and find that my whole body feels frozen. When I hear a man groan, and another curse, I am reminded that I am in a vehicle with two strange young doctors.

The high-pitched noise continues to drone on, and I realize that it is my cell phone. I reach down to my backpack and fumble to unzip it with my stiff fingers. The metal is cold and it makes me wince.

"Answer it already!" Owen says with sleepy annoyance.

"I'm trying," I say as I feel around for my phone. When my hand finally connects with the item, it takes me a few tries to answer. "Hello?" I finally say, bringing it close to my ear. My voice is hoarse and my hands are so cold that they hurt. When I breathe out, I can almost feel the cloud of water vapor hovering around my face. There is nothing on the other end of the line. "Helloooo?" I say again.

The sound of soft crying filters into my ear.

"Carmen?" I say with concern, sitting straight up and at alert. "Is everything okay?"

"No. No. I'm freaking out." She takes several deep breaths, trying to calm herself down. "I'm getting married today. *Today.*"

"Just relax," I command in a stern, take-charge voice. "What's going on?"

"Oh, Helen. I'm just so stressed out. Where are you? I was hoping you'd show up last night. Aren't you coming? I thought you'd be coming."

"Yeah," I tell her, groaning and repositioning my sore body. Liam has turned on the car to begin warming us up, but it hasn't started working yet. "I'm on my way to you. I was living in New Hampshire, so it's a bit of a trip."

"Thank goodness," Carmen says, and her tears abate almost immediately. "I can't wait to see you! How long until you get here?"

"Uh. I don't know. A few hours?"

"Great! Oh, I'm so glad you're coming home, Hellie. I invited a bunch of great guys that I went to school with, so maybe I can introduce them to you, and one of them can be your date!"

"Wait, what?" I say grouchily, blinking and rubbing my eyes. My vision might not work, but my eyes still feel gross after sleeping for a few hours. "A date? Why do I need a date?"

"Because you're my sister! You can't be single at your sister's wedding. Everyone knows that. We need to find a handsome man for you to wear on your arm. There's this guy, Brad—I met him in a philosophy class, but now he's a copyright lawyer. He's very passionate about intellectual property. I figured that you two might have something in common, since he sort of works with books?"

"Carmen, are you insane?" I say angrily, clutching my head. "I don't want to date some douchebag lawyer. I'm coming to your wedding because I care about *you*, not because I want to get set up with random freaks. With your horrible taste in men? Brad is probably a closet serial-killer."

"No way! He's a total sweetheart. You're going to love him. In addition to being Grayson's best man, he's also *so* sexy..."

"No," I say firmly. "Carmen, do you hear me? I swear to God. If you set me up with someone, I'm not coming. I am not in the mood for this garbage."

"But... Helen. You have to come. I told Daddy that you were coming, and he already bought your favorite red velvet cupcakes." Carmen sighs. "I didn't want to tell you this, but Dad hasn't been doing so well lately. He had a minor heart attack..."

"A heart attack?" I repeat dumbly. Remembering my mother's death, my entire body is seized by a panic. "Is he... is he okay?"

"Sure. He's fine, but he'll be better if you get your cute butt down here!"

I shove my forehead into the upholstery of the backseat. "Carm, are you lying to manipulate me?"

"No way, honey. I'm just reminding you of your responsibility to your family," Carmen says innocently. "And part of that responsibility is to date Brad!"

I gnash my teeth together angrily. An idea suddenly strikes me. It's horrible, but it just might work. I glance toward the front seats where the two doctors are sitting, and I bite my lip as a smile begins to transform my features.

"No," Liam whispers. "Whatever you're planning, don't do it!"

I have to ignore him for the sake of self-preservation. "I have to be honest with you, Carmen. The reason I didn't want to date Brad... is because I have a boyfriend. I'm bringing a date to your wedding."

Liam groans and Owen chuckles.

"You have a boyfriend?" Carmen

exclaims in shock. "You? No way! Little Hellie has a boyfriend? I don't believe it!"

"Yeah. I didn't want to tell you because... I wanted to surprise you," I lie awkwardly. "He's... uh... he's a doctor."

"Pick me," Owen whispers. "Pick me!"

I am stricken with a mental image of Owen enthusiastically discussing porn with my sister and family. I shudder. There is also the fact that he has a girlfriend, and this makes me uncomfortable—even for a fake date. I don't have many options.

"What's his name?" Carmen asks. "When do I get to meet him?"

I mouth the words *I'm sorry* to Liam before responding. I hope he's not too upset. Shutting my eyes tightly and making a face, I prepare to lie through my teeth. "His name is Dr. Liam Larson. He'll be arriving with me later today."

Owen immediately begins laughing, but he clamps his hands over his mouth to muffle the sound.

"Gosh, Helen! That's so exciting. A doctor! Wow! I'm so happy for you." Carmen lets out a feminine squeal. "So tell me, is he great in bed?"

I start coughing violently. I press a hand over my face to hide my embarrassment. Owen makes a low whistle; he has partly climbed over the seats in order to press his face close to my phone and listen to everything that Carmen is saying.

"Uh, yeah," I say awkwardly into my cell. "He's, uh, really great in bed. Like, the greatest."

"Oh, brother," Liam mutters under his breath. "How do I get myself into these things?"

"There's a porno that starts *just like this!*" Owen whispers excitedly to his friend.

Carmen sighs happily. "This is such good news, darling!" she says in a wavering voice. "I'm—I'm sorry to have called so late. I know I probably woke you up. I—I just wanted to hear your voice. I'm so glad you're coming. I have been hoping and praying to see you again for the longest time." She begins to cry again softly.

"Carm?" I say in concern. "Are you sure everything's good?"

"Oh, yes. I'm just—just don't mind me. You know weddings make me emotional. I'll see you soon, Hellie? You and your dashing doctor?"

"Yeah. See you soon."

She hangs up the phone, and I do too. I let my head fall into my hands for a moment, as I go over the entire conversation a few times in my mind. I am left with the urge to scream at the top of my lungs, and run out into the forest, never to see these doctors again. "This is so humiliating," I whisper. "I'm sorry. I don't know why I said that. Carmen just gets under my skin."

"Why didn't you pick me?" Owen said in disappointment.

"Liam's more suitable," I explain with a groan. "He's read my books, so he knows a little about me. He can bullshit that we have some previous connection. And also, he's less likely to talk about porn."

"Fair enough," Owen said unhappily, "but I would have liked to be a wedding crasher."

"Is your sister okay?" Liam asks. "Does she usually call you at 5 AM?"

"Whoa," I say in surprise. "Is it 5 AM?" My first thought is that something must be terribly wrong. I consider this for a moment. "It's probably just pre-wedding jitters," I tell the guys, trying to brush it off.

"So you really want me to come with you, as your date?" Liam asks me.

"Yes," I say quietly. "I'm so sorry. What can I do for you in return?"

"Well, since you offered," Liam responds, "I would like some information."

"Information?" I ask with a frown.

"Yes," Liam says. "Remember all those deep, dark secrets I said I'd extract from you? Well, if you share them with us, then I'll be your date for your sister's wedding."

This is probably the worst thing he could have requested. My mouth feels suddenly very dry. "Um. Isn't there anything else you might want?

Maybe I could dedicate my next book to you?"

He laughs lightly. "You're going to do that anyway once I get your sight back."

I rack my brain, searching for something I could give him. "I'll have my publisher put out a press release," I offer, "or maybe schedule an event, like a book launch. We can publicly declare that you're the hero who helped the semi-famous blind author Winter Rose to see. Even if it doesn't work, and I can't see, I'll pretend like I can, and you'll probably get tons of research grants and stuff."

"I'm pretty sure that you're going to do that anyway," Liam tells me, "because it's a good story that will sell books."

"Okay," I mumble, getting desperate. "How about I name a character after you?"

"That would be nice," Liam says. "I'll take all of the above, but I'll still need one additional thing to sweeten the pot. Information."

"Why?" I moan in protest.

"Because I'm curious," he answers in a good-natured way. "Come on. It can't be that bad. Tell me your deepest, darkest secrets."

I sigh. "Are you sure?"

"Yes."

"Really? Right here. Right now? In front of Owen?"

"Yeah, why not?" Liam says cheerfully. "He's been telling us way more than we need to know for a while."

"I want to hear, too," Owen chimes in. "Entertain us, storyteller!"

I spend a moment gathering my composure. I smooth my hands over my legs, and look around uneasily. Taking a deep breath, I try to mentally prepare myself for what I'm about to say to two complete strangers.

"Well... three years ago, I was raped."

A hush falls over the car. I can feel the men looking at each other. They obviously don't know how to respond, and the silence is growing tense.

"I guess it's not really a big deal," I say lightly. "I know it happens to a lot of people. I probably shouldn't have let it bother me as much as it did, but it was..." I pause in my narration, searching for the right words. "It was one of the first really awful things that had ever happened to me. I guess you could say I became disillusioned with life. A lot of really bad things happened three years ago." I bite down on my lip nervously. I'm not used to talking about this, and it's difficult to appear calm and emotionless. I just want this moment to be behind me forever. Maybe if I can reflect in an unaffected way, I can finally move forward with my life and be brave again. I look toward the window once more, and lift my hand to touch the cool glass.

We remain sitting in silence for a little

while, before someone finally speaks.

"That *sucks*," Owen says unhappily.

"Yeah," I agree with a small nod. "It did suck. I dropped out of school after that, because I couldn't bring myself to go back. I'd had amazing grades, too. I didn't tell my dad or my sister all the details, because they had enough to worry about. I just said I was mugged to explain the bruises and injuries. Actually, the only person I really confided in was Dr. Howard. I knew I could trust her with sensitive information..." I suddenly frown. It occurs to me that Leslie Howard might have sent Liam and Owen to find me out of pity for my situation. While this bothers me, even if it is true, it was still a thoughtful gesture. I try to cast this thought out of my mind. "So, that's my story," I tell the guys, trying to brush it off. "After that happened, I tried to act like things were normal, but I just couldn't be around people anymore. So I moved out of the city and changed my name. And here we are!"

"I'm sorry," Liam says in a low voice. His breathing is ragged, as though his chest might be shaking with bottled rage. "I wish that hadn't happened to you."

I am a little surprised by his tone. He sounds like he cares, and might actually be really upset on my behalf. "Maybe it was for the best," I muse, to myself more than the men. "Maybe it ended up pushing my life in the right direction."

"What do you mean?" Liam asks sharply. "How could *this* be the right direction?"

"Well," I say gently. "I had been working on a manuscript in my free time, but I was so busy with school that I probably would have never finished it. Even if I did, I wouldn't have had the time to look for a publisher. I probably would have kept pursuing my education until I was a doctor like you guys. But after that happened to me..." I laugh lightly at the situation. "There was nothing I could do *except* for writing! I couldn't leave the house due to crippling social anxiety. I couldn't even get out of bed for a while. Writing was the only job where I didn't need enough energy to get dressed and face the world. I only had to face what was inside myself." I hesitate. "This might sound silly, but it's like the universe *wanted* me to write. So it stripped me of my ability to do anything else. I wish it could have been a little less harsh with its methods, but what can you expect? It's the universe."

"That wasn't the universe," Liam says with a growl. "That was some fucking worthless jackass..."

"Shut up," Owen whispers to his friend angrily. "Stop talking about it, or you'll make it worse!"

"How can I make it worse?" Liam asks, also in a whisper. "It's pretty damn bad already."

Owen makes a noise of frustration. "Dude,

why'd you have to go and ask her about her secrets? Now you've made things all uncomfortable. We still have a few hours left of driving. Now I'm nervous and I don't know what to say to lighten the mood. Why'd you have to be so inappropriate and personal?"

"Me?" Liam whispers to his friend angrily. "You're the one who talked about graphic porn for almost four hours. To a girl who's been raped. Did you ever think that maybe the last thing she might want to hear about is kinky sex?"

"You both fail at whispering," I inform them. I hear them hanging their heads like sad puppies. "Guys, it's cool," I tell them, lifting my hands in a gesture meant to tell them to calm down. "I'm over it, really."

"You don't seem to be over it," Liam said skeptically. Something seemed to click in his brain as his voice changed. "Oh. That's why you kept flinching and getting upset when I tried to guide you earlier..."

"Yeah, so I have a few lingering issues," I admit. "It's not a big deal. I've mostly sorted it out."

"Mostly sorted it out?" Liam demands. "Mostly?"

I send him a curt nod. "I'm here, aren't I? I'm taking a chance and going on a road trip with two men I just met."

"But you need counseling," Liam said

with concern.

"I gave myself counseling," I explain. "You see, at first, I blamed my disability. I thought it was because I couldn't see, that someone would take advantage of me like that. I thought that it was a weakness; a vulnerability. I thought I wasn't fit enough for society. But I did some reading on the subject, and now I realize that... it happens to lots of people. It was just a random crime. Lots of people commit random crimes, and target people who are weaker than they are. Lots of people like to inflict harm on others, especially if the others seem like easy targets." I give the men a sad little smile. "So, that's why I generally try to avoid people. It's safer."

"That's really sad," Owen says in a depressed tone.

"I don't mind being alone," I tell him. "Writers need their solitude anyway. I think it suits me."

"Helen?" Liam asks softly. "Don't let a few bad apples ruin all of humanity for you. Most of us are good. Most of us genuinely care for others, and don't get pleasure out of hurting those who seem fragile and down on their luck. In fact— some of us thrive on healing others. Some of us will go out of our way to try to help someone we've never met. I hope you'll see that soon. I hope you'll see *everything* soon."

I send a smile in the direction of the

doctor in the driver's seat. He says such sweet things, and it's starting to get under my skin more than a little. "Maybe I will," I say in a flirtatious tone, "but for now, let's focus on getting our story straight. I hope you own a tux. How long have we been dating, honey pants?"

"Long enough for you to know that I don't like being called 'honey pants,'" Liam answers in dismay.

"What do you prefer? Sweet cheeks? Stud muffin? Cuddly bear?" I ask teasingly. "Help me out, Owen. I can't see what he look like."

"Hmm," Owen says thoughtfully. "How about 'handsome tiger'?"

"You think I look like a handsome tiger?" Liam asks his friend, and it's obvious that he's flattered.

I burst out laughing. "I think *you two* have some deep, dark secrets you need to discuss. Now I know what we're going to talk about for the rest of the drive. Owen, do you find Liam attractive?"

"Well, he has these intense hazel eyes," Owen explains, "and when he gets angry, he does sort of resemble a tiger about to pounce."

"Wow! That's really nice of you to say, man," Liam says. He puts the car in gear and begins to drive out of the rest stop. "I'm touched."

"This reminds me," I tell the men, leaning forward, "of a gay erotica story I read once. It started exactly like this, with two close friends and colleagues exchanging a casual compliment that turned into more..."

"I don't want to hear that story," Owen said sharply, cutting me off.

"What?" I say, feigning hurt. "But you shared all your stories! That isn't fair. Don't you want to hear the tale of two athletes, training late one day at the gym? One of them catches sight of his buddy in the showers..."

"Dammit," Liam says. "This is going to be a long trip."

"Maybe I shouldn't have been talking about porn so much," Owen says, wincing.

I smile and proceed to torture them with my words. If my words are the only power I have, I intend to use them well.

Chapter Eight

"This can't be right," Liam said in disbelief. "Helen, I think you gave me the wrong address."

"No. This should be the right house," I tell him with embarrassment.

"Jesus. This is where you grew up?"

"Yes," I say shamefully. People often have this sort of reaction upon viewing my childhood home. I hear the men staring at the house in silence. Groaning, I unbuckle my seatbelt and fiddle with the handle of my backpack. I know that I should leave them and go inside, but I'm a bit apprehensive about the reunion with Carmen and my father.

"How many rooms are in that thing?" Owen asked with a gulp.

"I don't know," I say with a shrug. "Fifteen?"

"Fifteen," Liam repeats. *"Fifteen!"*

97

"Something like that," I mumble.

"Why the hell were you living in a tiny cabin out in the middle of nowhere when you come from money like this?" Owen asks.

"Money isn't everything," I respond glumly.

"She's crazy," Owen tells Liam, "batshit crazy! But it's okay to date a crazy chick if she's rich and pretty."

"It's just a fake date for the wedding, man," Liam said in protest. "Stop taking it so seriously."

"But now you have to make it serious," Owen told his friend earnestly. "You need to seduce her, so you can move into this house and I can come visit you. We could shoot pool. I bet there's a billiards table in there!"

"I'm not going to seduce Helen just so that we can play billiards in her fancy house," Liam tells his friend sternly. Then he hesitates. "But I might do it for the tennis court and indoor swimming pool..."

"Indeed," says Owen. "Think of all the fun we could have! Maybe you could just quit your job and mooch off her."

"There *are* a few television shows I wish I had time to watch," Liam says thoughtfully.

"Guys," I say with mock annoyance. "I'm *right here.*"

"Sorry. Forgot all about you, little lady!"

Owen said exuberantly. "I'm too distracted by this big, shiny mansion. Look at those skylights! And the balconies!"

"Even the trees! Even the shrubbery!" Liam declares. "Owen, have you ever seen such perfect, nicely shaped bushes?"

"Yes. Haven't I been talking about porn for hours? I thought I mentioned those!"

I chuckle to myself softly. "Okay, boys. Calm down. It's just a house. You know, those things people live in? It's not really that special."

"Just a house! *Just a house!*" Owen repeats. "Are you blind? Oh—wait. Sorry, it's just a phrase. I meant, like—metaphorically blind."

I make a face at his lackluster attempt at humor. "Thanks." I fiddle with my backpack some more, trying to think of something to say to stall leaving the car. "I just..."

"What's wrong, Helen?" Liam asks.

Blinking, I shake my head. "I have a bad feeling," I murmur, feeling stupid as the words leave my mouth.

"Of course you feel bad," Owen responds. "You feel bad that you're a loaded super-millionaire while your new friends are just poor, struggling doctors who can't even afford a one-bedroom apartment because of their astronomical student loans. You feel bad and want to share the wealth, don't you?"

Liam clears his throat. "Maybe if you had

focused a little more in school, you could have gotten some scholar..."

"No!" Owen shouts, plugging his ears. "How dare you speak that word in my presence?"

"What word?" Liam asks with a chuckle. He raises his voice purposefully. *"Scholarships?"*

Owen lets out a mournful wail. "Nooo! Shut up, Liam. No one wants to hear about you and your stinking scholarships."

Liam turns to me with a chuckle. "I believe someone watched too much porn when he should have been studying."

"If they're playing doctor, it counts as studying," Owen said defensively.

My cheeks are hurting from smiling. These two men have kept me entertained with their outrageous banter almost consistently since we left my cabin. I haven't smiled this much in as long as I can remember. But I know that once I step through the front door of my old house, my smile will disappear. I remember how the atmosphere hung heavy with death and despair, so thick that I could barely breathe. It was my father's grief; he carried it around with him in a dark cloud that poisoned everything. Maybe things will be different now? Maybe now that Carmen is getting married, we can finally be positive and look to the future?

"Are you going to go home, Helen?" Liam asks me. "Didn't your sister need you?"

I fold my hands together in my lap and press them together tightly. "They're going to be angry with me for leaving," I mumble.

"Do you want to drive around for a few more minutes and gather the courage to go inside?"

"No, I should be strong and stop delaying this," I say with resolve. I am tempted by Liam's offer. I would love nothing more than to spend just a little more time relaxing with the guys and making ridiculous jokes. I have only just met them, but they feel like old friends. However, I did manipulate the poor boys into driving me all this way. I can't back out now. "It can't be that bad," I say, trying to reassure myself. "I'm sure things are different than when I left."

"Give me your phone," Liam requests.

I reach beside me to Owen's leather seats, and feel around for a moment before grasping my cell. I extend the small device toward Liam. He takes it from my hand, and immediately begins pressing buttons.

"I'm putting my number in here so you can tell me the details of the wedding," he explains. "You can call or text to let me know when and where I should meet you later today."

"Thank you," I tell him quietly, accepting the return of my phone.

"You can also let him know if your house happens to be infested with giant mutant cockroaches," Owen says with a chuckle, "and he can come to your rescue. Seriously, Helen. From the look on your face, you'd think you were heading into an alien war-zone."

"That's exactly the way I feel," I say with a grimace. I sling my backpack over my shoulder and run my hands over the car door, looking for the handle. "Thanks for driving me, guys. It was really nice of you."

"Well, we made a bargain that helps our careers!" Liam says in a positive tone. "It's a win-win situation."

Finally managing to unlatch the car door, I place one foot outside on the ground. "It was great meeting you, Owen. Thanks for educating me on the wonders of porn."

"Once we get your vision working, I'll have to make popcorn and schedule a movie night," Owen says gravely. "It will blow your mind."

"I can't wait," I say, half-sarcastically and half-enthusiastically. Yes—being able to see anything at all would be a blessing; even porn. The popcorn doesn't sound terrible either, I realize, as my stomach growls eagerly at the idea. My mouth begins to water in yearning for the fluffy, buttery kernels. It is my appetite that finally motivates me to step out of the car; even if there is nothing pleasant or welcoming in that house, at the very least, there will be a delicious meal waiting for me.

Not protein shakes, granola bars, popsicles, or potato chips. Real food.

A smile finally comes to my lips. "Well, I guess it's time to go in there and face the music! Will you pop the trunk, Liam?"

"Sure. Let me come out and help you," he says.

"No, no. I'll be fine," I assure him as I walk around to the back of the car. I place my hand on the trunk of the car to lift the lid, but I feel another hand rest lightly on top of mine. I am momentarily startled, but I do not pull away this time. I have grown more comfortable around Liam in the past few hours of chatting.

"Allow me," he says gently, as he removes my hand from the car. "I insist."

A feeling of warmth flushes my neck as I feel his thumb brush against the palm of my hand. His touch is gone as soon as it came, and I hear him lifting the heavy suitcase onto the ground. The sound of the metal sliding against metal is heard as he extends the handle, followed by a loud click.

"I'll walk you to the door," he says.

Reaching out, I firmly take the suitcase from his hands. "You've been a real gentleman, Liam, but I can take it from here. If my sister sees you, she's going to attack you with all sorts of questions. You should probably go home and get some rest."

"Are you sure? I don't mind a few

questions..."

"Liam, there's something worse than mutant cockroaches in that house," I warn him ominously. "There's a fearsome creature that no man can ever hope to vanquish: the neurotic Bridezilla."

He laughs lightly. "Do you think you can survive her reign of terror?"

"Sure," I say softly. "It's only one day. I owe her this much, at least—especially after abandoning her for so long..."

"Don't feel guilty for that," he assures me. "It sounds to me like you needed to get away for your sanity and your career. Sometimes, the best thing you can do for another person is to leave. You need to take care of yourself before you can hope to take care of anyone else—you have to shake off all the negativity that's smothering you so that you don't drag others down."

"But I don't know if I'm at that place yet," I confess. "This is so sudden. I was uprooted from my home before I really got a chance to decide that I was ready. I don't know if I can handle this— being in the city again. The air smells different, and it's so loud—even all the way out here in the suburbs."

"Just take it slow," he says. "Take it one day at a time. If you hate it here, you can always go back. I'll drive you myself, if you need a ride."

"Everything's a mess," I mumble. "I don't

know where to begin. How do I repair the relationships I ruined?"

"Just try," he tells me. "All you can really do is try."

Although his words are simple, I feel a little bolder. I realize that I am having trouble ripping myself away from him. Kicking the bottom of my suitcase while tugging the handle toward me, I set the heavy luggage at an angle that is easier to roll along the cobblestoned path to my front door. "Thanks," I call over my shoulder, as I begin to walk away. "I'll see you later."

"Good luck!" he shouts after me.

"Liam's really easy when he's drunk!" Owen yells from the car. "Just wear something nice, and make sure he has a few drinks later— you'll definitely get lucky."

I make a face and shake my head as I march along the path to my front door. The wheels of my suitcase rattle and jangle against the cobblestones with a rhythmic drumbeat. It makes the perfect soundtrack for my impending doom. I hear the sound of rushing water to my left, and I am surprised that the fountain in our front yard is running in the winter. It must be because we have family from out of town staying at the house for the wedding. This thought makes me even more anxious. I have never fared well in large crowds.

When I feel the ground become smoother beneath my feet, and my suitcase becomes quieter,

I know that I am walking on the concrete closer to the stairs. I slow down my walking a little, and slide my feet along the ground tentatively until my toes collide with the stairs. It occurs to me that I haven't heard Liam and Owen drive away, so I try to be as graceful as possible when I reach down to lift my suitcase, and drag it up the stairs. I count the five steps up to our porch, and place my suitcase down on the flat ground. I suppose the men are waiting to see me enter the house before leaving, and I turn to send a wave in the direction from which I came. If they aren't waiting, or even paying attention, this might look silly—waving at nothing like a fool. However, I would rather risk looking like an idiot than seeming impolite or ungrateful in this moment.

I hear an engine start, and the sound of the car pulling away. I breathe a sigh of relief. It looks like I was waving closely enough in the right direction, and they were actually still waiting for me. It's so hard to follow social protocol when you have no idea what's going on around you. So many assumptions need to be made.

Turning back to the front door, I move forward with a hand outstretched. Beneath my boots, I can feel the fabric of the large welcome mat. When my fingers collide with the stylish beveled glass panel set within in the door, I feel the contours in the design for a moment. Compared to my tiny cabin, this house really was filled with a gorgeous tactile landscape. My mother made a point of making sure that the décor was not only aesthetically pleasing to the eyes of our sighted family members, but also pleasing to my senses. I am surprised when the door shifts under my hand; I am able to push it open without much effort.

Without any warning, a divine scent assails my nostrils. Releasing my suitcase, I walk into the foyer in wonder. I close my eyes and breathe deeply, turning my body around slowly in a 360 degree spin.

Flowers.

I can imagine the softness of the petals and the glorious colors, in tender pastels or vibrant, rich reds. I have no idea what these words mean, but if the flowers look anything close to the way they smell, they must be unbelievably enchanting. I breathe in again, sifting through all the different aromas in the room; I feel like I am pulling apart a piece of fabric and examining each thread. I can just make out the delicate, intoxicating fragrance of jasmine, along with the spicy sweetness of gardenia. Finally, an unmistakable musky aroma; the dizzying and deeply refreshing aroma of roses.

The perfumed air invades my sinuses and lungs, filling me with memories. I recall springtime picnics in the grass, and my mother holding my hand as we walk barefoot through a gurgling brook. I remember my sister laughing and dumping dozens of fresh, velvety blossoms into my arms. I remember pressing my face into the cool softness of the petals, and feeling happy to be alive.

When I was younger, I would rub my fingers over the dresses in my closet, trying to feel the difference in their color. I hoped that there was some kind of special energy in each color that I could grow to sense, if I tried hard enough. But flowers are different—they are alive! They are exuberant to the touch, and they sing loudly to boast of their beauty; you can't *not* see the flowers in your mind when you smell them.

I hungrily inhale the fragrant air, trying to drink in the memories and squeeze every last drop of beauty out of this aroma. It's completely overpowering, and I stand there in the middle of the foyer, looking around in a daze. Have I really stepped into my old house, or did that doorway lead into a different dimension? It has been years since I have encountered a remotely nice smell. I have been content with merely agreeable aromas. But to be immersed in such hypnotic and mesmerizing natural perfumes, all mingling together in the perfect combination for my palate! It's almost unbearable. I almost want to cry at the loveliness of this moment.

I wish I had invited Liam and Owen in to see—but at the same time, I'm glad I did not. The fragrance is so uplifting that it's almost spiritual, and I would not want them to make fun of me; not in this moment. I wouldn't want anything to taint my enjoyment of the lush blossoms. I am almost trembling with gratitude for this moment alone with the posies. I feel like it was designed as a special gift, just for me. I stand in meditative silence for a few seconds, just breathing. I savor every breath.

When I am finally able to form coherent and practical thoughts, I realize that these must be decorations for the wedding. Carmen must have chosen to get married at home! This idea is both comforting and nerve-wracking. I am happy that the big event will take place in an environment that I know like the back of my hand; I won't need to rely on anyone, for I could never forget the precise number of stairs in every staircase, or the angles of every twist and turn of every passageway.

"Meredith?" says a man's voice questioningly.

I was so distracted by the flowers that I had not noticed the quiet footsteps of house slippers on hardwood. I turn toward the source of the sound, and I find myself facing the direction of the library. My father's favorite room. My father's voice. I feel my chest swell with nostalgia and tenderness. I remember the diligent man who was always up at the crack of dawn, working dutifully in that library before any of us had even considered getting out of bed. I remember him

Loretta Lost

reading the best articles in the newspaper to me each morning over breakfast—and sometimes the comics, to cheer me up when I was down. My heart leaps a little, in hope that this could be a normal, happy morning. Like the way things used to be. I have a delayed realization that he has called me by my mother's name. I swallow before speaking, to make sure that the emotion is cleared from my voice.

"No, Dad. It's me."

"Helen?" he says softly. "Heavens, child. I could have sworn you were your mother's ghost. You look just like she did on the day I met her."

I struggle to fight back tears. "Didn't Carmen tell you I was coming?"

"Yes. I haven't been able to sleep since she mentioned it to me," he admits. "But I have also been expecting your mother's ghost to show up for the big day, so I hope you'll forgive me for mixing up our party guests."

Even through my sadness, he is able to coax a smile from me. He seems better than when I left—still wistful and brokenhearted, but in higher spirits. "I missed you, Dad," I whisper, and this time the emotion does cause my voice to break.

"I missed you too, sweetheart." His gentle gait is almost noiseless as he crosses the room toward me. He places two big, warm hands on each of my shoulders. "Let me look at you. My little Helen! You're all grown up."

110

I nod, lowering my chin to look at the ground. "Dad, I'm sorry that I left..."

"None of that," he tells me kindly. "You were unhappy, and your happiness is the most important thing in the world to me. Now stop moping and let your old man give you a hug."

I don't need to be offered twice. I dive forward, burying my face against his shoulder. His arms encircle me, and for the first time in years, I truly feel like I have a home. I smell his familiar fatherly cologne, mingling with the flowers all around us. I am filled with such a deep joy, that I am almost sure I must be daydreaming.

"Are you going to stay with us, Helen?" he asks me in a quiet voice.

A pang of sorrow strikes my heart, and I remember how miserable and melancholy he was when I left home. I suddenly realize that the man I am hugging does not feel anything like the man my father used to be. His frame is skeletal and gaunt. His arms and shoulders are no longer large and firm with muscle, but wiry with bone. His skin is paper-thin, stretched over his bones like saran wrap.

I am stricken with the knowledge that I could lose him, just like I lost my mother. Carmen mentioned that he had suffered a heart attack. Has she been taking care of him? The big house suddenly feels very lonely. I realize that my father has no one. Even if Carmen hasn't been neglecting him, now that she is getting married, Dad will be even less of a priority to her. He needs me.

"I would like to stay," I tell him softly. "That is—if you're not too upset at me. If you want me to stay."

"Of course, I do!" he says, tightening the hug. "Who else is going to keep your sister from driving me mad?"

I smile. A pair of timid footsteps distract me, and I pull away from him and look in their direction. "Carmen?" I say with anticipation, but I know that the footsteps sound nothing like my sister's.

"No, no," my father says. "That's our new housekeeper, Natalia. She's here to help out with the wedding."

"Oh," I say in disappointment, realizing that I am actually eager to see my sister. "Hello, Natalia."

"Good morning, Miss," says the housekeeper.

"This is Helen, my youngest daughter," my father says, introducing me with a hand on my back. "She's a writer. She is blind, but don't let that fool you—she's the smartest person in the family, and she will give you much less trouble than Carmen."

I hear the tone of pride in his voice, and I am pleasantly surprised. This homecoming has been a lot less painful than I expected.

"Natalia, will you please take Helen's suitcase up to her room and unpack for her?" my father requests. "I want to have breakfast with my daughter and catch up on the last few years."

"Sure thing, Mr. Winters!" says the housekeeper. "It was nice meeting you, Helen."

I nod, following her footsteps with my eyes. I turn back to my father. "So, where's Carmen?"

My father laughs, a deep-throated rumble. "I don't know what's going on with that girl. She's probably just hung over from drinking too much last night at her bachelorette party. I guess it's just you and me, kiddo."

I frown at this news. When Carmen called at 5 AM, she did not sound drunk or hung over to me. But it would explain her crying and sharp mood swings. I shrug, and decide to question her later about the strange behavior.

"I went to the bakery last night and got some delicious red velvet cupcakes for you," my father says. "Will you join me for a completely unhealthy, sugary breakfast?"

My mouth begins to water, and my legs begin moving toward the kitchen. "Heck, yes!" I am still wearing my winter coat and boots, but I don't even care. I want those cupcakes.

113

Chapter Nine

I ate five cupcakes. Really. Five cupcakes.

I don't even regret it. They were so scrumptious and delectable that I could have died, right there in the kitchen. Death by cupcake. I could have just keeled over in a seizure of red-velvet-induced bliss. They were, hands down, the best cupcakes in the world. The best substance, period, that I have ever tasted in my life. I didn't even try to be polite. No, I shoved my fingers in there, getting them all sticky and covered with icing. I shed my jacket and kicked off my boots to curl up in one of our upholstered kitchen chairs as I gorged. I stuffed my mouth full to the brim and closed my eyes and chewed very, very slowly. It was heavenly. It was like a celestial encounter with dozens of tiny deities, tap-dancing on my tongue.

My father has been sharing various details of events I've missed over the years, and I'm trying my best to pay attention to him and not to the perfection on my taste buds. It's hard. Most of the conversation does not require my full attention, but I pause and grow worried when he begins discussing our financial situation. For a moment, I am regretfully distracted from my hedonistic joy as I listen to the story of how he lost his job at the pharmaceutical company shortly after my mother's death. Combined with the market crash, our finances were in a sorry state. He had needed to take out a mortgage on the house, which had previously been paid off in full. He complains that he has been incredibly dejected by the looming feeling of moving backward instead of forward. I nod attentively as I chow down ravenously on the cupcakes.

"But things are looking up," he says firmly. "I owe it largely to your sister's fiancé, Grayson. He's a smart boy, with a good head on his shoulders. He's given me some really good investing advice, and it looks like we won't need to sell the house after all."

"So you approve of this guy? He's decent, this Grayson?" I ask, nibbling the icing off the sixth cupcake. The sweetness is finally starting to overwhelm me, and my chewing begins to slow. I inwardly bemoan that I must be approaching my ultimate cupcake-capacity.

"He's wonderful," my father says with a solemn gravity. "I am so thankful, every single day, that he came into Carmen's life. And my life, too. He's been a blessing. He's been a true gentleman to your sister—he's been the son I never had. I am sure that he will also be an excellent brother-in-law to you. I can't wait for you to meet him."

I finish off my cupcake, and sigh in contentment. This news is inspiring. Since I returned home, I have been greeted with breathtaking smells, tastes, and heartwarming news. What more could anyone ask for in life? My thoughts return to Liam. I feel so grateful that he convinced me to participate in his research and helped me get back home in time for the wedding. I can't even remember what I was so terrified about. This is so wonderful. I should have come home ages ago! I can already tell that today is going to be amazing.

And I can't wait to see Liam again.

Something inside my chest flutters a little at the thought, and I feel silly for being so excited. However, it is out of my control now. He said one too many nice things, and I grew just a little too attached to him over the few hours we spent together. While I can strictly enforce my thoughts to be logical and sensible, I cannot keep the girlish giddiness out of my emotions. I blame my childhood home, and the stupid flowers and cupcakes for reverting me to my former optimistic and dreamy state. My mind begins to wander, but I quickly quell the fantasies and remind myself that it's only a fake date. He's going to be my doctor, for god's sake. Nothing can happen there.

But hearing about Carmen's happily ever after is making me crave my own. At the very least, maybe sometime in the non-too-distant future, I could be brave enough to try...

My father chuckles. "If you're finished binge-eating those cupcakes, darling, I'd love to hear about what you've been up to these past few years."

As I gulp down the last bite, it occurs to me that he might be the perfect person to consult about the clinical trial that could return my vision. My father has always known everything about everything. I part my lips, intending to spill my guts and divulge the dilemma that has been bothering me, but then I surprise myself by clamping my mouth shut again. I don't want to hear the downsides. I don't want to be cautioned. I don't want to give anyone a chance to talk me out of this.

I want to hope for the best, even if it's illogical. For the first time in forever, I want to have faith in something. I want to have faith in someone.

Searching my mind for something less sensitive to discuss, I think of my career. "I've written a few more books since I left home," I tell him instead. "Nothing special, just some thrillers.

Conspiracies, spies, revenge, action. That sort of thing."

"That's really wonderful, sweetheart. You'll have to let me read them later."

"I don't think you'd like them, Dad," I say with embarrassment, feeling the heat of a blush in my cheeks. "They're sometimes kind of cheesy, and not that intelligent."

"You're just being modest," he accuses. There is a brief, but heavy pause. "Who have you been staying with all this time? Why couldn't you come to visit? Is there a boy?"

I am a little upset by these questions. I wipe my fingers on a napkin, taking a moment to compose myself before responding. Of course, due to my blindness, he assumes I needed to live with someone so that they could help me on a day-to-day basis. Yes, I am more than a little miffed. "I was living by myself in New Hampshire," I respond quietly. "I bought a small cabin in the mountains, far away from society. I have been living on protein shakes and granola bars, so I haven't really eaten anything tasty in years. That's why I went nuts on the cupcakes."

"Good gracious, child. Why would you do subject yourself to such a life?" he asks in horror.

I shrug awkwardly. "I guess it was what I needed. It was a restorative little reprieve; very nun-like and ascetic. Also, very good for writing."

"You've always been an odd little bird,"

my father says fondly.

The old nickname brings a smile to my lips. It erases my previous annoyance. I have always adored my father, even if he often considers me to be mortally weak and incapable of basic tasks. I suppose that parents will always see their children as infants and invalids, regardless of whether they possess any glaring disabilities.

My father's phone receives a text message, and I hear him pull it from his pocket. "This is going to be a very busy day," he tells me as he responds to the text. "The ceremony won't start until 4 PM, but we need to do plenty of preparation beforehand. Guests will be arriving all day. The groom and his family will be arriving around noon. We had the florists come over early this morning, and the caterers are going to start making their deliveries." He laughs to himself. "I should keep you away from Carmen's wedding cake! You might scarf the whole thing down before the guests even get a chance to look at it."

"I think I won't be able to eat a bite of cake," I say, holding my stomach. "I'm all caked-out for at least a decade."

"I have no idea where you put it all," my father says in wonder. He receives another text message, and clears his throat. "You should probably go and wake your sister up," he encourages me. "Please help her out with anything she needs today—she can be quite the fussy bride.

But I'm sure she'll be overjoyed to see you."

"Sure, Dad. I'll try to keep her calm and stop her from stressing out," I say, rising to my feet.

"Wonderful, darling. I have no idea how we got along without you."

When he moves out of the room, I move in the opposite direction, heading for the staircase that leads up to Carmen's room. I do not even bother counting the stairs, or using the banister as a guide. I just let my muscle memory carry me up the stairs, and automatically stop me when I've reached the landing. I am impressed at how flawless my spatial memory is. Even if I'm not conscious of this knowledge, it resides deep in my brain, along with dozens of other secrets that I hope will surface as I need them. It's reassuring to know that my brain is far smarter than I am.

I stroll down the hallway toward Carmen's bedroom. It's adjacent to my old room; while we were growing up, I probably spent more time in her room than my own. I used to idolize my older sister, and try to be like her in every way possible. She was my hero and mentor for the longest while. I'm not sure exactly at what point we discovered that I was actually the more mature one. We were probably teenagers before it happened, but somehow, our dynamic changed. She began to rely on me.

Guilt floods my chest. She relied on me.

And I left.

I push these crippling thoughts away as I knock on her bedroom door. "Carm?"

There is no response. I open the door and walk inside, but I do not hear her breathing coming from the bed. I move over to the empty bed and place my hands down on the unkempt sheets. It's still warm. A muffled sound nearby startles me.

"Carm?" I say again, turning around and listening closely for the direction of the sound. When there is no response yet again, I begin to grow annoyed. "Carmen!" I call out. "We're too old for hide and seek. Also, you always had an unfair advantage with the seeking part."

The muffled sound grows louder. It sounds like something between a cough and a cry. I move toward its source, and find myself at the door to Carmen's bathroom. I knock again, politely.

There is a silence, and some heavy breathing, followed by more strange noises.

"Carmen, what's going on?" I demand. When I hear the guttural, incoherent vocalizations once more, I begin to feel afraid. I push open the bathroom door. The sound becomes clearer instantly, and I grow aware of the fact that Carmen is on the ground near the toilet, and vomiting into the bowl. I stare in surprise for a moment, before moving forward and placing my hand on her back. "Carm?" I say with concern.

She continues retching for a moment before sighing and resting her face tiredly on the toilet. I know this, because I hear her metal earring clink against the ceramic bowl.

"Hi," Carmen says weakly. "I swear—this isn't what it looks like."

Chapter Ten

"And what does it look like?" I ask her.

"It looks like I'm a psycho with bulimia and I'm trying to ensure that there's nothing in my body so I don't look fat in my wedding dress," Carmen says. "But really, I just drank *wayyyy* too much last night. The girls were just forcing me to take shots, left, right, and center. It was out of control. I'm never going to touch tequila again. Ever."

I lift my eyebrows. "I see that you're still the same old lovable, responsible Carmen."

"Shut up," she grumbles. "It's not fair. If you were around more often, you'd see my better moments. You'd see the highlights. You'd see that I've changed a lot and grown up. But the first time you see me in years, you happen to walk in on me while I'm on my knees and—" She trails off as her

123

body begins to shudder again. She wraps her arms around the toilet bowl and begins to retch violently.

With a frown, I crouch down to sit on the floor beside her. I rub my hand over her back soothingly. I can feel that she is wearing a tiny silk nightgown, and I worry that she must be freezing with her bare skin pressed against the cold bathroom tiles. When she finishes voiding the contents of her stomach, I try to think of something witty to say to distract her.

"Many women spend their whole lives dreaming about their perfect wedding day," I tell her. "Personally, I think yours is off to an excellent start."

"You jerk," Carmen says, hitting me in the arm. "Thanks for being a bucket of sunshine!" She pauses, and her playfulness disappears completely as her voice grows dark and quiet. "Why did I even invite you to come here? It's not like you care. It's not like you want to be here. Why would you? You're so superior to us, and you don't need anyone. I bet you enjoy sitting there and patronizing me."

"Hey," I say softly. "That isn't true. You know I love you. And today's going to be great! Come on, let's get you cleaned up."

"No," she says softly. She clings to the toilet bowl as her shoulders begin to tremble gently with the onset of tears. Her sobs are silent, but filled with misery. "I don't have the energy to move. Go away."

As my hand rests on her shoulder blade, I feel her anguish seep into me from the connection of our skin. Something is really wrong. I remember what Liam said about using touch to understand others. It's too powerful. It's too upsetting and heartbreaking to know that someone I love is so deeply hurt, and that she doesn't even trust me enough to tell me why. I know that it's my fault, and I need to prove that I care about her all over again. I need to be strong for her—today more than any other day.

Sliding closer to my older sister, I encircle her body in a cozy hug. I rest my head on her shoulder. "Fine. Let's just hang out here by the toilet! It's really comfortable here on the cold hard ground. In the years to come, we will often reminisce about this special day, and how you spent the entire morning puking and crying on the toilet."

"I hate you," she mumbles, but when her shoulders shake again, it's with laughter. "You're so stupid, Helen."

I am surprised when she turns toward me and hugs me back fiercely.

"I missed you," she mumbles into my shirt. "You stupid jerk."

For a moment, I just sit with her on the ground and hold her. I run my hand over her hair, and it feels as soft and silky as ever—I wonder what color it is at the moment? Her body begins to relax, and the tension leaves her shoulders. I feel relieved, like a great crisis has been averted. I also feel somewhat... maternal. Tears spring to my eyes as I acknowledge that it's my job to take over Mom's duties in this family. I should have been here to take care of both Carmen and Dad. But instead, I was weak and selfish. I can't be that way anymore.

"You need to get some water and eat something," I tell Carmen, pulling out of the hug and rising to my feet. I reach down to carefully tug on her arms to coax her into standing. "Come on! It's your wedding day. Isn't it going to take several hours to get your hair and makeup done?"

"Only four," she says tiredly as she struggles to stand. She leans on me for support. "Hey, Helen—can you bring me one of those cupcakes Dad got for you? He wouldn't let me touch them yesterday, and I was trying to stay away from anything that might jeopardize me fitting into my dress. But I could really use a pick-me-up right about now."

"Um," I say guiltily, looking down at the ground.

"Helen?" Carmen asks in horror. "Please tell me you didn't..."

"I ate all the cupcakes."

"Fuck you!" she roars, with the bellow of

a great beast about to trample a small city.

I flinch, a little bit worried that she's going to tackle me to begin an all-out brawl. We might be grown women now, and we might try our best to act the way we should, but we had more than a few physical fights when we were younger. They were always great fun. A good rough-and-tumble was always therapeutic in letting off steam. If she needs one now, I am more than happy to oblige—and to take most of the punches so that her face can remain flawless for the wedding photographs.

Carmen growls at me angrily, but she quickly breaks down into laughter. "All of them? Seriously, you ate *all* of them?"

"Sorry," I say sheepishly, and I feel a blush staining my cheeks.

"Psh, whatever," she says in frustration. I can almost hear her rolling her eyes. I know that she isn't really angry, and that she's feeling a bit better.

"You smell disgusting," I tell her, wrinkling my nose, "it's an interesting odor that's somewhere between manure and wet dog. You better take a shower, or your fiancé might change his mind and marry someone who *isn't* covered in vomit."

Carmen giggles and moves away from me to turn on the bath. "Thanks for coming, Hellie," she says softly. "This wedding stuff has been so stressful, and I'm just a pile of nerves. I really needed my sister."

Chapter Eleven

"Are your eyes closed?" I ask her nervously, grasping the hem of my shirt.

"Of course! Just hurry up, we don't have all day," Carmen says with annoyance.

I make a face as I quickly tug off my shirt and slide out of my jeans. I reach for the bridesmaid dress, and grasp it by the shoulder straps before stepping into the garment. I wiggle it up my body, and slip my hands through the armholes before reaching behind me for the zipper. It slides up easily. I move around a little, and the dress feels light and airy, and quite comfortable. "Okay!" I say happily. "You can look now."

"The dress fits," Carmen says with annoyance, "but you lied to me. I thought you said you had a boyfriend."

"What?" I said nervously. "I do."

"Then why aren't your legs shaved? And

why are you wearing *granny* panties?"

"You said your eyes were closed!" I exclaim in horror, covering my body modestly. "And these aren't granny panties—they're comfortable, *normal* underwear!"

"Why did you lie?" Carmen demands. "I'm going to have to set you up with someone..."

"No!" I shout, putting my hands up in a gesture meant to halt her. "Liam's coming a little later, I swear. You'll meet my boyfriend, and you'll see that he really exists! He's just super nice, and he knows that it's difficult for me to shave my legs, being blind and all—so he doesn't mind if I don't shave in the winter. It is winter, you know."

"Do *not* bullshit me, little sister!" Carmen says sharply. I imagine her pointing a finger at me accusingly. "You only ever blame your blindness when you're trying to elicit pity to distract someone from the topic at hand."

Damn. She knows me really well. I had forgotten that. A small smile touches my lips. "Okay, I'll tell you the truth," I say earnestly. "Liam and I—we're doing the long-distance thing. He's a doctor, and he's super busy doing research at the hospital. I need my alone time to work on my books—so it works out really well! We only see each other once every few weeks. It keeps things exciting—builds anticipation."

"Ohhh," she says, accepting this. "That

CLARITY

makes sense. So you *do* shave your legs and wear thongs once in a while?"

"Sure," I say awkwardly. "I mean, my lingerie probably isn't as nice as yours. A little touch of lace here and there." I shrug.

"Good grief. Your poor doctor must be bored out of his mind," Carmen says with pity. She moves over to her dresser and begins pulling out drawers. Finally finding a satisfactory undergarment, she tosses it at me.

"Ow." The tiny thong hits me squarely in the eye. I am not happy about this. There must have been small jewels or metal charms attached to it, for my cheek is actually stinging from the impact. "If I had known that you were going to throw your dominatrix panties at me, I might have reconsidered coming here," I tell her, rubbing my sore face.

"Men are visual creatures," Carmen lectures me. "You need to keep them interested with pleasurable aesthetics. I know that you're obviously *not* a visual person..."

"That doesn't mean you can panty-bomb my eye," I say grouchily. "I might not be able to see, but it still hurts!"

"Just put those on," Carmen commands me. "They'll look better under that dress than the outdated garbage you're wearing."

The novelty underwear is sitting on my bare toes, and I wiggle them apprehensively. "I don't think so. It's not really my style."

"Fine," Carmen says. "Then I'm calling Brad and telling him that you are going to be his date. Since you obviously don't have any real men in your life."

"I do!" I protest. I feel tingles of shame spreading through my chest at how correct she actually is. "I swear, Carmen. Stop embarrassing me. This makes me uncomfortable."

"Then call your boyfriend," she challenges me. She moves over to the bed where my discarded clothes are, and pulls my phone out of the pocket of my jeans. She advances on me and shoves my phone against my stomach. "Call him! Call him so I now so I can see that he exists."

I make a sound of annoyance and exasperation. "Really?"

"Really," she says with severity. "Or else."

Sighing, I resign myself to making the phone call. I feel stupid. This whole situation is very juvenile and high-school, but I need to protect myself from Carmen's whims and fancies. I know that she has always been a magnet for trouble, and has a tendency to drag me down into her mayhem. I do not want to be set up with anyone. I am terrified at the prospect. While Liam is also a stranger, I have somehow grown to trust him a tiny bit—enough to think that he might be mostly a decent human being.

CLARITY

After what I've been through, I have made it a personal policy to always choose the devil I know.

However, standing there with the phone in my hand makes me a little queasy. I have never spoken to Liam on the phone before, but I will need to be convincing in my lie. I will need to act like we have been dating for a while. I can feel my face growing red at the realization that I have dragged my new *doctor* into this infantile charade. I reassure myself that it won't scare him away or jeopardize my potential treatment—after all, he is friends with Owen. His tolerance for juvenile must be extremely high.

"I knew it," Carmen says triumphantly. "There isn't anyone. You're just standing there with your phone and looking like an idiot. I'm calling Brad."

"No, no," I say firmly. "I was just feeling shy for a moment. I don't really like talking on the phone much, these days." Taking a deep breath, I press the circular button on my phone. "Dial Liam."

"Calling Liam! Please stand by."

I bite my lip as I wait for the phone to begin ringing. It feels like an eternity. And then, once it is ringing, it feels like it's happening far too quickly. The ringing noises come at me like gunshots I can't possibly dodge, and I try my best not to flinch at each one. When a voice finally answers, it's more masculine than I remember and ragged with sleep.

"Hello?" he says with a yawn.

"Hi honey, how are you feeling?" I ask with concern, quickly getting into the character of a loving girlfriend. I press my hand over the phone and whisper to Carmen. "He's been a bit under the weather."

"I'm good," he responds in a husky tone. "Helen? Is that you? Your voice sounds so sweet over the phone. Say something else. I could listen to you for hours."

I feel an odd little ache in the pit of my stomach. I know we're just play-acting, but it feels more real than anything I've had in years. "I'm beginning to regret coming home," I tell him. "My sister is trying to pimp me out to strange men, and I'm getting assaulted with a blitzkrieg of scandalous intimate apparel."

"Let me talk to him!" Carmen says, reaching for the phone.

I step away, keeping it out of her grasp. I am worried she'll ask him something about me that he doesn't know, and figure out that I'm lying.

"Sounds brutal," Liam responds with another yawn. "Do you still want me to come to the wedding? I found an old tux in the back of my closet."

"No, babe!" I say nervously, while dancing away from Carmen's grabby hands. "If you're still feeling tired, you should get some rest. You've been working so hard."

I hear him chuckling on the other end of the line. "I'm guessing your sister is there? It's no trouble, Helen—I don't mind coming to the wedding. I'm actually really excited to see you again! I love spending time with you, and I'd like to do it again as soon as possible."

"I—I miss you, too?" I respond in confusion. For a moment, I am not sure whether he actually meant what he said, or if it's somehow part of our ploy. I forget to move away from my sister's grasp, and she manages to pry the phone from my distracted hands.

"Hello!" she says into the phone. "Is there a real person on the other end of this line?"

I move forward to listen to his responses, but Carmen darts away briskly, and I'm not in an aggressive enough mood to follow her and fight to retrieve my phone.

"Wow!" Carmen says in wonder. "An actual man with an actual penis! You do have a penis, right? And it's healthy? Describe it to me."

"Oh my god," I say in horror, moving to sit on the bed and lifting a pillow to smother my face.

"Lovely. I'm so glad to hear that," Carmen says with approval. "It's great to meet you, Liam. I'm Helen's sister—also known as the bride. Am I going to be seeing you later?" There is a pause as Carmen waits for the answer. "Awesome! The ceremony starts at 4 PM, so just arrive a little before that. Do you know where the house is?" When Carmen pauses again, her voice grows ominous and dark. "Wonderful. Now Liam, I have a few serious questions for you. What are your intentions with my sister?"

I remove the pillow from my face, my eyebrows lifting in puzzlement. Is Carmen being protective of me? I have never seen this side of her, or heard this tone in her voice. It warms my heart to think that my big sister could actually be my big sister for a few minutes.

"I see," Carmen says thoughtfully. "Well, you sound like a tolerable guy. Please be good to Helen. She deserves the best. She's a really sweet, loyal, and intelligent girl. Anyone who can't see that is blind—far blinder than she is."

Warmth spreads through my chest at my sister's kind words. "Carm," I say softly, getting a little choked up. I had forgotten her ability to go from being a shallow, mindless ditz to a sincere and loving human being quite suddenly and without warning.

"Also," Carmen adds, "I apologize for the bleak state of my sister's wardrobe. You'll be happy to know that I'm hooking her up with some irresistible new lingerie that should really spice up your sex life."

"Carmen!" I shriek, launching myself off

the ground and tackling her. I wrestle my phone away from her hastily while she laughs, and I growl. Her sentimental mood didn't last for very long. Stepping away, I press the phone against my face, huffing furiously. "I'm sorry about that, Liam." I am relieved to hear that he is laughing.

"Your sister sounds like a female Owen," he says in amusement. "It's too bad neither of them are single—we could hook them up. They would be instant soul mates."

I am surprised at the pleasant thought. "Wow, you're right. They would really hit it off."

"Oh, well," he says in disappointment. "Maybe in another lifetime!"

My face softens. "Maybe," I agree with a small smile. In the brief time that I have known him, Liam has made some rather whimsical and philosophical comments. I imagine him being a lonely person who spent a lot of time with his nose in books as a child. He seems so thoughtful and romantic—especially for someone in the sciences. I wish I had met him under different circumstances. I wish he wasn't my doctor, and I wish this wasn't a fake date.

"So, I made some phone calls. I can get you in for diagnostic tests on Thursday," he tells me. "I want to try to expedite the procedure as much as possible."

"Sure," I tell him, my stomach flip-flopping in excitement. "That sounds good."

137

"But forgive me—I shouldn't talk about medical stuff today. We should just focus on having fun at your sister's wedding." His voice takes on a roguish and guttural quality. "Are you going to wear something sexy for me under your clothes, *kitten?*"

I press a hand over my lips to try to contain my laugher from bubbling out. "You know it, *tiger.*" I hang up quickly so that he doesn't hear me dissolve into giggles at the nicknames.

"Look at you," Carmen says in wonder. "I've never seen a smile like that on your face before. Helen... are you in love with him?"

Her astonishment and questioning quickly returns me to reality. My enjoyment of the ruse is dampened by the guilt from lying to my sister—and the reminder that I am actually just a lonely hermit writer without any friends. "I don't know," I tell her, "but I think I'd like to be."

"I'm glad for you, Helen. I was really... worried. For the longest time." Carmen breathes a sigh of relief. "You have no idea, darling—how I worry about you."

"Really?" I say in surprise.

"Yes." She hesitates. "Hellie? If I ask you something, do you promise not to get mad?"

"Sure," I say in confusion.

Carmen moves over to me, and places a hand on my arm tentatively. "Are you okay? Are you really, truly okay? I just—I always thought...

138

Well, I got the feeling that something terrible happened three years ago. Something more than you were telling us. You really changed, almost overnight."

I turn my head to the left to look in the direction of the wall. I want to conceal my expressions from her as all traces of my smile disappear. "I just took losing Mom really hard," I explain in a distant voice.

She moves forward to hug me. "I know. We all did. Just when you got mugged, and you came home with all those bruises, and locked yourself in your room..."

I clear my throat loudly, pulling out of her hug and standing up. "Hey, isn't it time for your hair and makeup? Won't your photographer be here soon? I should probably go and shave my legs."

"Yes!" she shouts. "Get rid of that forest, fast. If you need help, give me a shout."

"Pfft," I say in contempt. "I can shave by touch quite easily. I just like to complain because I'm lazy. You know that."

She laughs lightly. "I've missed you, little sister. I can't wait to meet your doctor—and I can't wait for you to meet my fiancé! I'm not usually separated from him for this long, but we're doing that whole traditional thing where the bride and groom don't see each other for a little while before the wedding. It's supposed to make it more magical and emotional when we see each other again later today."

"Sounds romantic," I say with a yawn.

"Don't make fun of me," she says, shoving me a little. "You'll understand someday. Now go and get ready." She stoops to pick something up, and hooks it over my arm. "And for heaven's sake, *wear the thong.*"

Chapter Twelve

"I thought that *I* was going to be your maid of honor," says Carmen's friend jealously. Her voice is small and whiny, and it's unpleasant being in the same room with her.

"Yes, but that's before I knew Helen would be coming home," Carmen explains. "I'm sorry, Sabrina. She's my sister."

I feel a little embarrassed for stealing the poor girl's joyful moment. She must not have too many. Shifting in my chair, with my ultra-soft, newly shaved legs rubbing against each other, I allow the makeup artist to apply foundation to my face. I feel the fabric of Carmen's thong nestling into my bottom, and it does somehow give me an odd burst of confidence. "I haven't been around for a while, and I don't want to step on anyone's toes," I say as the makeup artist dusts blush across my cheekbones. "Sabrina can be the maid of honor if she wants."

"But I'm the bride, and I want you, Helen," Carmen insists. I hear the click of a curling iron releasing a section of her hair. She makes a noise of frustration. "Where's Emma? She should be here by now."

"Oh, didn't you hear?" Sabrina asks in the gossipy tone of a schoolgirl. "Emma's having some issues."

"Issues?" Carmen repeats with concern. "She didn't tell me anything. Is she going to miss my wedding?"

"I don't think so, but she might be late." Sabrina sighs. "Haven't you heard? She caught Jacob cheating on her a few days ago. They've been fighting since then, but she finally decided to move out this morning. They're getting a divorce."

"No way," Carmen whispers. "Jacob and Emma split up? But they've been together since high school. They're the best couple I know."

"I guess none of us are safe," Sabrina laments. "Frankly, I don't know why you're getting married at all. Shit's just going to go horribly wrong. It always does."

I simply cannot believe how dumb and insensitive Sabrina is being. As the makeup artist deftly applies my eye shadow, I try very hard to keep from interjecting and yelling at the annoying woman. It's clear to see that Carmen is under enough pressure, without stressing her out more about her impending wedding. I can hear the catch in my sister's breathing, indicating that she is about to begin hyperventilating.

"I can't... I can't..." Carmen pulls her hair out of her curling iron and the barrel clicks shut. She tosses it onto her dresser, and it clatters to a halt. Standing up, she begins to pace and tries to calm her breathing. "I can't believe he'd do that to her. Why? Jacob has always been the sweetest guy."

"Who knows why men do half the things they do?" Sabrina mutters callously. "They all end up revealing their true colors eventually."

"Oh god," Carmen moans. "Oh god, what am I doing? I'm not ready. This is crazy. I'm going to ruin my whole life..."

"Hey, hey," I tell her softly, holding my hand up to instruct the makeup artist to pause. I am sorely vexed with Sabrina for aggravating my sister. "It's going to be fine, Carm. I don't know your fiancé, but from what you've told me, he sounds like the type of guy who would never hurt you like that."

"I don't know," Sabrina says skeptically. "Jacob and Emma were together for twelve years, and we all thought they were solid. If they can fall apart so easily, then nothing's safe."

Carmen takes several quick, shallow breaths. "Get Grayson. Please. I'm freaking out."

"What?" Sabrina says with a frown. "But you haven't finished your hair and makeup yet, or even put on your dress. It will ruin your first look."

"Fuck the first look!" Carmen shouts. "I need to see Grayson. Now. Please, Sabby. He should be here by now. Will you go get him? I need to see my man. I need to remember why I'm doing this."

Sabrina makes a sound of displeasure. "At least get your dress on first. This destroys a perfectly good tradition."

"I really don't care about tradition right now," Carmen says, as she struggles to breathe.

Pushing my makeup artist aside slightly, I move over to my sister and touch her arm. "Hey," I tell her softly. "It's going to be fine, Carm. You're going to be happy."

"What if—what if something goes wrong?" Carmen demands. "Almost half of all marriages end up in divorce. What if I end up being another statistic?"

"You won't," I tell her firmly. "You're too smart. You're too funny, beautiful, and amazing. Any guy would be an idiot to let you get away. Come on, Carm. Pull it together." I grasp her wrists gently and squeeze them in a reassuring way.

"I'm going to cry," she says with a small, derisive laugh at herself. "I can't do this, Helen. I want it so badly, but I'm just not ready."

"Forget Grayson," Sabrina says solemnly. "What you need is a drink! Shall I get us a bottle

CLARITY

of champagne to sip on while we get ready?"

"No," Carmen says. "I need *him*. I need my fiancé. If you don't bring him for me, I'll go to him myself."

"No, no," Sabrina says in disappointment. "I'll go find Grayson. Just put on your dress!"

When Sabrina leaves the room, I breathe a sigh of relief. "God, Carm! Didn't you have any better choices for women to have as bridesmaids?" I ask her.

"You might find this hard to believe," she tells me, "but I actually don't have too many female friends. I can't deal with how catty and superficial they are. They're also always jealous, for one reason or another. Sabrina and Emma were just going to be there to make it look like I'm not a total loser."

I smile at this. I do know that while other women tend to be attracted to Carmen, and while she is polite and friendly to most of them, she keeps them at an arm's length. "Let's get you into that dress," I tell her.

"Okay," she says anxiously, moving across the room to retrieve it from its plastic packaging. She heads toward the bathroom to change so that the makeup artists and hair stylist won't see her nude. "I guess this is really happening," she murmurs.

"What kind of dress is it?" I ask as I follow her across the room.

"It's a strapless mermaid-style gown," she tells me, closing the bathroom door behind us. I can hear her running her hand over the embroidery. "I wish you could see it. It's covered in pearls and Swarovski crystals. It's really something."

"I bet you'll be unforgettable," I tell her with confidence. "Now put it on!"

A rustling is heard as she fumbles with the material. She thrusts the dress into my hands.

"Hold this for a moment," she tells me as she unties her robe and steps barefoot onto the ground.

I feel Carmen unzip the dress in my hands and step into it, and I help to lift the heavy garment around her body.

"Oh, I'm feeling better already," she says with a sigh of contentment. "Will you zip me up?"

When she turns around, I brush my hands over the gown, searching for the zipper. When I finally locate it, I begin tugging it up. I am surprised when it gets stuck near her lower back. Biting down on my lip, I try again. The zipper won't go up. I grasp the sides of the fabric and pull them closer together, before trying to zip once more. A frown settles on my face.

"It doesn't fit?" Carmen asks me in alarm. "God. Did I get too fat?"

"Put your arms straight up and stretch your body out," I instruct her. She follows my

146

directions, and with some gentle pulling and tugging, coaxing the zipper up and down, it finally travels up the length of her back.

"Oh my god," she breathes. "I was seconds away from having a full-blown panic attack."

"Pfft," I say in dismissal. "You're fine. It's a good thing you didn't have any cupcakes, though."

"Helen..." she begins saying softly. Her voice is breaking like she might cry.

A knock sounds on the bathroom door. "Miss Winters, we really need to get back to doing your hair and makeup," says the makeup artist. "We're running out of time before the wedding photographs."

"Okay! Be right out!" Carmen shouts, before turning back to me. She sniffles, as though trying very hard to fight back her tears. "Helen, I just—"

"What is it?" I ask her.

"I—I need a Tylenol," Carmen grumbles, moving over to the medicine cabinet. She is struggling to open the cap on the bottle when a male voice is heard coming from her bedroom, she abruptly drops the container of pills into the sink.

"Carmen?" says the man's soft and tender voice.

My blood runs cold.

"Are you here, honey?" he asks gently. "I

couldn't wait to see you either."

I stumble back against the bathroom wall, my face frozen.

"Oh, thank god!" Carmen says. "He's here. Helen, you have to meet my fiancé!"

My heart is pounding like a stampede within my chest. There are a thousand beasts racing across the savannah of my insides, spurred on by crushing fear. My mind has trouble forming logical thoughts, as my body reacts in sheer terror. No. This isn't possible. Prickles of hot panic spread through my neck and spine. A thin film of cool sweat has instantly covered my freshly showered skin from head to toe.

"Gray!" Carmen whispers as she runs out of the bathroom in her wedding dress, and throws herself into her fiancé's arms. I hear her dissolving into tears. "I've missed you," she sobs. "I missed you so much."

I hear him catch her and plant a kiss on her lips. "I've missed you more, darling. Let's make sure that's the last night we ever spend apart."

I feel like I'm going to throw up. This can't be right. I have heard that people have doppelgangers who look almost identical to them—perhaps Grayson's voice just happens to be very similar to the voice that haunts my nightmares. It's highly unlikely that he is who I believe he is...

CLARITY

The sound of Carmen's crying filters into the bathroom.

"Shhhhh," says Grayson in a soothing voice. "Just relax, honey. I'm here."

"It's been so hard—I'm freaking out about everything," Carmen says through her tears.

For a moment, I almost can convince myself that this isn't really happening. If my sister loves this man, he must be a good person. There is no possible way that he is the monster who...

"Think about calm ocean breezes," Grayson tells her in a soft and melodic whisper. "Shhh, Carmen. My beloved Carmen." He runs his hand over her back and presses a kiss against her forehead. "Think about soft waves of the ocean. Shhh. That's all we are. Soft waves of the ocean."

Something explodes inside me. I see red.

Although I can see nothing, I see everything. Everything is red.

I lunge forward and slam the bathroom door shut before the man can see me. I lock the door. Staggering back into the bathroom, I reach out and grasp for something, anything to give me support. Everything is spinning, and I cannot stand.

I grasp the shower curtain and tear it off the hooks as I fall to my knees. I hit my head on the ceramic edge of the tub, but I barely notice this due to the pain, dizziness, and nausea that has already seized my body. I press my face into the

149

folds of the shower curtain, and scream. I scream at the top of my lungs. I scream bloody murder. I scream with years of pent up fury.

But no sound leaves my chest. It's like I have forgotten how to speak.

He has stolen my breath, along with everything else.

CLARITY

Book Two

Will our life not be a tunnel between two vague clarities? Or will it not be a clarity between two dark triangles?

– Pablo Neruda

Clarity 2

by
Loretta Lost

Chapter One

Everything is soft, dark, and peaceful. I sway in suspension, comforted by the silence. A sweet, feminine voice calls for me from somewhere distant. Only then do I become aware that I have been sitting on the ground and staring forward vacantly for several minutes. I have withdrawn so deep inside myself that even several sharp knocks on the bathroom door cannot draw me out of my stupor.

"Hellie?" a woman says with a sniffle. "Are you okay? I heard a crash."

I try to respond, but I am locked inside the maze of my own mind. I try to navigate toward the sound and climb out of my subconscious, but there are thick stone walls all around me. I keep slipping back down into my quiet, isolated pit of protection. The voices on the outside sound faraway and muffled, and I can't reach them. I don't know if I want to reach them; it's safe here. Still, there is something tugging at the edge of my soul and reminding me that I have an urgent responsibility. I try to remember what it is, but my brain feels like

157

slush. I can't speak. I can't think.

"Who's in there?" Grayson asks. "One of your bridesmaids?"

"No," Carmen says. "It's my sister."

He pauses. "Your sister's here? Your blind sister Helen?"

Carmen huffs in exasperation. "Yes, Gray. Who else would I be talking about? I don't have any other sisters."

"I—I just..." Grayson makes a sharp and jagged intake of air. He seems suddenly agitated and alarmed. "You—you said she wasn't coming. You said you hadn't seen her in years. You said she wouldn't..." He gulps so loudly that I can hear the saliva barreling down the tunnel of his throat. I imagine the liquid swirling and sizzling into steam as it mixes with the raging hellfire of guilt in his gut. "You said she wouldn't be at our wedding."

"Yes, but she called me last night," Carmen says softly. "I told her to come home and be my maid of honor. Helen!" she calls again, rapping gently on the bathroom door. "Sweetie, is everything okay?"

A searing pain pierces behind my eyes and abruptly brings me back to reality. I blink rapidly. I lift my fingers shakily to touch the side of my head. There is a bit of warm, sticky moisture seeping between the strands of my hair, and a quickly forming bump just over my temple. I wince, and rest my elbow on the side of the bathtub so I can keep my hand pressed against my forehead. *Okay, Helen. There's no time for you to fall apart. Get it together. You need to think clearly. Quickly.* Try as I might, I can't seem to make heads or tails of the situation. My heart is racing, my breathing is labored and uneven, and my whole body is shaking with silent fury.

"I thought you hated your sister," Grayson whispers. "I thought—I thought you were angry that she left without a word. She doesn't give a shit about you! Why would you invite her here?"

"I was just pretending to be pissed to hide how hurt I was. She's my best friend! I missed her nonstop, every day." Carmen is close to the point of tears again, and I hear her voice breaking. "What the fuck is wrong with you, Gray? Don't you know me?"

"I'm sorry, honey. Come here."

My ears are assaulted with the sound of them embracing again. I can hear him pressing kisses against her face to soothe her, and each time their skin connects, I feel my insides churning in disgust. The cupcakes in my stomach rebel at being confined within their gastric prison, and fight to make their exit in a gushing eruption. I clamp my hands around my middle and shut my eyes tightly, trying to avoid duplicating Carmen's performance from the morning—it will not help this situation in the least if I need to stuff my face into the toilet. *What is happening?* I ask myself weakly. *This can't be real. Please let this be a nightmare. I've had so many nightmares about that man—just let this be one more awful dream that I will wake up from at any moment. I just want to be tucked away safe in my little cabin, light years from humanity... any moment now. I'll wake up. Please.*

"I thought my wedding day was supposed to be wonderful," Carmen tells her fiancé softly, "but this is just one headache after another. I just want it to be over so we can be together."

"We'll be happy—soon. I promise you," Grayson says to her gently. He trips over his words slowly and clumsily, with the trepidation of a man who is aware that he is one misstep away from unraveling the fabric of his entire life. "Soon— soon, we'll be family. And nothing—nothing will ever stand between us again. Nothing."

Family. He's going to be family? My stomach lurches again. This is madness. Does he really love her? What is going on? I dig my fingertips into my new head injury, and the pain confirms my darkest dread.

Yes, this is a nightmare. The absolute worst kind of nightmare; real life.

I have to struggle to stay conscious. My mind is still reeling from the shock, and is trying urgently to shut down to shield itself from harm. Sadly, I wish my problems amounted to a simple concussion, but the trauma that's affecting me is much deeper than the mild impact against my skull. I fight to take charge of my own disengaged faculties. Even my body is no longer under my control; I regretfully acknowledge that I am curled up into a tiny ball and shaking like a frightened animal. I realize this is counterproductive and worthless behavior, and I am furious with myself. I try to gather my wits so that I can pick myself off the ground and deal with this situation.

My sister is marrying my rapist, I inform myself. These words feel unreal. They sound ridiculous. The sentence does not pierce the murky depths of my brain, and I try to process the information again. *My sister is about to marry the man who raped me.*

Before I can form a plan of action, I hear the doorknob being jostled violently. My head snaps sharply to the side, and I am stabbed in the heart with multiple daggers of fear.

"Helen?" Grayson says, in a familiar and deceptively humane fashion. "Honey?"

I grind my teeth together. I would have been perfectly happy if I had never heard him speak my name again for the duration of my entire existence. The whole reason I changed my name was to escape the vile memory of him repeating it, over and over in a sadistic song...

"Honey, are you okay in there?" he asks again. "Will you come out so that Carmen doesn't worry about you?"

Pressing my hand against the tub for support, I slowly lift myself off the ground. I find my chest heaving with deep, panting breaths. My tongue circles in the extra bit of sweet saliva that has gathered in my mouth, and all my muscles clench until they grow painfully taut. My body is gearing up for a fight. I don't care if he's a two-hundred-pound football player—or ex-football player. This time, I'm going to tear him limb from limb like a savage beast. I have replayed the event from three years ago in my mind several thousand times. Each time, I do something a little better; I'm a little faster, a little wiser, a little stronger. He will never hurt me again. I won't allow it. But even if he does...

I know one thing for damned certain. There is no way that demon is marrying my sister. He might have gotten the best of me, but I will never allow him to do the same to her. I won't allow him to touch her, ever again. I need to kick this man out of my home, and out of my life for good.

The doorknob jostles again, but this time, it doesn't scare me. I puff out my chest and ball my hands into fists so tightly that my fingernails cut into my palms. How dare he? How dare he violate me and terrorize my family? I remember what my dad said about him being the perfect son-in-law, and my insides shudder with revulsion.

"Excuse me, Miss Winters," says the

makeup artist who has been waiting from somewhere distant in Carmen's bedroom. I have to strain to hear her words, because she is speaking softly and the syllables do not perfectly carry through the door. Her voice is impatient and tired. "We haven't finished working on your face."

"Oh, I forgot," Carmen says in horror. "We're running so late! This is awful, Gray. We're probably going to have to delay the ceremony."

"All the guests will wait," Grayson tells her. "You're worth waiting for."

Carmen lets out a shaky little laugh. "At least I cried *before* my makeup was complete..."

"Honey, your bathroom has an entrance to the adjoining room, right?" Grayson asks quietly. "Your sister's old room?"

"Yes," she responds. "Why?"

"Just wait here, love," he tells her with another kiss. "I'll go check on Helen. Why don't you finish getting your makeup done for the wedding photos? Just sit down and relax, honey."

"Gray," Carmen whispers. "Just tell me one thing. Are you sure about me? One hundred percent sure about us?"

"I've never been surer about anything in my life," he tells her. "You need to calm down, love. The day will be over soon, and we can curl up in bed and sleep in tomorrow, for as long as we want. We just have to get through these next couple hours, and satisfy all the family members—

we just have to go through the motions for tradition's sake."

"Okay," Carmen says, and there is strength in her voice for the first time in several minutes. "Thank you. You always make me feel better when things get rough."

"That's what I'm here for," he tells her lightly. "I'll be right back."

Now it's time for action. I move to the adjoining door that leads into my bedroom, and I lock it hastily. I wait until I hear Grayson leave Carmen's room, and then I burst through the bathroom door into her room, and push past her. Moving as quickly as I can, I run across the carpeted floor, tripping over beauty supplies and knocking over chairs as I rush to lock her door. I turn back to her in righteous rage and terror, my chest still expanding rapidly with my heavy breathing.

"You can't marry him," I tell her adamantly.

"What?" Carmen says in surprise. "Why? Oh, Helen, you're bleeding..."

"I'm fine," I tell her, gasping for air. "Just listen to me for once in your life. You need to call off this wedding."

"Why are you saying this?" she asks me, her voice wounded. "First Sabrina is a downer, and now you? Why can't anyone be supportive of me?"

164

CLARITY

"I know him," I tell her, as I continue wheezing. I bend over slightly and place the palms of my hands against my knees to support me. My hands are clammy and cold against my soft and newly-shaved legs. The salt in my sweat causes a mild burning sensation against the slightly razor-burned skin of my thighs. I realize that I haven't decided how much I should tell Carmen. It could be very damaging for her to learn the whole truth; that's why I protected her from it in the first place. But now? Now that she has fallen in love with him, I'm not sure what might be the proper protocol for this situation. "I know him from school, Carmen. He's a criminal. He's done horrible things."

"Stop," she hisses sharply. "Just stop. I don't want to hear about it."

I frown at the tone in her voice. "You're about to marry this man, and you don't even know who he is! He's going to ruin your life. Call it off. Please call it off, for your own sake."

"I can't believe you," Carmen whispers. "Why would you do this to me? You're supposed to be happy for me."

"I would be happy if it were almost anyone else," I say in a deadly serious voice. "Carmen. You need to call it off."

"Why?" she demands.

How can I say anything without hurting her? I part my lips, trying to think of the right

165

words. I can't just blurt out the truth, can I? No. It would devastate her. She would be upset enough about her cancelled wedding, and the embarrassment to all her friends and relatives—but then she would also need to deal with what happened to me. It would be too much for her to handle in this moment. "He's going to hurt you," I tell her, closing my eyes. "He's not a good person."

"Look," Carmen snaps in annoyance. "We're all flawed in some way. We all make mistakes. If I spend my life waiting for the perfect man, I'll be waiting forever."

"Flawed? He's not just flawed. He's a fucking monster."

"Helen!" she says in shock. "You're talking about the man who's going to be my husband in a few hours."

The makeup artist clears her throat. "We really need to get the bride's face ready for photos... unless you're calling the wedding off?"

"I'm not!" Carmen declares. "I'm getting married."

Just then, to add another horrible element to the chaos, Grayson tries to re-enter the room. He turns the knob, and finds that it has been locked. "Carmen?" he says in confusion as he fiddles with it. "Will you let me in?"

In a panic, I move over to the dresser where I had left my phone. I pick it up with shaking hands, and hastily shove the single circular button. "Dial 911," I speak into the phone anxiously.

"What the fuck are you doing?!" Carmen asks, leaping forward and grabbing the phone from my hands.

"Calling 91..."

She interrupts my phone call before it can be completed, but places a hand on my arm. "Helen," she says quietly. "Did he really do something worthy of arrest?"

"Yes," I say, swallowing nervously. "Give me my phone. I'm calling the cops."

"Please don't," Carmen begs. "If you destroy him, you'll destroy me. Our lives are already so intertwined. We are practically married as it is! Anything that happened? Anything he did? It's a family matter now. We'll deal with it right here, between us."

"You're being so weak right now," I say to her in surprise. "This isn't like you. Why would you ignore important information and go ahead with a decision that can only end in tears?"

"Is everything okay in there?" Grayson calls from outside the room, jostling the doorknob.

Carmen takes a deep breath. "Listen to me, Helen. I'm not young and idealistic anymore. I've grown up, and I know that I need to make compromises."

"You can't compromise on *this!*" I hiss.

"You can't compromise on your safety!"

There is the sound of an item being tossed across the room and I flinch when it smashes into the wall. Carmen has snapped. I just hope it was a random beauty implement that fell victim to her rage, and not my cell phone.

"You weren't here for me!" Carmen screams. "You were gone! Do you know how much you hurt me? Who the hell do you think you are? You left! You'll probably just leave again tomorrow. This family obviously means nothing to you. *I* mean nothing to you!"

I can feel her breath on my face as she moves close to me so that her yelling can pierce my ears more painfully. I can also feel the eyes of the makeup artist on us. I am embarrassed as I wonder what she thinks of us—is this normal wedding behavior? It might be. There is also a hair stylist in the room, but it sounds like she is sitting and typing on her phone, and not bothered. There was another makeup artist in the room earlier, but it seems like she might have left when I was helping Carmen put on her dress. My sister is still screaming at me, and I wince as her already shrill voice increases by a few decibels.

"Don't think you can come in here at the last minute and stick your nose in my business! Don't think you can order me around and interfere with my choices like you give a fuck! Grayson has been there for me every single day, for years. I'm not throwing that away because you're a bitter little bitch."

I lift my hands into the air, and they float there in confusion and bewilderment. Although I know that my leaving was justified, I still feel terrible. I wonder for a moment if Grayson really can be healthier for my sister than I am. Is it possible that he is trying to be good to her to atone for what he did to me? Is this all part of some kind of twisted plan for redemption? I can't imagine what an appalled and horrified look I must have on my face, because Carmen gasps and sobs.

"I'm sorry, Helen," she says, placing my phone against the palm of my hand. I am relieved to feel that it is in one piece. "Just—stay out of it, okay? Grayson is my guy. I accept him for who he is. Please understand that."

"But Carm—" I begin in protest.

"No. I won't listen to any more of it. This is a seriously big and empty house, and I can't be alone here for another day. The silence is deafening. Every little noise, every creak and sigh drives me insane." She pauses. "But worse than that... my whole *life* is a big and empty house that people just walk in and out of as they please. No one stays with me. I need to start building a home where I feel welcome and wanted. I need to start building the foundation of my future. You understand that, don't you? I'm much older than you, Helen. I can't play games or life will pass me

169

Loretta Lost

by. It's time for me to move forward. Grayson treats me well. This is what I need."

I stand in stunned silence as I allow her words to sink into my brain.

"Look. I need to get my makeup on," Carmen says softly. "Can you please just be happy for me, little sister? Can you please just be supportive?"

"Carmen!" Grayson shouts from outside the room. "Please open the door, love. What's going on? You never lock your door—I'm getting worried."

"Excuse me," Carmen says to me as she moves toward the door.

My legs feel like lead, and I remain rooted to the spot. Only when I hear Carmen unlocking her door do I realize that Grayson is about to enter the room. The thought of coming face-to-face with him sends a violent shiver through my body. There is a sharp pain in my shoulders and neck where all my muscles are clenched and bunched up tightly. For a moment, it is difficult to force myself to move, because my brain seems disconnected from the rest of me.

But then I hear his footstep.

I suddenly spring into motion as though he has set the ground beneath me on fire with his presence in the room. I can't bear the thought of him looking at me, and I hope I can move quickly enough that he barely glimpses a flash of my hair

170

disappearing. I find myself bolting back into the bathroom and ripping the door open to my bedroom. I need locked doors between me and that man. As many locked doors as possible. I know that they don't offer complete protection, but they certainly help my anxiety. Once I have successfully barricaded every entrance, I move to grasp the post of my bed.

I close my eyes and press my forehead against the cool varnished wood.

With a sigh, I non-too-gently thump my forehead against the bedpost. "Why," I grumble to myself blankly. "Why. Why. Why." I don't even have the energy to speak the word in the form of a question. The universe isn't going to answer me; it doesn't need to justify itself. It's just having fun. I don't think it even cares whether that fun is at my expense.

I fight the urge to lift my fist into the air and give God an excellent view of my middle finger. I have never been very religious, but for one single moment, I am almost completely certain that there must be one single, sick bastard responsible for this. I fight the urge to call him names, or ask *why* a few more dozen times.

I fight the urge to throw myself out of the second-story window.

An object vibrating in my hand startles me, and I jump and reflexively toss it away, as though stung by an insect. I then register the sound of ringing. My mind has been spinning so wildly that it takes me a moment to process that I am receiving a phone call. *Why?* I inwardly ask myself again. Even this phone call is too much to bear. I went so many days with zero contact from the outside world—so many weeks and months, with only the necessary communication for my job. Now, in one day, I am suddenly popular. I suddenly have to talk to people and touch them, and answer phone calls. It's too much. It's terrifying. But my phone continues to ring.

I fumble for the small device that I had dropped on my bed. Collecting it, I quickly answer it in a curt and businesslike voice. "Yes?"

"Helen! Sorry to call again so soon," says the voice on the other end of the phone. "I am having a bit of a wardrobe crisis—I don't go to special events very often. I thought I'd just ask to make sure. Do I wear a bow tie or a normal tie?"

My nose wrinkles with irritation. "Don't bother," I say in a dry tone.

"What?" Liam asks, sounding somewhat surprised. "What's going on? Just a few minutes ago, you said..."

"Forget what I said!" I snap harshly. My entire face contorts with heat and rage. "Just—forget it. Don't bother coming here."

"Did something happen, Helen?" He pauses, and his voice sounds almost hurt. "You're acting different. I thought we were going to have

172

fun with this fake-date thing. Is everything okay?"

"Everything's fine," I tell him quietly, "but it looks like my sister isn't getting married after all."

"What? But she said..."

"I don't care what she said," I hiss into the phone. "I'm going to stop this fucking wedding."

And with that proclamation, I hang up the phone. I stand victorious in my resolve for a moment, breathing heavily in fury. Then it occurs to me that I have no clue in hell how I'm going to stop this wedding without trampling on my sister's heart, and destroying the hopes of my fragile father. Feeling suddenly drained of my strength, I move over to collapse facedown onto my bed. My face sinks into the fluffy duvet atop the lovely farmhouse bed that I haven't slept on in three years. It is much larger and softer than the tiny, hard cot I slept on back in my cabin, but in this moment, I cannot appreciate the luxury. I would gladly lie down on anything; even a bed of dirt in the slums of India, if it meant I would be far away from this house and *him*.

"Why," I mutter again into the pillow as my makeup surely gets smudged all over the fabric. I can't seem to form any other utterance. "Why."

Chapter Two

I'm not sure how long I've been lying flat on my face before I can no longer stand the inertia. I have been running dozens of possible scenarios through my mind, and trying to choose the best course of action. I have been hovering in a strange meditative state somewhere between wakefulness and slumber, and it has been calm and serene. I can hear people rushing about the corridor outside my room, but I have been able to block it out and listen only to my inner voice. I have been able to reach inside myself and grasp a few morsels of wisdom and patience, to help me combat my overpowering anger and fear.

I need to tread carefully.

With a few words, I have the power to drop an avalanche on my sister's head. It's the right thing to do, but I shouldn't be hasty and careless. I need to be graceful and delicate in my delivery, or I could hurt her just as much as

Grayson. The fact is that Carmen doesn't trust me. She sees me as an outsider, or even an enemy, and anything I can say or do to protect her will seem malicious and spiteful. I hear a female voice in the corridor, and I recognize it as an older family member.

Rising to my feet, I head to my bedroom door and unlock it before bravely swinging it wide open.

"There you are, child!" says the old woman's voice. "Oh, look at you, Helen. You're absolutely darling in that gown! You look just like your mother. I've been sent to collect you. It's time for the family wedding photos!"

"Aunt Edna," I say firmly. "My sister is making a huge mistake. She can't marry Grayson."

"What do you mean, dear?" The older woman chuckles softly. "Why, I've never met a finer boy than that Grayson. Your sister sure got lucky and picked a good one!"

"No. She didn't." I grip the door frame tightly, and almost expect the wood to shatter under my fingers. "Aunt Edna. You have to talk to my dad and get him to convince Carmen to stop the wedding. I have evidence that Grayson is... only after our family's money."

"Good gracious, child!" Aunt Edna scoffs. "I hardly think that's true. From what your father tells me, that boy single-handedly saved the family fortune! Grayson helped your dad make hundreds of thousands of dollars from investments in only a few short years. He's the only reason you could keep the house!"

"But Aunt Edna," I say sharply. "I have reason to believe..."

"Rubbish! Stop this nonsense immediately. Grayson is a lovely young man, and your sister is going to be just fine." Aunt Edna reaches out to slip her hand under my arm and guide me into the hallway. "Besides," she says in a conspiratorial whisper, "they have a pre-nup. My husband saw to that, and it's iron-clad. If something goes wrong and your sister needs to divorce him, he doesn't get anything! So, you can stop worrying, dear."

I groan and stiffly follow the woman as she guides me through the hallway.

"Really, I understand your concerns," Aunt Edna chatters on. "Why, when my daughter got married, I was in such a fright..."

"Excuse me, Aunt Edna," I say, pulling my arm away and trying to escape as gently as possible. "I forgot something important that I need to do." I slip away from her and move toward the staircase. The scent of the flowers decorating the main foyer fills my nostrils again, but it does not enchant me the way it did before. I don't have even a millisecond to pause and appreciate them. There are dozens of voices in the house, and I realize that many of the guests have begun to arrive.

I should not have waited so long. By being depressed and indecisive, I have probably made cancelling the wedding far more painful to Carmen. People start to greet me as I descend the staircase, and dive into the confusing sea of voices. My head begins to spin a bit, as I try to move through the crowd without colliding with anyone.

"Helen, dear! Oh, you've grown so big, sweetie!" says a deep woman's voice.

"Thank you," I mumble with a nod as I slip past her.

"Well, if it isn't little Helen Keller," says a cheerful man's voice—I think it's one of our uncles. "I heard you've written some books! Boy, you never cease to amaze me. Being blind never slowed you down, kiddo!"

"Thanks," I say again as I move past him. I am startled when I feel a large hand on my shoulder. I jump and rip my body away from the physical contact.

"Cousin Helen? Holy shit! The last time I saw you, we were both four feet tall. You turned out a lot prettier than I expected."

"Thanks," I say again as try to move away, but the male voice follows me.

"Can you believe Carmen's getting married? She's such an airhead. I always figured she'd just spend her life moving from random dude to random dude. But I was sure that *you'd* settle down and get married. You've always been the serious one!"

"Excuse me," I say, trying to pull away from him.

"Hey, you don't recognize my voice?" he asks, sounding hurt. He grabs my elbow gently. "It's Cousin Charlie! Remember, we shared our first kiss in the attic when we were ten?"

"Sure. Great to see you," I say as I remove his hand from my arm. I deftly maneuver around him so that I can escape. I cringe a little in memory of the kid that Carmen and I had dubbed Creepy Cousin Charlie—yet there is a bit of wistfulness in my expression. I long for the days when our biggest problem was an awkward young boy who wanted to play spin the bottle a little too often. Now that we are larger, it seems that the dangers have grown along with us, escalating from tiny annoyances into real threats.

I push these thoughts aside as I continue to navigate through the crowd, heading for my father's library. Like me, he has never enjoyed crowds very much, and chances are that he will be locked away in the quiet privacy of his study until it is absolutely necessary to socialize. A few more people try to accost me for conversation as I move through the foyer, but I excuse myself. I accidentally bump into a fat woman's squishy body, and quickly apologize and step away. I wince in embarrassment and aversion. Every time I come into contact with another person, my insides quake in momentary terror. But it's unavoidable.

Trying to move gracefully through a crowded room when you're blind is kind of like dancing in a swarm of bees and expecting not to get stung.

After great effort, I finally arrive at the doors to my father's library. I am pleased to see that they are closed, and I quickly slide them open and slip inside. Tugging the doors closed behind me, I release a sigh of relief as the noise from all the wedding guests is instantly—but not completely—muffled. I feel as though I have placed all the bees into a jar and fastened the lid tightly closed; for a moment, they are no longer an issue. I hear breathing in the room with me, and I am glad to know my father is in his library, as always. Now I can finally discuss the situation and stop this wedding.

"Dad?" I say with determination. "I need to talk to you about Grayson."

There is a silence. "No," he responds quietly. "You don't need to say anything to anyone."

My heart feels like it has been jabbed with a taser. For a moment, my insides are paralyzed. It is *his* voice—I am in the room alone with *him*. I am too frozen to escape before I feel two hands circling around my waist.

"Helen," he whispers. "I thought I'd never

see you again."

I am torn between wanting to run, scream, lash out and hurt him, or say something profound and wise that will fix everything. However, my mind can't work quickly enough to decide what to do, or what I could possibly say, and I end up immobilized in anxiety.

I can feel his face descending close to mine. The bristles of his chin scratch against my cheek as he puts his lips close to my ear. His breath tickles the tiny wisps of wayward curls framing my face.

"You shouldn't have come back here," he tells me. "I'm never going to be able to let you go. Those mesmerizing amber eyes of yours—it's such a pity they're useless."

Finally, I am so appalled that I am able to break through my barrier of fear and push him away. "Don't touch me," I hiss, and my voice is filled with snakelike venom. "I don't know how you weaseled your way into my home and into my family, but you are *not* going to marry my sister."

He laughs softly. "You're delightful when you're pissed. Unfortunately, I *am* going to marry Carmen. We've been together for years—and in case you haven't noticed, your entire extended family is already here, eagerly anticipating the wedding."

"I don't give a flying fuck," I tell him. "They don't know who you are and what you did

180

to me. I'm giving you one chance, Grayson. Call the wedding off and tell them you changed your mind. Or I'm going to expose you and send you to jail."

"That's the first time I've heard you say my name," he says in wonder. "It sounds so refined coming from your lips. Say it again."

I close my eyes briefly. This man is beyond infuriating. I need to find a way to overpower him with my words. "Three years ago, you raped me. All I need to do is tell someone that it was you..."

"How do you know it was me?" he asks. "You have no idea what I look like."

My face twists into a scowl. "No one is going to doubt my judgment."

"Maybe I'm not who you think I am. Did you ever think that maybe you have me confused with someone else?" He moves close to me again, and reaches for me. I back away, but he grabs me and pins me to the door beside the wall. "You can't positively identify me. You have no evidence."

"That's where you're wrong," I tell him quietly as I peel his hands off my body. "After you beat me unconscious and I woke up, I immediately filed a police report. They checked me out and created a rape kit." This time, I'm the one stepping forward and lifting my chin to put my face close to his. I need to be as intimidating as possible. I need to show that I won't back down. "If I ask them to reopen my case and test my rape kit, whose DNA do you think they'll find? If you don't call off the wedding *now,* then we'll find out. I wager you won't be too happy with the results."

There is a moment of stillness as he considers this. I hold my breath, thinking that I might be victorious. Did my threat work? Can he tell I'm bluffing? Of course, there is no rape kit. I was so depressed that I was unable to file a police report or do much of anything after the event. I only had the presence of mind to call our family doctor, Leslie Howard, and have her bring me emergency contraception. I listen to the silence, trying to figure out what Grayson is thinking. Does he believe me? This is my trump card; if this doesn't work, I have no other ideas.

I hear a little metallic click, and I feel a cold nozzle pressed against my forehead, between my eyes.

"Do you know what this is, Helen?" he asks me softly.

My heart starts racing. Is he going to kill me? Right here in my father's library? I am so terrified that I can't reassure myself with the reminder that there are dozens of people just outside the door who might hear the shot. I know what this man is capable of—but I don't know how smart he is.

"This is a gun. Don't worry, sweet thing.

I'm not going to put a bullet in your head." He slowly drags the nozzle of the gun down along my nose, and roughly over my lips. He rakes the gun down over my neck and collarbone, until he slides it into place over my heart. The gun lingers there for a moment, between my breasts. "I'm not going to put a bullet in your chest, either. But let me tell you this..."

He lowers his voice to a deathly whisper as he lifts a hand to cup my cheek. "If you tell anyone *anything* about what happened three years ago—or if you do *anything* to jeopardize my marriage to your sister—I will kill Carmen. I will put a bullet in your sister's head. I will put a bullet in your sister's chest. And then I'll shoot myself. I love your sister more than I've ever loved another human being. If you take that away from me—if you take that away from *us*—you might as well be killing us both."

All the energy drains from my body. I am defeated.

"Do you understand me?" he demands, shoving the gun forward painfully so that it digs into my chest and pushes me slightly off balance. "If you don't keep your mouth shut, I'll kill Carmen. Why are you just standing there? Can you hear me? Nod if you understand."

Very slowly, and with great effort, I force myself to nod.

"Great. But don't worry," he says gently,

removing the gun from my chest and returning it to his blazer. "There's no need to be jealous. I still have plenty of love to give to you."

"Go to hell," I whisper.

He laughs and grasps the back of my head, leaning down to force a kiss against my lips.

I am stupefied and speechless by his gall. Thankfully, he doesn't try to do more than this, because I no longer have the strength to fight. I feel like the blood has left my veins and been replaced by empty air. I won't risk my sister's life, and he must know that. He has won. When he moves away, I hear him wiping his mouth with his sleeve to remove any telltale traces of lipstick. For a brief moment, a spark of fury fills me with fire. I consider tackling him and trying to steal the gun away from him—maybe I could shoot *him* in the chest. But the thought disappears as soon as it comes. Even if my limbs didn't feel lifeless and weak, I am not sure I could be capable of such cruelty. I am not even sure if he deserves such treatment. After all—he did not take my life. It would be unfair to take his.

"It's been a pleasure catching up with you," Grayson says as he walks to the library doors. "But I've got to get back to my wedding. Haven't you heard? It's the most important day of my life." He pushes open the sliding doors and moves back into the foyer. There are joyous sounds of welcoming as the other guests greet him

with good cheer and claps on the back.
I am left standing alone and staring into my familiar nothingness.

Chapter Three

"Here she is! I've found her!" announces a female voice loudly. I recognize it as Carmen's bridesmaid Sabrina. She rushes into the library and grabs my arm. "Where have you been? You missed the photos!"

I am still slightly in a daze as I allow her to pull me out into the cacophony of the crowd.

"Oh, Helen," Carmen says in disappointment. "You forgot your shoes in my bedroom. I've been looking for you. I can't believe you're walking around barefoot when all the guests are here. Stop being ridiculous."

I feel a pair of high-heeled shoes thrust against my chest, and I lift my arms to grasp them. The sharp heels poking into my skin do not bother me nearly as much as the cold metal cylinder just did.

"They're such lovely shoes," Sabrina says with a sigh. "Most women make their bridesmaids look hideous, but Carmen really picked out exquisite clothes for us. It's too bad you can't see the shoes, Helen."

I can hardly be bothered to care, but I try to force myself to go through the motions. Skimming my fingers over the satiny shoes, I feel some kind of jeweled embellishment on the front. They have a peep toe and a small kitten heel. I don't know why I bothered to examine the shoes, because I can't even try to make my face seem interested.

"Put them on!" Carmen urges. "Today, you are merely one of my decorations. You have to dress up exactly as the bride wishes, and I am *not* doing a barefoot-on-the-beach style wedding."

The excitement in her voice makes me feel ill. All I can think about is the sensation of the gun nozzle pressed against my chest. *If you don't keep your mouth shut, I'll kill Carmen.* How can she be so happy, when just a few minutes before, her fiancé threatened to kill her? She is so innocent—and there is nothing I can do to inform her. My trump card failed. I have no other ideas. Unless I can think of something really ingenious, it looks like Grayson is going to get his way.

"Put on the shoes, Helen," Carmen commands in an annoyed voice.

"Fine," I say miserably. I allow both of the shoes to clatter from my arms to the ground. I then use my toe to poke around, searching for the entrance to the footwear. As I do this, I try to maintain my balance on one foot, but I'm sure I look wobbly and pathetic—which is precisely the way I feel. When I finally discover a shoe and try to insert my foot, of course, it happens to be the wrong shoe. I utter a very unladylike curse.

"Allow me to help you with that," says a deep male voice. I am not sure who it is, but I am comforted by the fact that it is not Grayson. At this moment, any other man is a potential ally. I can feel that he has crouched down before me, for he gently takes my wrist and positions it on his shoulder so that I have some support. I don't even have the energy to protest, for I feel that I might actually fall over without his assistance. I am so discombobulated. His hand carefully encircles my foot and guides it into the correct high-heeled shoe. I am expecting him to immediately release me and disappear, but he holds my foot there for a moment, until I feel steady again. After a second, he picks up the other shoe and helps me place my second foot into the encasement.

"Thank you," I whisper, pleasantly surprised by the tenderness of his touch.

"Not a problem," he says kindly.

His voice is somehow calming to me. There are dozens of voices all around me in the crowded foyer, but his is soft and serene. When he speaks, I feel like I've discovered the solitary safe place in the middle of a raging storm. There is shelter and protection in his quiet strength.

"Helen? What's wrong?" he asks me with concern. He reaches up to clasp my hand as it rests on his shoulder. "You're so pale—like you've seen a ghost."

I am suddenly even more confused. First of all, I am stricken by the fact that I am supposed to know this man. Is he one of our family members? Another distant cousin? I search my memory for his voice, but I am drawing a blank. Second of all, how does he know me so well? How can he see that I am pale and shaken, while my own sister is oblivious to this?

"Whoa," Carmen says with a strange tone in her voice. "Who's Prince Charming over here with the glass slippers?"

The man on the ground laughs lightly. He removes my hand from his shoulder as he rises to his feet. "That's right. We haven't been introduced. Helen, will you do the honors?"

I am worried that my face betrays how clueless I am. Luckily, I am saved by my father's booming voice.

"Ladies! How are we all doing over here?" my father asks happily. "I think it was a splendid idea to serve cocktails to the guests before the wedding, Carmen. Everyone is in such good spirits—pardon the pun!"

"Oh, Dad," Carmen says with a giggle. "How much have you had to drink?"

189

"Just enough, darling. Just enough."

There is a twinkle in his tone, as though he might be winking at my sister. His voice makes me feel much better, too. I wish I could take him aside and tell him what I know, but I can no longer try to save the day with the grave threat looming over my head.

"Oh, there you are, my good fellow!" my father says, and his voice is directed at the person standing next to me—the man who helped with my shoes. "I just ran into this fine gentleman a few minutes ago. Imagine my surprise when he introduced himself as my daughter's boyfriend!"

For a moment, I am bewildered. Carmen has a boyfriend? In addition to Grayson? Does Grayson know about this? I immediately start to hope that there's a chance for the wedding to be halted by other complications. My mind runs away with me, and I imagine a brave prince coming to the rescue and beating the shit out of Grayson.

"Oh my god," Carmen says in astonishment. "*This* is Liam? *This* is Helen's boyfriend?"

I am stunned by this information and deeply embarrassed that I *forgot* the voice of my supposed suitor. I am shocked that he is here at all, considering I told him not to come.

"That's right," Liam says, placing a hand affectionately on my back. "We've only been dating for a year, but it's been the best year of my life. Helen is an incredible woman."

The palm of his hand is warm against my spine, and I can feel my cheeks growing red. This is so absurd and embarrassing. I can't remember why I decided to do this. Now, after all that's happened, it feels so pointless and bizarre that I ever asked Liam to be my fake date to this wedding. How stupid was that? Why did I even care about such trivial bullshit? My sister's life is on the line, and I feel like a fool. I can't believe I thought it would be fun. Still... I can't help but be glad that Liam is here. His presence is somehow reassuring.

"Holy shit!" Carmen exclaims in amazement. "Helen, you didn't tell me that he's gorgeous!"

"Yeah," Sabrina adds solemnly. "Wow."

I shrug to hide my mortification and annoyance. "How could I have told you that? I have no idea what he looks like."

"Well, you could have told me more about what he *feels* like," Carmen says with an audacious giggle.

"Oh my god," I mutter softly, turning to Liam. "I'm so sorry about this."

"It's quite alright," he says with amusement.

Sabrina clucks her tongue in disapproval. "Helen, didn't you know you that you're not supposed to bring a man to the wedding who's

191

more handsome than the groom? It's bad etiquette!"

"Uhh." I don't know how to respond to their flattery, and my cheeks flush even darker. I'm not sure whether I'm more embarrassed at being the center of attention, at the fact that dating Liam is a lie, or at the fact that it is now confirmed that he's incredibly attractive, which makes me feel a little uneasy. If I was going to create a convincing lie, I probably should have chosen someone plain and forgettable, who was a little more in my league.

"Alright, children. That's enough of teasing poor Helen," my father says with a laugh. "She's red as a beet! Don't we have a wedding to get started? It's about ten minutes to show time! Grayson's standing over there and looking very impatient."

"Oh, let him wait," Carmen says flippantly. "He's been pressuring me to marry him for years. I'm sure he can handle another ten minutes of waiting."

"That's your fiancé?" Liam asks. "He seems a bit... angry."

"No, no," my father answers. "I'm sure it's just the wedding-day pressure getting to him. It's a lot of stress. I can assure you that Grayson is the nicest guy in the world."

I can't keep a small grunt of derision from leaving my throat. It goes undetected by everyone around me, except for Liam. His hand on my back moves up and down in a soothing manner. I am surprised at how attentive and intuitive he is.

"Well, I suppose we might as well start getting ready," Carmen grumbles. "Let's usher everyone to their seats."

A moment later, Carmen, Sabrina, and my father are gone. The wedding is about to begin, and it will proceed as planned. I have failed in trying to stop it. Unless...

"Hey. What's wrong?" Liam asks me again. "Come on, Helen. Talk to me. There's this look on your face, like you just stepped on a landmine."

"I did," I say softly. Then I turn to him with a frown. "What are you doing here anyway? I told you not to come."

"You sounded distraught," he tells me. "I don't know—I was worried. What's the matter? Something is bothering you; I can see that. When I walked in, you were as white as death."

"Liam," I say quietly, moving close to him. My eyebrows knit together in consternation. "Thank you for coming. I just..."

A passionate female voice interrupts me. "Hellie! Can I speak to you in private for a moment?"

"Carm?" I say in surprise. "Uh, sure."

"I hope you don't mind if I steal her, Liam." Carmen says this as she slips her hand on my arm, already prepared to drag me away. I am a bit disappointed at the interruption, but I appreciate one final chance to talk to my sister.

"Not a problem," Liam says. "I think I see someone I know—Dr. Leslie Howard. I'll go chat with her in the meantime."

"Great!" Carmen chimes in as she leads me back into the privacy of the library.

I am nervous that Grayson might be suspicious of me speaking to Carmen alone—if he can see us. And I'm sure he's keeping an eye on me. Nonetheless, I can't waste this opportunity to tell her. *Should* I tell her? Is it worth the risk? I am startled out of my thoughts when Carmen pulls me into a hug.

"I just wanted to congratulate you, Helen. I know we were joking around about Liam's hotness a few minutes ago, but I wanted to be serious for a sec. He seems so sweet and loving. The way he helped you with your shoes! What a gentleman. You two seem perfect for each other, and I'm so happy for you. I think this is the first time I've ever seen you with a guy—the first time you ever brought someone home. Gosh... he's your first *real* boyfriend!"

I flinch at her words. He's certainly my first fake boyfriend.

"My little sister's growing up," Carmen says affectionately. "Sorry. I'm just so emotional today. This is so special."

"Yeah," I mutter in frustration. "So special."

"Honestly, I'm jealous," Carmen whispers. "Grayson is pretty cute, but Liam is a *stud*. Gosh. Aren't you glad you wore the thong?"

"No. Not really."

"Why can't you be a little excited with me, Helen? Seriously. I'm just trying to enjoy the moment and bask in our happiness." She moves over to the library doors to peer out at the crowd with a sigh. "I mean, if only you could *see* this adorable man who's all yours..."

"There has to be more to a man than his appearance," I tell her briskly. "I really don't care what he looks like."

"But doesn't it help to know that... oh. Hey, Helen?" Carmen pauses and hesitates. "How well does your boyfriend know Dr. Howard? They seem pretty close."

"Liam and Leslie?" I ask in surprise. I immediately frown at how nice their names sound together. "Well... they're colleagues."

"They seem like a little more than just colleagues to me," Carmen observes.

"What do you mean?" I ask, without really wanting to. It's none of my concern.

"Well, he just hugged her and she kissed him on the cheek. They seem really affectionate."

"Oh," I say in disappointment. "I thought she was close to Mom's age?"

"Yes," Carmen responds slowly, "but she's very well put-together. I'm almost positive she's had some work done. She might be a bit of a... cougar."

I make a face. This upsets me. Why does it upset me? Liam isn't actually my boyfriend, and I don't actually care if he has something going on with an older woman. How do I even have the ability to care about anything other than the situation with Grayson? I am shocked at my endless capacity to be even more hurt and upset that I was a few minutes before.

"Maybe I'm wrong," Carmen says. "I shouldn't judge things so easily. You know how I always jump to conclusions and make the wrong assump..."

"Grayson is a rapist."

My sister abruptly stops her prattling. There is a silence in the library. I did not mean to say this, but I was unable to keep it inside any longer. I immediately regret having spoken, and wished I had delivered the information in a different way. I just didn't have any time to think. It needed to be done *now*. Finally, when Carmen speaks, her voice is a tiny whisper.

"I know."

"What?" I say in horror. "You know? You *know?*"

"Yes. Helen..."

"Then why the hell are you marrying

him?"

"It's not what you think." She takes several deep breaths and pulls me further into the shadows of the library. "He—he has a problem. I've done some research... psychological research. I think it's like a mental illness. Or just part of who he is. Either way, I accept this about him."

"Carmen, are you insane?" I struggle to keep my voice down because I'm moments away from screaming at her or grabbing and shaking her. "Has he ever hurt you?"

"Well, he's aggressive sometimes. He's never hit me, but sometimes..."

"Sometimes what?" I demand.

She hesitates. "If I'm sleeping, or if I'm not feeling well. Like, if I'm on my period, and I have cramps... he will force himself on me." She gulps loudly. "Look, it's only been a few times, and he's always really apologetic afterward. We've gone to counseling. I swear, it's just this one thing—he's a great guy in every other way."

I feel so sick at hearing this. "You can't marry him."

"I have to. I love him. Please... please respect my decision, Helen. I know it seems messed up—but even though he hurts me, I know he doesn't *really* mean to hurt me. I've talked to him about it. I don't know what it is, but he has some kind of issue. He can't control himself sometimes."

"There are no excuses. If you marry him, it will only get worse."

"It's just sex, Helen! He's been nothing but supportive and openhearted in other ways. In every other way."

"Carmen, I can't believe what you're saying. You can't do this." I am losing my temper and trying to be calm, but I find myself grabbing her shoulders. "Did you know that in a lot of countries, it's *legal* to rape your wife? Even here, it's only been taken seriously in recent history. Traditionally, wives are supposed to be submissive to their husband, and that attitude is still a huge part of our culture. You can't agree to a life with someone who doesn't respect you."

"He respects me," Carmen insists. Her body trembles under my hands as though she is silently crying. "I swear to you, Helen. He respects me."

"Are you insane?" I shake my head in disbelief. "You're throwing away your freedom and the sanctity of your body. You're subjugating yourself to abuse! And you're *defending* him?"

"Yes, I'm defending him!" Carmen says sharply. "Believe it or not, I've had worse boyfriends. I've dated guys who tried to interfere with my school or my career. I dated guys that were jerks to Dad. I dated guys who were emotionally abusive and got drunk on an almost nightly basis, and said the cruelest things to me. I

198

dated guys who drove recklessly and got into several accidents with me in the vehicle. I dated guys with drug problems who tried to get me addicted and waste our days away being high. Yes, I'm sad and pathetic. But Grayson is the best guy I've ever met. He's the best guy I've ever been with, even with his flaws. And I'm marrying him!"

"Are you fucking kidding me right now?" I ask her in shock. "He just threatened to kill you if I told you what I know about him."

"He doesn't mean it," Carmen says tearfully. "Trust me, he's just using scare tactics— he really doesn't mean it, and he would never hurt me."

"You just told me he *raped* you."

"Yes, but... it's not complete rape. I want to have sex with him most of the time. Look, it's just a super small issue, Hellie. It's my fault too. If I had just been in the mood..."

"Oh my god," I say in disbelief and horror. "Who *are* you? What the fuck are you even saying right now? I thought my big sister was strong and brave. I thought she didn't take crap from anyone."

"I've changed since we lost Mom," Carmen tells me. "Now... I'd rather take a little crap from people than be completely alone forever."

"I won't let you," I tell her firmly. "You won't be alone, but you can't marry *him*. He's an animal. You deserve better!"

Carmen sighs. "I'm too tired, Helen. I'm too old to meet someone new and get to know him all over again. I've been with Grayson for a long time, and we are good together. I don't want to start all over again with someone else who could be even worse once I discover who he really is—it takes *years* to really figure a person out."

"You haven't even figured Grayson out!" I accuse her. "You don't even know how foul he is. Let me tell you what he did. Maybe if you know that you're not the only one he's hurt, you'll understand and take action."

"Helen," she says brokenly. "Don't."

"Do you remember when I came home with all those bruises? When I said I was mugged?"

"No!" Carmen almost shouts at me. Her words are laced with small, heart-wrenching sobs. "Please. Stop. I can't know this. Don't say another word. I'm fucked, Helen. I'm so fucked."

"You need to hear this," I insist. "He's the one who..."

"Helen, I'm three months pregnant."

The words get caught in my throat. I find myself rendered speechless.

"Whatever he's done?" Carmen whispers. "I can't know. He's the father of my baby. I can't... I can't back out of this now. I need him. I want my baby to grow up with a good father, like we did."

My hands fall to my side, quite limp and robbed of their fire. I lower my head.

"I need to sit down," Carmen says as she moves over to a chair in the corner of the library. She takes several deep breaths. "So now you know. I think it's why I've been so hormonal," she says with a small, miserable laugh. "It's why I've been crying so easily. Oh, and of course, it's why I was throwing up earlier. Why I had Tylenol instead of Advil, and no champagne while getting ready..."

"Is it also why you've lost your mind?" I ask her quietly.

"Yes," she answers. "I know that Grayson will be a good father. I don't care if he hurts me sometimes. That's the price I'm willing to pay to have the security of a good man and a strong family. As long as he takes care of my baby, nothing else matters."

I close my eyes, trying to un-see the horrible images in my mind. In this moment, I see too much. I vividly remember calling Dr. Howard to get me the morning-after pill when this happened to me. She tried to get me to file a police report and do a rape kit, but I just wanted to put the attack behind me. Now, I wish I had. If only I had known that my rapist wouldn't stop there, and that he would take things even further and hurt my sister? Or any other woman?

I was being selfish. I just wanted to run away to save myself, when I should have stayed to fight. This is all my fault. And now, this man has raped my sister into fathering my niece or nephew. He's trapped her. Emotionally, financially, and probably in dozens of ways I can't begin to guess, he's made her his prisoner.

"What if he hurts your child?" I ask her softly. "What if it's a girl, and when she's a teenager..."

"No. Don't even say that," Carmen tells me. "He wouldn't—"

Music starts playing from the ballroom where the wedding is being held. It's the music meant to announce Carmen's entrance into the room.

"Oh god," she says quietly, leaping up from her chair. "Oh god. How's my makeup? Shit, you can't even see my makeup. Oh god."

"Your makeup is the least of your worries," I tell her dryly.

"Look, Helen. I've made my choice. Maybe it's a bad choice, but I can't change my mind now. It's too late. I'm in too deep." She sniffles and wipes her face. "I have to go now. I love him, and I know he'll be a good father. I just want to present a good image to everyone else. I want to seem strong and happy to all our family and friends. Who cares if I have some private issues that bother me behind closed doors?

Everyone has skeletons in their closets. I'm going to head inside now."

"Can you think about this for a moment?" I implore her. "Carmen, I just want you to be safe. You're my big sister. I want you to be happy for real. Not just put on a show for everyone. Years of faking it and silently suffering will destroy you. It will suck the life out of you, and you'll be dead inside."

"I will be fine," she assures me, putting a hand on my arm. "Don't worry about me. Besides, I can live vicariously through you—at least you have Liam! He seems like a great guy who would never..."

"Ha! I just met him yesterday."

"What?"

"He's a stranger," I admit shamefully. "Sorry, Carm. He's just my doctor. I asked him to pretend for me."

"Oh." Her voice is empty and disappointed. "Well, then we're both fucked."

"Yeah," I agree.

"I guess... I'm going to go get married now," she says quietly. "Are you going to come stand beside me at the altar?"

"No." There is zero hesitation in my voice. "I don't support your decision. I can't be part of this celebration." My face contorts into a nasty frown. "But if Grayson dies, please invite me to his funeral."

"Okay," she says softly. "Thanks for coming to my wedding, Hellie. You're—you're the only one who *really* cares." Carmen throws her arms around me in one final, tight hug before leaving the library.

I could feel all her love and fear in the fierceness of her embrace. It brings tears to my eyes. I listen to her hurried footsteps as she turns and rushes across the foyer to do her duty and walk down the aisle. I know that she's just trying to be strong and do the right thing. Who am I to judge? Maybe it is the right thing to do. Maybe Grayson really is a good person with some sort of mental illness, and maybe the good he does in the world makes up for his sins. Maybe the good he does for my family makes up for what he did to me. Maybe he really will be a good father.

Somehow, I have trouble believing this.

The news of my sister's pregnancy is bittersweet. She seems excited at the prospect, and I will be happy to be an auntie. I wonder if Dad knows? Either way, I'm sure he would be thrilled. I just always imagined this happening under different circumstances. I imagined more laughter and safety. I imagined that it would be slow and carefully planned. I imagined throwing baby showers and parties, and celebrating with friends. I imagined that Mom would be there to help Carmen and guide her with good advice.

I imagined looking up to my big sister as

she succeeded in life and accomplished huge milestones. I imagined patterning myself off her, and using her achievements to give me direction. I imagined her guiding me with her greater years and wisdom, and helping me feel certain on my own path. I imagined so much stupid bullshit that will never happen. Sure, I somewhat expected to use her mistakes to guide me on what *not* to do, but not to this extent.

This is not a mistake. This is a tragedy.

I slowly make my way out of the library, but I only get as far as the doorframe before I have to lean against the wall for support. It's my fault. If I had been braver, and tried to find my attacker instead of simply running away... I could have prevented this. I knew some information about him—although I'm not sure if it was accurate. I knew that he was an engineer and a football player. Those could have been lies, but I could have provided a general description of his physical build. I knew where he was, and at what time—there could have been security footage on the campus to show who was in the vicinity.

I was selfish and self-absorbed. I thought it was just about me, and my drama. I thought that if no one else had to hear my story and deal with the event, that they would all be safe. I thought that pretending it never happened could make it go away.

I thought it only happened to me because

of my disability. I thought that by being blind, I was somehow asking for it. I thought that by crying in a stairwell, I had made myself vulnerable and an easy target; I announced myself as a victim, and it was almost entirely my fault. I thought that other women—normal women—would be able to look at a man and instantly see all the evil and cruelty inside him written on his face. Shouldn't those things be glaringly obvious?

It's my fault. It's all my fault. I could have protected her. I believed I was protecting her from the harshness of the truth, but really, I was concealing knowledge from her and exposing her to the harshness of reality. Now, she's pregnant. *He* made her pregnant. Probably without her consent or any planning. I failed her. I failed my sister.

She's not even thirty years old, but her life is over.

I hear the music quiet down and the minister begin to commence the ceremony. Each word is more grating to my ears than nails on a chalkboard. I can't stay in the house and listen to this anymore. I hate myself for what I've done. For letting this happen. How could I have been so stupid?

I hear footsteps on the hardwood floor of the foyer. Footsteps moving toward me.

"Helen?" says a worried male voice. "What's going on? Why aren't you in the ceremony?"

My mouth opens for me to speak, but I find that my lips are trembling. My eyebrows crease as I fight back tears of failure and self-hatred. "I shouldn't have come here, Liam." I take a moment to compose myself, trying to detach myself from the doorframe and stand up properly. My knee quivers slightly under me, threatening to cave. I did not walk around very much during the years that I spent confined to my little cabin, and I suppose I am kind of skinny and weak. My emotional state does not help. In this moment, I wish more than anything that I could be back home in my cabin. This place is not my home any longer.

"Is there anything I can do to help?" he asks me.

"No. Just..." I shut my eyes tightly to restrain my tears. "Please go away. Do your experiments on someone else. I don't want to be here. I don't want to be able to see."

"But Helen, we made a deal..."

"I don't even know why you bothered," I tell him. I am suddenly filled with rage, and I step forward to glare at the spot where I believe his face is. "Why do you even care? What the hell is your problem? Searching me out, and digging me out of my comfort zone. Dragging me back here, and trying to change everything about me? Trying to improve my life? What is your deal? Maybe you should mind your own business, Dr. Larson."

"Helen, this study really could change your life. Your vision is important. I don't know what upset you, but it has nothing to do with..."

"Fuck you!" I snap at him cruelly. "Vision is nothing. Vision is worthless. I am more than just a pair of broken eyes!"

"I never felt that way! I just wanted to help. I never meant to imply that..."

"No. I am not some pitiful disabled patient you can jerk around as you please, to suit your purposes. I *liked* my life in New Hampshire. I liked my shitty food, and I liked my shitty job, and I liked being alone. I *like* not being able to see, because I know there's a whole lot of ugly shit in the world. Isn't it bad enough that I have to *hear* it, and *feel* it? Did you ever think that being able to see it would cause my brain to explode in a sensory overload? You know I was on anti-depressants. Did you ever think it might be too much, and I might end up in a mental institution for the rest of my life because I was forced to see things too clearly? See all these terrible things?"

"There are wonderful things too," Liam tells me. "Please, Helen. Just trust me. I wanted to show you so many beautiful things. Of course, it will be a huge adjustment when you first gain your vision, but it will make life so much easier in the long run. Trust me; it will be worth it. For every horrible thing you will see in the world, there will be a thousand amazing sights that far outshine the negative ones."

His voice is pleading and kind, and it cuts right down to my soul. I really do want to trust him and believe in the good things. I want to embrace the good that life has to offer, but how can I after this wedding? In the background of our conversation, wedding vows are being spoken as my sister signs away her soul to the devil.

"I, Carmen, take you, Grayson, to be my lawfully wedded husband from this day forward. In the presence of God, our family and friends..."

A tear that has been gathering in the corner of my eye finally breaks free. I feel helpless and overwhelmed. I feel even worse for being mean to Liam when I know that he has only been good to me in the short time we've been acquainted. I breathe deeply and exhale. "I'm sorry," I manage to say through a constricted throat. "This is the worst day I've had in years. Possibly the worst day of my life. I just... I need to go."

"Helen, I..."

"No. Thank you for everything, Liam. Please excuse me." I turn and run through the house as quickly as I can. I need to get out of this place.

Chapter Four

I head toward the back of the house. My high-heeled shoes pound the ground as I run across the dining room, carefully stepping around chairs and other decorative pieces of furniture. I skirt around the kitchen counter as I head for the large glass doors that open out onto our patio. There is a small wooded area behind our house. It's not the perfect time of year to be going outside without a jacket, but I can't pause to properly prepare. I need to get out *now*. I am filled with rage, desperation, and guilt. I cannot seem to breathe, and I need fresh air.

Stepping through the door to the backyard, I slam it shut behind me. The cold air immediately pierces directly through my flimsy bridesmaid dress, and begins to stab at my skin like a blanket of tiny needles. Oddly enough, the first place it strikes me is my chest. I am not wearing bra, and my nipples begin to ache before any other part of my body. It feels like they have been dipped in liquid nitrogen, and scalded so badly that they might fall off at any moment. I ignore this and continue to run across our backyard in my pumps, ignoring that the snow is seeping through the open toes of the shoes, and snapping around my ankles like bear traps made of ice. As I move down the patio steps and into the grass, the snow gets deeper, and begins to freeze my calves. Nevertheless, I move forward. I run through the snow until my skin is searing and blistering from the cold.

A couple times, I stumble, but I just manage to keep my balance and prevent myself from entirely falling. Finally, my heel catches on a dense snowdrift, and I do fall completely. My hands plunge forward into the snow to steady myself. It feels like icy fists have gripped my wrists as I struggle to pick myself off the ground. I realize that I'm not going to get anywhere in these shoes, and I reach down to rip them off my feet and angrily toss them across the backyard. Fuck this wedding, and fuck those shoes. Fuck this whole fucking day. I trudge through the snow barefoot, and get a kind of sick pleasure from the pain running up my legs, stabbing me like lightning bolts made of ice. I imagine getting serious frostbite and having to cut my feet off. It makes me move even faster.

Finally, knowing that I am nearing my destination, I begin to stretch my arms outward. I move around frantically, feeling for the impact of a familiar structure. It takes a few minutes, and I begin to panic as I am lost and disoriented and standing knee-deep in bone-chilling snow. What if the structure I'm searching for has been moved or replaced in my absence? I sigh thankfully when my arms connect with the wooden walls of the garden shed. The cold surface feels sticky under my hands due to being coated with a thin layer of ice. Dragging my hands across the exterior of the shed, my fingers glide over the frosty glass windows. I slide my hands lower as I wildly search for the doorknob. It takes me a few seconds to locate the frigid metal knob, and I grasp it and turn violently, yanking the door open.

Stepping into the old garden shed, I hastily close the door behind me. Only then do I exhale in relief. When I breathe in, my nostrils are filled with the scent of old wood and rusty metal gardening tools. There is also the lingering aroma of potted soil and dead plants. These decaying herbs used to be alive and flourishing when my mother tended the garden, and taken inside annually to be protected from the winter. Now, they are neglected and crumbling into dust. I begin moving through the garden shed to the other end, and my knee knocks over what must be a shovel. It clatters loudly to the ground, startling me. I always get really clumsy when I'm upset. I simply stop caring about the fact that I'm blind, and pretend that I'm invincible and magically know where everything is all around me. I boldly take another two steps, as though defying all inanimate objects and daring them to collide with me. On my third step, my heel jams down on the hard spikes of a rake. I curse and reflexively rip my foot away from the painful metal implement. My bare feet are already very sensitive and sore from the cold, so the agony caused by the impact is amplified at least tenfold. I clutch my sore foot with a wounded expression on my face as I glare down at my attacker.

There is a burst of fire in my gut as I reach forward and grasp the handle of the offensive rake. My arms move without my permission, swinging the rake madly and smashing it into the wall of the cabin, as though everything is its fault. I let out a scream as I slam the rake into the cabin's window, and the sound of shattering glass is heard. I let it fall down around me like lethal rain. It is extremely cathartic. For a moment, I feel strong and powerful. I feel like I could do anything.

Then it's gone. I am powerless. I remember everything.

I can't bear the crushing weight of these vile memories, and I need to escape them somehow. Running away to the ends of the earth won't help, and neither will smashing everything in sight. I need to disappear into my own mind.

Feeling guilty for my violent outburst, I try to carefully step around the stray shards of glass as I move toward the corner of the little shed. I put my back toward the wall and slide down to the ground, and my bottom lands against the floor with a small thud. The cold ground sends icy shockwaves up through my dress, and I seriously regret wearing Carmen's thong. It is not offering much in the way of protection from the weather. This entire ensemble is worthless, and I might as well be naked. She even forced me to shave my legs! What I wouldn't give for even that extra protective layer of tiny hairs right now. Rubbing my hands up and down my clammy, cold legs, I try to get warm. I try to no avail. Blowing some hot air over my legs, I slap my toes to make sure I can feel them. They are so cold that it's excruciating. I press my hands against my chest, trying to soothe my stinging nipples. The coldness is no longer jabbing me with needles, but with dagger-like intensity.

However, I am glad for the pain. It distracts me from the memories that are playing across the inside of my mind—the memories that I can't seem to shake away. So many parts of my body are screaming at me for attention that I don't even know where to begin. I reach forward I wrap my fingers around my frozen toes to try to massage the sensation back into them, but before

214

long, my hands start feeling too cold to assist my toes. I stick my fingers under my armpits to help them defrost, but I am soon distracted by the throbbing ache in my ears. I lift my hands to cup my tender ears for a moment. As I close my eyes, I hear Grayson's voice echoing in my mind. I am frustrated to find that even though I have left the house, and even though I have my hands clamped over my ears, the man is too deep inside my head for me to find sanctuary. It's completely futile to fight against both the cold and the past.

The strength and fire within me quickly dissipate. I slump weakly against the side of the wall. I stop caring about my painful ears and toes, and just wrap my arms around my legs. I hug my knees tightly against my chest and curl up into a little ball. I rock slightly back and forth in an attempt to soothe and warm myself. I can't think. I want to comfort myself with reassuring thoughts about my own strength and resilience, but I just can't think.

I sit there by myself for several minutes, enjoying the solitude.

My mind floats away, and I am at peace again.

I remain in this state until a loud noise causes me to jump in fright. I realize that someone is opening the door of the garden shed. I gasp and freeze in panic, as my heart rate instantly doubles. Is the wedding over? Is it Grayson? Has he come looking for me? I want to move forward to grab the metal rake for protection, or maybe a sliver of broken glass from the window I smashed, but I can't seem to make my body move. Is it him? Is he here to torture me again?

I hear the man's breathing, and my cold fingers are suddenly reenergized. I reach forward, fumbling for the rake. I grasp the handle firmly, ready to swing it again—this time, directly into that bastard's skull.

"What is it with you and little wooden shacks?" says Liam's teasing voice. "I bet you were the kind of kid who played with a cardboard box even when you were given really expensive, fancy toys."

I open my fingers and let the rake clatter to the ground. I am so thankful to hear Liam's voice. I am so relieved that it's him. I feel a rush of emotion pouring through the floodgates. I can't restrain this onslaught of gladness mixed in with anguish. It shakes me to my very core. I place my face in my hands.

"Helen?" he says softly. "My god, you're shaking like a leaf. What happened?"

A few tears tumble into my hands, and my shoulders shudder slightly. I take a deep breath, and find my resolve. "I'm just cold," I say in a small and halting voice. It is the best explanation I could muster, and quite obviously a blatant lie.

"Of course you're cold!" he says angrily.

216

"You're running through the snow half-naked like a madwoman. Do you want to get hypothermia? Jesus, Helen! I said I could fix your eyes. I can't get you a new pair of legs, too."

In spite of myself, a smile tugs at my lips. My moment of mirth is interrupted by a violent shiver, and I hug my knees closer to my chest. I have never felt such severe, almost unbearable pain in my nipples before. I did not know how much they could hurt. "Why didn't you just go home?" I ask him.

"I thought about it," he says, entering the cabin and closing the door behind him. "I got in my car and turned on the engine. But then I looked down and saw that paperback you signed for me. With that personalized inscription. 'Please leave me alone.' I suppose it's the rebel in me, but I simply couldn't let you have the satisfaction."

"Thanks," I tell him quietly. "Sorry I was such a bitch earlier. I'm actually... glad you're here."

Liam moves over to my corner of the shed, stepping over the shovels and rakes. When he's standing directly above me, I hear the rustling of fabric as he removes his coat. In the next moment, he is laying the thick garment over my bare legs and arms.

I stare down at the coat in surprise. Of course, I see nothing, but the kindness in his gesture has caused me to feel as though he has

217

placed a glowing cloak of magical diamonds at my feet. I am overwhelmed with emotion; I value this so much. I know that it's a tiny, basic thing that any person should do, but not every person *does*. Grayson wouldn't. When faced with someone sad and down on her luck, he wouldn't help. He would take advantage of the situation. I am so thankful that Liam is not like him.

The truth is that I am already so frozen that his coat does very little for my temperature. Still, I treasure the thoughtfulness of the act. I probably needed a bit of sensitivity and caring far more than I needed to be warm. I carefully extend my fingers to touch Liam's coat. It's difficult to move my hands, because my fingers are so stiff. I run my fingers over the lining of the fabric, just to convince myself that this is real—the coat is a symbol that there is at least one good person in the world. I can barely feel the coarse fibers under what is surely the beginning of frostbitten digits, but it is reassuring to know that they are there. Liam's compassion causes a tiny spark that begins to thaw the cold and dead parts of me that matter far more than my skin.

"It's dangerous to be out here like this," he tells me, crouching down to my level. "Jesus, Helen. Your lips are turning blue. We should go back inside."

"I'm not going back into that house," I say adamantly. "I'd rather die here."

"But Helen..."

"No. I told you I had a bad feeling. I never should have come back here."

Liam takes my hands into his and begins to rub them between his own to generate some heat through friction. "You're shivering way too much. Let me go inside and get some warmer clothes and some blankets..."

"No, I'm fine." I pull my hands away from him and wrap them around myself.

I hear him standing up and moving briskly toward the exit of the shed. "I should grab some hot cocoa at the very least, and maybe a portable heater..."

"No—no. Liam. Please don't leave. Just stay with me?" I can't believe how pathetic I sound. I can't believe that sentence even left my lips. My embarrassment is quickly assuaged when I feel the floorboards creak as he moves back over to my corner, and lowers himself to sit next to me. I am relieved to have him near me, but I am swiftly seized with a fear that he will get *too* close. I remember Grayson's hands on my body, and the gun against my chest. I remember the disgusting, degrading kiss. I flinch away from Liam, pressing myself against the wall of the wooden cabin. I feel a sudden suffocating claustrophobia. I am not usually one to dislike small spaces—in fact, I usually prefer them—but being confined in close quarters with other people is entirely unnerving.

I am grateful when Liam maintains his distance. He does not try to embrace me or move any closer; not even under the pretense of keeping me warm. He seems to be able to sense my anxiety. When he sits beside for over a full minute without trying to touch me or even asking why I'm upset, I begin to relax. I stop holding my breath, and I feel the erratic pounding of my heart slowly ease. I reach down and lift his coat, arranging it so that it covers his legs as well.

"Can I at least keep trying to warm your hands?" he asks me. "I'm worried."

"Yes," I tell him softly, "but I think my toes are the real problem. They feel like they're going to fall off."

I feel Liam slide his coat over my ankles to study my feet. "Helen... okay. This is going to sound awful, but you need to listen to me." He speaks in a brisk and commanding tone that I haven't heard him use before. "Put your feet in my lap."

"In your lap?" I say awkwardly.

"Yes. Unless you want to risk losing your toes."

"You're probably exaggerating," I accuse him, but the cold is so agonizing that I am beginning to grow desperate for any warmth. I try to flex my toes, and wince, because even that tiny bit of motion hurts like a bitch.

"I'm not really exaggerating. It's damn

cold out here. But I won't let you get severe frostbite," he tells me firmly, "because I'll drag you kicking and screaming back into that house before any permanent damage is done. However, if you don't follow my instructions right away, you'll probably develop blisters and swelling so painful that you can't walk for days."

I make a face, for this sounds almost as unpleasant as my feet already feel.

"Trust me," he says. "I'm a doctor."

"You know that every time you say that I get even more suspicious, right?" I ask him lightly.

"Feet. Lap. Now." He demands this while vigorously rubbing my fingers.

Biting my lip, I angle my body perpendicular to his and place my feet in his lap. I carefully rest my toes against what should be the warmest part of his upper thigh, while still being as respectful and polite as possible and not plunging my toes directly into his genitals. Unfortunately, I am so numb that I can't feel any of his body heat and it offers no immediate relief to my stinging pain.

Liam arranges his coat more closely around my legs as he continues to rub my fingers.

"Thanks," I tell him softly.

"You don't need to thank me," he responds, and there is a bit of anger in his voice. "I'm just trying to keep you all in one piece. Jesus. It's like you're determined to sabotage yourself! If being blind isn't bad enough, you have no appreciation for your fingers and toes. Your body parts aren't just expendable, you know!"

"No," I tell him. "That's not what I meant. Thanks for not asking what happened in the house."

"Oh," he says in surprise. "Well... you're welcome. I figure that if you want to tell me, you will."

I am quiet for a moment, except for the noise of my teeth chattering and my short, rapid breathing. "Can I sit a little closer to you?" I ask quietly.

"Sure," he says, but he moves toward me instead, pinning me into the corner of the shed. He slips his arm around me, trying to cradle me in a cocoon of comfort and warmth.

I lean forward and press my shoulder against his body, trying to burrow into the warmth of his armpit. My ears and nose have been stinging with pain, and I press my face against his chest to steal the heat of his torso, through his tuxedo jacket. My feet are still positioned in his lap. I am shivering quite uncontrollably now, and running out into the snow no longer seems like it was the perfect rebellious and dramatic idea. It feels like it was immature and self-destructive. I wouldn't have cared if Liam hadn't followed me; if it was just me alone, shivering and getting frostbite and possibly dying, I might be comfortable with that.

But forcing him to take care of me? Making him deal with my stress and my crisis? That's selfish of me, and it's not right. I feel so childish and needy, and I hate myself for being like this.

"I'm sorry," I mumble against his chest. "I didn't mean to involve you..."

"I involved myself," he responds. "Are you feeling a bit warmer? Does it hurt anywhere?"

"Just my ears and face," I say quietly. My nipples are also hurting a great deal, but I am far too embarrassed to mention that. The cold is starting to make me sleepy.

I feel one of Liam's hands leave mine, and a warm palm is pressed against my exposed ear. He gently rubs my ear between his fingers, and I wince at the pain. I feel his fingers under my chin, lifting it so that he can examine my face. He presses his thumb against my nose, massaging it gently, followed by my cheeks. He leans down and breathes hot air into my face, and it tickles my eyelashes. He skirts his thumb over my frozen lips, while breathing more hot air onto my skin.

"Um," he says awkwardly, suddenly pulling away. "Sorry about that."

"About what?" I ask in confusion.

"You know..." He clears his throat. "The situation in my lap."

"Oh!" I say in surprise. I'm not sure why, but I try to wiggle my toes around to figure out what he's talking about. I am almost disappointed when all I feel is the burning pain of my toes. "Unfortunately, I'm too numb to feel anything and I hadn't noticed."

"Dammit. Then I shouldn't have mentioned it," he grumbles. "How humiliating. Can you please stop poking your feet around now? That's not helping."

"Is something happening in your lap?" I ask innocently. For some reason, this is somewhat amusing to me. The gentle beginnings of a smile cause the corners of my lips to crinkle, and this hurts my face as though my skin is made of ice which has begun to crack and shatter.

"Helen," he says with warning. "Stop teasing me. You refused to go inside or let me go in the house and bring something warm back—so I'm improvising. This is the best I can do."

"Thanks," I tell him sincerely. I lean forward and press my face against his chest again, but this time it's not entirely for warmth. "Why was there a situation in your lap?" I ask him.

"Oh. I was just thinking of ways to help you get warm... and for an instant, the thought of kissing you might have crossed my mind."

Luckily, my face being hidden against his chest conceals my surprise. "Thanks for not doing that. I don't think I could handle it right now."

"You don't have to keep thanking me for being a decent human being, Helen. Besides, logically, my armpit is warmer, so you should probably stick your face there—it was just a fleeting thought I couldn't control."

I try to conceal a frown. I told him on the car ride over here that I had changed my name, and no longer wanted to be called Helen. My recent encounter with Grayson has only made it worse. I hate that name. I hate the way he says it. I hate everything associated with it. I wish that I could escape it, but I already tried that once. Someone still found me and brought me home. How could I escape even further? How could I really get away and disappear from all this?

My thoughts take a sinister turn, and I start wishing that Liam had not found me. I start to grow comforted by imagining a perfect silence and darkness, one even more complete than my usual silence and darkness. I think that Liam senses my train of thought, for he rubs his hand up and down over my back.

"What are you thinking about?" he asks softly.

I can't respond. How can I tell him these thoughts? How can I tell him that I am wishing I would freeze to death? He will think I'm insane. Still, I can't stop wishing that my existence would come to an end, so that I would never have to be afraid, anxious, or alone again. The last of those three qualities, the loneliness, is not something that I have allowed to bother me in the past. But after feeling a brief period of hopefulness and happiness, brought to me by Liam and his dorky friend Owen, I'm not sure how I can return to my previous life. After imagining for hours how glorious it could be to have my vision returned, and after hugging my dad again for the first time in years, and eating scrumptious cupcakes—how can I give up all of this? Worst of all, is this precious feeling I currently have.

I feel like Liam has dropped everything to take care of me—not just to prevent my potential frostbite, but to comfort me emotionally. He hasn't mentioned it, but it is quite obvious in the careful way that he is holding me that he's not just here because I'm a patient. There was no need to follow me out into the backyard to check on me. Coming to the wedding *at all* was unnecessary, especially after I told him not to. Heck—it was crazy that he sought me out specifically for his experiment when there were probably dozens of other excellent candidates. Why would he go out of his way to be so nice? Everything he's done for me has been over-the-top and extraordinary. I haven't had to ask repeatedly for assistance, or pressure him, and grow to feel uncomfortable and desperate. He has just taken action, so easily and happily, almost completely without prompting. We did make a few silly bargains, but I think that was mostly having fun. He has helped me and been there for me, almost as though he might *enjoy* doing things for me.

226

CLARITY

And he's here right now. Suffering through the cold with me. Protecting me. From the weather, from Grayson, and from myself.

For the first time in as long as I can remember, I feel important to someone.

I feel like the center of his world.

It's ridiculous, I know—and I won't be foolish enough to say anything of the sort. It's just that since my mom died, I haven't felt this kind of sympathy and understanding. I haven't had any intimate connections with any other people—I haven't had anyone in whom I could confide. I've only known Liam for a few hours, but he really does feel like an old friend. It's so easy to talk to him, like we might have always been around each other, moving in the same circles, reading the same books, sharing the same experiences. I know this is insane and untrue, but there's just something calming about his energy. There's something true and solid in his voice.

Gone is the boisterous, animated sound of Carmen's shrill tone—she somehow managed to be peppy and animated even in her darkest moment. I don't think anything could keep that girl down. Thinking about her makes me feel a little sick. Our previous conversation really got under my skin. Sometimes listening to her speak can be exhausting, but that had to be the most depressing conversation we ever shared. In contrast, when Liam speaks, in his slow and careful way, I just want to hear more.

It baffles me that even though he has no idea what's wrong with me, or the reason why I ran out into the snow, he's helping anyway. No questions asked. I am suddenly overcome with the urge to tell him. I am not sure why—do I require validation for my reckless act? Do I feel I owe him an explanation in exchange for his kindness? Or is the memory of Carmen and her situation destroying my insides like a cancer, and do I need to share it with someone in order to get it out of my system?

"Do you want to know what's bothering me?" I ask him, taking a frosty breath.

"I'm dying to know," he admits, "but only if you want to share."

Nodding, I try to find the words. "Remember the story I told you in the car? About my past? What happened to me?"

"Yes, of course," he answers.

I shut my eyes tightly. It feels like that car ride was a lifetime ago. So much has happened since then that I feel like a different person. I clear my throat as I prepare to deliver the awkward words. "The man that my sister just married... is the man who... yeah."

Liam sits up a little, and I feel his entire body tense up in understanding. He does not respond right away. He seems dumbstruck to the point of speechlessness. I can also feel that he has not taken a breath in several seconds as he processes the information. "You're saying that the groom—Grayson—is the one who..."

"Yeah."

He remains wordless for another little while. "Does your sister know?"

"Not exactly. I mean—not about me. I tried to tell her, but I think she doesn't want to know." I hesitate and frown, rubbing my hands together for warmth. "He's exhibited the same sort of behavior with her."

"Then why the hell did you let them get married?" Liam shoves my legs off his lap and rises to his feet. "We have to call the police!"

"Liam, Liam... she's pregnant." I lower my face in disappointment at the situation. "She accepts him. She forgives him. Or at least that's what she tells herself," I mutter under my breath.

"I don't understand. How can—how can she...?" Liam pauses. "Is this a joke, Helen? I know you're a writer, so..."

I sigh and shiver at the freezing floorboards which are beneath my toes once again. "I wish it was a joke."

"This is possibly the most insane thing I've ever heard," Liam tells me.

I bitterly shrug my cold, bare shoulders. "Personally, I prefer fiction. This is what happens when I try to participate in real life."

Liam makes a derisive noise. "Fuck that

guy. Don't let one assface ruin real life for you."
The floorboards creak and the glass crunches as
Liam paces back and forth in the garden shed. "I
just don't understand how this happened. Was it a
coincidence? Or did he do it on purpose?"

"I don't know," I say quietly. "I think it
was on purpose—maybe because he felt guilty and
wanted to help my family as repentance. Or maybe
because he liked hurting me so much that he
wanted the opportunity to emotionally torture me
for the rest of my life. In addition to the other
stuff."

"Jesus," Liam says harshly. "Jesus! Fuck."

"Yeah," I say again dryly, rubbing my
arms.

"And your sister didn't care? She was cool
with the whole thing?" Liam demands.

"She said she loves him," I respond. "She
says that she considers it a mental illness and that
she's going to counseling with him."

"Dammit!" Liam says, his voice escalating
in volume. "What is wrong with these stupid
women! Why do they always subject themselves to
such bullshit? Do you know how many female
patients I've seen not because of some random
accident, infection, or congenital disease—but
because of domestic abuse? And then they come
back again. And again. And they beg me not to do
anything about it. It's fucking bullshit!"

I am a little startled by his outburst. I

didn't expect him to be so passionate about this subject. He is also defending me—he is on my side, and I feel like I have an ally.

The floorboards creak again as Liam paces furiously in the tiny garden shed. "It's a bit more understandable when they're from other cultures," he says heatedly. "I figure they have certain traditions, and that's just the way they've been raised to behave. It's hard to break ancient habits. But your sister is American. What the fuck is wrong with her?"

His righteous anger thrills me a little, and I do feel validated. "Thank you."

"Dammit," Liam says again. "I'm really upset. I don't even *know* Carmen, but I'm so pissed at her. I kind of want to grab this shovel or rake and just smash it into the wall a few times."

A sardonic smile comes to my lips. "Be my guest. Try taking out the other window. Smashing this one really helped me feel better."

"Oh, you did that?" Liam pauses. "What are we going to do? We need to do something about this, right? Should we call the cops anyway?"

"I don't know. That could make things worse." I suddenly find that my lip is quivering and I'm getting emotional. I was trying to remain aloof and above this, and not let Liam see how much it's affecting me, but it's getting increasingly difficult the more we discuss this. "He has a gun—

he threatened me," I say quietly. I lift my hands to massage my temples gently, and take a deep breath. "When I spoke to him... he seemed to genuinely want to be with Carmen. He said he would shoot her and then himself if I did anything to stop the wedding. He put the gun against my chest so I could feel it."

"Oh, Helen," Liam says. "I'm so sorry..."

"Don't call me that," I whisper. I slightly shift my hands so that they cover my ears. "Why does everyone call me that? I'm not her anymore."

I feel the floor shift beneath me as Liam comes closer. He kneels before me and places a hand on my shoulder.

"Winter," he says softly, as if testing it on his tongue. "Winter, please listen to me. You're right. You're not the same person, and that man is not going to hurt you ever again. Do you believe me?"

His words filter through my hands, and I cautiously remove them from my ears. I swallow, trying to fight back tears. "But he's going to hurt *her*. He literally has a *license* to hurt her. He's going to hurt my unborn niece or nephew. And it's all my fault."

"Don't say that," he tells me firmly. "This is definitely not your fault. Not in any way."

"But it is," I say brokenly. "I ran away from home. I kept everything to myself. If I had stayed here, I could have prevented this. I could have protected her. I would have recognized him sooner—I could have warned her early on, before she was so attached to him and *pregnant*. Now it's too late."

Liam hesitates. "What if... what if the gun thing was just bravado? What if he really has changed?"

"You're just saying that," I accuse him. "You're just trying to make me feel better."

"Not entirely. I'm being serious. Do you believe in redemption?"

I blink a few times as I consider this. The intensity of the conversation and our emotions have almost entirely distracted me from the cold, and I shiver a little. "Redemption? I don't know. Have you ever known someone who really changed?"

"Not really," he responds. "I just—I guess I just think it's a nice idea." Liam comes to sit by my side again, and he takes my feet back into his lap. He begins to rub my toes to stimulate circulation and keep them warm.

We sit like this, in silence for several minutes. My thoughts turn to the future, and what my plan of action should be. I feel so weak and miserable, and incapable of dealing with this.

"So this is why you don't want to participate in the study anymore?" he asks me.

"What?" I say in confusion, startled from my thoughts.

"Earlier when you were yelling at me, you said you didn't want me to try the gene therapy on your eyes. Were you just upset, or did you mean that?"

I shake my head, with my eyebrows drawn together in a frown. It's difficult to speak. "I wish I could do the study. I wish it more than anything. But now? I can't stay here in this house. In this city. I have to get the hell away from this place."

"But don't you regret running away last time?" he asks me.

"Yes, but..." I try to think of how to phrase my thoughts. "I already failed. What more damage could really be done? Even if I do stay— I'm powerless to protect Carmen or make things better. I might even make things worse with my presence."

"You have to stay," Liam insists. "You can't just leave again. You have this huge opportunity, and if you run away... then he's won. You can't let him destroy your life."

"Luckily, I hardly have any life for him to destroy. Not here. I don't have any ties to this place. My life is sitting in a small cabin up north, and that's where I should return. I haven't called to cancel my grocery deliveries yet. I should just go back there."

"I won't let you," Liam tells me. "The life you were living was no kind of life at all. It was some kind of masochistic self-punishment for something that wasn't even your fault. You need to stay here and be strong, Hel—Winter. Stay here, and let me try to give you the ability to see."

"I don't think I can..."

"You can't let a ghost from your past destroy your future."

"It doesn't feel like he's in the past anymore, Liam. He's right here. He's standing a few steps away in my family home... he's probably laughing and feeding my sister cake right now."

Liam makes a sound of exasperation. "Well, fuck him! You can't go on running and hiding from everything good just because of this one man. What about me? I mean, ignoring the fact that you *promised* that if we drove you home, you'd let us do the research..."

"I'm sorry to go back on my word," I say glumly. "I didn't expect that it would be unsafe to be here."

"*Ignoring* that fact," Liam repeats with emphasis, "what about us?"

"Us?" I repeat slowly.

"Yeah. Am I crazy," he asks, "or is there something here between us?"

My lips part to deliver a response, but I press them together again tightly to save myself from saying something impulsive and possibly stupid.

"Maybe it's just friendship," Liam says. "Maybe... there's the potential for something more.

I don't know, but I just... I really like being around you." He clears his throat awkwardly. "Am I nuts? Do you feel the same?"

I close my eyes before speaking, almost ashamed of the answer. "Yes," I say weakly.

"Good," he says, exhaling in relief. "It's just special, you know? It's rare to meet someone and have such an awesome connection right off the bat. You can't just toss *us* away before we even know what *us* could be." His voice grows firm and demanding. "I'm sorry if saying this is uncool, or if it makes you uncomfortable. I just won't accept you *banishing* yourself from the realm to live in exile again. This house is your kingdom, and you can't let some fool shove you out of your domain."

I can't help but smile sadly in spite of myself at the adorable metaphor.

"If this is a territorial dispute, you need to mark your space and hold your ground," Liam says with determination. "He doesn't deserve to take everything that's yours. He doesn't deserve to win. He doesn't deserve to steal your family, and steal all possibility of you having friends or lovers..."

I lower my face to conceal a blush at that last word. Somehow, even though I am literally freezing my ass off (it is now conclusive that I despise thongs with a great passion) my cheeks begin to feel very hot at the concept of having a lover. My feet are still in Liam's lap, and my mind

236

drifts back to his earlier apology about his body's responsiveness to me. The thought that someone kind and intelligent might actually desire *me* is quite wonderful. It gives me a little injection of self-esteem and strength. But then I remind myself that it's so wonderful it's almost *unbelievable*. Something about the whole situation seems too good to be true.

"I just want to see you again," Liam says. "That can't happen if you go away. I want to be your friend. I want to read your new book before everyone else. I want you to be happy. I want to be there on the day that you get your vision back, and see the look on your face."

"Liam," I say softly. "That's all a lovely fantasy, but..."

"It's not a fantasy," he assures me. "All of this can happen if you just stay here and *trust me*."

I take a moment to consider his words before responding. A deep frown settles into my face. I try to breathe slowly and evenly to clear my mind as I carefully choose my next words. "Do you want to know what I'm afraid of, Liam?"

"What is it?" he asks, squeezing my knee.

I take another deep breath before responding. Tears prick the back of my eyes, and I fend them off with a halfhearted smile. "What scares me most is that even if I *could* see, I would still be blind to the truth about people. Like Carmen." I wrinkle my eyes, struggling to repress

237

the waterworks. "She can't tell what a demon he is—and I'm supposed to be the blind one. What if being able to see actually distracts a person from the truth of things, beneath the surface? What if I saw a pretty face and thought there must be an equally beautiful soul behind it? I'm sitting here with you, and I have no clue what you look like, except for other people's descriptions. But I can hear your voice, and your words, and feel your touch—and I think you're wonderful. But I could still be wrong. This could all be deception. I have been wrong before. What if I could see you, and you were beautiful? What if I were enchanted by your outward appearance? How would I have *any* indication that there could be a monster deep inside you? How could I possibly protect myself? What if having perfect eyesight actually made things worse for me—what if being able to see more made me understand less? What if the world became less clear?" I pause, realizing that I have been going on and on in an emotional tirade. I lift my fingertips and press them against my closed eyelid as a tear squeezes itself through the crevice. I sigh and utter one final sentence to Liam in closing:

"You can give me vision, but you can't give me clarity."

Liam reaches out and presses his palm against my cheek. He stares at me silently for a brief interval before speaking. "Winter," he says softly. "The name does suit you. You're as pure as the snow. Your mind is like the crisp, clean winter air."

I puzzled by his romantic response.

"I will give you clarity, Winter," he promises in a low voice. "I'll give you everything I possibly can."

The tone of devotion in his oath is so strong that I can't bear it. I press my hands against my face as the tears begin to fall freely. I want to believe him so badly. I want to believe that things will be fine. "I was so happy, Liam. Earlier on, with you and Owen. I was the happiest I've been in ages. Everything seemed good."

"I know," he says, hugging me gently. "When I texted Owen, I told him to try his best to make you laugh."

Once again, I am stunned by Liam's thoughtfulness. That he would care at all about making a stranger laugh is unreal. It causes more tears to slide down my cheeks. "What am I going to do?" I ask him. "How can I live in the same house with that man? He threatened to kill my sister and her baby."

"Just take it one step at a time," he tells me. "One day at a time. You might find that once you rid yourself of fear, life will surprise you and you'll learn a great deal."

His words of wisdom are somehow soothing; even when I'm in this state. For an instant, I recognize how vulnerable I am. Liam is already incredibly nice, but compared to Grayson, he seems like a storybook hero. I am not in a good place to be making decisions or judgments about anything or anyone. I really don't have any clarity. Maybe I never did.

"I would like to invite you out on a date," Liam suddenly says.

"A date?" I ask guardedly.

"Yes. I spoke to Dr. Howard earlier, and I told her about your granola-bar-and-protein-shake diet..."

"Don't forget the wine. I also drank wine," I inform him stubbornly.

"That doesn't help too much with your overall nutrition," he says lightly. "Leslie is concerned about your health and wants to run a full physical on you and some diagnostic tests on Thursday, before we proceed with the clinical study. At this rate, she might also have to treat you for frostbite."

"That doesn't sound much like a date to me."

"Oh, not that!" He laughs lightly. "I meant that maybe I could pick you up and take you to the appointment, and we could hang out afterwards."

"I would like to—but isn't that unethical?" I ask him.

"Yes," he says softly. "It would technically be unethical for me to date you until

240

after the study is complete, and some time has passed. Otherwise, it puts my career in jeopardy."

"Oh," I say in disappointment. "Well, we shouldn't risk it. I understand."

He seems to ponder over this briefly. "Or maybe... I could *not* be ethical," he suggests.

"Yes," I tell him quietly. "Please. Please—don't be ethical. I don't need ethical right now."

He takes my hand and puts reassuring pressure on my palm. "Then I'll see you on Thursday," he says decisively. "I'll plan something awesome for us to do, to take your mind off all of this."

"I doubt you can take my mind off this," I say skeptically.

"I'll consider that a challenge," he says with a chuckle. "But for now, let's get you inside and get you warm. For god's sake, woman. What will your father think of me? It's not a good first impression that I let his daughter get turned into a popsicle."

The mention of popsicles makes me smile in memory of Owen's stories. After sitting and chatting with Liam, I am definitely feeling better and stronger. When I let him guide me to my feet, I am not so terrified of the future. It helps to have one pleasant thing to look forward to.

Chapter Five

I toss and turn between the sheets.

I have been locked in my bedroom for days. I have no idea how I'm going to last until Thursday.

After the wedding I had the housekeeper help me move my suitcase from my old bedroom to one of the guest rooms on the other side of the house. It is closer to my dad's bedroom, and as far as possible from Carmen and Grayson's new room. Of course, it also has its own bathroom, and *not* one that opens into any other rooms. Choosing this strategic location has made me feel slightly more at ease. I even asked the housekeeper to study the outside of the house and make sure that the window wasn't easily accessible by climbing up any drainpipes. She probably thought I was crazy. I figured that I could keep to the safety of this room for the most part, but venture out into the rest of the house when Grayson was at work. But it just so happens that he was able to get many vacation days to celebrate his wedding.

Unfortunately, he didn't use them to go on vacation.

I'm not sure why they didn't go on a honeymoon—I think it's because Grayson wanted to keep an eye on me. Either way, I have been unable to leave the room. That in itself is not so terrible. I am used to being confined to a small space and not moving around much. However, I have been entirely unable to work. Every time I tried, I found myself sitting uselessly before my braille typewriter, with my hands resting lightly on the keys. Try as I might, I could not seem to make my fingers move to produce anything worthwhile. All I could think about was that *he* was right outside my door.

Sometimes my father tried to coax me out to join the family for dinner, but I tried to decline as politely as possible, making excuses about how I needed privacy for my writing. In the middle of the night, I was able to scavenge for a large case of bottled water, in addition to a six-pack of soda. I also secured a few jars of peanut butter, some raisins, bags of chips, and cheese. These items are my only sustenance, and they must last until Grayson leaves the house again, and I can finally get more food. I locked the bedroom door and used several pieces of furniture to barricade myself inside. Pushing the dresser was difficult, but once I temporarily removed the drawers, it became easier.

Now, I have no idea what day it is. Possibly Tuesday or Wednesday. I am also unsure whether it is night or day. Liam has called me a few times to make small talk, but he has been busy at work and hasn't had much time to spare. For the most part, I have been trying to sleep to pass the time. (It also requires the least expenditure of energy and helps my food last longer since I don't need to consume quite as much.) I have been rolling around in bed for hours, trying to think of my story and imagine the scenes I intend to write later on, so there is at least some meager attempt at working. Mostly, I just let my mind run away with me and dream, and do as it wishes to do. This could be therapeutic in clearing the blockage in my brain and allowing my imagination to flow freely again.

I am focused on the bright colors and stories of my dreamscape when a knock sounds on the door. I try to coax myself into being awake as I pull myself off the bed.

"Dad?" I ask in confusion. "I can't come out to eat today. Not until I finish this book."

"It's not your father," Grayson responds.

In an instant, I am extremely awake. My hands tightly grip and twist bunches of the comforter.

"Your dad told me to bring some of your favorite cupcakes for you," Grayson says gently. "Why don't you come downstairs and spend some time with us? We can catch up."

I can't believe his gall in acting like nothing is wrong. In acting like we could be a happy family and eat cupcakes together. "No, thank you," I say through the door. "I'm not hungry." My stomach immediately growls at this lie.

"You don't have to come downstairs if you don't feel like it," Grayson tells me. He pauses. "I could just hand you the cupcakes and leave."

"No, thank you," I say again. My mind begins to race, and I begin to grow worried. "Where is my sister?" I demand.

"She went out to a doctor's appointment for the pregnancy," Grayson tells me. "She's fine—it's just a routine checkup."

"Why didn't you go with her?" I ask him.

"I told her I had some things to take care of here."

My eyebrows furrow deeply. "Then go take care of them," I tell him.

"I am," he says.

I sit up straighter in alarm when the doorknob starts rattling as he tries to gain entry to my room. Swinging my legs out of bed, I walk over to the dresser that blocks my door from opening, and I abruptly sit down with my back against the furniture. I figure that even if he is able to somehow unlock my door, maybe I can use my body to push against the dresser and keep it from opening.

"Come on. Let me in, Helen," he demands. "I just want to talk."

"Go away," I tell him.

"Really, your dad's getting worried about you. I think it would ease his mind if you came out of your room and ate a few of these cupcakes."

It occurs to me that my dad probably took Carmen to her doctor's appointment. That means I'm alone in the house with Grayson. My cell phone is over on my night table, but I decide to bluff anyway.

"If you don't get the hell away from my door and stop bothering me right now, I will call the cops," I tell him quietly.

"Don't be like that," Grayson tells me. He sighs, and I hear him put his back to the door and slide to sit down just outside the bedroom. "I just want to talk about what happened between us. I mean, don't you wants answers? Aren't you curious?"

"No."

"I'm your brother-in-law now, Helen. You should be nicer to me. We should be friends."

"Fuck you," I hiss. Anger and fear are bubbling up inside me like a storm. I don't think I can take living in this house anymore. Not even for Liam—not even for the prospect of getting my vision back. This is not living. I have no freedom and I am completely unable to work. Liam said that staying was the stronger thing to do, but I don't feel like I can keep fighting against my fear on a daily basis. It wins. Each and every time, it wins.

"I know what I did to you was wrong," he says, "but I just couldn't help myself. That day, when you were sitting and crying on the stairs in the engineering department, it wasn't the first time I had ever seen you."

I sink my teeth into my bottom lip to try to keep from responding and betraying how upsetting this is.

"I'd been watching you for weeks," Grayson admits softly. "I thought you were really cute, and I wanted to ask you out... but I didn't know how to do that. I used to be really shy when it came to women. So, I followed you. I memorized your schedule, and I would watch you enter your classes, and wait until they were over, and watch you head back to your dorm."

I was being stalked. The realization that I had no idea that this was happening hits me like a ton of bricks. All this time, I thought it was just a random attack. If I could see—if I had been able to see, I might have noticed that I was being followed. I press the palms of my hands into my eyes, hating my body for being so flawed. I inwardly curse my disability.

"There was just something special about

you, Helen. There always was. I watched you moving through the crowds of people with this serene look on your face. You just seemed like someone holy to me. Someone greater than everyone else. I spent weeks following you, and studying you from afar, and trying to gather the courage to talk to you."

I take a shuddering breath. Listening to this story is filling me with horror. I don't want to hear his perspective. I don't want to revisit this event. I just want it to be finished and over.

"Your hair was the color of mahogany, but when you stepped into the sunlight, it burst into flames like the strands were made of copper. I couldn't stop staring at your tawny locks, and the way they curled around your perfect face. I was just so drawn to you, Helen. I've never felt that way about anyone. It was like you were calling out to me. Like touching you was part of my destiny."

"Please stop," I say in a hoarse voice. "Please stop talking about this. Please go away."

"Then a day came when something changed. I could see the change in your face. Your eyes, they used to shine like burnished amber. But on this day, they were just dead. They were empty, like sand or rust. You didn't go to class. You wandered aimlessly until you just collapsed and crumbled into tears. You were sad. I've never seen you so sad, Helen."

I can't listen to this. His retelling makes

everything fresh. I can feel the way I felt that day, even before he made my day worse. I shake my head, unable to believe that this is happening to me.

"That was the first day I could find the courage to talk to you," Grayson said. "I had to say something. I had to try to lift you up and be your hero."

I swallow a bit of saliva that has been gathering in my throat. "When I first heard you speak," I manage to croak out, "I thought you were nice. You could have asked me out. I would have probably agreed."

"I wanted to," he admits. "More than anything, I wanted to. I just... I don't know what was wrong with me."

This is so painful. He sounds like a wounded little boy. I don't know how it's possible, but I'm beginning to feel a pang of sympathy for him. His voice still sounds as kind as it did the first time I heard it—the first time it deceived me. I press my face into my hands, hating myself for pitying him.

Grayson sits silently outside my door for a few minutes before speaking again. "I couldn't control myself," Grayson says softly. "You were just so beautiful, sitting there on the stairs like a broken angel. I needed to touch you to see that you were real. And once I started touching you, I couldn't seem to stop. I felt like you might disappear right before my eyes. I needed to have you, while you were still here on this earth, in human form. I couldn't waste a second not being inside you. I needed to drown in your beauty; I needed to feel you around me. I needed to feel every inch of you, whether you would have me or not." His voice has been growing quieter until it is a barely audible whisper. He pauses to take a deep, mournful breath.

"I felt like I could fuck you into being real. I felt like I could fuck you into being mine."

I am so horrified that I do not know how to respond. I wrap my arms around myself and double over, trying to push his voice out of my mind.

"You were an angel," Grayson says again. "I was guiding you through the halls, and staring at you. And I just started getting more and more... excited. I thought that if I could just have you once, just one taste—that it would somehow be everything I ever needed."

I am struggling to breathe. I am struggling to think. My lips are parted in shock and disbelief. "I was never an angel," I say dumbly, because it is the only thing I can manage to say. "I was just a girl."

"You were so much more than a girl," Grayson says with complete certainty. "Maybe you didn't even know, but I could see it. And I just couldn't wait. I couldn't stand the thought of you rejecting me. I don't know what came over me, but even your hand on my arm... I couldn't bear it. I needed you. Right then and there. I needed to have you. You understand, don't you? I needed you, Helen. I needed you."

I find myself breathing very rapidly, as though I have just finished running a small marathon. I lift my fingers to plug my ears to drown out the sound. This can't be real. This can't be happening. His voice is so soft that my fingers actually do manage to muffle him completely, but once I am unable to hear anything, I begin to panic. I am already so oblivious to my surroundings. He could use a ladder to climb in the window, and I wouldn't even hear it. He could have found a secret entrance to my room and be standing in front of me right now, and I wouldn't even know. I rip my fingers out of my ears to keep from sending myself into a panic. Of course, he is still talking.

"... went to counseling with her. Your sister thinks there's something wrong with me. Sex addiction, or something of the sort. But I think she's wrong, Helen. It's just you. It's just the thought of you that makes me feel this way. Don't get me wrong, I grew to love Carmen over the years. But I only started seeing her because I saw a tiny bit of your spark in her." He sighs. "Don't you understand? Fucking her was the closest I could get to having you again."

"Oh my god," I moan in horror. "Please stop. Stop. Stop."

"You need to hear this," Grayson insists. "I was so disappointed when you stopped going to school. You even left your dorm. You headed back here, to your home. And I followed you. I watched you, and I was waiting for an opportunity to see you again. To touch you again. To taste you again. But somehow, you escaped me. You disappeared, and I needed to find you. That's why I first spoke to Carmen. To find out where you were. She had no idea, and I was heartbroken. But Carmen wasn't like you. She was friendly, flirtatious, and she expressed interest in me. At first, I was too upset over losing you to consider dating her, but as time went on, and my wounds healed... Carmen became my consolation prize."

"I wish I didn't have to hear any of this," I say miserably. "I need to go back in time and un-hear everything I just heard."

"I'm glad you're home, Helen," Grayson says quietly. "I do love your sister, but I was thinking that we could work out an arrangement of sorts. I want to see you sometimes. When Carmen is away from home, or busy at work—I want to be with you. I need this. We're family now, so you'll help me out, right? I want to see you on the side. I want you to be my mistress."

I finally snap. I finally start laughing hysterically. My laughter sounds zany and bizarre.

252

CLARITY

I allow my body to fall to the side until I am lying on the ground and clutching my stomach and laughing. I have completely cracked. I am laughing so hard that I almost don't notice my phone ringing.

"Is that your boyfriend, Helen?" Grayson asks angrily. "That fucking jerk who was here at the wedding? Don't answer it. Forget about him. I'll fucking kill him."

I slam my fist into the dresser which is blocking my door. This time I am filled with aggression and fury. "Maybe I'll kill you instead," I tell Grayson in a cheerful voice. "You've driven me insane. Doesn't that make me the dangerous one?" I am just talking out of my ass, but it feels good to turn the threatening around on him. I am sick of being the victim.

Placing my palm on the ground, I push myself off the ground and move across the room to answer my phone. "Hello?" I say in an upbeat tone.

"Winter?" Liam says. "Hey! So I had some questions I wanted to ask about our date tomorrow..."

I suddenly frown. "One sec." Holding the phone against my ear, I move over to my closet and open the doors. I move inside and shut the doors, and position my body between rows of hanging dresses to conceal my voice. "What's up?"

"Well, I have some really awesome ideas of things we could do after the appointment. Owen's been helping me with something he calls 'The Ultimate List of Best First Dates.' I know, that sounds ridiculous, but I was actually surprised to see that he had some really great ideas! They're not all even based on porn. I tried to incorporate them with my own, and..."

The frown on my face has been growing deeper and deeper the entire time that Liam has been speaking. "Look," I tell him in a snappish tone. "I'm going to have to cancel."

"What? Why?"

"Because Grayson is harassing me, and I can't deal with this," I say angrily. "Liam, I'm sorry. I can't stay here another day. I want to go home. I'm going to pack my suitcase and wait until he goes to sleep, and get the hell out of here. I need to leave. ASAP."

"Don't." Liam says the word softly, and then he sighs. "Okay. Just give me an hour. I'll come and rescue you from your tower, and the fearsome ogre. We'll do our date today instead of tomorrow. I have a strategy. I'm sure I can make you feel better. What do you say?"

"No," I say firmly. "I don't want to leave my room. Not unless it's to leave for good."

"Just trust me, Winter. You said you'd trust me," Liam says forcefully. "Please."

"You can't come here," I say with

concern. "He said he'd kill you. He has a gun, remember?"

"I'm not afraid of a coward like Grayson," Liam says urgently. "Come on. I am sure that if you go on this date with me, you'll feel better about everything. It will change your life. I promise. Please give me a chance?"

"And if it doesn't change my life," I tell him softly. "You'll take me home to New Hampshire?"

"It's a deal," he agrees. "Put on a sports bra and some comfortable clothes. As though we were going on a jog."

"A sports bra?" I say in surprise.

"Just trust me," he repeats solemnly. "No asking questions—just do as I say."

"Fine," I say grumpily, hanging up the phone. Even as intelligent as Liam is, I highly doubt that he can magically change my life with a single date and a sports bra. Still, some part of me really wants him to, and dearly hopes he can.

Chapter Six

Getting out of the house was a great idea. I am sitting in the passenger seat of Liam's car, and it is a lot nicer than Owen's old vehicle. The seats are ultra-cushiony, and the leathery smell is soothing. The car drives a lot smoother too, and I feel fewer of the bumps and potholes on the road. It is very relaxing.

The best part is that Grayson isn't in the car. And with each passing mile, he is farther and farther away. I do feel free and liberated—like a princess rescued from an ogre. Even if Liam's planned date fails to change my life, I still appreciate that he forced me to get out of the house. I feel like myself again.

"We're almost there," Liam tells me. "Now you might think this is weird at first, but just trust me and go with it."

"Should I be worried?" I ask him with a quizzical smile.

"Nope. You should be delirious with

excitement."

I snort at this. "You sure are confident."

"No one is *ever* disappointed with my surprises," Liam assures me.

"Maybe I'll be the first," I say, making a face. "I barely know you! This could be awful. You could be taking me to... a hypnotist. You could be trying to change my life by erasing all my bad memories. And when hypnotizing me fails, you could give me a lobotomy or something. What if you're actually a crazy mad-scientist type of doctor?"

Liam laughs as he parks the car. "With an imagination like that, I can see why you write such excellent books. Don't worry, I'm not going to erase your memory. Wait there for a sec." He turns off the engine of the car, and exits the vehicle.

A moment later, I hear the sound of him opening my car door. I smile at this, and unbuckle my seatbelt before stepping out. "Where are we?" I ask, trying to identify our location through listening to the street sounds.

"No asking questions," he says in a teasing voice. "It might ruin the surprise. Do you want to take my elbow?"

"Sure," I say cautiously, reaching out to circle my hand around his upper arm. He guides me slowly and carefully toward a building, and opens a door. Once we step through it, he places my hand on a railing.

"There's a narrow staircase here," he tells me, as he begins to climb the flight of stairs.

I climb behind him until we reach a landing. Once we are there, I feel that the material on the ground has changed. It's rubbery.

"Take off your shoes," Liam tells me, "and hand me your jacket."

Smiling to mask my confusion, I comply with his commands.I can hear him removing his shoes as well. He gives me his elbow again, and guides me through another set of doors. I am surprised to feel that the ground has grown quite soft beneath my feet, which are now only clad in a pair of socks. I am even more surprised when I feel Liam stopping and bowing deeply.

"Liam!" says an older man's voice with a hearty laugh. "Shame on you for getting me out of bed this early for an 'emergency session.' Where's the fire, son?"

"I'm sorry, Sensei," Liam says respectfully. "I would like you to meet Winter, the girl I told you about on the phone."

"Ah, a lovely fire indeed," says the older man. "I'm James. Nice to meet you, Winter."

"Hello," I say shyly.

"James has been my judo teacher since I was a kid," Liam explains to me. "He's the best. He's also partially blind."

"Judo?" I whisper in surprise. "You want me to learn how to fight?"

"Yes," Liam says, "but it's so much more than that. I considered taking you to therapy, but you've already studied psychology—they can't tell you anything you don't already know. I believe you need something stronger than counseling."

"Can a blind person really learn how to fight?" I ask in wonder.

James laughs. "Of course! You can ask my blind students who medaled at the Paralympics. The Judo competition is reserved specifically for the visually impaired."

I did not know this. I feel like a door has been opened, and a huge tidal wave of information has gushed through and smacked me in the face. I also do feel excited. Scared, but excited. I am already grateful to Liam for teaching me that there was a possible power that I *could have* that I had never considered exploring.

"I was hoping you could give her a personalized crash course in basic self-defense," Liam tells his instructor. "I think she's a fast learner and will pick it up quickly."

"Sure," James says, "but I think we need to start with the philosophy of the art. You see, Winter, many sighted folks consider us blind people easy targets. Muggings, violence, abuse— you name it. We can often seem disadvantaged and defenseless, and that encourages attacks against us. The solution? Well, we need both to stop *seeming* defenseless, and to stop *being* defenseless."

"How do we do that?" I ask him curiously.

"You need to learn how to carry yourself," James tells me, and I hear his voice moving closer. "Sighted people can use body language to convey a sense of confidence and strength. This automatically wards off many attackers. However, body language is learned through visually observing the postures of others. I will be teaching you how to be strong and aggressive in your stance."

I nod, for this makes a lot of sense. "I would like to learn."

"If you're going to study under me, the number one rule is that you should not be afraid of touch." The teacher's voice is calm and pleasant, and I am eager to absorb his every word. "If someone tries to grab you or hit you, then they are stepping onto *your* battlefield. Your body is your turf—and the moment someone steps onto *your* turf, you are no longer blind. If they touch you, you touch them back. You grab whatever you can. If you can *feel* your attacker, you can *see* your attacker."

"Okay," I say softly.

"Do you see this?" James reaches out to touch my shoulder. "Now you know exactly where I am. Now you have valuable information about me—all the information you need to take me down."

I nod in understanding.

CLARITY

"And now—observe this," James says removing his hand from my shoulder. He steps around me, slowly circling my body. "Now that I am no longer touching you, I have become invisible to you. I could be anywhere around you. You have some clues, but not all the clues you need. You don't want to run away. You don't want more space between us. You want to move *into* me so that you can *see* my body and neutralize it so that it is no longer a threat. It might seem counterintuitive at first, but you'll soon understand once we begin training."

My mind is blown. It makes so much sense. When Grayson attacked me, I ran away. I am always getting nervous and flinching away from contact with people. I never realized that doing so gave *them* the power.

"Remember this concept," James says again. "If they're not touching you, they're invisible. So take advantage of touch, and make it your friend—not your enemy."

I take a deep breath and nod thankfully. "I will," I say with determination. It also occurs to me that I have psychological issues with running away. Going to New Hampshire might have saved my skin for the time being, but it did not erase my problems completely. Instead, it exposed my home to infiltration from my attacker. If I had stayed, and pushed forward instead of caving in, I could have changed everything.

I want to change everything.

"It's good to keep your enemies close," Liam tells me, "so don't worry. We'll teach you what you need to do."

"And I have the perfect way to start!" James says happily. "Winter, how would you like to kick Liam's ass a lot?"

A laugh bubbles out of my throat. "Really? I think I'd love that."

"Darn," Liam says in dismay.

The teacher gets to work on showing me what to do if someone has placed a hand around my neck. He shows me where to place my thumb and how to twist my opponents arm until he is disabled. He shows me how to follow through until my opponent is on the ground. He has me try it gently a few times in slow-motion before turning to Liam.

"Alright, son," James says cheerfully. "I want you to grab Winter by the throat."

Liam hesitates. "Do you feel comfortable with that?" he asks me.

"Just shut up and do it already," I say with a smile. "I want to try this."

"Okay, here goes," he says, before reaching for my neck.

For a moment, I do feel a bit of fear. I do remember Grayson's hand on my neck. For only a fraction of a second, as his hand comes into contact with my skin, I am paralyzed in terror.

Then, as his hand clamps around my neck, I remember that he is now 'visible' to me. Comforted by the fact that this is a safe environment, and I have simple instructions, I grab his hand and twist it until Liam is on the ground, and my body is positioned over his, pinning him down.

Liam laughs. "Ouch! I knew you'd be a fast learner. That was almost perfect, and it was only your first try."

I blush in embarrassment when I realize how close my body is to his, and I begin to pull away.

"No," James says, placing a hand on my back. "Touch is your weapon, remember? You want to move your knees closer to his body. If you pull away, he'll get free and attack you again. Remember, you are not only blind, but you are a woman. Which means you will be much smaller than most of your opponents. Although you may not weigh much, if you position your body correctly, you can overpower someone who weighs twice as much as you do. Really *press* your body down on his and *lock* him down. Knees and arms closer! Closer!"

"Okay," I say nervously, pushing aside my modesty and focusing on the technique. "Like this?"

"Yes! Yes! That's it," James says. "Now, Liam, try to break free."

Liam struggles against me, and I hold my position fast. A few times, he nearly breaks my hold and I am worried that I'm doing it wrong. After a few seconds of struggling, he gives up.

"I'm down," Liam says in approval. "She's got me."

"Great," says James. "Now let's move on to the next technique."

The rest of the lesson passes by in a whirlwind of energy and struggling to achieve perfection. I feel so honored by the way that James and Liam treat me; like I am truly capable of doing this. It really does strengthen my confidence in myself, and makes me want to try to do more and more. My muscles quickly begin to ache, having not been used very much in years. However, I welcome the feeling and push onward, feeling exhilarated from the exercise and motion.

I feel like Liam has dumped me into a swift-moving river and demanded that I swim. I love it. I love the challenge, and I love being immersed in fast-paced new information. It's intimidating, and it could certainly drown me, but I won't be tugged under by the current. I'm going to swim.

Chapter Seven

"You were really good," Liam says as he drives me home. "Are you sure you've never done any martial arts before?"

"No," I say with a laugh, "I haven't. Unless you count years of wrestling with my sister—almost every day, for every tiny thing. Even when I first came home, we got physical a few times."

"That must be it. The source of your great talent," Liam says solemnly.

"Don't be ridiculous," I tell him, but I *am* really happy about my performance.

Snapping his fingers, Liam makes an excited exclamation. "Oh! I have an idea. Let's delay your surgery so you can be blind enough to compete in the Paralympics. What do you say? You just have to train really hard, then we can head to Rio de Janeiro for 2016. I was just going to watch it from TV, but being there would be so much better. And James can add your picture to his impressive wall of successful students."

"Are you joking?" I ask him incredulously.

"Nope."

"Liam!" I burst into laughter.

"What?" he asks in a wounded tone. "What's so funny?"

"I just had my first lesson today. Cool your balls, buddy."

"My balls are... at the perfectly appropriate temperature," he assures me. "I'm just thinking of the possibilities!"

I growl at him softly. "Are you my pimp now, or am I a dancing circus animal?"

"Can't it be both?" he asks whimsically.

"I know you're just trying to make me feel better," I tell him, "and it's working. Just remember that I'm learning to fight to stay alive and protect my sister, not for the glamor of showing off my smooth moves on TV."

"Can't you do both?" he asks glumly.

I can't help smiling at his attitude. Liam is possibly one of the most positive people I've ever met. His enthusiasm is apparent in everything he does—it is obvious that he's very passionate about both judo, and his job. Being around him makes me feel like anything is possible. "Even though you're insane," I tell him, "and you push me around way too much—I still think you're sweet."

"I solemnly vow that whenever I manipulate you, I will always have your best interests at heart," Liam says with complete seriousness.

"Wow," I say in mock admiration. "That was really romantic. I need to save those words." I pull out my phone and press my thumb down on the solitary circular button, and request that it make a recording. Then I repeat his words into the machine: "I solemnly vow that whenever I manipulate you, I will always have your best interests at heart."

He laughs at this. "Why are you recording that? Are you going to use it in one of your books?"

"Maybe," I say teasingly, "but also, if this dating thing works out? You can use it in your wedding vows."

"No way," Liam says. "My wedding vows would be so much more interesting than that."

"Like what?" I ask with a challenge in my voice.

"Hmm," he says thoughtfully. "Like... 'I vow to love you so much that I will always let you choose what we watch together on TV. If I don't like what you're watching, I'm just going to go watch my own thing in a different room anyway.'"

"Really, really romantic," I say in amusement.

"Also," he adds, picking up momentum, "this one's really good: 'I vow always to leave the last potato chip for you. But it's the only one you're getting, because I call dibs on the rest of the bag.'"

He finally manages to get a real laugh out of me. I have to catch myself to try and stop from laughing too loudly. I have been holding this in for some time and trying to appear cool and sardonic, but now he's definitely won. I can't help relaxing a little. "I envy the lucky lady who gets to tie the knot with you," I tell him with a grin.

"I can be a regular Casanova," he assures me. "I picked up a lot from watching Owen over the years. For example, the date we just had? The truth is that I just chose this because it involved a *lot* of physical contact. I'm pretty sure we got to third base there. I got to cop a lot of feels."

I twist my face up in what I imagine must be a skeptical look.

"Winter, what are you giving me that look for?"

"I highly doubt that *this* was on Owen's list of ultimate first dates."

"Maybe it was," Liam says.

"No," I tell him. "It was special and meaningful, and you chose it specifically for me. I won't let you cheapen it with jokes. It was amazing."

Liam's voice lowers a little. "Did you

really like it?"

"Yes," I respond sincerely. "It was a lot of fun. It was also just what I needed. You didn't just help me. You helped me help myself, which is far more valuable. I can't thank you enough."

"You're very welcome," he responds, "but you're not a master yet. We'll have to keep training, and keep going back, dozens of times."

The idea of more training gives me a thrill. I am somehow bursting with energy—even though I have spent much more energy today than I would on an average day, I seem to have more because of this. It's ironic and puzzling, but I love the sensation.

"When can we do this again?" I ask him shyly.

"Soon," he responds instantly. "Let's make a promise that we'll train with James at least three times a week, for a minimum of two hours. Even if things don't work out with us—we'll just quit going there on dates and go as friends. It's important to do this. It will change your life."

"You already have changed my life," I tell him softly. I think about where I was earlier today, sitting with my back to a dresser and feeling terrified of a door opening. I think about where I have been for several days, confined to my room and unable to get out of bed. Unable to do any work. Unable to think of anything other than my overwhelming fear. I know that I probably don't know enough about judo yet to actually stand a chance in a fight, but I feel like I have broken through some barrier today. I am not afraid anymore. Tears spring to my eyes, but they are tears of happiness. "Liam," I say, and my voice is all choked up. However, having learned that touch can be my friend, I decide not to speak and simply reach out and place my hand on his leg. I place a gentle pressure on his thigh to try and convey my gratitude.

He removes one of his hands from the steering wheel, and places it over my own. He interlaces his fingers with mine, in a gesture which clearly conveys him accepting my sentiments.

The touch is so powerful that there really is no need for speech.

A few more minutes and miles pass, and our fingers remain woven together. It is so comforting and natural, and I wish that the moment would last forever. I feel like my skin just melts together with his, and disappears into his body. It is like his hand belongs attached to mine—like it always had been there before, but was separated for this lifetime, and only just reunited.

He feels like the missing part of me that I never even realized I was missing. I never thought I could feel so secure and complete. I don't know how I'm going to rip myself away from him. All I can seem to think about is how I *need* to be even closer to him than this. I want to be around him all the time—I want to spend as much time with him as possible. He makes me feel like life could be a good thing. He makes me laugh, even when I'm trying to be standoffish and snobby. He easily breaks down all my walls with his gentle persistence. He believes I can do anything, and makes me into a better version of myself. He helps me to see the things I cannot see. He makes me feel fulfilled.

"We're almost at your place," he says quietly.

There is a silence, and we both seem to feel the ache of the impending loss. However, as he continues to drive onward, my thoughts begin to focus less on how incredible Liam is, and more on the horrible hellhole that is looming in the distance. I have been enjoying myself so much that I had almost entirely forgotten about Grayson. I had forgotten how soon I would be thrust back into the same dwelling with him. I had forgotten that date had to end. I had forgotten how quickly we were approaching my house.

"We're here," Liam says, as he removes his hand from mine and begins to turn the steering wheel.

His words are like a slap in my face. I am seized with a great panic and I reach out to grab his wrist to halt the turning. "No. No, please." I take a few quick breaths. "Liam, I'm not ready to go back in there. Can we just drive around for a little? Just a little more?"

"Sure," he says, without hesitation. He pulls back onto the road and begins driving again.

"I'm sorry," I tell him. "I just couldn't—I need a minute to prepare."

"It's okay," Liam says. He hesitates before speaking. "I'm really not supposed to do this—it could present problems for my job. But if you really want, you could stay at my place. It's very small, but I could take the couch..."

"No, no," I say softly. "I appreciate the offer, but I don't want to impose. You've already done so much for me. I just need a few minutes to gather my strength."

"Would you like a distraction?" Liam asks.

"What do you mean?" I ask him. I am surprised when he pulls the car over sharply into the shoulder.

He parks the car and unlocks his seatbelt before leaning across the center console to place his face near mine. He slides his hand along my neck, just under my ear. His thumb rests lightly on my earlobe. "May I?" he breathes.

I cannot find the words, so I force myself to nod.

Liam presses his lips against mine with a soft and tender pressure. At first, the kiss is barely a whisper of a touch, as though I am fragile and made of glass that might shatter. Once my surprise eases away, and I am able to respond, he notices this and begins to deepen the kiss. His hand slips around the back of my head, and his lips become more intense and demanding.

I find myself swept away in the sensation. His touch is so strong and forceful, yet filled with sweetness and compassion. He seems to have discovered that I am not fragile glass, but a real woman made of flesh and blood—and he treats me accordingly. I kiss back ardently, eager to lose myself in the loveliness of the connection.

I can taste a little bit of masculine sweat lingering on his skin from our earlier workout. It is salty and pleasant, and with a bit of a spicy flavor. I can also smell the muskiness of cologne on his jacket. I am just beginning to relax and pour all of my pent-up emotion into the kiss when he pulls away.

He clears his throat, and speaks in a husky voice. "I had better take you home."

"Yes," I say quietly, in disappointment. I lower my chin and try to catch my breath as my heartbeat races—for the first time in forever, I have butterflies in my stomach from an emotion other than fear. "When can we do that again?" I ask him, trying to conceal my desperation. I want to see him again so badly.

"Soon," he says with an upbeat tone. "Maybe next time we can go on a true Owen-style date."

"I can't wait," I tell him with a smile.

Chapter Eight

"You're underweight," Dr. Howard accuses me. "Before you get your eye surgery, I'm going to recommend you gain at least ten pounds."

"Ten pounds!" I repeat in dismay as I step off the scale. "But I feel fine. Maybe this is just a good weight for me."

"As you currently are, you may experience slower wound healing," Dr. Howard says. "It's safer if you gain a little weight."

"Well, I've begun working out a little," I tell her as I return to my seat. "I've begun going to judo classes. So I might gain some muscle."

"That's great, honey. But you need to *eat*. A lot."

I think about the situation at home where I need to stockpile non-perishables in my room to avoid running into Grayson. If I felt my comfortable going into the rest of the house, I could happily eat a dozen cupcakes every day and fatten myself up.

"Dr. Larson told me that you haven't eaten real food in years," Dr. Howard says, tapping her pen on her folder. "So I'd like to get some blood work done and determine if you have any deficiencies."

"Okay, Leslie."

I hear the flipping of paper as she closes my file. "So you've begun dating Liam?" she asks me curiously.

I suddenly feel embarrassed. I remember that Carmen had mentioned that Liam and Leslie seemed close at the wedding. Am I stepping on her toes? "Uh, yes," I tell her nervously. "Do you think it's a bad idea?"

"Not at all!" Leslie says with enthusiasm. "Remember, I'm the one who gave him your books in the first place and recommended he take you on as a patient. He's always been a really sensitive guy—really interested in improving every aspect of his patients' lives, not just their eyes. I thought you two would get along."

"And *you* don't have any... interest in him?" I ask her awkwardly.

"Good grief, Helen!" Leslie says with a laugh. "Just because my husband is dead doesn't mean I'm going to go rob the cradle. I'm nearly twice that boy's age."

"I was just curious," I tell her. "I feel like

Liam's too good to be true, and there must be something wrong here. Is there? Is really... a good guy?"

"He's the best guy," Dr. Howard says without hesitation. Then she pauses. "But you should still be careful, Helen. Don't rush into things too quickly."

"I'm not," I assure her. "That's why I'm asking your opinion."

"You might be a little eager to fall for him, considering you've been isolated for so long. Especially with your past, Liam must seem like the best thing since sliced bread. Just try to be cautious and logical." Leslie sighs. "I suppose that since your mom is gone, I feel the need to give you motherly advice. Even the best of men have huge flaws. They need to be... worked on."

"What does that mean?" I ask her.

"Oh, I don't know," she says. "Just ignore me; I like to ramble!"

"No, Leslie. Please tell me."

The doctor begins tapping her pen on her desk. "It's just that you young girls seem to think that relationships are all rainbows and butterflies all the time. Back in my day, when we had a problem with our men, we just made it work. No matter what. Even your mother—she was upset for years about the way your dad didn't take care of himself. Richard was a very heavy smoker. But Meredith didn't leave him and go off in search of greener grass. She just made him stop." Leslie stands up and moves to the other end of the small room. "Your mom refused to have kids with Richard unless he promised to seriously begin fixing his health so he'd be around to see you girls grow up—to be there for your graduation and weddings. It's a good thing she made him promise that—none of us had any idea that *she* would be the one who wasn't around."

"Yeah," I say softly. "Why are you telling me this?"

"I'm just thinking about Carmen, the poor girl," says Leslie with a sigh. "She's been coming in for checkups since she got pregnant, and really flying off the handle. Do you want to know what she said a few months ago? 'Please tell me there's something wrong with the baby so I can get an abortion and don't have to marry that bastard.' I couldn't believe my ears. Why would she say something like that? Grayson seems like a perfectly nice guy. Even Richard loves him. They seemed really happy at their wedding."

I groan and lower my face into my hands. "She said that?"

"Yes. Right when she found out she was pregnant. I think it was shock or something. I better not ever hear you speaking about Liam that way, young lady. If something goes wrong—and it will—just stick it out and fix it, okay? He's a gem. Don't toss him into the trash heap if you find one tiny flaw in the jewel."

I press my fingers into my aching temples. This is about as much motherly advice as I can handle. It does make me wonder what our actual mother would have said about the situation with Grayson. She was pretty close to Dr. Howard, and she might have had a similar opinion. Somehow, I feel that we never would have gotten into this situation at all if we hadn't lost Mom. We all just seemed to fall apart without her. "Thanks for the checkup, Leslie," I tell her, "and thanks for the chat. I'd better get going now."

Dr. Howard snaps her fingers. "I nearly forgot. You should get a pap smear."

"No way!" I shout. "I don't need one."

"Helen. Your mother had pre-cancerous cells on her cervix. You're getting a pap smear."

"Yes, but it's not what killed her. She just got a hysterectomy and she was fine."

"Thanks to *my* early detection," Dr. Howard argues. "Look, it's just a basic screening test. I know it's uncomfortable, but you haven't had one in years. We need to do a complete physical."

"Can we do it later?" I grumble. "Liam is going to be poking giant needles into my eyes, along with a huge tube for a camera, and possibly other things. I'm going to have enough strange objects being shoved into my body soon enough— can we just skip the pap?"

"No," Leslie says, growing impatient. "This is important. Helen, you're dating a doctor. How about I call Liam and tell him you're refusing to have a pap done?"

"No, no, no!" I say, lifting both of my hands anxiously. "Don't tell him about that. This is super personal and intimate..."

"Poking needles into your eyes is as intimate as it gets," Dr. Howard says teasingly. "It's a level of trust that most couples will never need to reach; an activity most will never share!"

"Leslie!"

"Fine, I won't call Liam since you don't seem to enjoy the idea of having your cervix discussed with him. I'll call your father."

I drop both of my hands to my sides in defeat. "Fine," I say weakly. "Do the damn test."

Chapter Nine

A few days later...

"I have something planned that will blow your mind," Liam says while giving me a hug in greeting.

I no longer doubt his ability to blow my mind. I gingerly return his hug and rest my cheek on the lapel of his coat for a second. "Thank you for trying to make every day so special for me," I tell him softly.

"Hey, it's my pleasure! I love surprising you," he says in an upbeat tone. He takes my arm to guide me to his car, and opens the door for me. "And here's the first surprise of the day! I promised you a true Owen-style date, but I bet you didn't expect it to actually include *Owen*."

"Yo," says the cheerful doctor from the

backseat of the vehicle. "What's up, Winter?"

"Hi Owen," I say pleasantly as I climb into the passenger seat. When Liam closes the door and begins walking around the vehicle, I turn back to Owen with a smile. "What are you doing here? Should I be worried?"

"Naw," Owen says with a drawl. "Liam was afraid that he had used up all his best topics of conversation. He has maybe three subjects tops that he can speak about without boring everyone to sleep and sounding like an idiot. So he got me to come along to be his wingman—it's my job to act really dumb so he will seem way smarter in comparison."

"That's not the reason at all," Liam protests as he climbs into the driver's seat. "I just wanted to demonstrate my smooth social skills to impress Winter. Have you introduced her to Caroline yet?"

I have noticed the additional person sitting in the backseat, even though her breathing is very quiet and she hasn't spoken. I am curious, but I didn't want to ask.

"This is my lady-love," Owen says proudly. "The gorgeous, enchanting, and very flexible Caroline."

"For god's sake, Owen," Caroline mutters angrily. "Why do you have to introduce me like that? What if I introduced you to people as 'the dorky man-child who only thinks with his penis and barely survived med school'? How would you like that?"

"It would be accurate," Owen says in confusion. "But I'd appreciate if you added something about my stamina in there. Maybe a little compliment on my girth? You have to highlight my positive attributes."

Caroline releases a stream of furiously-spoken words in a foreign language.

"Is that German?" I ask nervously.

"She just insulted my manhood," Owen explains, "and called me a bunch of names I'd rather not translate. I bet she just wants me to kiss her to keep her filthy mouth shut."

"You pig," Caroline says, but in the next moment she unbuckles her seat belt and moves over to sit on Owen's lap. Soon, the two are lip-locked and there are sounds of a passionate make-out session coming from the back seat.

"Um. Did I miss something?" I ask Liam, screwing up my face in confusion.

"Don't look at me," he says as he starts the car, "I don't understand those two in the least. Owen! Do whatever you want back there, just don't get my seats dirty!"

"Aye, aye, Cap'n!" Owen responds.

"It's nice to meet you, Winter," Caroline says elegantly, as though she had not just been shoving her tongue down Owen's throat.

"Uh, it's great to meet you, Caroline," I

say, trying to hide my shock at their behavior.

"You'll get used to it," Liam assures me as he drives away from my house. "And if you don't, at least I'll seem like a much more civilized and cultured human being than those two animals in the backseat."

"I resent that!" Owen says between bouts of loud, amorous lip-smacking.

I listen to them for a few minutes before a grin breaks out on my face. I shake my head in amusement.

Liam reaches over and pats my leg. "If it really bothers you, we can make Owen drive on the way home and we can torture them with our own gross tonsil-tango."

"That sounds lovely," I tell him. My shoulders shake in a small giggle. "Disgusting, but lovely."

Liam drives for a few minutes before he starts to slow down. "This is interesting, Winter. The GPS just made me turn down a street I don't know. I don't come to your neighborhood often—I didn't know you had all these adorable little art shops!"

"Yes," I say with a smile. "Many of the locals are obsessed with decorating their homes with the perfect paintings and potteries and..."

"Antiques!" Liam exclaims, slamming on the brakes.

My body is propelled forward slightly

before being rammed back into his cushiony leather seats. I hear Caroline giggle as her body is thrust against Owen's. "Antiques?" I repeat in confusion. "Is this where we're going?"

"No," Liam says cryptically. "Just a quick pit stop. Wait here!"

The car swerves sharply as he pulls into the parking lot and swiftly exits the vehicle. He even leaves the car running.

"Okay," I say slowly. "What's happening here? What did I miss?"

"Liam likes old things," Owen explains when he can manage to pull his mouth away from Caroline for a moment.

"Old things?" I ask again.

"He collects antiques," Caroline explains. "You should see his apartment. Very small, but very stylish. Everything artsy, everything vintage."

"To be honest, I thought he was gay for a little while," Owen admits. "It seems unnatural for any straight man to like funky furniture as much as he does."

I smile at this. I like the fact that Liam has an artistic side. Still, I am a bit confused. "You thought he was gay?" I ask Owen. "Hasn't he dated many women?"

"Very rarely. Too rarely. It takes a lot for him to find a woman interesting. He's too picky," Owen explains.

"It's the story," Caroline says softly. "The

man likes old furniture because it has a history. He can touch the wood, and it tells him a beautiful tale of love and loss. He likes his women the same way; vastly complex with endless layers and depth. He wants to look into her eyes and see a touch of tragedy and the promise of victory."

"Wow, Caroline," Owen says in amazement. "That's astute. Hey, I have refined tastes too. I like my women to be... female."

Caroline curses again in German before slapping Owen in the face.

"I'm kidding!" Owen whines. "Relax, baby. You know I love how fierce and fiery you are. Come here. Bring it home for Papa."

"Whoa," I say in discomfort, feeling like I am intruding on a very private moment. The sound of incessant lip-smacking is less tolerable now that Liam has stepped out of the car. "Does anyone know where we're going?"

"He said that he needs to fatten you up before your eye surgery," Owen says, groaning as Caroline makes noises that indicate she might be nibbling his neck. "So we're going to some fancy-schmancy food thing."

"Food thing?" I ask, pressuring the pair for details.

"It's a wine and cheese party," Caroline explains. "I could not refuse free booze—it will help me forget that I've wasted five years of my life dating a boy who will never grow into a man."

"Hey!" Owen says in a wounded tone. "It will also help me forget that I'm dating a B-cup who won't get implants or let me try her back door."

"Too much information," I tell the couple, "too much information!"

"I think he mentioned a competition too," Caroline says. "Something about a blind tasting?"

"A blind wine tasting competition?" I say very loudly. "Are you kidding me? Really!" Just as I say this, struggling very hard not to squeal in excitement, Liam opens his car door.

"Darn," he says in disappointment. "You two ruined my surprise."

"Liam!" I exclaim, grabbing his sleeve. "Really? A wine tasting competition?!"

"Yes," he says with a laugh. "When I first met you, you were hugging a bottle of Cabernet Sauvignon from the Napa Valley pretty tightly. Remember how I asked for a sip? That was some good stuff. I was impressed. I thought we could test your mettle and see whether you have a good palate for identifying wines from all over the world."

"Of *course* I do!" I tell him with excitement. "My mom and dad used to take me to wine tasting parties all the time when I was a teenager. They used to show off my skill. It was totally illegal for me to be drinking, so I just swirled it around on my tongue and spit it out—I felt so grown up and sophisticated. I can tell you what anything is. *Anything!"*

"I was hoping you'd get excited about this," he says with pleasure. "I just didn't think you'd get *this* excited! If you're half as good as you say you are, I'm going to have to bet money on you."

"I wish Owen would do something nice like that for me," Caroline says with disappointment and envy.

Owen ignores her, leaning forward. I can tell because his voice gets closer, and his breath tickles my ear. "Hey, Liam," he says curiously. "What's in the bag, bro?"

"Dammit. Why do you keep ruining my surprises?" Liam snaps at his friend.

"Oh no," Owen groans. "Don't tell me you brought more fruity antiques."

"Fruity?" Liam says in dismay. "Is that what he's been saying about me? None of my antiques are fruity in any way!"

"What's in the bag?" Caroline echoes. "Show it to us, Liam."

"Alright," Liam mutters. "You bunch of spoilsports. It's a gift for Winter." He reaches into the cloth bag and begins unwrapping an item that has been tightly wound in wrapping paper. He then places the item in my hands.

I am surprised by the heft of the object. There seems to be an ornate and slender handle which leads up to an oval frame. I run my hands over the center of the object and discover a smooth surface. "Is it a... mirror?" I ask him.

"Yes," he tells me, reaching over to brush a few wisps of hair behind my ear. He leans over and places a kiss on my shoulder. "And soon, you'll be able to see your reflection in it. Then, you can finally discover every aspect of how amazing you are."

I stare down at the object in my hands, and squint as though I might already be able to see a tiny beam or flicker of light reflecting off its surface. Of course, there is nothing. Is it possible that I might actually be able to see into this mirror soon? "Stop getting my hopes up," I tell Liam softly. "Thank you for the gift, but you're being *way* too optimistic."

"Give the boy a break," Caroline says gently. "He's completely smitten with you, Winter. It's adorable."

"What if the operation doesn't work?" I ask them as I lift up the mirror and stare into it with determination, as though I must be able to see if I try hard enough. "What if I can never see *anything* reflected in this mirror?"

"I'll make sure you do," Liam says. "Besides, I won't be working alone. Owen will help me! I know he seems like a dolt, but he's actually really brilliant. There's no one I'd rather have beside me at the operating table."

"Gee," Owen says. He turns to Caroline and speaks in a hushed whisper. "I better not mess up and poke the needle in the wrong place. That would be awkward."

"I heard that," I tell him, "and it's not funny."

A feminine hand rests gently on my shoulder. "Don't worry, Winter," Caroline says in a grave voice. "Owen never has any trouble poking things into the right place."

I clear my throat. "I'm not sure if that's supposed to be reassuring... but thanks."

Liam laughs. "Alright, you crazy people. Let's get back on the road. There's a party waiting for us."

As Liam begins to drive away from the antique shop, I continue staring at the ornate mirror in my hand. I can feel the heavy metal object, and I can trace its intricate details, but I can't even see a speck of light illuminating a single corner. It might as well not exist. What if nothing actually exists, and nothing can actually be seen, and it's all some elaborate lie everyone has fabricated to torture me? It's a silly thought, but I often wonder if this darkness is all there really is. Having lived so long with this reality, it's terrifying to think of how great the change would be. How could I accept and adjust to anything else?

I continue to search the obscured mirror

for answers as we drive along. What if when I can finally see a girl staring back at me, I don't like what I see? What if she's just another stranger I wish I could escape?

Chapter Ten

I gently circle my wrist as it cradles the wine glass, swirling the liquid around to release its aroma. I inhale deeply, allowing the piquant scent to fill my sinuses.

"There's no way she can guess this one," someone in the room whispers.

"Why not?" says Caroline. "She's guessed everything so far."

"But this wine isn't quite so mainstream. I bet she doesn't even get the continent right."

The corner of my lips curl in pleasure at everyone's whispers. Needless to say, I have been able to impress Liam's peers with my vast knowledge of the grape. I have easily beaten out every competitor, which isn't saying much; forced to drink blindfolded from dark glasses, some of the people at the party have been unable to tell red from white. They have made some ridiculous guesses that have caused me to erupt in laughter.

Now, as the sole victor, everyone is continuing to test me to see how far they can strain my knowledge before I break. Liam has been standing off to the side and boasting about me, and I must say that it feels good to be the best at something. Due to my genuine love for wine, it is also quite effortless. It is one of my few hobbies and interests that I kept up with even when I was isolated from society. I still took the time to order a good wine now and then. I would frequently browse the award winning wines for various competitions, and have a few of the more affordable selections sent over to my address. I don't think I could live without the soothing flavors to transport me away on a bad day.

"Well, Winter?" someone prods me. "Are you going to taste it?"

"I bet she has no idea what's in the glass," another person says in a snooty tone.

"You'll bet?" Liam says, and I can hear the sound of him pulling out his wallet. "How much, my friend? A thousand bucks says she gets it spot on."

"Really, Liam? You're nuts. I don't have a thousand dollars on me—but sure. If she gets it, I'll write you a check. If not, you can write me a check."

"Deal," Liam says, shaking his colleague's hand. From what I understand, many of the people at the party are his old college buddies.

"Look at you, Liam," says a woman's voice. "Tossing around your wad. I remember when you were in school, you could barely afford a sandwich."

"That's because I was saving up for my down payment, Alyssa," he tells her.

"Enough suspense!" declares the party host. "Winter, what's your verdict?"

I take another deep whiff of the aroma. "It's red. Vintage. Australia. I'm going to say... South Australia."

"She hasn't even tasted it yet!" someone exclaims in horror.

"Oh, that's right," I say as though I have forgotten. "The taste! That will help me narrow it down." I press my lips against the rim of the glass and tilt it to allow the liquid to seep into my mouth. I swish it around my tongue carefully, allowing the flavor to dance around my taste buds. "Oh, this is very distinctive. You guys are trying to trip me up by using a very small winery, aren't you? It's not going to work. This is from Clare Valley. Specifically, Wakefield Estate." I take another large sip, but this time, just for enjoyment. "2008, Shiraz."

"Fuck," curses the guy who lost his money to Liam.

"Yep. Hand it over, John," Liam says smugly, clapping his hand on his friend's back.

I can hear the other man pull out his checkbook and begin writing, while muttering insults.

"It's not fair to bring a blind girl to a blind tasting, Liam," says a jealous female spectator in the room.

"Why is it not fair?" he asks innocently. "Do you mean to say that it's not fair she is *only* limited to blind tastings? That it's unfair she has never been able to experience the color of various wines? Or to see their stylish bottles and labels?"

"I—I didn't..."

"Sarah, she has no idea what the colors *red* or *white* even mean. Is that fair to her? Do you think her life is easy? Stop discriminating against the disabled!" Liam is obviously slightly drunk and messing with this woman, and I find it hilarious.

"You're right," says the woman meekly. "I'm sorry."

"Hey, wait!" says another person in the room. "It actually might be unfair. Really unfair. I think I recognize this chick." He comes close to me, and looks into my face. "Aren't you Helen Winters? Yeah! Her family owns a whole fucking winery!"

"Is that true?" Owen asks.

"Not exactly," I say in puzzlement. "We sold it years ago. We owned a small private vineyard in Northern Michigan. We made a special

295

ice wine that we called The Winter Grape. My sister and I would spend summers there and help with the cultivation. We never really sold the product commercially, though, so I'm surprised you'd know about us."

"I knew it! Didn't your dad purchase a vineyard out in Long Island last year?" a man insists.

"I don't know," I say in confusion. "Maybe."

"Excuse us for a minute," Liam tells everyone as he places his hand on my back. "Winter and I are going to step out onto the balcony."

"Wait!" says another partygoer, shoving a glass into my hands. "Can you tell what this is, Winter?"

I bring it to my nose and sniff it, and immediately make a face of disgust. "Ugh," I say in displeasure. "You can't expect me to taste this stuff? Is it even wine? It smells like rancid nuts."

Everyone in the room begins to laugh.

"It looks like we've final stumped her," someone says triumphantly.

"Yes, but this doesn't count," another person says. "That wine is sort of a trick question."

"Give me a second," I tell them, wrinkling my nose. I gather my courage and toss the wine down my throat. I scrunch up my eyes and try to avoid gagging on the bitter taste. "That tastes like cat urine," I declare, causing more laughter from the room. When the laughter calms down, I sip the wine again. "But it's actually a 2001 Riesling from Southern Ontario. That horrible taste and smell comes from the fact that the region was invaded by Asian ladybugs around that time. It's a rare wine flaw called ladybug taint. I believe they trashed most of this stuff so it wouldn't be sold."

"Damn," says the party's host, and there is a tone of respect in his voice. "She wins. I give up. I can't stump her."

"Of course, you can't," Liam says as he guides me away from the crowd. "She's too damn good."

I let him lead me out onto the balcony, and I am immediately refreshed by the cool night air. The party is being hosted in a penthouse apartment, and the wind is rather strong; it tosses my hair around my shoulders a little.

"Here," Liam says, pushing a plate toward me that has been sitting out on the patio. "You're supposed to be eating too. You'll never get fat enough for the surgery at this rate."

I feel around on the plate and discover toothpicks shoved into little cubes of cheeses. I pop one in my mouth to try to overpower the taste of the ladybug-tainted wine. "Mmmm. That's nice," I say, taking another piece of cheese.

"You were amazing in there," Liam tells me. He laughs lightly. "I made a few thousand bucks off betting on you."

"I noticed that," I say with a smile. My words feel a bit slow and slurred. "You shamelessly capitalized on my skill—you exploited me for personal gain!"

"I hope you don't mind," he says gently. "I don't mean to keep treating you like a circus animal."

"Or like you're my pimp," I add as I pop a few more pieces of cheese into my mouth.

"It's an interesting dynamic," he agrees. "I don't know why things seem to go that way. It might be due to the fact that you're just so good at everything."

"Flattery will get you everywhere," I tell him playfully, poking him in the ribs. I suddenly cast my eyes downward. "Liam, this was a lot of fun."

"It was," he agrees. "Plus, I got to learn fun facts about your past. I knew you loved wine, but I had no idea your family used to own a vineyard!"

"You seem to have this weird intuition when it comes to me," I tell him suspiciously. "I don't know how you do it, but it's like you can see into my head. Every activity you choose for us is amazing."

"I think I'm just getting lucky," he admits as he puts aside the empty tray of cheese. "It seems like I'm putting all this effort into choosing events specifically for you—but we might just genuinely like the same things."

"And maybe I'm just easy to please?" I say in a seductive tone, moving closer to him.

"Maybe," he says, reaching out to slide his hands around my hips, "but I think I still have a lot to find out about that." Lowering his lips to mine, he kisses me deeply. His hands slide around my back as he angles his face for better access to my mouth.

His touch makes me feel dizzy. Combined with too many wine tastings, I almost feel like I might fall over. He senses my unsteadiness and pushes me back against the balcony railing. I gasp a little, afraid of the considerable plunge to dozens of stories below. I cannot see the drop, so I imagine the street to be an enormous distance away—maybe hundreds of miles below. His kiss makes me feel like I am falling even though I am standing still. We must be up in the stratosphere, for I am having difficulty breathing. The air is thin up here. All I can taste is Liam—I seem to be breathing in his skin. The scent of his cologne and the sweetness of his lips make me more light-headed than any wine or drug possibly could. I still feel like I am falling, directly through the atmosphere now. There is a heat blossoming inside me. My heart is pounding fiercely, and I really feel like I might somehow be in outer space. I can no longer feel the familiar tug of gravity weighing me down. I cling to Liam, somewhat terrified of the vast expanse of space below; but I trust that he won't let me hit the ground. His arms are wrapped tightly around my waist, and they grip me with certainty and protectiveness. I continue to kiss him, allowing my body to melt against his rock-hard frame, holding him desperately for stability. I fear that if I let go, I'll go hurtling out into some infinite abyss.

"Hey!" says someone stepping out on the balcony. "Liam, isn't she your patient? What are you doing, bro?"

"Well..." he says nervously, hesitating. His voice sounds faraway and confused. I know that whatever distant place to which my mind had been flung, he was there with me.

"It's my fault," I say, trying to gather my composure and pull myself away from Liam. "I've had way too much to drink, and I forced myself on him. Just consider him my helpless victim."

The intruder laughs. "You're wild, Winter. Come on back inside. We just opened up some more wines I think you'll love."

When he disappears, I sigh in relief. "I'm sorry, Liam."

He pulls me close again and places a few more kisses on my lips. "Worth the risk," he whispers.

"Come on," I tell him, grabbing his hand and leading him inside. "I'm going to tell your friends the story about how I lost my virginity among the grape vines, when I was only twelve years old. To a French kid named Pierre. "

"Is that true?" Liam asks in shock.

"Maybe. Maybe not." I shrug mischievously. "Who cares? I'm a writer and it will make for a really great story."

Chapter Eleven

The car driving along the highway feels as smooth as though it might be a boat cruising through water. I have no idea what time it is, but it's very, very late. The party ran into the early hours of the morning, and Liam needed some time to sober up before driving. Owen and Caroline were so drunk that they were nearly unconscious, and it took some considerable effort to stuff them into the car. Luckily, by the time Liam drove to their apartment, they were conscious enough to walk and use the elevator on their own.

Now, I am sitting in Liam's passenger seat as he ferries me home. I am imagining that we are in a yacht, steering through the rocky waves of the ocean. Every bump in the road feels like a large swell of water rocking the boat. My head rolls from side to side slightly, and I acknowledge that I am also somewhat drunk—but the perfect amount of intoxication. The world seems a little more magical, but I haven't completely lost my senses.

"Is it normal how Owen and Caroline argue about everything?" I ask Liam. "They only seem to get along when their lips are connected."

"Their attraction is mostly a physical one," Liam explains. "They do seem strange to the uninformed onlooker. But they have their own... language. Underneath all of that craziness, they really are good friends."

"I like them," I say to him with a lazy smile. I reach out and try to touch his leg, but my hand accidentally drifts a bit too far up his thigh. I giggle to myself a little. "And I really like you."

"Winter," Liam says with warning, clearing his throat. "I'm driving."

"Mmm, am I distracting you?" I ask sleepily. I let my hand brush against his manhood, stirring him to life. I suddenly feel curious and explorative, like when I was swirling the glass of wine within my hand. I trace my fingers in a teasing circular pattern along the front of his pants.

"Whoa," he says, his voice suddenly hoarse. "Remind me to give you wine more often. It makes you really bold."

"Yeah," I murmur, releasing my seatbelt. "I feel so good. Like nothing bad has ever happened. Like nothing bad ever could happen. I feel no pain. I feel like I can see all the colors in the whole world. I feel like I'm floating. Floating over the water with you."

"The water?" Liam asks in confusion.

"Yes," I say, leaning over to rest my face against his shoulder. I snuggle closer to him and wrap my arms around his torso. I let my hands caress his firm abdominals which must have been developed from plenty of judo. "In the boat," I explain sleepily, "over the water."

"Okay," he says with a little laugh.

I doze off against his shoulder, until I find him gently shaking me. To my surprise, the car has stopped moving. It feels like I was barely asleep for a second, but several minutes must have passed.

"We're here," Liam tells me softly. "At your house."

"Dammit," I say, sobering up almost instantly. It's time to cautiously sneak up into my bedroom once again while trying to avoid Grayson. Even though I feel very weak and sleepy, I will also have to slide my dresser in front of my door. I release a loud yawn. "At least he's unlikely to be awake at this hour," I assure myself. "So the coast should be clear."

"You'll be fine," Liam says, caressing my hair. He places a kiss on my forehead. "Just ignore that asshole. He can't hurt you anymore."

I nod in agreement.

"I'll open your door for you," Liam says. He pulls away from me and exits through his side

CLARITY

of the vehicle.

I feel cold due to the sudden removal of his body heat, and I pull my coat closer around me. When my door opens and he offers me his hand, I accept it and step outside with a smile. "This was a really great night," I tell him, "as always. Thanks for inviting me out."

"We're going to have a lot of amazing nights," he assures me. "I love spending time with you. I want to take you everywhere. I want to experience everything with you."

"I'd like that," I say softly, reaching for his tie to tug him down for a goodnight kiss.

Liam responds with gusto. He holds nothing back as he dives into my lips, whisking me away to that outer space again, almost instantly. I am not sure how he does it. No one has ever had this effect on me. I am dazed with pleasure when he plasters my body against the side of his car and slowly presses kisses along my chin and neck. His touch sends shivers of excitement directly through me, converging at my center. In an effort to be closer to him, I hook one of my legs around his, pulling him tighter against my body as I wrap my arms around his neck and kiss him deeply.

"I wish you didn't have to go," Liam groans between kisses.

"Me too," I whisper.

"This feels right, doesn't it?" Liam asks me. "You and me?"

305

I sigh and murmur against his mouth. "Yes. Definitely."

"Soon," he says quietly, pressing his lips against my cheek and then my earlobe. "Once we get past this doctor-patient stuff, I'll make you mine. And I'll keep you for good."

"I'm impatient," I say, tugging on his tie again. "I want to be yours now."

"But Winter..."

"Stop talking and kiss me," I command him.

He does not hesitate to comply. He slips his hand behind my head, letting his fingers get tangled up in my hair as he kisses me soundly. He lets his other hand trail over my collarbone and underneath the neckline of my blouse. I feel his fingers exploring downward to trace the edge of my bra. The sensitive, warm skin there responds to the cold and gentle touch of his fingers, and I arch my back to encourage him. He tenderly cups my breast in his hand and begins to massage my flesh. A small moan escapes my lips, and I am about to give him permission and beg him for more when I am startled by the noise of a door slamming. Liam rips his hands away from my body, and straightens himself.

For a moment, I am worried that it's my dad. I feel like a teenager terrified that my father has caught me fooling around in the car with my boyfriend. Then, I recall the greater threat. I am too stunned, being brutally yanked out of my bliss, to properly register the danger.

"Get the fuck away from her!" Grayson shouts as he moves toward us.

I feel like ice has been poured into my spine. I am suddenly frozen and unable to move.

"Relax, man!" Liam says. "Just relax. Helen is an adult, and she can do whatever she wants."

"I said to get the fuck away from her!" Grayson yells again, his voice rising to a fanatical screech.

My stomach contorts with nausea at the loathsome sound of his voice.

"Get in the car," Liam whispers to me, opening the door and swiftly guiding me inside. "Duck down below the glass."

When he shuts the car door, I follow his instructions and lean forward, lowering my head and torso. Only after I am crouching below the protection of the metal panel do I realize why he has asked me to do this. Grayson's gun. Just as I realize what's happening, the deafening sound of a shot being fired causes me to jump. I no longer care about my own safety, and I grab the handle of the car door and try to swing it open.

"Liam!" I scream in horror.

"Stay down!" he yells at me, shoving the car door closed again. "I'm fine!"

Another earsplitting shot is fired, and I

flinch as I feel the glass window above me shatter. My heart sinks as I imagine Liam shot and bleeding to death a few feet away, outside the car.

"Who the fuck do you think you are?" Grayson shouts. "Keeping her out all night and treating her like your little whore?"

Another shot is fired, but this time I hear Grayson grunting in pain. There seems to be some sort of struggle, and the sound of a metal item clattering to the floor. There is a loud thump followed by Grayson howling bloody murder.

Another gunshot.

Everything goes quiet.

"Liam?" I whisper fearfully. With a shaking hand I reach for the handle and push open the car door. I swing my legs out, causing pieces of the shattered glass window to fall from my lap and clatter to the ground. I move forward in a daze, afraid of what I'll discover. I take a few more tentative steps before my toes collide with a motionless body. I stand completely still, staring down in shock. I wish I could see the scene before me so I didn't have to crouch down on my hands and knees and try to identify the lifeless man on the ground.

This can't be happening. Liam was laughing with me and kissing me just a moment before. I have only just found him, and the thought of losing him like this rips my heart in half.

I can't lose him before I have ever had the

chance to really call him mine.

Please, God. Don't let him be gone.

"Liam?" I say softly again, into the emptiness of the night. I can feel my frosty breath tickle my lips. I wait. Nothing. No response. Tears spring to my eyes. The panic in my chest builds to a feverish scream as my voice bursts out of my chest like one of the gunshots echoing into the distance. *"Liam!"*

Loretta Lost

Book Three

Clarity of mind means clarity of passion, too; this is why a great and clear mind loves ardently and sees distinctly what he loves.

- Blaise Pascal

CLARITY

Clarity 3

by
Loretta Lost

Chapter One

The night is deathly still.

I can hear the moonlight. It's dripping all around me like liquid silver, and making my blood run cold. Crickets are calling out to each other and singing about the stars. I can hear all of this, but I can't hear the sound that I want to hear most.

A man's breathing.

I press my hands against my heart to keep it from pounding right out of my chest. It feels like a jackhammer is trying to drill through my breastbone. My knees tremble, and I struggle to remain upright in my high heels. I am empty and numb and weak. I wobble a little, and my toes graze along the shoulder of a lifeless human being. A bit of bile lifts in my throat, and I force myself to swallow down the bitter combination of stomach acid and saliva.

There is a possibly dead body resting against my toes. It's still warm.

I'm afraid that if I fall to my knees, I will touch the man's face and recognize the familiar curve of Liam's chin. The warm tickle of a tear squeezes itself through my lower eyelashes. It slowly slides down my cheek, but I am so mannequin-stiff that I cannot lift my arm to brush it away.

Please, I repeat mentally as I press my eyelids together tightly. As if I could possibly see any less. The stars and streetlights are all obscured, but try as I might, I can't block out the horrible images in my mind. *Please. Please let him be okay.*

My thoughts continue to race as I begin to lower myself to the ground. I reach out to touch the man before me, but I pause. I'm afraid to know. I remember the light stubble of Liam's five-o'clock shadow, brushing against my cheek only moments ago. My fingers twitch as they imagine tracing the hard angle of his handsome jaw, only to discover blood seeping from a gruesome wound. I need to identify the body, but I am terrified of plunging my hands into a pool of blood that used to be a bright young man. I don't think my heart could take it. I hesitate.

A sound breaks through the darkness. A groan.

"Liam?" I whisper desperately. All hesitation leaves me as I throw myself to my knees. My skin scrapes roughly against the cobblestoned ground, but I ignore the bruising. My hands dart out to clutch the body before me. If he has a moment's life left in him, I want to spend that moment holding him. I want to feel his final heartbeat against mine. I want to taste his last breath.

My hands brush against the fabric of a cotton collar. I lift my fingers higher and touch the man's face. It's smooth. Freshly shaven.

I jerk away with a gasp, recoiling from what must be Grayson's body. I fall back onto the cobblestones, my palms slamming clumsily against the cool ground. I shiver in horror at having touched my enemy. I draw in a deep breath. He was motionless. I was unable to touch his vile skin long enough to determine whether he was dead or alive. But if he's on the ground, does that mean...

"Winter," says a hoarse voice, a few feet away. He groans softly. "It's okay. I'm okay."

"Liam," I sob. "I thought you were..."

"No," he tells me. "I was just dazed. I don't get shot very often."

I feel like a small grenade has detonated within my chest, and I experience a sudden inability to breathe. I scramble back onto my knees and move around Grayson toward the sound of Liam's voice. "You've been shot?" I whisper. "Where? How bad is it?"

"It's fine," he assures me as he reaches out to pull me close. He wraps his arms around me and presses his lips against my forehead. "Hey. I'm—I'm fine. Don't worry."

I gratefully accept his embrace, collapsing into the warmth of his chest. I bury my face into his shirt, pressing my ear against his heart so that I can listen to it pounding nearly as fast as mine. He doesn't sound fine. I run my hands over his body, searching for his wound. "Where were you hurt? What happened? Should I call an ambulance?"

"No, no. It's nothing. I'm a doctor, remember?" he speaks in a soothing tone as he brushes my hair back from my cheek. "This is a minor graze. I can handle it."

"Are you sure?" I ask him as I move my hands all over his chest and sides, followed by his arms. When I move to his thighs, he finally winces and pulls away. I gasp at the feeling of sticky moisture soaking the side of his pants. "Liam! We need to get you to a hospital."

"For this little thing?" he says in the tone men always use when they're trying to be tough. "Don't worry. He got me in a lucky spot. A fifth-grader could patch this up with a basic first-aid kit."

"Are you crazy? This is a bullet wound!" I try to put pressure on his leg because I can't think of anything else to do. "What kind of fifth-graders do you know?" I ask him angrily.

"Well, I was a boy scout," he explains, "and I played a lot of Operation."

I can't believe he's making a joke at a time like this. I glance over at my silent brother-in-law who remains motionless on the ground. "What about him? Is he..."

"He's alive. I just broke both of his arms and took his gun. I think he passed out from the pain—or it might have been my left hook." Liam shrugs as though he does this every day.

I exhale slowly. "Are you serious?" I ask in wonder, releasing a little hysterical laugh of relief. *"You broke both of his arms?"*

"I told you judo was useful," Liam says casually. He pulls away from me and grunts as he slowly rises to his feet. He reaches out to help me stand. "Lights are being turned on in your house. It seems the shots woke up your family. We should go tell your dad and sister what happened— Grayson is going to need medical attention. They're probably going to call the cops, and we'll have to file a police report..."

"No," I tell him softly as I clutch handfuls of his shirt to help keep myself upright. The idea of having to go through all of that bureaucracy gives me headache. Why is it that immediately after surviving a traumatic event, you are always faced with a great deal of equally traumatic paperwork? I step closer to Liam so that our bodies are almost touching, but not quite. I can feel his warmth surrounding me. I release his shirt and slide my hands over the taut muscles of his torso.

He feels tense, like he is still in the middle of a fight and ready to spring into action. I take a deep breath. I can't seem to stop touching him. After that terrifying moment of uncertainty, I need constant proof that he is alive. "Can we just... go?" I plead. "Somewhere. Anywhere. I don't want to deal with this right now."

He is quiet for a moment, and he reaches out to cup my face. "Winter," he tells me softly. "You're shaking."

I try to breathe slowly to chase away my terror and regain control of my body. I had not noticed my pathetic state until he mentioned it; I know that my mind is tough and resilient, but my body is a mess. My hands are trembling and my shoulders keep shuddering sporadically. I must look like a bundle of exposed nerves, all frayed and split. Liam senses my anxiety, and moves forward to wrap his arms around me. He cradles me against him, locking his arms around my back fiercely. After a moment, I close my eyes and sink into his embrace. I feel my tension begin to ease away, and my body begins to grow calm. He is so strong; so amazingly strong. He is overflowing with so much quiet power that it seeps into me. I feel shielded against everything. The gunshots and Grayson seem far away, almost in another lifetime. I know that Liam would never allow any harm to come to me.

But Liam hasn't always been around. He

won't always be around.

I grow suddenly aware of the large bulge in his pocket. I am confused for a moment, but then I realize that it's Grayson's gun. I move my hand to touch the metal instrument curiously through his coat. A horrifying thought crosses my mind; I consider taking the gun and shooting the unconscious Grayson in the face. It would permanently remove him from my life. I can see myself pulling the trigger—I can hear the gunshot ripping away his life. I immediately feel ill, but intrigued.

"What if I... got rid of him?" I ask Liam breathlessly. My voice is so soft that it blends with the wind. As I taste the whisper of dark words on my tongue, the idea begins to seduce me. I know that I'm not capable of such a thing, but my hands are inching over the edges of his pockets anyway. I slip my index finger between the folds of fabric and touch the cold metal. It sends a little jolt of excitement through me, along with a shiver of dread.

I know that my sister would never forgive me.

But I almost don't care. I'd be protecting her. I'd be protecting myself.

"No," Liam says, taking my wrists and guiding them away from his pocket. "You're not thinking clearly right now. No one deserves that—it's not for us to decide. You're not that type of person."

Anger rises in my chest. "How do you know what kind of person I am? *He* made me into a different kind of person." I pause as I my indignation gives way to helplessness. My hiss fades into a whisper. "Liam... shouldn't I do something? He hurt Carmen. He tried to *kill* you."

"That doesn't make it right," Liam tells me, gently squeezing my wrists. "We need to be better than him."

I shake my head in dismay and confusion. I wish I could be tough enough pull the trigger. But if my sister and dad are coming downstairs to investigate the gunshots, then I wouldn't like to need to explain why Grayson is lying on the ground unconscious, with both of his arms broken, and a bullet in his body. He's defenseless; it would be in bad taste to hurt him now. It would be low. It would be despicable. But he just shot at us! He just wounded Liam. If I don't do something now, will he try to hurt us again? Am I missing my last opportunity to gain the upper hand?

My head begins to ache. Could I live with myself and accept the consequences if I did this? I haven't given hurting him any real thought. I haven't really felt a great need for revenge—just the need to get away. Maybe I *should* get revenge. Maybe it was what I really needed all along. Maybe this is the only way I can *really* get away—while simultaneously remaining in one spot.

CLARITY

Would it be somehow liberating or healing? Would life magically get better if Grayson was gone? Would I return to who I was? Could I reclaim my innocence and optimistic look at the world? Could I be around people again without falling apart?

My breathing is quick and labored as the adrenaline and panic courses through me. *No, I* command myself. *You could never. You're out of your mind for even considering this. Snap out of it.* I try to purge the images of revenge from my thoughts. At the same time, I feel disgustingly powerless and upset with the idea of doing nothing at all. I can't live like this. I can't live in constant fear. I can't let Grayson live, and let him keep doing this to me. But I can't take his life either. Guilt and remorse would consume me, and living under that shadow might be more difficult than living with constant fear and anxiety. I pull my hands away from Liam and let them fall to my sides.

A few feet away, I hear Grayson stirring and groaning on the ground.

My eyes widen as I turn to the sound, and I flinch ever so slightly. The knowledge that his arms are broken does nothing to comfort me. I move back a step, wishing there were walls and fortifications between us. I wish I could turn and run—run away from here forever. But I already tried that. I feel lost and overwhelmed, and trapped in this mess. I feel my knees trembling, and my ankles bending as I lose the strength to keep myself upright in my high heels. I close my eyes and clench my fists, trying to maintain a bit of dignity and not let myself fall to the ground and collapse into tears.

"Fuck it," Liam says suddenly and harshly. He slips his arm around my waist to help me stand. "You're coming home with me. I'm not letting you sleep in the same house with that man anymore."

"Thank you," I whisper.

"Come on," he says as he guides me over to his car. He curses when he sees his shattered windows. "At least he didn't hit the tires," he says furiously as he stoops to survey the damage on his vehicle. He pulls the passenger door open wider, as I had previously left it ajar. He brushes some glass out of the car before guiding me into my seat and shutting the door.

"Liam," I whisper, seeking an answer to a question that escapes me.

He has taken a step to move around the car, but he returns and reaches through the shattered window frame to hug my shoulders. "We're okay. It's going to be okay. Do you trust me?"

I give him the tiniest of nods. He leans forward to press his lips against mine, but I am too emotionally numb to feel comforted by the kiss.

He lets his mouth linger against mine for a moment, until the warmth of his skin reaches that dark place inside me and pulls me back to him. Once he feels my frozenness thaw, he squeezes my shoulders and pulls away. Liam briskly walks around the car, but I hear a change in his step. Even though he moves quickly, I can hear the new limp in his gait as he tries to avoid putting his full weight on his wounded leg.

When he climbs into the car, he winces in pain.

"Are you sure you don't need to go to the hospital?" I ask him as he starts the engine.

"I'll be fine," he tells me with a low growl. "Good thing that motherfucker has terrible aim."

"What an awful night," I say softly, pushing my head back against the headrest. I just want to get away from here and lie down. I want this to be over

I hear the sound of footsteps on the cobblestones, and a feminine gasp.

"Helen?" my sister calls out from a distance. "Helen! What the hell happened?"

I hesitate, hearing the panic in her tone. My first thought is to comfort her and explain the situation. Then a frown warps my features. I have nothing to explain. "Just go," I tell Liam quietly. "I don't want to deal with Carmen right now."

Liam doesn't waste a second in slamming

his foot on the gas pedal, and the car peels away from the driveway. I feel my body pressed back against the seat with the momentum as we turn out onto the main road.

"I can't believe that just happened," Liam says angrily. "What the fuck is wrong with that man? Why would he shoot at us?" Liam slams his hand down against the steering wheel. "Dammit! And I just bought this car. I've been taking it to the car wash every day and wiping off every speck of dust. Then that asshole goes and puts *bullet holes* in the side of my car. Great. Just great."

"Liam," I say, wrinkling my face in frustration. "I'm much more concerned about the bullet hole he put in you."

"I can stitch up my leg! The bullet just tore a minor cut into the side of my thigh. It's not that deep. It's mostly stopped bleeding already, and it will mostly heal itself—and probably leave a cool scar. But my car can't heal itself! I'm not a mechanic—I don't know how to fix the bullet holes in the metal! Dammit." He takes several deep breaths. "I should have never taken you to that house. This is my fault. I'm keeping you far away from that man from now on. You never have to go back there."

A thought suddenly strikes me and I bolt upright in my seat. "My computer. My braille notetaker. It has my story on it."

"We can just get you a new computer,"

Liam says.

"No—my book was half-finished," I say miserably. Sinking back into my seat, I sigh in frustration. "I haven't been able to make any progress since I came home, but I had written a good chunk of the novel when I was back in New Hampshire. I can't lose all that work."

"I'll get it for you in a few days once things have calmed down," Liam says. He suddenly lets out a laugh. "Look at the two of us! We just escaped a life-or-death situation, and you're worried about your computer, while I'm worried about my car."

Somehow, even in this moment, he is able to make me smile.

"I guess life isn't worth living unless we also have our stuff," I say in a feeble attempt at humor. The sound of ringing causes me to jump violently. In the second before I identify the sound, my body has already jerked and recoiled as though I have been stung by a bee. My heart pounds fiercely again, and I bite down on my lip. After hearing the gunshots, even the sound of a phone ringing seems to send me into a state of fear and paralysis. With stiff fingers, I reach into my pocket for my cell phone and answer the call.

"Hello?" I say into the small box as I bring it to my ear.

"What the fuck, Helen?" My sister's voice hisses at me through the cell phone. "Grayson's in so much pain! What did you do to him?"

For a moment, I can't respond. I shake my head, caught somewhere between anger and hysterical laughter. "What did *I* do to him? Your beloved husband *shot* Liam."

There's a pause on the other end. "I don't believe you," Carmen says hesitantly. Then she repeats herself with more conviction. "I don't believe you! I'm calling the cops."

"Go ahead!" I encourage her viciously. "Let's have a nice long discussion with the police. But I would advise your husband to get a fucking lawyer. After what he did tonight and what he's done in the past, he's probably going to spend a very long time behind bars. Long enough to miss your kid growing up; that's for sure."

"Helen," Carmen says softly. "Grayson doesn't deserve to go to prison. I don't know what happened here, but he's a good man. For god's sake, he's injured. He can't move his arms. Isn't he suffering enough? I need to get him to a hospital. Will you come home and help me out? Dad's freaking out."

At the mention of our father, I clench my teeth together. I know that Dad is innocent in all this, but I can't help lumping him together with Carmen as one of Grayson's allies. He said that Grayson was like a son to him. The three of them are family, and I'm the outsider. I'm sure Dad would defend me and take my side if he knew the whole story, but I don't think I can break his heart like that—maybe it's better that he remains innocent. All three of them were doing fine until I came into the picture; maybe if I remove myself, things will go back to normal.

"I'm never coming back to that house again," I tell Carmen firmly. "I'll send someone to pick up my things, but this is it for me. Before you married Grayson, you knew he had violent tendencies. You could have prevented all this, but you chose to put us all at risk. You have never given a fuck about me or anyone else, Carmen. You only think about yourself. I'm done. I can't be your sister anymore."

"That's not fair!" Carmen yells back. "I never meant for you to get hurt. I told you that I'm pregnant! I have to think about my baby. Why can't you understand that? I chose not to put my baby at risk of growing up without a dad."

"Sure. But now your kid will have to grow up without an aunt," I tell her in a quiet voice. "Goodbye, Carmen."

"Helen! You're being emotional and rash. Just come back home and we can sort this out. I need to take Grayson to the hospital. I don't know what happened, but we'll just tell them that he was mugged."

"He shot Liam," I tell her again. "Do you even care?"

"I do. It's just so hard to believe. Is Liam

alright?" Carmen asks.

Annoyed at her delayed fake concern, I hang up the phone. I toss it to the ground of Liam's car and put both of my hands in my hair. "Fuck!" I say in exasperation to Liam. "I'm so sorry I dragged you into this."

"I'm the one who dragged you away from your sanctuary," he responds softly. "I should be apologizing. But are you sure you want to cut ties with your sister? It's not her fault."

"Carmen chose this. I was already gone— she's the one who begged me to come home. I was looking for a reason to stay, but instead, she reminded me of all the reasons I left. She ruined our relationship when she chose to go ahead with marrying that monster. If she's going to call *him* family, I can't call *her* family. If I keep associating with her, she'll get me killed."

"Maybe they'll break up now that he's tried to hurt you," Liam says.

"I doubt it. He had already hurt me, and it seemed to make no difference to her. She didn't even want to know."

There is a silence in the car after I speak these words. Liam seems unable to respond, and I think we both need a moment to ponder the events. After a few minutes pass, he reaches over to place his hand on my leg in a gentle caress.

"Let's look on the bright side," he says softly. "Now that you'll be staying with me, we can spend a lot more time together. I hope you'll like my apartment. It's very small, but it's home."

"I'm sure it will be lovely," I tell him, putting my hand over his. "Thanks for helping me get the hell away from that place." I finally begin to relax and calm down as I interlace my fingers with his. I can't believe that just a few hours ago, I was tipsy and having a good time. The gunshots somehow made me instantly stone cold sober.

It suddenly occurs to me that I might be moving in with Liam. We haven't talked about it at all, and our relationship is certainly not ready for this. I don't have the energy to stress out about this tonight, as my main concern is putting my aching head down on a pillow and drifting off to sleep. However, it does seem like I might be stepping out of one dangerous situation and into another.

"I should be getting a royalty check by the end of the week," I tell Liam. "I could look for my own place after that, or use the money to get back to New Hampshire—so you don't have to worry about being stuck with me."

"Winter," Liam says lightly, tightening his grip on my hand. "You can stay as long as you like. It will be my honor to have you for as long as you can stand me. Besides, I'm already stuck on you pretty bad. You occupy my thoughts all the time; you might as well occupy my apartment!"

I lower my chin in embarrassment at his sweet words. "I must have done something

331

amazing in a previous life to deserve a guy like you. You're a hero, Liam. Rescuing the damsel in distress and whisking her away into the night—taking a bullet for her. This is classic hero stuff."

"Wow!" he says in surprise. "I guess you're right. I am a hero!" He seems thoughtful for a moment. "I'll have to brag about it later to Owen. He can add getting shot to his list of romantic date ideas."

My lips curl upward in a smile—I still feel puzzled at my ability to smile after all this. With Liam beside me, even the worst situations don't seem so terrible. He is able to lift my spirits and help me feel positive about the future, even though my present and past are impossibly dark.

Maybe the future really will be brighter, in every sense of the word. Maybe, with Liam's help, I will actually be able to see a sliver of light someday soon. Both visually and emotionally. I feel like it could be possible. I feel like we really are leaving everything dark and horrible far behind as we race forward along the highway, toward something brilliant.

For the first time in ages, I find myself craving that light. I want to feel the warmth of the sun on my face, and actually be able to see the sunbeams streaming down from heaven. I want the sunlight to wash away everything hateful until I feel clean, radiant, and new.

CLARITY

Chapter Two

"Are you sure you don't need any help?" I ask Liam nervously as he stitches up the wound on his leg.

"It's a pretty simple job," he says through gritted teeth. I can tell that he's trying very hard not to make pain-noises to betray how much it hurts. I can still hear the catches in his breathing every time he jabs the needle through his skin.

"There must be something I can do," I insist.

"Alright. Go and wash your hands thoroughly with soap," he instructs. "The sink is in the middle of the kitchen, and the soap is on the left side of the counter. When you're done, there's a roll of paper towel above the sink, and you can grab a few sheets to blot away the blood so I can see what I'm doing."

I place my hand on his coffee table to help me rise to my feet. My fingers encounter the edge of a book, and I can't resist the urge to let them lightly scan over the cover. I am surprised to discover that it's the same book I signed for him on our very first meeting. I am flattered that he keeps it in such a prominent place in his apartment. However, I don't have the time to tease him or mention this now.

I rush to the sink to follow his instructions. The apartment *is* very small, and the kitchen is not completely separated from the living area—it was easy to get a sense of the layout quite quickly. I find the soap without difficulty and begin scrubbing my hands. "I'm glad that I can't see you bleeding," I admit as I dry my hands on the paper towel and pull out a few more sheets. "I think it would stress me out a lot."

"I'm just glad you can't see me sitting here without my pants," he admits.

"Why?" I ask curiously as I reenter the room.

"I didn't know I was going to get shot today, but I did know that my friends would be gambling. So—I wore my lucky boxers. They're covered in hearts, four-leaf clovers, and horseshoes. It would be quite embarrassing if you could see this."

The edge of my lips quirk slightly. "But you just told me what they look like."

"Knowing and seeing are two different things," he says solemnly. "Now come over here before I bleed all over my new couch."

I move over to kneel on the ground near where he's sitting and gently press the paper towel against his leg. "Is that okay?"

"Here," he says, guiding my hands. "You can press it directly on the wound and be a bit more aggressive to really soak up the blood," he tells me.

"Okay," I say with a grimace, "but I still think you should go to the hospital."

"And wait three hours in the emergency for something I can do in five minutes? No, thanks." Liam prepares himself for doing another stitch in his leg. "Besides, this way you get to see a preview of my excellent skills as a surgeon. You need to trust me if I'm going to be poking holes in your eyes in a few weeks."

I pull the paper towel away from his leg and shudder at the thought. I did not realize that my shoulder was lightly touching his knee until I feel his body twitch at the pain of the needle piercing his skin. I immediately curl my arm around his calf and gently hug the bottom half of his leg to both soothe him and steady him.

"Almost done," he says after a sharp intake of breath. "Blot the blood away?"

I immediately comply and press the paper towel back against his wound. I can't tell how bad it is, but I feel a small trickle of moisture slide down my wrist. "Liam," I say softly, with concern.

"Just one more stitch," he says with determination.

I remove my hand so that he can get to work, and I dab the dribble of blood off my wrist. This time, he does release a small groan when the metal impales his skin. It takes him a second to finish the stitch and tie a knot in the thread. Finally, he tosses the needle onto the coffee table and collapses back in the sofa, breathing deeply.

"Is that all?" I ask him softly as I press the paper towel against his cut.

He exhales slowly. "Just one more task. Can you hand me the gauze on the coffee table?" he asks me weakly.

I hate the sound of him in such agony. I place the paper towel down and retrieve the gauze, but instead of giving it to him, I begin to unroll the fabric. He seems exhausted, and he shouldn't have to do everything himself. I place the end of the fabric over his stitched up wound, and hold it in place as I begin to wrap the roll slowly around his thigh. I try to focus on the task and not notice how hard and muscular his leg is under my hands. I am stunned by the large circumference and the amount of gauze it takes to encircle his limb. I bite down on my lip and concentrate as I make several laps before he reaches out to halt me.

"That's perfect. Thank you, Winter," he says, taking the gauze from my hand and finishing up the job. He leans forward to place the empty roll on the table and sighs. "You know, you've really been a champ tonight."

"Me?" I say in surprise. "I would have fallen apart if it weren't for you—and I probably would have been shot. Or worse."

"Nonsense," he says, cupping my face in his hand. He runs his thumb over my cheek gently. "You've been through shit like this before and you found a way to cope. You're a survivor, and you would have been fine without me. Heck, this is the first time *I've* been in such a situation. I've never had a gun pointed at me before. I have trained in judo for years, but I've never had to *actually* fight someone. For a moment—I thought I was going to panic and screw up."

"Really?" I ask him in wonder. "You handled it so smoothly—like you do this every day."

"No. My mind was spinning. I don't even remember fighting with Grayson. I just remember the pain in my leg and then a burst of anger. I remember intending to disarm him, and I think another gunshot went off—I saw him reaching for me, and in the next instant we were both on the ground. I remember lying there in a daze and trying to figure out what had happened. It was like my body moved so fast I couldn't keep up. I was outside myself and looking in on the action."

"Oh, Liam," I say softly, turning to press my forehead against his knee. "I was so worried. I thought you were dead."

"For a second, I wasn't sure," he admits. "I was lying there and staring at the stars, and they all seemed to be dancing and spiraling around each other rapidly. I was so full of adrenaline that everything was distorted and I had no idea where I was. But then I heard you calling my name, and it cleared up all the cobwebs. In that moment, I knew that your voice was the sweetest sound I had ever heard."

I don't know how to respond. I feel like something has irrevocably changed between us due to the night's earlier events. Maybe it's impossible to go through something like this without being drawn closer together. Liam seemed so strong throughout the whole situation, but now that we are alone and safe in his home, he is choosing to be honest with me about the fact that he was scared. Of course, even the strongest of heroes are human beings who feel lost and afraid at times. His ability to share this with me endears him to me even further. I feel like we must be truly on the same side, if he is able to trust me with such intimate details.

I place my hand on his thigh to comfort him, trying to avoid the location of the wound. My fingers accidentally graze the edge of his lucky boxers, and I am surprised to feel that they have a satiny texture. I find myself taking the fabric between my thumb and forefinger and rubbing it curiously. It's strange to find such a soft and luxurious fabric on a male body—but I suppose I don't often get to examine what men wear beneath their clothing. Maybe many of them wear silk boxers. I feel a little embarrassed for my curiosity, and I clear my throat.

"You really shouldn't wear these boxers anymore," I inform Liam.

"Why not?" he says in surprise.

"They seem to bring bad luck more than anything," I point out with a frown. "You did get shot while wearing them."

"You're wrong," he says, his voice growing husky as he leans forward in the sofa. He reaches out to brush my hair back over my shoulders. "I believe they are, in fact, very lucky."

His voice gives me a little shiver. I am a bit startled when I feel his hands sliding down over my arms. I swallow to combat the sudden flush of warmth spreading across my neck and chest. "Why?" I manage to whisper.

"For one thing, the bullet completely missed everything vital. But more importantly, you did come home with me tonight, didn't you?" He slides his hands gently around my waist. "I'd say I'm pretty damn lucky. You're here; nothing else really matters. I think the boxers are doing just fine."

"Liam," I murmur in surprise. I feel a sudden weightlessness as he lifts me up onto his lap. "But your leg!" I exclaim with worry. I try to pull away and place my weight on the sofa. "Am I hurting..."

"Shhh," he says as he holds me fast. "Having you close to me is the best possible therapy for speeding up my healing. Trust me, I'm a doctor."

I release a small laugh and give in to the urge to curl up against him. I press my ear and hand against his chest, and I can feel that his heartbeat is a lot slower than earlier. Mine is, too. We are both calm and comfortable together. It's nice. It really feels like we've left all of the earlier drama far behind. I let my eyes close and I inhale deeply, savoring the mild scent of Liam's cologne, still lingering on his shirt. I feel myself drifting away with the relaxing sensation of his arms around me.

All my fear easily subsides into bliss. I think I am also rather lucky.

I am trying to soak up the serenity of the moment when I feel his fingertips brush along my spine. It's a tiny touch, trailing an erratic zigzag pattern beneath my blouse. I hold my breath as he weaves between my vertebrae, drawing invisible lines from the clasp of my bra to the waistband of my skirt. I am not sure why my stomach begins to tingle with heat and yearning. His other hand skims over my leg, caressing up and down the length of my thigh. As he draws closer to the hem of my skirt, his hand pauses. His fingers slide a few inches up under my skirt before retreating, hovering somewhere between boldness and respect. Something about the way he places his hands on me is tantalizing. I can feel that there are infinite unspoken sentences and secrets in his touch, and I try very hard to read their meaning. Something vital seems to be escaping me—it hides just out of reach within the silent spaces.

All I know is that he sets me on fire.

My very bones seem to quiver and melt beneath his hands. I try to remain very still, afraid to move and ruin the precious feeling. Is this a magical enchantment he's casting on me, or some kind of medical manipulation? The electricity flows through my spine to the very tips of my fingers and toes. I never want it to end.

It feels like he is trying to unravel my soul.

I wish someone would tell him that he doesn't have to try so hard. He doesn't need any of this voodoo or science to conquer me. All he has to do is whisper my name, and I am his. He is the only good thing in my life, and I would give him anything he asked. I trust him completely, especially after tonight. Without Liam, I would surely be all alone in the world. Before the kindness and strength of his embrace, I was barely alive. Not like this. I lived every day in quiet solitude, thinking deeply about everything, but feeling absolutely nothing. Now, every part of my body is humming with excitement and energy. I am awake and aware.

Thanks to him, I am alive. In every way, alive.

I didn't know I could ever feel this way again. I wouldn't have dared to try.

A prickle of coarse stubble grazes against my nose, informing me of the extreme closeness of Liam's face. I am feeling terribly sensitive, like every feather-light touch is simply too much to bear. I can feel my heartbeat increasing again, and the atmosphere grows thick and heavy around us, blanketing our bodies with a certain gorgeous tension. Does he feel this way, too? My eyelids flutter open, and in a way, they do help me see. I can feel the warmth of his breath tickling my eyelashes and can sense the location of his lips. I gingerly lift my chin and let my mouth barely brush against the corner of his lips. I shiver at the tremendous sensation.

There are small jolts of lightning passing between us.

I feel like a storm cloud that hasn't rained in a century. That's how long I've been bottling up all my emotions, and keeping them from spilling over. Now, I fear that if that if he keeps touching me like this, I might burst. I might shatter in a mighty blizzard of passion, and take him down with me. I have so much love to give; it has been brimming inside me and begging to be set free. I have been lost and isolated for so long, with no one with whom I could share all of this feeling. I have kept myself busy to try to distract myself from how much I needed this.

People are meant to love other people. It was unnatural to starve myself from affection, even though I convinced myself that it was safer and the only way. I was just scared. I wasn't strong enough to try; I couldn't deal with the pain of losing another person I loved so dearly. I couldn't trust anyone enough to love them with complete and utter abandon. But something has changed now. I feel like I deserve to be happy. I'm ready to stop my self-punishment and exile. I'm ready to be happy.

How do I tell Liam all this? I want him to know. I slide my hand across his chest, and I can feel that his heartbeat has quickened, too. Does he feel the way I do? I exhale slowly, feeling my breath mingle with the electricity between us. I want this so badly. I want to love him so badly. I am tired of living and loving only in my stories, and mingling only with fictional people. I tried so hard, for so many years, to pour all of my emotions into the pages—but it was never enough. They never became real. The people I created never jumped from the pages and became my friends or lovers. I tried as hard as I could, and gave them everything I had, but I could never bring them to

CLARITY

life.

Now, for the first time, my life is on the verge of becoming just as beautiful as my stories. Can this be real? I remember my book resting on Liam's coffee table, and tears spring to my eyes. Did he feel all of that emotion, and instinctively know how much I needed him? Is that why he came all that way to find me? Was my writing some sort of beacon? Was I sending messages out into the world all along, and asking someone to come and save me?

Feeling a bit desperate, I place my lips against his, trying to phrase all my questions within the confines of a single kiss. He does not respond, but instead, he becomes suddenly and strangely still. I wait for a moment, growing afraid. I kiss him again, more deeply, trying to elicit a response from him. His hands have stopped moving against me, and he seems to be considering something. Anxiety bubbles up within me, and I press my lips against his again and again, growing more demanding.

"Liam," I whisper against his mouth. "Liam?"

His hands tighten around me, and he returns the kiss with more urgency than ever before; he steals my breath away. I am overwhelmed by his power as his hands tighten around my body, and he pulls me even closer. He kisses me so forcefully that my neck cranes

345

backward slightly and hurts a little. I feel like I have gotten the answer to my question. He feels just as desperate and lonely as I do. He needs me just as much as I need him.

I am relieved by this answer. My body responds to his, becoming more aggressive and trying to meet his strength with my own. My tongue searches further, delving and hunting between his lips for the answers to all the questions I've ever had.

Why are things so much harder for me?

I find myself twisting in his lap so that I can gain better access to his body. I sit up and straddle his thighs so that I can focus all my attention on the kiss, and take the pressure off his wound; I don't want to hurt him. He slides his hands over my legs, causing my skirt to ride up and bunch up around my hips. I wrap my arms around his neck and hold him so tightly that my breasts are mashed against his chest. I can't seem to get close enough. I try to soak up all of him, and bathe myself in his strength.

Why do so many bad things happen to me? What have I done to deserve this?

Liam's hands grab my hips and drag me down firmly against him. I gasp a little at the feeling of his hardness straining through the thin material of his lucky boxers and pressing on my most sensitive spot. A tremor runs through me at the contact, and I feel myself growing moist as my body instinctively prepares for him. I am unable to resist rubbing myself along his length, trying to feel all of him. He groans into my mouth and cups my bottom, pushing me against him harder. The two thin pieces of fabric between us are powerless to dull the sensation or separate us. They are already so soaked that they might as well be nonexistent.

Liam moves his hands to the sides of my blouse, grasping the material and tugging it up over my head. Our lips only break for a moment in order for the garment to be torn from my body. In the next moment, his hands are on the clasp of my bra, and it is removed with similar efficiency. My breasts are only exposed to the cool air for a second before his warm hands gently encircle them both, kneading the sensitive mounds with the perfect amount of pressure.

I grab his shoulders tightly as the mind-numbing pleasure overwhelms my senses. He continues to massage my flesh, masterfully rolling my nipples between his fingers. I break the kiss as my head tilts back in ecstasy, and he uses the opportunity to take my breast into his mouth, twirling his tongue around the tightened bud of my nipple. I gasp as he suckles on my breast, sending more of those little lightning bolts dancing through my stomach. He simultaneously bucks his hips against me, sliding his manhood between my increasingly slick folds. I can't think of anything else but him.

Make me forget. Make me forget everything bad that has ever happened.

Liam removes his lips from my breast, and kisses the tender, exposed area of my neck, raking his stubble across my sensitive skin. Somehow, even this is pleasurable. Every aspect of him is torturing me with its sublime masculine perfection. It suddenly occurs to me that he is still wearing a shirt, and I feel the need to remove it from him hastily. I want to feel his skin against mine. I reach out and begin to fumble madly to undo the buttons. He helps me, and when I push the fabric off his arms, he leans forward to shrug the material away and slide it off his arms. He flings the shirt aside before putting his arms back around me, and crushing me against him.

"Winter," he groans against my face. "God, I want you."

He attaches his lips to mine again hungrily, and runs his hands over my naked back. He circles his hips upward to tease me with his erection until I gasp out his name. My soaked panties are plastered against me and becoming cumbersome. He must sense this, for he reaches down to peel them away from my skin and places his fingers there instead.

When he rubs his fingers in a slow circle amidst my wetness, I can't restrain a moan. This encourages him, and he continues to massage between my folds until my desire builds to an ache deep inside me. I feel like my body is ablaze. My tender flesh is throbbing against his fingers and begging him for more.

All my logic seems to have flown from my skull; there is only devastating pleasure.

I find myself squirming wantonly, and behaving very unlike myself. When he plunges his fingers inside me, I cry out at the precious invasion. I haven't been touched this way in forever, and never so skillfully and lovingly. For a few seconds, as he pumps his fingers into me, I find my body quaking as my muscles tense around him, unused to the affections. It soon grows to be too much, and I have to push him away and try to catch my breath.

"Are you okay?" he asks immediately. "Did I hurt you?"

"No, no," I tell him breathlessly. "It's wonderful. I just..." I place my hands on his face and give him a look of pleading. "I just want *you.*"

He understands my need and he swivels to toss me down onto the sofa. He reaches under my bunched up skirt to completely remove my ruined panties, pulling them over my legs and tossing them in the direction of the coffee table. I worry that he has placed them on my book, but I imagine he has better aim than that. I am startled when he pushes my knees apart and looks at me for a moment.

"Liam?" I say nervously.

"You're beautiful," he says, lowering himself to place a kiss between my thighs. His tongue darts within me, lapping up my juices and massaging my sensitive bud.

My hips quiver at this feeling, and I place my hands in his hair. A strange moan of pleasure leaves my lips, and I feel dizzy and delirious. I can't take much more of this. It's too much to bear. "Liam," I murmur, trying to pull him away from my body. "Stop. Come here."

He immediately halts his activities and moves back over me to place a kiss on my lips. I can taste the residue of myself on him, and it's sweet and pleasant.

"What's wrong?" he asks softly. "I was enjoying myself."

"Please," I whisper, reaching down to tug at the waistband of his lucky boxers and beginning to slide them off. I wrap my hand around the warm flesh of his engorged member and firmly stroke his entire length. "I want you inside me."

"Winter," Liam says hoarsely. "Are you sure that..."

"Yes, yes," I mumble. "Please."

He hesitates. "I just don't want..."

"Take these off already," I implore him as I reach down to wrestle with the boxers, "so you can *actually* get lucky."

A deep chuckle rumbles in his throat. He

complies in removing the offending garment, but I feel him wince when the waistband scrapes against his wounded leg.

"Does it hurt too much?" I ask him with worry.

"I'm fine," he tells me as he moves back over me. He lets his forehead drop to rest gently against mine as he positions himself at my entrance. "Are you sure you want to do this? We're not moving too fast?"

"You're moving far too slowly," I complain as my body writhes in torment beneath him. I feel so much burning need that it is causing me physical pain. I need to quench this fire before it reduces me to ashes. I push my hips against him, trying to beg him with my body. "Please, Liam? Will you make love to me?"

"Gladly," he whispers, gently combing his fingers through my hair. He seems to be exercising great restraint in not plunging himself inside me. I can feel his body shaking above me with the effort. "I just want to take it slow and enjoy the moment."

"I don't have the same self-control that you do," I tell him weakly. "I never feel this way. I never let myself feel this way."

"I know," he says softly, as he pulls away from me a few inches. "And I also know from your medical records that you've never been on birth control."

"Hey! Those are private," I say with a

frown. I am flattered that he cared enough to check, but having trouble caring about that right now. "Can you just... be careful?"

"I could," he says softly, "but it's a risk."

"I want to take a risk with you," I say as I wrap my arms around his large torso. He feels so good on top of me. "Please."

"Alright," he says, placing his hand against my cheek. He positions himself against my wetness again, and gently prods my entrance by moving his hips ever-so-slightly. "I swear to God, Helen, if you say 'please' one more time, I'm going to lose my mind. I don't have as much self-control as you think."

My body suddenly stiffens. Time seems to slow down all around me. I try to speak, but my lips are locked shut. My chest feels very constricted, like there is a great weight on top of me. I try to breathe.

"What did you..." I manage to croak out. I gasp for air. "What did you call me?"

He responds, but I can't hear the words he's speaking. It suddenly feels like he is very far away. The darkness around me grows darker, and I stare into it with terror. A strange pain shoots through my eyes, and I feel like I have been plunged underwater. My lungs are heavy. I feel like I am drowning.

I feel a finger trail down across my neck. It is gentle, but somehow, I still feel like it is suffocating me. I gasp for breath, but I can't seem to get any air. My windpipe is being crushed. The darkness spins, growing heavy and dragging me down. I shut my eyes tightly, wondering if I am close to death.

"Winter?" Liam says sharply. I can feel that he is shaking my shoulders. "Winter? Are you okay?"

I open my eyes, and inhale deeply. In an instant, the panic is gone, but I do feel a thin film of sweat covering my chest. I try to quickly rid myself of the old feelings. I know them well—it's part of a nightmare I've had a thousand times. "I'm fine," I tell him weakly. "I'm so sorry. I just thought—I thought I heard you call me Helen."

"Did I?" he asks. "I don't think so. I'm sorry if I did. We should probably stop."

"What?" I say with a different kind of panic. I realize then that Liam has pulled away from me completely, and that his body is no longer close to mine. I reach out to grasp his arm. "Liam! It was just a moment of—something. Please don't stop."

"Winter," he says slowly. "Your pupils just dilated."

"So?" I say in confusion.

"Your disease prevents your eyes from perceiving any light. You could look directly at the sun and your pupils wouldn't change size. But you just looked at me and your pupils dilated—with fear."

"I'm not afraid," I say, but it's a blatant lie. I am afraid—terrified of the fact that he's walking away from me now after we nearly shared something so intimate. Am I too damaged for him to love me? "Liam, please," I whisper brokenly. "Come back. I'm sorry."

"Look," he says softly, squeezing my hand. "We've had a rough night. Maybe this just isn't the right time. Besides, I'm a little worried that my stitches might break open. I could feel them straining. I should probably let my leg heal first."

"Really?" I say skeptically. "Are you sure that's bothering you? Because it's the right time for me."

"There's also the fact that you're my patient," he says hesitantly. "I really shouldn't..."

"What the hell!" I say angrily, ripping my hand away from him and gesturing to the sofa. "And all this—haven't we already done enough for you to lose your job?"

"Yes," he says quietly. "But the truth is that I think we're doing this for the wrong reasons. After what we've been through tonight—this is just stress relief. It's understandable that we would want to lose ourselves in this and forget. But it's not right, Winter. It's just going through the motions."

"How can you say that?" I whisper in

horror.

"I want to have something real with you," Liam says. "I wanted this to be about you and me. I don't want you to be thinking about anyone else. I don't want you to be with me while remembering someone else. You can't just use *us* to erase something bad."

These words hit me like a stab to the heart. I try to conceal the hurt from my face. "I can't control my bad memories."

"Maybe you just need time," he tells me. "Maybe we were just moving way too fast. It's probably my fault. I'm sorry. If we did this now, you would just be using me to override someone else."

"I've had time," I say quietly, turning away from him to face the inside of the sofa. I wrap my arms around myself and stare forward blankly. "It's just the first time since..."

Tears begin streaming down my cheeks and I cannot finish my sentence. I try to remain very quiet and still so that he won't know that I'm crying. I feel so humiliated.

Liam places a hand on my waist, and the contact against my exposed skin makes me flinch. I try to hold my breath so that he won't feel my tears. I remain very still, praying that he'll go away.

"I have a large t-shirt that you can wear to sleep, if you want," he says kindly. "It's an old

Yankees jersey. It's very comfortable."

The fact that he is being so sweet causes more tears to slide across my nose in a veritable torrent. I would normally try to make a joke about actually being a Mets fan, but I haven't the energy. The idea of wearing his shirt to sleep sounds lovely—I still want to be close to him, but he seems so withdrawn. It feels like it's over between us.

"I have clean towels if you want to take a shower," Liam says softly. "In case you don't remember, the bathroom is the door near the entrance. Also, if you'd like to sleep in the bed, I could take the couch if that would make you more comfortable."

I wrinkle up my face at these words. I must be extremely repulsive to him if he doesn't even want to sleep in the same bed with me. It is especially painful due to the fact that I was really looking forward to cuddling with him and being held. Now, all these fantasies are shattered. I feel miserable and unwanted.

"Just..." Liam emits a small sigh of defeat. "It's been a rough night. I think we're both feeling a little vulnerable and not thinking straight. I just... I didn't want to take advantage of you."

The phrase causes my stomach to turn over in disgust. He's treating me like fragile glass. Like a child. I suppose I deserve it, because I certainly feel like both of those things at the moment.

"Let me know if there's anything you need. Goodnight, Winter."

As soon as his hand leaves my side, I silently release the breath I have been holding. I wait until I hear his footsteps walking away before I breathe in and let a small sob shake my shoulders. I can't believe that I dared to think I could be happy. Only a few minutes ago, I felt like I was in heaven. I felt like I was loved, or at least wanted. But now, I'm lonelier than ever. Even more so than when I was actually alone, in the middle of nowhere. I was so close to having something perfect. Something normal.

I really didn't need this little taste of all the things I'll never have.

It hurts so much. Far more than I thought it would. How long until I get over this? And where do I go from here? Liam's rejection stings and grates my insides in a much more personal way than Grayson's violence.

Of course, it would so happen that when I'm begging a man to touch me, he isn't interested. He has better things to do. Yet when I'm begging a man to stop... he doesn't.

Typical. That's just my luck.

I close my eyes and command my weary heart to sleep and forget.

Chapter Three

I am woken up by a brutal pounding in my head that could only be one thing: a wine hangover.

Why does wine always give the *worst* hangovers? I press both of my hands against my forehead to try to quell the dull throbbing. My body aches and feels sore all over. I am also rather weak, and I need to lie in place for a moment before I can even attempt to sit up. When I reach out to push myself off the bed, I am surprised to find that I'm not on a bed at all, but on a leather couch.

I open my eyes and feel around quickly to get a sense of my surroundings. There is a thin blanket draped over me that I don't remember at all. I am shocked to find that under the blanket, my chest is bare and I am mostly naked.

The previous evening comes rushing back

to me, and the memories make my head throb even more. I sigh and crane my neck to listen for sounds of Liam moving around the apartment. There is only silence. Maybe he's still asleep? I swing my legs off the side of the sofa, and wrap the blanket around me to form a makeshift dress. I move toward his bedroom and listen for the sounds of breathing.

"Liam?" I ask softly. Hearing no response, I move forward to touch the bed. I slide my hand over the comforter, and I discover that there is no one in the bed—and the sheets have been folded perfectly smooth. It's not even warm. He must have been up for a while.

Has he left the apartment? I am not aware of his schedule, and he might have needed to go to work today. I am a bit anxious at the thought that he might have abandoned me, but also relieved that he doesn't have to see the way I look right now. I can feel that the light makeup Carmen helped me put on the day before is smudged, and I am sure my hair needs to be brushed quite badly.

Thinking about Carmen makes my head pound harder. I remember the fact that I "broke up" with my only sister. The entire night feels like a bad dream. I move through the empty apartment toward the bathroom to freshen up. I keep one arm extended before me to feel out my surroundings, and one holding my blanket-dress up against my chest. I knock on the door lightly to make sure it isn't occupied.

"Liam?" I say a little more loudly. A ghastly thought strikes me as I imagine him lying on the bathroom floor, dead from having bled out from his bullet wound. I shake my head to clear the ridiculous thought. I just can't help worrying about him. I wish that I knew where he was—but even if he'd left a note, I wouldn't be able to read it. Wherever he is, I know that he'd rather be there than here with me anyway.

This is the thought that finally clears the fog from my mind and jumpstarts my day. I would like very much to get cleaned up and get out of Liam's apartment before he returns. After the humiliating night before, I would rather *not* see him again. I just need to take some time to figure out where to go, and how on earth I'll get there. Maybe a quick shower will help to lubricate my mind.

I am growing annoyed with this new landscape. It was very inconsiderate of Liam to

CLARITY

leave me to wake up alone in an empty apartment that I barely know. If he wanted to dump me after finding out that I was horrible in bed, there were better ways to go about doing so. After having hunted for what I hoped was a clean towel, and a bar of soap, I managed to scrub the makeup from my face and rinse my entire body. I was also embarrassingly forced to steal Liam's toothbrush. Nonetheless, after the difficult task of getting clean, I do feel much better and more clear-headed. I have also developed an epic escape plan for fleeing the city.

The only issue is that I can't seem to find my underwear.

I have spent several minutes crawling around Liam's coffee table on my hands and knees as I hunt for my bra and panties. This whole day has been one mortification after another. It doesn't help that my hands and knees are bruised and sore from falling on the cobblestoned ground last night. I didn't feel it back when there were almost equal parts wine and blood in my body, but it sure does suck the morning after. The only thing that protects me from completely losing my dignity is a healthy dose of anger. I utter small curses as I battle to figure out the layout of the land.

This must be exactly what a blind lioness feels like on the savannah as she prowls for scraps. When I bang into a piece of furniture for what must be the twentieth time, I release a frustrated

361

growl and decide to give up. I have already put on my skirt, but I now pull my blouse on without my bra, assuring myself that my coat will cover everything I'm wearing anyway. I just need some fresh air as soon as possible.

I move to the coat closet and retrieve my coat and purse hastily. As I slip my arms into the coat, and fasten it around me, I feel around on the ground for my shoes. Once I locate the discarded footwear, I hold the wall for balance as I slide my feet into them. Glad to have finally conquered the difficult task of getting dressed, I head to the exit, clutching my purse tightly in my hand and eager for my freedom. However, once I place my hand on the doorknob, a brilliant idea strikes me. I return to the coat closet and fish around for the coat that Liam was wearing last night. I hope that he hasn't decided to wear it again today. When my fingers encounter the precise woolen texture, I nearly jump for joy. I reach into the pocket and retrieve Grayson's metal pistol.

If I'm heading out into the world on my own, I'm going to need protection. This seems like it might do the trick.

I stuff the weapon into my own pocket and unlock the apartment door with more confidence. As I step into the hallway, it occurs to me that I have no idea where the elevator is. I was too focused on worrying about Liam's injury to notice which way we were going last night. I begin moving awkwardly in one direction, before I hesitate and head the other way.

A door in the hallway opens and someone steps out.

"So," says a woman with a distinctly New Jerseyan accent. It sounds like she's chewing gum and taking a moment to appraise me. "Are you the doctor's new girlfriend?"

I cringe at this question. "No," I respond. "I don't think so."

"Ah," she says, chewing her gum some more. "So you're doing the walk of shame, then?"

"Yes," I respond bitterly. "I suppose I am."

"What's he like in the sack?" asks the woman. "I've been trying to get Liam in bed since he moved in here, but I guess he likes 'em younger. He's *such* a hottie, no?"

"Look, lady," I say with annoyance. "I'm blind. Can you tell me where the fucking elevator is?"

"Oh, you got a mouth on you. Relax, honey, I was just curious. The elevator is that way."

"I can't exactly see where you're pointing," I tell her impatiently. I feel a rush of rage bubble up inside me, along with a sudden loathing for this woman. She is not a real threat, and certainly not worthy of the gun in my pocket, but I still experience a great urge to rip her face off. At least my inner lioness has found her claws.

"Just turn around and walk in the other direction," she tells me.

"Thanks," I say, glowering at her before I swivel to march down the hallway. I trail my hand along the wall, hoping that I'll notice the elevator buttons.

"Turn right!" shouts the woman. "The elevators are right there."

"Thanks!" I call back to her, a little uncomfortable with the fact that she has been staring at me walk down the hallway. I can't wait to get away from this city and all its crazy inhabitants.

I find the elevator button and push it, hoping that there will be braille on the inside of the elevator to indicate what to press for the lobby. That is, if the elevator *ever* arrives! I stand in place waiting for a full minute before I begin tapping my foot in annoyance. Another full minute passes, and I begin to boil with fury. I am sure that it is visible on me in some kind of red glow, or steam coming out of my ears. I continue to stand there, seething at the elevator and vigorously jabbing the *down* button until my phone rings. I am embarrassed to admit that all my anger instant leaves me and turns into hope as I rip my purse open and fish inside it for my phone. I answer it rapidly.

"Liam?" I say breathlessly into the phone.

"No, Helen. It's your father."

I am filled with a strange combination of disappointment and relief. "Hi, Dad," I say quietly into the phone.

"Darling, I'm so sorry for everything that's happened. I've been at the hospital all night with Carmen and it's just been madness." His voice is tired and drained. He pauses for a moment, as if trying to gain his composure. "It's good to hear your voice. Are you okay?"

"I'm fine," I tell him softly.

"And how is Liam? Heavens, child. Carmen said that he was shot!"

"It wasn't serious. He stitched it up last night. I think he's doing well."

"Thank goodness," my father says with a sigh. "I was so worried about you two, but I haven't had a spare moment to call. Oh, sweetheart. I never expected something like this to happen in a million years."

"I did," I mutter quietly.

"Grayson is a fine young man, and it's so upsetting to see him like this. I don't know what's gotten into the poor boy. I think it's just the pressure of the baby on the way and his work getting to him. He seems to have... cracked."

"No kidding," I murmur.

"Yes, well... I just wanted to apologize for all of this and tell you that it's safe to come home. We took Grayson to the emergency last night, but he kept muttering your name and saying that he was going to kill Liam. He didn't even seem to recognize Carmen, and he attacked a nurse. Yes— even with his injuries, he managed to attack someone. They had to sedate him, and he's been sent to a psychiatric facility. They're not sure what's wrong with him. Some kind of mental illness or breakdown."

"Oh," I say in response.

"Carmen says you warned her before the wedding but she didn't listen. Why didn't you tell me, darling?"

"I tried, but..." I shrug my shoulders limply. This all seems so pointless to discuss now.

"Helen, I am always here to listen to you. Carmen said you two girls had a fight? She's really upset about it. Will you please come home and make things better, darling? The poor girl is so distraught, and it's not healthy for her pregnancy."

A deep frown settles in my face. "Dad, can you please do me a favor?"

"Anything, dear."

"Go up to my room and put my computer into my backpack, along with the power cord and my phone charger. Also, please put some basic clothes into my suitcase. Some underwear and socks, a few pairs of pajamas, dresses, shirts, and jeans. And some shoes."

"Helen, please don't go off to the godforsaken middle of nowhere again! Do you need money? I have money for you. I can help you get your own place nearby. I could even live with you if you needed a hand with the chores—or heck, we can kick Carmen and Grayson out of the house and live here together."

"Dad..."

"Please don't be so bullheaded, sweetheart. Sometimes you remind me so much of your mother that it scares me. I'm an old man, and I can't lose you again for so many years, without a word. You're my favorite daughter. What do you say?"

I release a sigh. "Please, Dad. I need to get away. I just want to go home. To my home. Can you please do this for me? Leave the suitcase and my backpack on the front doorstep. I'll be over to pick it up shortly."

"Helen, won't you at least talk—"

The elevator dings to signify its arrival. "Gotta go, Dad. Thanks in advance." I hang up the phone and step forward into the elevator, which I can immediately tell is empty. I scan my finger over the buttons and I'm relieved to find braille beside each one. I hit the button for the lobby. I miserably lean against the side of the elevator, glad to finally be moving. My hangover has returned with full force, and my head is throbbing again. The idea of losing my family again causes tears to prick the back of my eyes—and I try not to think about Liam at all. I just know that it must be done. The elevator does not make any stops to collect other passengers on the way down, and I am grateful for the privacy.

When the doors open and the elevator announces that we have arrived at the lobby, I clear my throat and straighten myself before stepping out of the cabin. I listen for the sounds of the street, and head in the direction of freedom. People are bustling past me and the lobby is full of strange noises. I had forgotten how difficult it is to navigate in the busy downtown area. I hate crowds. People bump into me at least twice, and I haven't even reached the revolving doors. Finally, when my fingers do connect with the glass, it takes me a moment to figure out how to exit. The rotating doors seem to be on my left, and they are spinning so quickly that I'm quite certain I'm going to get chopped in half.

I am somehow able to dart into the rotating doors at the correct time, and dash out on cue as well. I sort of just allow my body to be pushed by the people around me who are rushing around and occasionally snapping at me or making grunts intended to make me feel guilty for not moving faster. I *really* hate crowds. When I am finally out on the busy street, it is even worse. People are moving past me in every direction, and I am overwhelmed by the commotion.

I feel like I am stuck between two colliding schools of fish, and being torn in both directions. I'm not sure whether I should follow the trout or the flounder. Or stand foolishly in the middle and wait for the piranhas that are chasing the fish to devour me.

"What the hell is wrong with you?" someone shouts. "Move!"

I turn to the man who said these words, because I assume that he's looking at me. "Can you please tell me where we are?" I ask him.

"Where the fuck do you think, you dumb bitch? Jesus." He pushes past me without giving me any information.

I stumble backward a little, clenching my teeth together disgust at his lack of manners. I am always unlucky enough to run into the worst sorts of people. Did I mention that I really, really hate crowds? I slip my hand into my pocket to feel the cool metal barrel of Grayson's gun. I doubt I'd ever use it, but it reassures me to know that it's there. It gives me a small sense of power.

"Are you okay, sweetie?" says an older woman who kindly takes my arm. "Can I help you?"

"I'm blind," I tell her immediately. "Could you please flag down a cab for me?"

"Certainly, dear!" she says at once, moving to the side of the road. *"Hey, buddy!"* she shouts loudly, before letting out a loud whistle. "Over here!"

I smile at her spunk. A moment later, she is taking my arm and guiding me toward the cab.

"Here you are, sweetie. Be safe!"

"Thank you so much, ma'am," I tell her kindly as I move to climb into the cab. I am precisely halfway into the vehicle, with one of my feet resting on the ground, and one of my butt cheeks already making contact with the seat, and I am about to slide in further when a strong hand clamps around my arm and pulls me out of the cab. I gasp when I find myself stumbling into a large man's body. I try to pull away hastily, but I am not used to walking in heels and I find myself tripping over my own feet in my panic. However, it would be impossible to fall because the man effortlessly maintains a strong grip on me.

"Let go of me," I demand, trying to twist away like I learned in my judo lessons. I am surprised when he counters my move, and I fearfully stuff my free hand into my pocket. Before I can touch the gun, the large man grabs both of my wrists.

"Winter?" he says with worry. "Where are you going?"

Relief courses through me at the recognizable voice and I stop struggling. Only then do I notice the familiarity of Liam's hands, and the fact that he is holding several large shopping bags which brush against my leg. I would have noticed these details earlier, but I was in too much distress about being caught in a vast swarm of humans.

"Get off her, you sicko perv!" shrieks the

little old lady from earlier. She must have noticed Liam pull me out of the cab and rushed back to save me. She pummels him with an item that I imagine must be her purse, because it makes a loud *thwack* which causes Liam to flinch.

"It's okay!" I tell the old woman kindly, smiling at her efforts. "Thank you for your help, but I know this man. He's a friend."

"Oh! My apologies, dear," says the lady with slight embarrassment, before scurrying away.

"Ouch," Liam says, rubbing his arm. "At least she didn't hit my leg. I seem to get attacked a whole lot when I'm around you, Winter."

"I'm sorry," I tell him, reaching forward to touch his wounded arm to see if there has been any real damage. When he laughs lightly, I am relieved to see that he has not been hurt in the slightest.

"You vaunt ride or no?" snaps the annoyed cab driver with a thick Russian accent.

"Yes!" I tell the driver. "Just a second. You can start running the meter." Everything is so chaotic with so many people around—there doesn't seem to be a spare moment. I turn back to Liam and look up to where I believe his face is. I am not sure if I'm glad that he caught me, so that I have a chance to say goodbye, or if I'm upset that I now need to feel the pain of ripping myself away. Either way, my heart flutters in my chest. This is not going to be easy. "I'm going home," I tell him.

"Home?" he repeats. "To your dad's? I don't think that's safe."

"No, no. I'm just going to pick up my suitcase from my dad's and head to a bus station to go back to New Hampshire." I try very hard to keep my face expressionless and to remain focused. I feel a terrible ache stirring in the pit of my chest, and I realize that I really am going to miss him. I shake the emotions away briskly. "Thanks for everything," I say softly, before pulling away and moving back into the cab.

"Winter!" Liam says, following after me quickly and taking ahold of me before I can fully enter the cab once again. "Why? Why are you leaving me?"

His grip on me is tight and desperate. It almost feels like he wants me to stay. This idea is silly, but the thought almost makes me want to cry. I need to dig up my anger and bitterness to keep me strong. "This isn't working out between us," I tell him coldly, "I think you should date a healthy woman. Someone who isn't blind—but more importantly, someone who isn't fucked up in the head."

He seems stunned by my words, and he abruptly releases me. "That's not fair," he says. "You're just upset. You can't leave like this or you'll be filled with regrets. Let's just take five minutes to relax and sit down and talk about this. After all we've been through, you owe me that, at least!"

"I don't owe anyone anything," I inform him stubbornly. "Goodbye, Liam."

He intercepts me and blocks me from entering the cab. "What about your eyes?" he demands. "You can't let petty issues between us ruin this opportunity for you!"

"Find another candidate," I tell him quietly. "I like myself just the way I am. I don't need to improve for anyone." *Not even you,* I think inwardly.

"I don't need you to improve for me, Winter. I just want to make things easier. I just you to be happy."

"Please step aside so I can enter the cab," I tell Liam with a shaking voice.

"No," he says firmly. "I'm sorry. I'm not letting you walk out of my life. Not like this."

"You need cabby or no?!" the driver shouts.

"Yes!" I say while Liam simultaneously says, "No!"

"Get in or I leave!" the cab driver says irately. "Other customer waiting."

"I'm getting in," I say frantically, trying to maneuver around Liam. For the first time, I am strangely aware of how tall and large he is—he seems to be blocking the entire doorway. The shopping bags hanging from his arm are taking up a lot of space, too. I am growing frantic as I try to push past him. I know that I need to get away this instant to save myself from future humiliation and grief. "Liam, please!" I whisper.

"You said you trusted me," he says, and his voice is full of hurt. "Why would you want to leave?"

I turn my eyes to the ground, feeling guilty and miserable. "I just need to go. Now."

"Is girl getting in car?" the cab driver demands

"She isn't. Thanks, but we no longer require your services," Liam says to the driver, guiding me back away from the vehicle and slamming the door. The car immediately pulls away.

Now, I really do feel like crying. "Liam," I say softly as I stand in the street and struggle to fight back my tears. "It was really hard for me to hail that taxi."

"We had one bad night, Winter. *One* bad night. I know that your first instinct is to run away, but I really care about you. I'm not giving up so easily." He moves closer to me, and I can hear the rustling as he dumps his shopping bags down right in the middle of the street. A car honks at us, but Liam ignores this and places his hands gently around my shoulders. "I know that you don't really want to leave. You just got here. At least *try* to give us a chance? I want you to stay more than anything."

374

"You could've fooled me," I mumble under my breath.

"What?" he asks.

I'm feeling restless and confined and emotional. I pull myself away from Liam and walk away quickly. Unfortunately, I walk into the traffic. A car horn blares fiercely at me, and I am quite certain I am about to get bulldozed, but I keep moving forward anyway. I run a little faster, until I find myself in the middle of another stampede of people. I put my hands up to protect my face as the beasts rush by, heading with determination to their destination.

"Winter!" Liam shouts as he follows me. "Are you crazy? You're going to get yourself killed."

I hold my breath as the mob flocks around me, overwhelmed by the deafening noise, movement, and suffocating smog. The pollution is thick and tangible, stinging my eyes and throat. There are *so* many people. I haven't been out in the middle of a jam-packed metropolis in years, and the experience is terrifying. It does not seem safe, logical, or healthy to cram so many individuals into such a small space. I am craving the fresh mountain air and a drink of clear water. When Liam catches up to me, he places his hand on my back and says my name.

I turn around and bury myself into his arms, seeking the shielding power of his embrace.

I hate myself for being so weak. "I'm not cut out for this, Liam," I tell him quietly. "I'm just so worthless here. I can't even do basic things like cross the street. It's so loud. I have no idea what's going on all around me. I just want to be in a simple place, where I don't need to rely on anyone."

"I know that you're scared to trust people," he says, placing a hand gently in my hair, "but just bear with me for a little longer. I will try my best to give you the independence that you deserve. More independence than you've ever had before. The life you were living was full of fear and restriction. It was peaceful, but it was lonely. Just try to be a little brave, for a little longer, and you could have so much more. You can have a life that's rich and full of joy—any sort of life you choose."

"I don't want to be a burden on you," I tell him. "I don't want to... need you."

"It is my honor to be needed by you," he tells me. He places a kiss on my forehead. "I need you, Winter. I need you to need me. Just put a little faith in me, and let me take care of you. I promise you that you won't need to rely on anyone for much longer."

I shift uncomfortably. Part of me is desperate to cling to any reason to stay with him—but another, wiser part knows that leaving is the safest route. "I don't know..."

CLARITY

"You're the most important person in my life," he tells me quietly. "I need you to stay."

My eyebrows knit together in confusion. "That's bullshit," I tell him plainly, thinking about the night before. Damn this man and his mixed signals. "Maybe you want me to stick around for the operation, but you don't actually want *me.*"

"You're wrong," Liam says as he places a finger under my chin to lift it slightly. He places a demanding kiss directly on my lips. He slips a hand under my coat to pull me more tightly against him. He kisses all the fight out of me, and leaves no question of his intent. He kisses me until tears tumble from my eyes and I surrender to his touch.

"I want you," he says softly, once he pulls away. "I want you more than I've ever wanted anyone. I want you in every possible way. Don't you dare tell me to find a fucking *healthy* woman. You're healthy. In your heart and soul, you're the purest, wisest person I've ever met. You see more than anyone can dream to see. I wanted you long before I'd even met you."

I am left standing there speechless and embarrassed with a tear-soaked face.

"Come on," he says softly, as he takes my arm and gently guides me back across the street, weaving between the slow-moving traffic. "I got you a few things so you'll be more comfortable. Some clothes, a toothbrush, and a razor."

"That was thoughtful of you," I say

quietly.

"I couldn't find a braille computer, but I'll go pick up your old one as soon as I can. I'm on call at the hospital later, so I could grab it before work."

"Thanks," I whisper.

Liam pauses to retrieve the shopping bags that he had dropped in the street earlier. I'm surprised that they are still there, but when he thanks someone, I realize that the doorman of his building was taking care of them for him.

"I'm sorry about last night," Liam tells me as he guides me into the revolving doors. "I know it was a huge mess. Maybe let's go for breakfast and talk about it?"

I only then realize that I am quite hungry. "Sure," I say with a grateful nod.

"Oh!" he says, as we enter the busy lobby. "I nearly forgot. I also got this." He digs into his bags and retrieves a small box, which he places in my hands.

"What's this?" I ask him curiously. I make a face of puzzlement as I run my hands over the box.

He chuckles to himself as though something is extremely funny before leaning forward to whisper into my ear. "It's a box of twelve condoms."

"Liam!" I shriek, shoving the box back at him hastily before blushing furiously. "Why would you make me hold that in public?"

"Why would *you* doubt whether I want you?" he demands as he guides me into the elevator.

"That was uncalled for," I say glumly, but I am fighting back a smile.

"Don't worry," he says as he pushes me against the wall. "No one was looking. And no one's looking now."

When his lips descend to mine again, I realize how close I was to losing him. I feel a lump of emotion in my throat as I acknowledge my self-sabotaging and fearful behavior. This really does need to change. I really do need to become braver and learn how to live again. "If you didn't stop me from getting into that cab..." I whisper.

"It doesn't matter," he tells me. "I would have gone after you."

Chapter Four

"*Glaucoma is often called the 'silent thief of sight' because it destroys the eyes slowly, causing permanent harm long before any noticeable vision loss. The disease is mysterious, for although Glaucoma has been known since antiquity, modern researchers still struggle to understand its causes. While some treatments can stall the loss of vision, there is no cure, and it remains leading cause of blindness all over the world. Patients with glaucoma usually experience damage to the optic nerve, the cable behind the eyes which connect them to the brain...*"

I suppress a yawn as the monotonous drone from the audiobook lulls me to sleep. I have spent all day snooping through Liam's old laptop and trying to learn more about him. I have little else to do while I wait for him to finish his day at work and retrieve my computer from my dad's. Unfortunately, instead of finding something scandalous like kinky erotica, I keep stumbling upon things that reaffirm that he actually is a good boy. For example, his boring medical textbooks.

Does the man ever have fun? I know he has some of my books in paperback, along with a few other fiction titles on his shelves, but I can't determine what they are. They could be extremely interesting.

It's very difficult and frustrating to try and snoop in a man's apartment when you can't see any of his stuff. There could be disturbing paintings on the walls depicting graphic murder scenes—or any other telltale signs that I'm dating a serial killer—and I would have absolutely no inkling.

My imagination is running away with me, and I dearly miss having my computer nearby to jot down my thoughts. Liam said that I could use his to write, but it's just not the same. This isn't mainly due to the lack of accessibility features, but to my emotional attachment to the little machine. I never realized how important my computer was to me until this forced separation. Even on the days when I was at my dad's and unable to work due to Grayson's nearness, I was comforted by knowing my computer was nearby in case it was needed. I even kept it in the bed with me while I slept, like an electronic teddy bear.

For so many years, my computer was my only friend. I suppose that if I could bring one thing to a desert island, it would be that computer. And some sort of portable, infinite power source.

I suppose I'm going a little crazy. Being

stuck in a new environment and unable to work is making me restless. I was never the type of girl to do nothing and wait around for a man to come home from work. Even if he is a doctor—even if the ideal thing to do would be to put on a little dress and prepare a sweet-smelling dinner for his return. That's just not me. The very idea makes me ill. I have my own work to do.

Besides, I'd probably burn the building down trying to cook in the unfamiliar kitchen.

I shift onto my back as I lie on Liam's bed, ignoring the narration about various types of glaucoma. At breakfast, he insisted that I sleep in the bed from now on, for he felt uncomfortable about me taking the couch. We actually had a really nice conversation over waffles, and sorted out a lot of the awkwardness from the night before. I am now wearing his old baseball jersey as I nestle between the sheets, and it's rather soft and perfect for sleeping. I probably shouldn't be napping in the middle of the day; he did give me lots of options of things I could do with the spare time while he was out. He gave me James' phone number, so that I could call the judo master to take me to the dojo and train. He said there was also a gym downstairs in the building which we could use.

I might have liked to practice some judo, but I won't have suitable attire until Liam returns with my suitcase. Isn't it funny that we have to wear specific clothing for self-defense training? A sports bra and athletic gear. I never seem to be wearing appropriate clothing whenever I get attacked.

I wonder if I would have been tougher last night if I had been wearing the right clothing. Maybe I leave all my toughness in the sports bra, and when I take it off, I go back to weak old me. I wonder if the solution is to wear the sports bra forever, or whether I should try training in ordinary clothes. Does anyone train while wearing high heels and a skirt? It seems to make sense to me that if you're going to get attacked while wearing those things, you should also train in them.

Maybe such feminine and compromising clothing should never be worn. Maybe I should always wear athletic gear. Or maybe I should just never go out in public. Maybe I should go home.

I sigh at these thoughts, and shift my body to turn off the annoying audiobook. I'd rather lie in bed and paint my own stories across my mind. I might not be able to work at the moment, but at least I can prepare for writing; I can play the ending of the book over and over in my mind until it's perfect.

I try to do this for a few minutes, but my thoughts run away with me. I keep thinking of a book I'd love to write called *Snowfire*. I'm not sure where I heard the word, but I think it's a beautiful oxymoron, and would make for a great romantic suspense. I would love to create a character based on Liam. I wonder if he'd help give me feedback before I send it to my publisher? I've never had anyone that I trusted enough to read my writing before it was finished and bound in a book. At that point, there's very little anyone can say or do to improve it.

The real magic happens in the process. Could Liam be part of my process? Could he contribute to my work and be healthy for my career? I could try my best to be good for his—it is the reason I'm staying in this congested, stuffy city, after all. Well, it's part of the reason. My mind wanders again, imagining the perfect relationship where both parties feed each other's success; is it possible? Could we really support each other and make each other larger instead of dragging each other down and sucking the other person dry?

All the relationships I've witnessed have been parasitic. One person would bleed the other person of all their energy and love so that they could perform better in their own life, without any consideration for the other person's fulfillment. The only exception to this was my parents—but of course, my mother died. She left my father brokenhearted, and our whole family easily crumbled without her. She was our pillar of strength. We all leaned on her so much that we didn't even realize how quickly we would fall flat on our faces without her. We also seem to have lost all connection to each other.

I realize that I'm making the classic writer's mistake of dwelling too much on own life. I have been way too absorbed in my own story. This hardly ever happens to me, but it's been a huge issue lately. This is another reason I prefer to be solitary—when there's too much drama in my own life, it really distracts my mind from my work.

It's a great problem for writers, trying to maintain focus. Sometimes you feel inspired to work on something entirely different from what you should be working on. Sometimes you're even forced to live your own story instead of contemplating and creating a better one.

When my phone rings, I jump slightly. I move to reach for it, eager to hear Liam's voice— hopefully with news of my computer. I turn over in the bed, and feel around for the place where I dropped my phone. It takes me a few seconds to find it, but I quickly fumble to answer and place it against my ear.

"Hello!" I say in a pleasant voice.

There is only static and a strange rustling on the other end of the line.

"Liam?" I say with confusion.

The sound of heavy breathing filters through the phone.

I sit up in bed, beginning to feel worried and anxious. My body grows tense. "Who is this?" I ask again.

"Do you think I'm evil, Helen?"

Hearing the voice from my nightmares causes me to sit up even straighter. I feel as though ice water has been poured down my spine.

"I never wanted to hurt you. My sweet Helen. I don't know why I did any of those things. I just couldn't control myself. Do you think I'm evil? I must be evil. What other explanation is there?"

My lips part slightly as I look around the bedroom nervously, paralyzed in a sort of terror. I know that Grayson is not here with me, but I feel as though he might be. I am suddenly very aware of how alone I am in this apartment.

"I'm a monster," he says quietly. "I know that now. They said there's something wrong with my brain, but I don't believe them. I'm just evil. Pure evil. The things that I've done to you... they were more than just criminal. They were sinful. Do you believe in Satan?"

"How did you get this number?" I finally manage to ask. It's not the forceful demand I intended; my voice leaves my throat hesitantly, in a feeble squawk.

"They told me I needed to call you and apologize," Grayson says. "They said I needed to make peace with you and myself in order to get better. Carmen gave me the number and the nurse dialed for me. They gave me some privacy to talk to you. But they're all idiots; I can't make peace. You should stay far away from me, Helen. If I ever see you again, I will do things to you that you could never imagine. I will do far worse to than I've ever done before. I want to take you—in the worst possible way. I want to feel you bleeding and crying and screaming. I can't control the monster inside me."

My entire body is seized by a spasm of dread. I feel a great pressure in my chest, and a sudden inability to breathe. The muscles in my arms and legs constrict until the tension causes me pain. Even though they are just words, I can imagine them so clearly that it is almost as though he is right here, doing those things to me now. It seems to be too much for my brain to handle, and it has hit the pause button on my entire central nervous system.

"There's something special about you," Grayson whispers. "Only you, Helen. You make me want to do things I would never do. I think it's your innocence. It hangs around you like a cloud. Like an aura of light, glowing around you. I have tried to figure out what it is, Helen, and I think I finally know. It must be innocence. Only innocence could be so beautiful. So pale and fragile that it shouldn't exist. Like fine porcelain. Like precious glass. I wanted to break it before anyone else could—but I didn't succeed. It's still there."

There's a pause on the line, filled only with his ragged breathing.

"You're still innocent," he whispers, "and I still want to break you."

I finally remember how to breathe, and I remove the phone from my ear. I press the button to end the call, but it takes me a moment to find it with my shaking hands. I take several deep breaths as I lower my head to the pillow. I curl my knees up to my chest and wrap my arms around myself. It has never taken such a great effort just to breathe. I can feel the tension in my shoulders and thighs as my body feels strangely stiff and locked into place.

All my beautiful thoughts have been chased away.

I can't think about work anymore. I can't think about anything. I don't want to think about anything. If I ponder his words, it will drive me insane. There is no sense to them; they are just ramblings of a madman. But more terrifying is the fact that there might be some logic in them. What if I did take a moment to think about what he said, and I understood him?

What if it really is my fault? What if I brought out the worst in him? What if I do the same to Liam? What if that's my curse, and no one will ever love me? What if there's just something about me that people can't stand? What if I really do have this strange aura he's talking about?

All I know is that I'm going to have to change my number again. And maybe my name.

Maybe I should assume an entirely new identity.

Maybe I should go home. Maybe I should find a new home, even further away.

Maybe I should just...

Maybe...

Chapter Five

"Helen. My sweet Helen. You're an angel. Such fragile innocence..."

A hand slides gently over my hip.

I instantly snap awake, and grab the person's wrist. My heart begins pounding fiercely.

"Whoa," Liam says softly. "It's just me."

Sharp pain shoots through my chest as my heart struggles to go from a peaceful resting state to instant fight mode. I have to remind myself to breathe as my body feels paralyzed with fear. My hand is still clenched tightly around his wrist. "Liam?" I ask nervously, unable to relax my fist.

"Yes. Who else would it be?"

I let my head fall back onto the pillow and release him, pressing a hand against my racing heart. It takes me a moment before the pain subsides and I can catch my breath. My heart is beating so uncontrollably that I swear I can hear the pounding in my ears. "I just... I had a bad dream," I tell him weakly.

"What happened?" he asks me, slipping his arm around my waist.

I swallow in embarrassment at the answer. "The same thing that always happens." His touch is slightly comforting, and I try to let my body relax. This extreme anxiety can't be healthy. It never used to happen to me when I was younger, but lately, my heart seems to behave like an engine being pushed to the limit whenever I'm given a fright.

Liam moves closer to me so that the warmth of his body is pressed along my back. "I'm sorry," he says tenderly. "Do you want to tell me about your dream?"

After a moment's silence, I bite down into my lip. "It was worse this time. Just like he promised it would be."

"He promised?" Liam asks.

I reach up to run my fingers through my hair as I release a shuddering breath. "Grayson called me earlier. He was told to apologize and make peace. That's not what he did."

"Oh, Winter," Liam says, holding me closer and pressing a kiss against my neck.

"I think that I should probably go home," I whisper, turning so that my cheek rests against his face. "There are too many people here. I can hear your neighbors through the walls, but at home it's just quiet. I can't take this. I can't even take a goddamn phone call or you touching me without jumping out of my skin."

Liam kisses my cheek before resting his head against mine. "I've been thinking about you all day. I was thinking about what you said about your sister. That you were looking for a reason to stay. I spoke to Owen about my ideas, and he helped me make a plan. I want to be the one to give you a reason to stay."

A tired smile touches my lips. "That's sweet, but—"

"No buts," Liam says, kissing my lips to cut off my sentence. "Give me two weeks. If I can't give you tons of great reasons to stay in that time, I'll drive you home myself."

I cuddle closer against him. "Deal. Then I get to give you reasons to stay in the forest with me."

He laughs lightly. "You think I should sell my apartment and run away with you?"

"Definitely," I tell him. "We could find a little cave somewhere and become cave-people. You could grow a huge beard and wield a gigantic club."

"As long as you're there, it sounds charming," Liam says, nuzzling my neck. "I'm in a really great mood tonight."

"Oh? Why's that?"

"You know the last time I came home from work and there was a pretty girl in my bed, wearing my t-shirt?"

"I don't know. A few weeks?"

"Never."

I make a skeptical sound. "I don't believe you," I say with a lifted eyebrow.

"It's true," he assures me. "I also have some really good news that might cheer you up."

"Oh?"

"I stopped by your dad's and picked up your computer," he tells me.

I sigh with relief, immediately turning over to give him a hug. "Thank you," I say softly. "That does make me feel better."

"I also picked up all your stuff. I talked to your dad a little, and he gave me a gift for you." Liam moves away slightly to retrieve something, and I miss his body heat for the moment he isn't pressed against me.

When he returns, I find myself clinging to him and quickly grow annoyed with myself for being so needy. *Get a grip,* I tell myself—but he's so comfortable that I ignore this command and nestle closer to him anyway. I find that he's sliding a piece of paper into my hand.

"What's this?" I ask him curiously.

"A sealed envelope for you," he informs me, "from your dad."

"Why did he bother sealing the envelope? You're just going to have to open it and tell me what's inside," I say with frustration. I hate the fact that I need to depend on him like this.

"I know what's inside," Liam says quietly. "It's a check for five hundred thousand dollars."

I am motionless for a moment, and then I burst out laughing. "No, seriously," I tell Liam, pressing the envelope back into his hand. "You have to open this and read it for me."

"Winter, I'm being dead serious here. Your dad gave me that check for you, and told me to let you know that he hopes you'll use it to stay in the neighborhood."

I stare at Liam with my mouth slightly open in surprise. "Really?"

"He says he can get more if you need it. Just give him a call."

"Are you—no way—are you kidding me?" I mumble, tripping over my words. I pull away from him slightly and wave the envelope between us. "Do you seriously mean to say that I am holding half a million dollars in my hand right now?"

"Yep," Liam says cheerfully.

"Holy crap," I say in wonder. "You'd think the envelope would be heavier."

"I was hoping you'd be more excited," Liam says in disappointment. "If half a million dollars can't impress you and make you speak in capital letters, then I doubt that I can ever make you excited about anything."

"You want capital letters? Just give a

minute." I sit up in the bed and prepare myself as though I am getting into character. I stretch my shoulders and neck and take a deep breath. "HOLY CRAP!" I say again with all the enthusiasm I can muster. I hold the check up with a surprised look on my face. "Ohmigod, ohmigod! I'm rich!"

Liam erupts into a fit of laughter at my performance.

"Do you find me more attractive now?" I ask, bringing the envelope to my chest and smiling mischievously at him. "Does my big check make up for the fact that I don't have big boobs?"

"You were already devastatingly beautiful," he tells me in a low voice, "but the money doesn't hurt."

"Yeah, sure," I mumble, skeptical at his compliment. But somehow, acting excited actually did make me feel more excited about the situation. "How was that?" I ask Liam. "Capital letters and even some exclamation marks."

"It was perfect," he says, shifting his body so that his head rests in my lap.

"Any thoughts on what you'll do with your newfound wealth?"

"Breast implants," I answer immediately.

"What?" he responds in shock. "But…"

"I'm kidding," I assure him. "I probably won't even cash it." I pause for a moment, running my fingers through his hair. "What would you do if someone handed you a check like that?"

"I'd probably put it toward starting a private practice with Owen," Liam answers quickly. "It's our biggest dream, but it might be a while before we can get there."

"That sounds really nice," I tell him. "It must be great to work with your best friend—especially someone as fun as he is."

"You'd be surprised. Owen is actually very professional in the workplace. Speaking of which! I have some more good news for you."

"Hmm?"

"Owen and I pulled some strings and called in some favors, and we were able to move your surgery dates up. So if you come in tomorrow for prep and some tests, you could have some vision by the end of the week."

"Wow," I say softly. "That's very soon."

"I figured I have to work quickly to impress you. I only have two weeks, after all."

"That would definitely impress me, but I don't know if I'm ready."

"Just trust me," Liam says. "Things are going to get better from now on—in every way." He pauses. "You should cash that check. Your dad really loves you. He doesn't want you to leave."

"Yes, well... I'm not sure this is the way to get me to stay," I say awkwardly, leaning over to place the check on the bedside table. "Although it would really improve my standard of living if I

396

went home. I could afford to have a bottle of wine more than once every two weeks. Maybe I could even get slightly more expensive wine."

"That's all?" Liam asks in disbelief. He shakes his head, which I feel against my thigh. "Five hundred thousand dollars, and you only want to get better wine?"

"And better food," I say with a deep nod. "Money and luxuries don't really mean much to me. I grew up with plenty of both. The things I really want—they can't be purchased. But I guess it would be nice if I was no longer starving."

"Aha! You admit it. You were starving."

"No!" I say, trying to cover up my mistake. "I meant figuratively. I was a starving artist."

"Winter, I saw your cupboards. You were actually starving."

"Okay. Maybe a little." I sigh in memory of how boring my food choices were. "There certainly weren't any red velvet cupcakes."

"Then stay here," Liam urges me. "Stay here and have all the red velvet cupcakes you want. Why would you go back to that kind of life? Why would you have chosen that in the first place?"

I shrug my shoulders gently. "I wanted to punish myself."

"For what?"

"I don't know," I mumble, pausing to look

around in the darkness. I pull my lips tightly together before a sadistic smile comes to my face. "For being innocent, I suppose. Liam... do you think I'm innocent?"

"Hmm," he says thoughtfully. "Yes. I mean, I know that you've seen things, and been through a lot—but you still seem to be above all this. Untouched."

"What does that mean?" I ask him in confusion.

"You're just..." Liam sighs and turns to places a kiss against my thigh, at the spot where his t-shirt ends and my skin begins. "You're the most innocent girl I know—in a really wicked sort of way."

This answer pleases and puzzles me at the same time. I touch his arm, running my hand up and down the contours of his muscles. "How do I stop?"

"Stop what?"

"Being innocent," I say softly. "Is it something I can get rid of? Does someone have to take it from me?"

"Where is this coming from, Winter?"

I hesitate and shift uncomfortably. "Grayson said—"

"Why are you listening to that cocksucking piece of shit?" Liam asks.

I blink in surprise at his language. "Whoa."

"Sorry," he says as he sits up. "That guy is just really pissing me off. I still haven't gotten my car fixed and my leg has been hurting like a bitch all day. Now I come home and hear that he's planting shit in your head?"

The tone in Liam's voice is harsh and angry, like I've never heard it before. I find myself stunned and unable to respond. I do appreciate the fact that he's angry in my defense...

"I'm just sick of him," Liam says angrily. "This isn't my world—I'm not used to this crap. Isn't life hard enough without worrying about being in physical danger? I have to worry about my mortgage, loans, and my career—you can't even get across the street—"

"Hey," I interrupt in a prideful way. "I can too cross the street. I was just in a rush earlier."

"We just don't need this. I don't need to get shot at, and you don't need him tormenting you. We have to permanently erase that man from your life."

"I do need to change my phone number," I say softly in agreement as I lie back down on the bed.

"Fuck him," Liam says again angrily. "Nothing can take away your innocence. It's an essential quality of who you are—something that exists deep on the inside. All the wounds that others inflict on you are only skin-deep. They can't even scratch the surface of your soul. You're pure.

Even if darkness surrounds you, you'll always remain innocent."

"I don't know if that's a good thing," I tell him. "Doesn't innocent mean weak and vulnerable? Doesn't it mean stupid? And how can I be pure? I wanted to kill Grayson. Doesn't that make me vindictive?"

"That was one moment—a fleeting thought. I have seen the way you live your life. You don't focus on the pursuit of pleasure. You aren't selfish or greedy," Liam says, pausing slightly. "Trust me, I know. I'm selfish and greedy. I act only in my best interests."

I frown. "How can you say that about yourself? It isn't true. You've done so much for me."

"Everything I've ever done has been in my best interests," Liam admits. He moves to lie down beside me and places his hand on my stomach. "But you're not like that, Winter. You know it's true. There's something precious and pure within you, like a flawless diamond. That's why you hide away and try so hard to protect yourself from the world. You can't let anyone take that away from you."

My eyebrows knit together as I consider his words. "You have a very distorted perception of me, Liam. I'm not nearly as great as you think I am."

"You're probably way better," he says,

sliding over me to place a kiss on my nose. "I'm only going off a few dates, a few books, and a few long conversations. I've probably only seen the tip of the iceberg."

"So I'm a pure, innocent iceberg with a diamond in me," I say with annoyance. "No wonder my life sucks. No one can see that I'm just a girl."

"I do see that," he says, playfully pinching my side, "a skinny girl who needs to eat! Come on. Let's have dinner. I got some Thai takeout. But if you prefer, I could cook something for you."

"You can cook?" I say in surprise. My own kitchen skills are sorely limited.

"Of course," he says proudly. "It seems that you're the one who needs to learn more about me. Haven't you noticed yet? I'm not your average bachelor."

Chapter Six

"Would you like your coffee refilled, miss?"

I look up from my computer in surprise. I was so absorbed in the story that I hadn't noticed the waitress approaching. "No," I tell her, "but do you happen to know the time?"

"It's almost noon," she informs me.

"Oh! Thanks." I grab my backpack and begin stuffing my computer into it roughly. "I have to get going."

"Is a friend or family member sick?" asks the waitress with concern.

I have been sitting in the hospital café and working for a few hours. The waitress has been very friendly and sweet, and has kept me adequately pumped full of caffeine.

"Actually, it's for me," I tell her shyly as I sling my backpack over my shoulder. "I'm completely blind, but this crazy doctor thinks that he can give me the ability to see."

"Wow!" the waitress says happily. "That's awesome. Why don't you seem more excited?"

Why does everyone keep asking me that? I inwardly wonder. I hesitate before responding. "I guess I don't want to get my hopes up in case it doesn't work out. If I don't expect too much, I can't be too deeply disappointed."

"You're a pessimist," the waitress says with a laugh. "That's not healthy. You're going to be disappointed in life whether you get your hopes up or not. You can't fool yourself into wanting something less by pretending that you aren't excited."

I lift my eyebrows at this surprising bit of wisdom.

"It's like that feeling," the waitress explains, "when you start dating someone and the relationship is new. Even if things are perfect, you could be miserable and expect it to go horribly wrong, like it always does. Maybe it will fail—but even if it does—not allowing yourself to enjoy it when things are good only robs you of happiness. Joy is something you need to feel, and it's not any less joyful if it's temporary. If those happy moments at the beginning are all you have, you need to let go and just hope for the best. Imagine the best. Otherwise, you ruin all the good moments by focusing on the possibility of losing them or being hurt. You can't go through life like that."

"That... makes a lot of sense," I say in wonder. "I wish I could be more optimistic. I think too many horrid things have happened in my life for me to be positive like that."

"No way," the waitress says. "It's not about your past or your former experiences. The possibility for an amazing outcome is always just as likely as a horrible one. If you only dwell on the worst possible outcomes, it will take away your ability to create happy memories in the moment and sabotage your future. You need to let go of your fear. You need to let yourself be excited."

"You're so sweet," I tell her thankfully. "I need a friend like you."

The waitress laughs again. "My name's Krista. I work here almost every day, so feel free to stop by and chat whenever you need a fresh perspective."

"Thanks," I tell her softly, giving her a smile before turning to leave. I paid for my coffee ages ago, but I am now wishing I had left a better tip to show my gratitude. As I move through the hospital, following Liam's directions, I consider the waitress's words. Have I really allowed myself to get excited about anything in my life, lately? I haven't truly allowed myself to really believe that things could work out with Liam. Even in the best of moments, I do hold on to that lingering fear that something could go easily go wrong, and probably will very soon.

I have been sabotaging myself.

For a second, I pause in the middle of the hospital halls. I temporarily forget Liam's instructions. I squint with realization as I take a moment to regret my pessimistic thinking. Things aren't really that bad. I have a career that I absolutely love, and my new book is coming along quite well. I am not rich, but I am self-sufficient enough with money that I don't think I need to cash my dad's check—but if I needed money in an emergency, it's nice to know I have a backup plan. Grayson is gone from my life—hopefully for good—and my health is looking to improve. I have begun practicing martial arts, and I might even be able to see soon. Even being able to see a tiny amount would be life changing! To top it all off, I have a budding romance with a really wonderful, intelligent guy.

I smile, realizing that I have a lot to be thankful for. Maybe if I can only change my thinking, everything could get better. Maybe Liam will be my happily ever after. Maybe I'll be a famous, successful writer. Maybe I'll be able to have a family someday. All I need to do is keep moving forward and accept the help that's being offered to me. I just have to put myself in destiny's hands and let her take care of me. For once, maybe she will.

I begin walking again with renewed

purpose until a little ding alerts me to the location of the elevators. I alter my path and move quickly toward the sound of heavy doors sliding open. I cram my body into the cabin along with several other people. Earlier today, Liam gave me a ride to the hospital, but I had to keep myself busy with my writing while he saw his other patients. Now, it's my turn, and I'm a little nervous. People are chattering all around me, but I can't seem to focus on their conversations. When we arrive at the third floor, I exit the elevator and turn right—at least I think Liam said to go right—and head down the hallway.

I listen closely for the sounds of people talking, trying to determine whether I'm in the ophthalmology area. I hear a pair of women's voices and move closer to them, only to discover that they are talking about how annoyed they are with their husbands.

"He does absolutely nothing all day, and he expects me to cook and clean for him like some 50s housewife. Excuse me? I make more money than he does."

"At least he isn't sleeping with his secretary," the other woman grumbles. "And the bastard thinks I don't know!"

"You have to leave him."

This conversation doesn't help to situate me much, other than to inform me that I might be in some sort of waiting area filled with extremely bored women. I hope that I won't be forced to sit and wait here among them. It might drive me insane. I consider asking someone for help, but I don't really want to talk to anyone. I hear a door open, along with a shuffling of papers, and I move awkwardly toward the sound.

"I think there's been enough improvement that we won't need surgery."

"That's great news!"

I feel a bit embarrassed at needing to eavesdrop on everyone's conversations. A low masculine grumble alerts me to the charming sound of Liam's voice. I move toward it like a ship sailing toward a lighthouse in the dark, empty ocean.

"—just keep monitoring him for me."

"Yes, Dr. Larson. You only have one more patient today and then the other doctors can take over. I've got a break coming up shortly, too. Any plans for lunch?"

"I'm afraid I have to go straight home after work today, Melanie. Why don't we go for sushi tomorrow when I have more time?"

"You work so hard, Dr. Larson," says the woman's voice in a very tender way. "It was supposed to be your day off today. Why did you come in at all? Was it because you missed me?"

I narrow my eyes at this conversation.

Liam clears his throat. "Actually, Melanie, our next patient is very special. She's the test subject that Owen and I mentioned to you a while back. We needed to bump her surgery up, so we're doing the prep today."

"Oh," Melanie says in disappointment. "Yes, I remember. The girl who's supposed to be 'the master key' to all your research."

"That's right. We're so close to success that I can almost taste it!" Liam says, and there is a peculiar excitement in his voice.

I don't think I've ever heard him sound like this, and for a moment, I feel like he's a complete stranger. *The master key?* A little seed of anxiety begins to sprout in my gut, but I try desperately to push it down and hold onto my positivity.

"Will you take me out to dinner to celebrate?" Melanie asks coyly.

"Sure! We'll all have to go," Liam says, "the whole department."

"Oh," Melanie says in disappointment, understanding his subtle rejection. "Great."

I feel a bit reassured by his little show of loyalty. At least, I think it was loyalty. It doesn't matter. I am not going to go looking for little signs of trouble and start overanalyzing them until I drive myself crazy and ruin this. I just decided that I was going to be happy and stop the self-sabotage. If Liam wanted to be with this nurse instead of me, I'm sure he would be.

The door that I am standing near swings

open wider, and Liam and the nurse step outside. I don't even care that I've been caught eavesdropping.

"Am I in the right place?" I ask Liam with a sly smile.

"Yes," he responds at once, and his tone is familiar again. He moves forward to touch my arm before turning back to the nurse. "Melanie, this is Winter Rose, the test subject I mentioned to you."

"That's a fancy name," says Melanie again, in jealous tone. She looks at me for a moment. "Well, aren't you a lucky duck?"

"Excuse me?" I respond.

"To have been chosen for this," she clarifies. "I have met a lot of patients who would die for an opportunity like this."

"Yes," I respond in a voice filled with a confidence and strength that is rare for me. "I am very lucky and grateful."

"If you just come into this room, I'll begin prepping you with eye drops so that the doctor can run some tests." Melanie reaches out to take my hand, but I pull away from her reflexively like I have been touched by fire.

I might be trying very hard to be optimistic, but it's still difficult to be touched.

"Why don't you let me prep her?" Liam asks. "I can tell her a bit about the procedure while I do that."

"Sure," says Melanie a bit skeptically as

Liam pulls me into the examination room and shuts the door.

Liam guides me over to the chair and places my hand on it so I can determine where I am. I slide my backpack off and place it on the ground before climbing into the chair. It is extremely comfortable.

"Winter," he says in a whisper, leaning close to me. "I don't know what you heard, but there's nothing going on with her. I swear."

"It's okay," I tell him. "I'm not worried. We were never exclusive or anything, anyway." My face suddenly twists up in confusion. "I guess we were never really even *together*."

"But that's just the problem," he says. "That's been bothering me."

"What?" I say impatiently and nervously. "Liam, will you just get the damn eye drops? I don't think this is the time or place." I feel a bit sensitive and unprepared for this conversation. More importantly, I'm still afraid of a negative outcome. The momentary high from the philosophical waitress's pep talk is fading fast.

"But I want to be exclusive," Liam insists. "I've been meaning to ask you a question."

I feel him take one of my hands in both of his, and his entire body lowers. My eyes widen in surprise and confusion as I realize he is down on one knee—or possibly both knees. "Liam..."

"Winter Rose, author of many astounding

books, will you please be my girlfriend?"

I burst out laughing. "What are you talking about?"

"We haven't had this talk. We haven't made it official. I don't want you to have any doubt in your mind that I want to be committed to you. I want us to be together."

There is heat spreading through my cheeks, and I'm quite sure that I must be very flushed. My stomach does little flip-flops, encouraging me to respond with enthusiastic agreement. I just decided that I was going to let myself be excited. I gulp before trying to speak. "I don't know..."

"You're supposed to say 'yes,'" he instructs, nudging my leg.

"Um, okay," I mumble with embarrassment. "I guess? Yes?"

"Great! Now for a second question. Winter, will you please move in with me?"

"I'm already staying at your place," I inform him.

"No, no," he says, and clears his throat before repeating himself. "Will you move in with me as *my girlfriend*? And seriously consider staying with me and *not* running away to New Hampshire?"

"I don't know," I tell him honestly.

"You need to say '*yes*,'" he reminds me impatiently.

"Fine, fine." My lips curl upward in a smirk. "Dr. Liam Larson, great fixer of many broken eyes, *yes*, I will move in with you. And consider not running away."

"Good girl," he says softly, rising up to press a kiss against my lips.

The way he says that gives me a little shiver. "I reserve the right to change my mind if you act like a jerk," I warn him.

"I will try my best to make you happy," he promises. Then he hesitates. "And I'll stop holding back. I think we've both been holding back."

"Yeah." I nod slightly in gratitude. It was a lot more painful than I care to admit when he held back the other night.

"I think we both just needed a little security before really allowing ourselves to dive in," Liam explains. "At least... I did. But I'm ready to dive in now, if you are. I'm sorry. I'm sorry it took me so long to say all this."

"Don't worry," I say gently. "It took me a while to realize that I wanted this. But now, I know that I do. And I'm... excited about you."

"Good," Liam says, gently pushing me back in the exam chair. "Now, it's time for a whole bunch of boring and tedious tests. I will also be giving you antibiotic eye drops to reduce the risk of postoperative infection. You'll have to keep taking them at regular intervals for a while before and after the surgery. We usually do one eye at a time, and leave a few weeks in between surgeries so that the first eye can heal—but I want to do both of your eyes as soon as possible. It won't be exciting at all, and some of it will be uncomfortable or even painful. Do you trust me?"

"Always," I tell him softly. I don't want to question it anymore. I feel completely safe in his hands.

Chapter Seven

"Do you want to watch a movie tonight?" Liam asks as he holds the door for me to step into his apartment. "You should take it easy and relax before the surgery."

"No, I think I'll just work," I tell him as I enter and begin removing my shoes. "I am way behind on my book and I feel really guilty. I got a little work done earlier at the cafeteria, but other than that, I've been so unproductive. I should probably try." I slip off my backpack and place it on the island of his kitchen counter. "Feel free to watch your movies: the noise won't bother me."

"I'd love to read what you have written, if you'd like some feedback," Liam offers. "Maybe I could encourage you or give you some ideas."

I turn to look at him with puzzlement as I pull my notetaker out of my backpack. "Are you for real? You want to help me with my work?"

CLARITY

"Sure!" he says eagerly. "I'm excited to get to read your stories before everyone else."

"You're too good to be true," I accuse him as I slide onto his kitchen chair and begin preparing my work area. "Don't worry about me. I'm sure you'd rather just relax and watch TV or play video games or something."

Liam moves forward to stand behind my chair and gently squeezes my shoulders. "Winter, I have been relaxing, watching TV, and playing video games in my spare time for years before I met you. Now, there's this wonderful girl in my life, and my apartment, and I have the opportunity to either amuse myself with brainless activities for fun, or try to participate in her world. I could make a little effort to connect with her, while also showing her that I care." He combs his fingers through my hair, lifting it away so he can begin to massage the back of my neck. "Plus, helping her means I get to read awesome stories that are better than any TV show or video game. I get to take a little glimpse deeper inside her beautiful mind. You do the math. It's not a difficult decision."

My head tilts back a little as I enjoy the sensation of his massage. I consider his words for a moment, and a swell of emotion rises up in my throat. When I try to speak, I'm a little choked up. "I've never had anyone that cared about me that much before," I tell him softly. "Before I ran away and committed to writing full-time, everyone around me only tried to interfere with my writing. Carmen and my dad were always dragging me away from my computer for one reason or another. To have fun, go shopping, or help them with their lives. I guess they thought that when I was sitting at my desk and working in my spare time that there was something wrong with me—that I wasn't having fun. They didn't understand that it was not only the most fun I could possibly have, but the most rewarding and meaningful part of my life."

Liam continues to knead the muscles around my neck. "I don't know if I have anything like that. I have ambition, but sometimes when I achieve my goals, I'm left feeling a little empty."

"If I stop writing for too long, I feel empty," I admit. His massage is making me a tiny bit drowsy, and I allow my eyes to close. The tiredness is making me more honest than usual. "It's usually the only time I'm really happy."

Liam's hands pause and rest against my shoulders. "I do understand how you feel. Real life can be hard, and when you get whisked away into a beautiful story—everything else disappears. You can be someone else, somewhere else. When I'm reading your books, I can completely escape into your world and feel the same happiness that you feel while writing them. It's a unique experience that no one else could create exactly the way you do."

I lean my head back to rest against his

chest, trying to fight against the small wave of sleepiness. "I think I'd just die or fade into nothingness without my writing," I confess. "It's the only special thing about me—the only thing that makes my life worthwhile."

"We need to change that, Winter. You're special in so many ways."

"I just don't know how to do anything else," I tell him. I clear my throat and try to shake off my exhaustion as I reach out to touch my computer. I let my hands rest lightly on the keys. "Every time I've tried to really experience something new, horrible things happen. I should warn you that I don't really know how to be a girlfriend, or even a normal person. I'm only a writer. It's like writing is the only way I can be alive—and be free."

"I wish I was artistic," Liam says softly. "I must admit that part of the reason I want to help is that I'll get to live vicariously through you. You're so independent. My job depends on so many other people, facilities, equipment, rules and regulations, standards—if I make one wrong move, it could all fall apart. I like the way you get to answer only to yourself, and create absolutely anything you want."

"I am still slightly limited by market trends and what the publisher expects," I tell him. "But those are mostly just general guidelines. I can take the basic story and run with it in almost any direction I choose. Or I could write something entirely my own and deal with the consequences of having trouble getting it published—and once I do, making hardly any money." I laugh lightly at myself, because I have done this before. "But I do love the freedom."

"Doesn't it ever get lonely?" Liam asks.

"Of course," I tell him quietly. "Loneliness is the price of freedom. It's a price I've always been more than willing to pay. It can be very hard to create, sometimes. It requires a lot of sacrifices."

"Maybe you won't have to make those sacrifices anymore," Liam tells me, leaning down to place a kiss on the top of my head. "Maybe you won't have to be lonely anymore. Maybe you just need someone who really believes in you and your work."

I bite down on my lip to suppress the emotion. He's basically promising me paradise, and I doubt he has any idea how much it means to me. "The only person who ever really supported me was my mother. And she's gone."

"Well," Liam says, resting his chin on the top of my head, "you can count on me to be in your corner. I'll be your biggest fan. I'll be your cheerleader—although I absolutely refuse to wear a short pleated skirt. Unless you're into that."

The image causes me to erupt in giggles, relieving some of the heavy tension from my mind.

The joke soothes me far more than his massage managed to do. Who is this man? How does he manage to make me feel good on both the inside and out? He must be some kind of fairytale prince. I am now convinced of this. I feel so happy that I'm sort of dizzy and worry that I might fall off the chair I'm sitting in. The laughter has caused me to double over uncontrollably, but I try to get ahold of my senses.

"Okay, mister. Stop being so charming and let me work," I tell him, playfully smacking his hand.

"Will you email me the first few chapters of your book?" he asks.

I hesitate, torn between giving in and maintaining a safe distance. Do I really want to let him in? I remember the sweet waitress who said that I should allow myself to feel excited and happy. I find myself nodding. "Sure," I say softly, letting my fingers fly across my keyboard. "Sending it now."

"Great," he responds. "I want to be there for you, Winter. I want to be the one who makes it easier. I want to try my hardest to give you something *new* to make life worthwhile. A new reason. A new way to be happy."

"Something new?" I repeat as I finish sending the email. I turn to glance in his direction as I hear him retrieving his own computer and moving into the chair next to me. "What do you mean?"

"What do you think?" he asks with a chuckle. He reaches over to place his hand on my thigh and squeezes it gently. "There's only one thing that could be more powerful than your art. More powerful than your personal fulfillment. It's the thing that everyone on this planet wants more than anything else."

Say it. Please say it. A little voice inside me yearns to hear the word. I hold my breath, imagining the sound of the word spilling from his lips. I can hear it in my mind. I know it's in both of our minds. I know it's the reason for everything. I just need to hear it anyway. *Say the word. Please, Liam. Promise me everything.*

"Don't you know, silly girl? You're the one who writes about it."

"Like I said," I tell him softly. "I'm good at writing; not so much at living."

"I'll teach you how to live," he says with determination. "And I'll try to give you what you've really been seeking all along..."

I wait, listening closely for him to say the word. I don't know why. I probably wouldn't believe him if he said it. Why do I want to hear it anyway?

A loud banging alerts me to the sound of someone at the door. It wasn't the sound that I was expecting, and it startles me.

"Excuse me," Liam says, removing his

hand from my leg and pulling away. I hear him stand up from his chair and move across the room to answer the door.

I exhale in disappointment, releasing the breath that I had been holding. My stomach is all in knots, and I can't believe how badly I wanted to hear those words. I have never been a fan of big romantic declarations, and here I am, sitting on pins and needles as I anxiously wait to hear the coveted syllables.

Instead, I hear a crash.

My head snaps to the entryway where Liam has just opened the door to his apartment. I am not sure if he is expecting someone. Has he ordered delivery food? I seem to vaguely recall him mentioning something about that. However, there is another crash that causes the apartment walls to shake. It sounds like someone's fist just went through the drywall.

"Liam?" I say nervously, standing up from my chair.

"No, Helen. It's me."

I stand there blinking and stunned at the sound of Grayson's voice. How is this possible? I thought he had been committed to a psychiatric facility.

"They let me go," he says in a hideous rasp. "It turns out that I'm not as crazy as you'd think."

"How did you find me?" I ask him. My

421

breathing is quickening.

"I found out where the doctor worked and followed you two home from the hospital. This is a nice little setup he's got here."

"What did you do to him?" I ask. I haven't heard Liam's voice since before he answered the door. I can't even hear his breathing or moving.

"I hit him on the head with a crowbar," Grayson says with a laugh. "Too bad his fancy martial arts couldn't protect him from that."

"But your arms," I say in a hushed tone. "They're broken..."

"This ugly son of a bitch only broke one of my arms. The other one was simply dislocated. And I can still swing a fucking crowbar into his skull. Too bad you can't see this, Helen. I'm going to do it again. This time, I'm going to smash his brains until all his memories of you leak out onto these shiny hardwood floors. You belong to me."

"No!" I shout as I spring into action. I am no longer paralyzed with fear. I reach to my side and grab one of the chairs I had been sitting on and throw it at Grayson with all the strength I can muster. I hear the chair smash against his body, and I run to the kitchen to grab the biggest knife from Liam's set. "Get the fuck away from us!" I scream as I brandish the knife and move toward Grayson.

A sharp pain shoots through my hand as he swings the crowbar and hits me in the wrist. I gasp as the knife clatters to the floor.

"You went with him willingly!" Grayson says to me hysterically. "You *wanted* him. You never wanted me. That's why this fucker needs to die. If I can't have you, he sure as hell won't."

"Stop!" I scream, but I hear another sickening sound as Grayson swings the crowbar. I dive forward and try to intercept the impact, but I'm too late. I stumble forward and feel the instrument embedded in Liam's head. A wail of grief leaves my throat as I press both of my hands over the wound. "Liam? Liam! No. No." I move my hands over his face, touching his shoulders and shaking him gently, trying to stir him to life. "No," I whisper in disbelief. "You can't go. You need to stay with me. I don't have anyone else. You were going to say that you loved me. I love you, too. We need to love each other. Please, please stay." The warm liquid is seeping out of his cracked skull and onto my hands and knees. I feel a sob shake my shoulders. "Liam!"

My heartache is interrupted as I feel a hand go around my throat, dragging me to my feet and pulling me up to a standing position. I am too weak and drained to fight.

"It's his own fault," Grayson says as he pushes me up against the kitchen island. He reaches down and begins to hike up my skirt. "He tried to keep me from having you. But I will have you again, Helen. I'll do anything to have you just one more time."

Like a lightning bolt shooting through me, rage fills me with power and strength. I remember my judo training as he puts his hand on my body, and I grab it and twist it until I manage to take him down.

"Fuck you!" I scream at him as I pound my hands into his face. "You monster! Liam was a good man. The best. You're worthless! I should have killed you! I should have killed you with your own gun, that night! Oh, god. This is my fault."

Realizing that my lack of bravery has resulted in Liam's murder, sobs of guilt and despair begin to rack my chest. Tears pour down my face. "Fuck you," I whisper. "I hope you burn in hell."

"I will," Grayson assures me, catching my wrist in his hand. "But first, I'm going to have a little taste of heaven. Inside you."

He releases my wrist and grabs a fistful of my hair, slamming my head into Liam's stainless steel refrigerator. I scream and struggle against him, but the dizziness overpowers me. I find myself being forced face down onto the kitchen tiles. The ground is cold against my cheek as Grayson tears at my skirt and underwear.

"I promised you it would be worse this time," he whispers as he shoves his knees between my thighs to separate them. "Let's do things a little differently, my angel."

424

CLARITY

I feel like I am drowning. I am sobbing and screaming hysterically, unable to properly defend myself as my heart aches with loss of Liam. I don't even care what happens to me anymore. I am enraged and devastated, vicious and lifeless all at the same time. I don't know what I am. I don't know what to do.

I struggle. I struggle and scream and cry. "Liam!" I shout brokenly, begging all the gods to bring him back to life. I need my knight in shining armor. Maybe if I just knew he was alive, I could be strong. "Please!" I shriek as I try to wrestle with Grayson. For a man with one broken arm, he is impossibly strong and somehow still able to effectively restrain me. I try to reach backwards and grab his broken arm and hurt him, but he doesn't seem to care. He grabs my hair and pulls my head back, twisting my neck so he can force his mouth down against mine.

"My sweet, sweet Helen. My pure, innocent angel. I will have you in all the ways I've always dreamed of having you..."

"Liam!" I scream through my sobs. I pound my fist into the floor, wishing that it would make the whole apartment building crumble on top of us. *"Liam!* Please. Please, no."

"Whoa, whoa! Winter, calm down. Wake up. I'm right here."

I suddenly stop struggling and grow very still. I feel a body pressed on top of mine and restraining me, but he doesn't seem to be trying to hurt me. I feel the tears staining my cheeks, but I don't feel the pain in my wrist or my head.

"Liam?" I whisper again.

"It was a dream," he tells me. "You were having a nightmare and flailing all over the place."

"I don't..." I can't seem to speak as the tears continue to pour down my face. "You're okay. You're okay." As soon as he stops restraining me, I reach up and wrap my arms around him tightly. I continue to sob as I cling to him for dear life and bury my face in his shoulder.

"Hey, hey. Shhh. It was all just in your head," he says tenderly as he holds me. "That was the mother of all nightmares, Winter. What the hell happened in that fertile brain of yours? Do all writers dream like this? Jesus. I thought you were going to break my bed in half."

I finally stop crying enough to speak. The sound of his calm voice is soothing and reassuring. Still, the bitter taste of the nightmare lingers with me—it was so realistic.

"He hit you on the head with a crowbar," I tell Liam. "You were gone. I felt you die."

"Oh, Winter. Who did? Grayson?"

I nod in response, my arms still tightly clenched around Liam.

"Honey, I broke both of his arms, remember? He's not going to be able to even lift a crowbar for a long time. Shhh, just breathe slowly.

426

You need to relax."

I realize then that I'm clinging to him like a child. I realize how pathetic and needy I must seem. If he had trouble with my issues before... he'll never be able to love me now. I have screwed this up for good.

"I'm so sorry," I tell him, pulling away and reaching up to wipe the sweat away from my forehead. "God, I'm so stupid. You shouldn't have to deal with my drama and bullshit. I should just go home and leave you to live your life in peace."

"Winter, you are my peace."

"You're just saying shit to make me feel better. Thanks." I rub my eyes with a groan. "I don't even remember falling asleep."

"You wrote for about two hours at the kitchen table, but then you fell asleep on your work. I think it was a side effect of the drugs we gave you. When our pizza delivery came, and holding a slice under your nose wouldn't wake you up, I carried you to bed."

"Pizza delivery?" I respond, remembering the knock at the door in my dream.

"Yes. Remember we decided we were going to get pizza on the way home? I told you about that gourmet place that does the super thin crusts with spinach and heaps of feta."

"Oh, god." I press both of my palms against my eyes and hold them there for a moment. "Liam. I am so fucked up. You shouldn't be with

427

me."

"I want to be with you. I don't care that you have nightmares. It doesn't make me love you any less."

"What?" I say in surprise, removing my palms from my eyes.

"I'm sorry if that makes me uncool. I know it's kind of soon to use that word. But it's what I feel for you, Winter. I love you."

"No," I say, shaking my head as tears stream down my cheeks. "This is another nightmare. You don't really feel that way. It's just a dream. Wake up. Wake up."

"Why would you think that I don't?"

"I'm not healthy. You didn't even want to touch me. This is fucked up. We're fucked up. I ruined this. I'm not normal. I'm not well-adjusted. I can't be excited or happy or hopeful. You don't want me."

"Will you let me show you?" Liam asks, pressing kisses against my tear-soaked face. He kisses my clammy lips, holding me close against him. "Will you let me show you how I really feel?"

"What do you mean?" I ask him miserably, torn between the need to cling desperately to him, and the urge to run the hell away and get on the first flight out of the goddamn country.

"I said I wasn't going to hold back

anymore," he whispers against my face. "So let me love you." He presses a kiss against each of my closed eyelids before moving lower to rain kisses down against my neck and chest.

Somehow, he instantly stirs the fire inside me. I go from being filled with terror to being filled with desire. I use the feelings that his touch causes within me to try and forget everything negative that I just experienced. The terror and fear dissipates and I let my body respond to his hands and mouth. My back arches and I slide my hands up over his muscular arms. My body is screaming at me and begging for anything good. For anything that means that I'm not alone. For anything that might mean that I could actually be loved.

"Please," I say again, so softly that I am sure that he cannot hear me. "Liam, I need you so much."

This time, he doesn't hesitate. He reaches under my skirt to grab the sides of my underwear and slide it down over my legs. He also quickly disposes of his own pants and shirt before moving back on top of me. "Are you sure you want this?" he asks me.

I nod and reach up to hug him tightly, praying that he won't change his mind again. Tears are still sliding down my face; I am trying but failing to keep it together. I feel like I am irreparably damaged, and his touch is the only thing that can mend me. In this moment, I need him like I need air.

He positions himself at my entrance and then hesitates. "I should get one of the condoms..."

"No," I say, grabbing him tightly in fear. I feel like if anything interrupts this now, it will never happen. "Please, Liam," I sob softly. "I don't care. I don't care. I just need you."

He leans down to place a kiss against my lips, lightly brushing his fingers across my neck. "Okay," he says softly.

When he begins to press himself inside me, the feelings flood my entire body. The vast volumes of fear and longing threaten to tear me apart. I tremble as I remember how it felt to lose him in my dream. In so many ways, he is my lifeline. He's my reason. I want to give myself to him completely. I want to hold him close and treasure his life and strength. I never want to feel that pain of loss again. But I know I will. I just want to forget. I want to feel like everything's going to be okay.

Life is a terrible thing that likes to rip away the ones that we love. At least, if I really do lose him someday, I could say that we had this moment together. I can lose everything else, but I can't lose this. Just one moment. I have been searching for it for the longest time.

Every time I get close to feeling any sort of pleasure, it feels like the sky cracks open to rain down thunder on me. Please. Don't let it happen this time.

I just need one moment.

One moment of peace. One moment of being loved.

Won't the universe be good to me for a change? I need one perfect moment to remember, in case I never have another perfect moment. Sometimes, I think I never will.

I lift my lips to place a kiss against the edge of his jaw. I am not entirely sure if I intended to kiss him here, or if my aim was off, but I can't seem to pull away. I love the taste of his skin.

That small touch seems to be all the encouragement he needs, for he releases all his inhibitions and plunges himself inside me. I gasp out and cling to him, angling my hips to give him better access. I want to feel him more deeply inside me than anyone has ever been. I want him to heal everything in me that's broken.

Liam groans, and he seems to lose control of himself as he gives into the sensations. Something carnal and raw takes control of his body as he moves inside me with the utter abandon of a man possessed. He is no longer the careful, polite doctor that he portrays on the outside; he is the powerful, savage creature that I always knew lingered just beneath his skin. He thrusts himself so deeply inside me that I cry out in pleasure.

And for a moment, I swear that I can see all the colors in the universe.

Chapter Nine

"No, I've never had any allergic reactions."

"Great. It says here that you've never had any other surgeries? Nothing at all? Even something small is important to know. Wisdom teeth, plastic surgery."

"Nothing," I tell the anesthesiologist.

"Wonderful," she says, flipping through her papers. "I'm sorry for taking so long, I just want to confirm everything to be really thorough. Moderate drinking? Non-smoker?"

"That's all correct," I tell her, suppressing a yawn at the endless questioning.

"Alright. Let's get this show on the road!" she says. "I'm going to be right back in a moment to put you to sleep."

"Peachy," I mumble as she leaves the room. "You could have just kept talking and I'm sure it would have knocked me out."

The door closes behind her, but it opens again a moment later. I hear the sound of shoes squeaking on the floor as someone else approaches. I smile when I recognize the soles of the footwear and the sound of the gait. "Liam," I say softly.

Without a word, he comes over to the operating table and places his hand on the curve of my hip. The warmth of his skin easily seeps through the thin fabric of the hospital gown. He does not speak, but he leans down to place a kiss on my lips.

I kiss back for a moment, and my body is instantly flooded with heat and yearning. I wish that I could pull him down against me and ask him to take me right here on this operating table. Instead, I place a hand on his chest and gently push him away.

"The anesthesiologist will be back at any moment," I warn him nervously. "Don't be careless. We can make out later."

"She's cool," Liam says, sliding his hand over my body in a way that makes me squirm and breathe a little faster. "We only really have to worry about the nurses. Some of them are really fond of me, and they might decide to try and kill you in your sleep if they realize you're standing in the way."

"Liam!" I whisper, smacking his arm.

"Jesus. That is not what a girl wants to hear minutes before getting knocked unconscious."

"I'm just kidding. Don't worry," he says, sitting on the edge of the bed and squeezing my arm. "I'm going to watch you like a hawk. I won't let anyone do anything to you that isn't perfect and precise and intended only to heal you. This is going to be great. I promise. You'll see! Yes, pun intended."

"That was terrible," I tell him, suppressing a smile. I sigh and reach out to touch his leg. "I wish this surgery wasn't today. I just wanted to stay in bed with you for as long as possible."

"You did," he tells me with a chuckle. "I'm sorry you didn't get to try any of the pizza I ordered—but I couldn't let you have any food or drink after midnight."

"It's your fault for distracting me until midnight," I say teasingly. "But I suppose I did need the distraction." I shift uncomfortably on the hospital bed. "Liam, do you think surgery is really necessary at this point? I've been like this for so long that I don't feel like there's anything wrong with me. Maybe I should just be content with who I am? I'm anxious. I don't feel... ready."

"Just leave it all to me," he says gently. "You said you trust me, remember? I'll be right here when you wake up. There are almost no risks to your health other than infection—but you've been taking the antibiotic eye drops, and I'll make sure we're extra careful. Let's consider this a gamble with a high probability of success. You're actually very healthy and much stronger than you think. I discovered that last night when you were able to completely exhaust me."

I laugh lightly in embarrassment. "I'm sorry. You're addictive. I couldn't seem to get enough."

"Neither could I," he says, placing a kiss against the palm of my hand. "We'll pick up right where we left off when we get home tonight—if you're up for it. If you're in too much pain, we can wait a few days."

"Days? I can barely wait a few minutes," I tell him shyly.

Liam gently brushes his hand through my hair, and he seems like he is about to speak when he gets interrupted.

"Hey!" shouts a familiar voice, and I look up in realization that Owen has entered the room. I hear a loud snap as he pulls a rubber glove down over his wrist. "Liam, get your hands off the patient! We'll have none of that hanky-panky in my operating room."

"*Your* operating room?" Liam says in amusement.

"Winter, don't worry about a thing," Owen assures me. "I'll be watching this one to make sure he does a good job and doesn't get distracted by your body. If his hands start shaking because he gets too turned on, I'll take over."

"Owen, I resent that," Liam says in a low tone. "You know I would never let my emotional state interfere with my work."

"Hey, it could happen. I've seen some interesting videos lately about eyeball fetishes in Japan. I have no idea what kinky stuff you're into, man. All I know is that Winter has really pretty eyeballs, and I need to look out for her best interests." Owen claps Liam on the back affectionately. "Just try not to lose your marbles while we're working on her marbles."

"Buddy," Liam says in an annoyed tone. "If you keep implying that I'm a bad doctor in front of my girlfriend who I'm about to *operate on*, you're going to be the one in danger of losing two *very important* marbles. If you know what I mean."

Owen gulps loudly, and I can only imagine the death glare that Liam is giving him. I laugh at their boyish threats.

"I know you guys will do a great job," I tell them sincerely. "Even if it doesn't work on me, thanks for trying."

"It will work," Owen says confidently. "We're essentially just giving your eyes a little push so that they can heal themselves. We'll be inserting the viral vector containing healthy copies of the RPE65 gene just under your retina..."

"I've gone over this with her dozens of

times," Liam assures Owen. "She knows how the gene therapy works."

"Oh," Owen says in disappointment. "Fine. I get it. Less talking, more action."

The clinking of feminine shoes alerts me to the return of the anesthesiologist. I hear the sound of her fiddling with an apparatus in the room. "Have these boys been bothering you?" she asks me. "Don't worry. I know they sound like idiots, but they're brilliant."

"It's okay. I trust them," I tell the anesthesiologist. "I'm a little stressed out, and listening to their bad jokes relaxes me a bit."

"Honey, I've got just the thing to relax you," she says, placing a plastic mask over my face. "Just breathe normally for a minute or two. I'm going to put some oxygen through here first, but in a moment you're going to encounter a sweet smell and find yourself drifting off to sleep."

"Okay," I mumble into the gas mask. The scent of plastic assails my nostrils, and I wrinkle my nose up slightly.

"I'll be right here when you wake up," Liam assures me. "I want to be the first thing you see, once you can see."

"Like a mother duck?" Owen asks him.

"Duck?" I respond in confusion.

"You know," Owen says, "how slightly after hatching..."

While he is in the process of responding,

his voice seems to get further and further away until I can't hear anything at all. This bothers me, because I was very curious to hear what he had to say about the mother duck.

Chapter Nine

"The surgery went very well. I promise you, sir."

Silence.

"Yes, she should start to see improvements within a few days. We'll be doing a lot of tests over the next little while to monitor the improvements. If she needs a stronger dose, after a few weeks we'll go back in and try again."

Silence.

"Absolutely. Thank you so much for the opportunity, sir. I really appreciate your support. It's been a pleasure to perform these clinical trials, and I'm so glad you chose me. Take care."

The voice stops speaking, and I feel someone sit on the bed beside me. I feel a bit groggy and confused when I feel a hand on my shoulder.

439

"Liam?" I manage to croak out. My mouth is very dry, and my throat feels rather hoarse. I try to move, but my body feels like lead. "Could you please get me some water?"

"I can't give you water right away, but let's start with some ice chips," Liam says. He moves away slightly and returns with a small piece of ice that he runs back and forth over my lips. "How's that?"

I sigh gratefully at the refreshing sensation as the ice melts over my lips and gently drizzles onto my tongue. I thirstily savor every droplet. I never imagined that waking up from surgery would feel like I'd been lying in the hot desert sun and baking for hours. No one ever mentioned that part to me. "More, please," I whisper.

He moves away immediately, with a small chuckle. "It's quite easy to get you to beg for more, isn't it?"

Only then do I snap fully awake as I try to open my eyes and glare at him. I am surprised to discover that there are soft patches covering both my eyes, and that there is a growing ache in each eyeball. The more I think about the area, the more it seems to hurt. When Liam returns with more ice chips, I try to focus on them instead.

"Were you on the phone with someone?" I ask him in a slight daze. "Before I woke up?"

"That was my boss," Liam explains as he runs the ice over my lips. "He usually supervises these surgeries, but he couldn't make it today since we moved the dates."

"Oh," I mumble, using my teeth to steal a piece of ice from his fingers and gently push it around in my very dry mouth. "So, how long until we figure out if it worked?"

"It's different for everyone," Liam explains. "Some people see a tiny improvement almost immediately, but it can take a few days for your eyes to be healed enough..."

"So I could be able to see right now?" I ask him. The idea finally sends a true pang of excitement through me. The muscles in my arms tighten and twitch with the urge to rip off the eye patches. "I want to try."

"It's only been a few hours since your surgery," he warns me. "You might need more time..."

"I don't care," I tell him, pushing myself into a sitting position. I immediately feel lightheaded and woozy, and regret moving so quickly. I clutch the sides of the bed as Liam helps arrange the pillows to prop me up a bit. I breathe and lean back. After a moment, I stop feeling like I'm going to fall over and I reach out to squeeze his shoulder. "Come on, Doctor. Show me how good you are at your job. Impress me."

Liam laughs lightly. "You know, I had a feeling you'd say that. Here, I'm going to remove these shields. But if you feel too much pain when you try to open your eyes, we'll replace them and try again later, okay?"

I nod eagerly. I am determined not to feel any pain, or to ignore it if I do. When I was a little girl, I dreamed of this moment for so many years. Now, here it is, and I don't know what to do with myself. Tears begin to gather in my eyes, and they sting and burn a little.

"Wait!" I tell Liam, as he begins pulling off one of the eye patches. I grab his wrists and hold them in my lap. "I just need a second." I try to compose myself before he reveals my eyes and sees my tears.

"Winter, it's okay," he tells me gently, holding both of my hands. "I've helped so many people to see for the first time, and it's a very emotional thing. I know what you're going through."

"It's not that," I say with a sniffle. "I'm just worried that you'll be hideously ugly." I try to swallow my emotion. "What if I don't find you attractive? We'll have to break up so I can go find a hotter boyfriend."

Liam laughs and runs his thumbs over my wrists. "That's just the drugs talking. Trust me, Winter. You're going to find me *very* attractive. I have absolutely no concerns about that."

"Well, aren't you cocky!" I say with a scoff, but I also smile a little. "Fine. Take off my eye patches." I take a deep breath to prepare

442

myself.

"Just relax," he says in a soothing tone. "The worst part is over. It only gets better from now on."

As he removes the shields, I find that I'm frozen with apprehension. What if it doesn't work? What if everything remains the same?

"Winter," he coaxes, placing a hand on my stomach. "You need to open your eyes in order to see."

"Okay," I say nervously. When I finally allow my eyelids to flutter open slightly, I am assailed by the bright light in the room. I reflexively shut my eyes again to protect them, but a little gasp escapes my throat. "Oh my god," I whisper. "Oh my god." I try again, peeking through a tiny slit in my eyelids. My eyes begin to throb with the unbelievable brightness of almost everything. I look around in wonder. Everything is blurry, and I can't seem to make out any aspect of the world around me, but it is no longer completely dark.

"Liam," I whisper, grabbing his hand so that I can squeeze it again. "Is this a dream? Am I going to wake up?"

"No. It's real. What do you see?"

"I don't know. It's just... not like before. It's not *nothing*."

"Look directly at me," Liam says, returning the pressure on my hand. "Can you see my face?"

I follow his instructions, and it takes me a moment to focus on him. I see a shadowy spot surrounded by light. I see an outline surrounding what must be the shape of a man. "I can't see you," I tell him, "but I can see all the light around you. I can see... a silhouette, I suppose."

"That's good. Just take a moment to look at me. Let your eyes adjust. You should be able to see a little more after a few seconds."

"This must be a dream," I whisper again. "Sometimes when I was younger, I used to dream that I wasn't blind. Sometimes I could see people or landscapes for a fleeting second, the way I imagine they might look. But then I'd always wake up to darkness. Is this one of those dreams?"

"Unless our entire existence is part of one very large computer-generated illusion and we're all actually in some alternate reality," Liam says, "you're not dreaming."

His face is becoming clearer to me, even though it still feels like I am looking through a hazy film. I can see the color of his hair contrasting against his skin. I can see the shape of his eyes and nose and lips. I reach out to run my hands over his face to try and make sure that what I'm seeing correlates with what I'm used to feeling. I find myself squinting slightly and trying to see more.

"Take it easy," he says with warning.

"Just close your eyes if it gets too painful, and I'll put the shields back on."

"You're beautiful," I tell him as I run my fingers over his chiseled cheekbones. I feel the warmth of emotion brimming in my chest. "You're more beautiful than I could have ever imagined. No wonder the nurses are crazy about you. And your slutty neighbor across the hall. You must be one of the most beautiful men on the planet."

"Whoa, Winter," he says with a laugh. "Slow down! At least give yourself a chance to see other people so that you can compare."

"I don't need to see anyone else," I insist with a big smile. "If you're the only man I ever see for the rest of my life, I'll be perfectly happy. You're so handsome." I sigh in contentment.

"While my ego appreciates the compliment, I can assure you that I'm quite average. If I were really as handsome as you think I am, I would have just become a male underwear model or an actor and not have to work so damn hard."

"Oh!" I say as my vision becomes a bit sharper and I can make out the details of my hands moving on his face. "Oh my god... Is that what a hand looks like? Is this my hand?" I bring my hand close to my face to try to examine it more closely. "It's so wrinkled. There are so many lines." My eyes begin to hurt, but I can't stop staring. I don't even want to blink. I want to see everything. My eyes have been closed for too long, and I never want them to shut again. I wiggle my fingers wondrously. "Wow," I say in awe.

"You know, Winter—when people wake up from surgery, they usually have their families there to greet them. Wouldn't you like me to call your dad and sister? Wouldn't you like to see them for the first time?"

I shake my head. "No, please. I just want you. I can't deal with anyone else right now."

"Okay," he says gently. Then his face breaks out into a smile. I can tell by the little flash of teeth visible between his lips; I think that must be the color *white*. "That reminds me. Owen said that I should call him once you wake up, but I think there's someone else you need to meet first."

"Who?" I ask curiously. "Do I have to? I don't really like people."

"You'll like this person." Liam leans forward and reaches on the bedside table for a small oval-shaped object with a handle. He offers it to me, holding it up so I can stare into it. "Winter Rose, I'd like to introduce you to yourself."

For a moment, I simply stare. Then I gingerly reach out and allow my hands to encircle the handle of the antique mirror. I bring it close to my face and angle it properly so that I can examine every inch of myself. "Wow," I whisper. "Wow. This is me? Oh my god! I can see my lips moving when I speak."

Liam laughs at this and I feel a little silly. I don't care. My hair is lovely in the way that it frames my face, and I love the structure and placement of my eyes and nose and mouth. If I tilt my head to the side, I can even see my ears. I run my hands over my face and gently tug on my earlobe.

"Wow," I say again. I laugh lightly and I immediately decide that I look adorable when I laugh.

"What do you think?" he asks.

"I'm a babe," I say with a sigh as I run my fingers over the mirror. "Wow. I'm definitely the prettiest girl I've ever seen."

"You're the only girl you've ever seen," he reminds me.

"Quit ruining my buzz," I tell him teasingly. "I'm so lovely. I'm like a princess."

"You are," he agrees. "I tried to tell you that when we met, but you didn't believe me!"

"You saved me," I tell him suddenly, staring at him with renewed awe. I don't care if the anesthesia is making me loopy. "I ran away from my castle and got trapped in a tower, guarded by evil trolls. You were my knight in shining armor; you rode your horse across the land to come and rescue me."

Liam begins to chuckle. "I think you should probably get a bit more rest, Winter."

"No, I'm fine! I was just stunned by the

447

exquisiteness of my own face." I nod decisively. "In fact, I think I'm *much* better looking than you."

"Hey, let's not get too carried away now," he says with a grin.

I tilt the mirror around so that I can get more light. "I'm serious. I could look at me all day!"

Liam laughs. "I could, too." Looking toward the door to ensure our privacy, he leans forward to put his lips close to my ear. "You think this is great? You should see the rest of you," he whispers in a low voice.

"Can I?" I ask him curiously. "Oh! I guess I'd need a bigger mirror for that."

"Do you think you can walk?" he asks me.

"I don't know. Maybe, with a little help."

Liam takes the small mirror out of my hand and places it on the bedside table. He detaches the heart monitor from my finger before sliding his arms under my body to easily lift me from the hospital bed. I feel extremely dizzy, and the world visibly spins around me as he carries me to the small adjoining bathroom. Once we are positioned in front of the large bathroom mirror, he gently places my feet on the ground. I might have fallen over if not for him standing behind me and wrapping his strong arms around my waist.

I stare into the mirror, and I can see myself from the waist up. I can also see Liam, and I'm surprised by how much taller and larger than me he is. He makes me feel tiny. Somehow, staring at us together is the most beautiful and perfect thing I've seen so far. I wish I could take a picture of what I see in this moment, and always keep it with me. I have never been a person who cared much about taking or being in photographs, so it sounded silly when other people obsessed over them; but now I understand. I understand the need to capture a beautiful sight and put it in your pocket.

"We look so good together," I tell him softly. "The perfect couple."

"Now you can finally see all the things I've seen all along," he responds, resting his chin on the top of my head.

"Thank you," I whisper to him as I reach up to place my hands on the arms he has wrapped around me. "If you hadn't found me and dragged me back here, and forced me to do this... I never would have been brave enough to try."

"You wanted to try all along," he answers. "I just needed to help you realize that."

"It's worth it all just for this moment." I bite down on my lip a little. "The last twenty-four hours have probably been one of the best days of my life."

"Same here," he responds, "but I'll give you way better days if you let me."

We continue to stand there for several moments, just staring at each other and savoring the moment. Then I remember the conversation that happened right before I was put under anesthesia. "What was Owen saying about a duck?"

"Oh," Liam says with a smile. "Imprinting. There's a critical period a few hours right after hatching when goslings imprint on the first thing they see and think it's their mother..."

"I know. The Konrad Lorenz experiments. I studied psychology."

"Owen thinks that because this is a vulnerable and critical time for you, it's sort of like a rebirth. You should become extremely emotionally attached to the first things and people that you see." He clears his throat. "So he thinks I'm using science to trick you into falling in love with me."

"Are you?" I ask him.

"Maybe," he says softly.

"I must admit that it's working so far," I inform him.

"Good," he says in a low voice.

We are both distracted by a sound from the room, and we look toward the doorway.

"I came to check on you two to make sure that everything's okay," says Owen. I recognize his voice, but it's odd to watch it coming out of this very large person. "Winter, he isn't trying to get you to do freaky things in the hospital bathroom, is he? She just had surgery, man! Let her rest."

"And this is Owen," Liam says in introduction.

"Wow," I murmur appreciatively as I let my eyes roam over his body. His hair is far lighter and curlier than Liam's, and he seems a bit taller and more slender. There is a funny little apparatus on his face which must be a pair of glasses. I do not find him as attractive as the first man I happened to see, but he has his own certain charm. "Very cute. You're right, Liam. You are average."

"You think I'm cute?" Owen says happily, pointing at himself in surprise. "Thanks! Hey, Liam. Keep your woman on a leash, bro. She just hit on me."

"You can't go around hitting on every man you see," Liam scolds me, tightening his arms around my waist. "You're mine."

"I may have committed to being your girlfriend too soon," I say playfully. "If this is what men look like, I want a few more of them."

Owen clucks his tongue in disappointment. "You should have let her stay blind, bro. Now you'll never be able to keep her all to yourself."

"I guess I'll just have to lock her up in a tower again," Liam says, "and make her grow her hair so that I can climb up and visit."

I glance back at the mirror as he says this in order to better appreciate my lovely locks. I have been told that my hair is brown, chestnut, auburn, mahogany, and a variety of other words. I will have to determine for myself what each color means in the near future.

"I hate to ruin the moment, but we're going to have to run a few tests on her eyes now," Owen tells us. "You can let her rest for a bit longer if she needs to."

"Just give us a few minutes," Liam tells his friend. "I'll text you."

Owen moves to leave, but then he snaps his fingers and turns back to us. "Hey Winter," he says excitedly. "Once your eyes heal up, you two have to come over to watch a movie with me and Caroline. I have the perfect one in mind. It's French, with lesbians."

Chapter Ten

"Why won't you tell me where we're going?" I ask Liam with a quizzical smile. We're driving down the highway in the middle of the night, and I can't see much other than the fuzzy lights on the dashboard and the pale circle of the moon. Liam says there are also plenty of stars out, but I can't see any of them. It's been a few days since the surgery and my eyesight has been steadily improving, but my vision is still pretty mediocre in dim lighting conditions.

"It's a surprise," he tells me. "Come on; you love my surprises! Stop asking questions."

"Fine," I grumble to myself as I begin to dig inside my purse, "but I'm going to get some studying done."

Liam chuckles. "You and your *studying*."

"I have a lot to learn," I tell him, adjusting my glasses on my nose. I've been participating in lots of tests over the past few days, and I was given glasses to improve my sight. The doctors seem to be very particular in fiddling with me to achieve near perfect vision, but I don't care anymore. I don't care about their arbitrary measurements and numbers. My life has already changed for good. Even the pitch-black darkness of night is not quite so dark. Now, there is so much more to discover that would have otherwise escaped me forever. I want to soak up every bit of life that I've been missing.

I finally encounter what I'm searching for in my purse, and I pull out a handful of little strips of paper. I dig a bit deeper to find my phone, and I use it as a flashlight to examine the rectangular boxes of color printed on the paper, along with small descriptive lettering—they are paint chips. Earlier in the week, Liam needed to swing by the hardware store to buy some new lights to brighten up his apartment for me. I accompanied him, and by chance, I discovered the magical world of paint chips. Thousands of gorgeous colors with adorable names to describe each one. Some of the names are straightforward, like Honey Mustard, Lipstick Red, or Soothing Sapphire. But some are a bit more abstract and cause my imagination to wander. Midnight Blue, Artic Pool, Emerald Valley, Last of the Lilacs, or Sunflower Petal.

Only hours after my operation, I found myself struggling to read written letters for the first time, instead of braille. Of course, the first book I picked up was Liam's signed copy of *Blind Rage*. I was embarrassed to see how dreadful and sloppy my inscription was compared to the neat and evenly printed words throughout the book. At first, I grew very frustrated with trying to read the tiny script. I tried to read until my eyes were literally bleeding and sore. While I knew the general shape of each letter, my eyes were unused to needing to put them together into words and comprehending them quickly.

Liam finally hooked me up with a computer program intended to teach children the alphabet. I was embarrassed at first, but it quickly began to help me. I was then able to pull up a document file containing my story, and make the text larger until I could easily read my own writing. I spent an entire day learning to read my own books with my eyes, and it was eventually just as wonderful as I'd always imagined.

Now, I am struggling to read the tiny lettering on paint chips to memorize the colors. I never dreamed that there were so many infinite shades. No wonder I was always confused when people spoke about colors.

"Pure Periwinkle," I murmur, as I flip through a few paint chips. "Purple Passion. Amethyst Reflection. Oxford Blue. Faded Denim. Pearl Drop. Ming Dynasty White!" I sigh a little in satisfaction. Even if I couldn't see each particular hue, the names would give me a great deal of pleasure; but the fact that I *can* see them causes my entire body to hum with excitement.

I never knew that seeing a beautiful color was tantamount to hearing a lover's whisper.

"Wow," I say as I hold the paint chips closer to my face. "There are so many descriptions that I've never even heard before."

Liam looks over at me and smiles. "Winter, you're going to overload your brain with too much information. You can't memorize the names for every shade of every color known to man. Besides, a lot of those are just made up."

"I don't care!" I say, waving the paint chips at him eagerly. "Don't you understand? I never knew. I had no idea. I've heard of red, blue, yellow, black and white. I just didn't realize there was so much more. Liam!" I gasp a little in horrified realization. "I wrote my books with complete ignorance of how to actually describe *anything*. How can anyone like my writing?"

"You described emotions well," he tells me, "and that's all that matters. That's why people really read books." He leans forward to grab one of the paint chips from my hand, and reads it a little mockingly while driving. "Purple Passion? You can call that color a dozen other things. Probably way better things. I can't think of any, but I'm sure there are some. What about these... Royal Indigo? Lavender Suede? Mysterious Mauve? Hey, those

CLARITY

are actually pretty good. Very Violet. Happy Hyacinth. Okay, I see what you mean. These are kind of addictive."

"I told you," I say with a triumphant nod.

"Most people don't need all of this detail," he says as he places the paint chip back in my lap and returns to driving. "Who cares if the purple of your character's dress is dark or pale? What really matters is what's going on in the story."

"But doesn't it change the feel of the story if her dress is eggplant purple instead of Tyrian purple, or even magenta or fuchsia? A few days ago, I would have picked a random word based on how it sounded."

"It's not the color that makes the story," Liam tells me. "It's the story that makes the color. For example, do you know the history behind the creamy-yellow color *Isabelline*?"

I shake my head and turn to gaze at his profile as he speaks.

"In the fifteenth or sixteenth century, some Spanish woman named Isabella—a duchess or a queen or something—said that her husband was so amazing in battle that she expected a quick victory, and she wouldn't wash her underwear until he came home from war. The siege ended up lasting several years, and, well, you can only imagine the color of her dirty underwear after that."

I have to put my hand over my mouth as

giggles bubble up uncontrollably. "Seriously?"

He smiles in response. "I'm not making this up. I'm not any good at making things up! Anyway, I am positive that your stories will grow to be much more detailed and visual from this point forward, but I won't let you talk crap about the stuff you've already written. The vision you had inside your mind was always stronger than the superficial vision everyone else has. I think you'll remember that soon, once you stop getting overwhelmed by the mountains of rainbows falling on your head."

"Mountains of rainbows," I repeat thoughtfully as I return to examining my paint chips. "I like that."

"If I can ever afford an actual house with more than one room," Liam tells me. "I promise I'll let you choose the paint colors for the walls. Especially for our bedroom."

"I have the perfect one: Crimson Sin," I say with a mischievous smirk. Then I pause and look at him. "Wait, did you say *our* bedroom?"

"Aren't you going to share my bedroom?" he asks, as if it's the most natural thing in the world.

I laugh nervously, turning away to hide the fact that my cheeks are blushing the color of Scarlet Inferno. "Maybe," I say softly.

He continues to drive for a few minutes, and I continue to examine the various shades on the strips. I especially like the ones named after flowers. I haven't seen too many flowers yet, but I can imagine the memory of the various scents and the texture of their petals paired with the colors on the paint chips. Tender Daffodil, Iris Impact, Rich Bluebell, Morning Glory.

"We're almost there," Liam tells me. "Can you see the sky getting brighter?"

I glance up from my paint chips, and look toward the horizon. I do see that the sky is no longer completely black, but there is a faint glow of blue stretching across the east. I am held spellbound by the changing colors before I turn to Liam. "Is it... dawn? Are we going to watch the sunrise?"

"We're already watching the sunrise," he tells me. "It starts off small, with a few notes of color. Then it grows and builds, like a piece of music. Pay attention, or you might miss the best moment."

"You're insane," I tell him, but my eyes are glued to the sky. I have never seen the sunrise, and it seems almost surreal how the horizon is beginning to be touched by light. I am staring for a few minutes before I feel the car go over a large bump as Liam drives over a barrier of some sort. "What was that?" I ask him.

"You'll see," he tells me.

I am a bit nervous, as I try to look around and examine our surroundings. I can feel that the car is no longer driving on the hard road. I look out at the skyline again, and I squint my eyes to try and see better. I suddenly realize that there seems to be a harsh line directly through the sunrise. Like half of it might be a reflection—on water. "Are we on... a beach?" I ask him in surprise. "Are you driving on *sand?*"

Liam nods and smiles. "It's something my parents used to do with me when I was a kid. It was the best part of my childhood. We'd drive out onto the beach and watch the sunrise. My dad used to say that we had 'front row seats.'"

"That sounds so lovely," I tell him as I gaze at his face in the dim light. All I can see is the shadowy outline of his nose, but I'm glad that I can even see that much. He seems a little guarded and withdrawn as he mentions his past. He hardly ever talks about his family, and I am honored that he's sharing this with me. I feel like he's really letting me get close to him.

"You should really visit your dad," Liam tells me as he parks the car. "Wouldn't you like to see what he looks like?"

I turn away and look back to the sunrise. "I don't think I'm ready."

"You could see pictures of what you looked like as a child!" Liam says to me. "Aren't you curious? You could see pictures of your mother."

The idea has crossed my mind. I close my

eyes and take a deep breath. "I really wish I could," I tell him. "I just feel really uncomfortable about going anywhere near the house where Grayson lives."

"But he's in a psych facility," Liam says. "Wouldn't it be better to visit your family while he's not there? Before he's released?"

"Liam, I still have nightmares almost every night. I need physical and mental distance to start to get better. I don't care where he actually *is*. I need to get him out of my *head*."

"Maybe," Liam says, unbuckling his seatbelt and leaning over to slip his hand around my waist. He lets his lips linger just above mine as he speaks. "Or maybe you just need to watch the sunrise." He gives me a single, resolute kiss before pulling away and returning to his own seat.

I glance over at him before looking back to the sky. The horizon is now being touched with splashes of rosy pink and a deeper lavender. The blue of the sky above is changing rapidly, going through a gradation of different shades so quickly that I can't keep up. I can't even begin to think of what to call them. Azure, Cobalt, Ultramarine. There are so many beautiful shades of blue that it defies description and takes my breath away. Suddenly, I notice something strange interrupting the sunset.

"What is that?" I ask Liam, pointing through the windshield of the car. "It seems like...

Loretta Lost

is it a star?"

"I was hoping you'd be able to see it," Liam says with a happy smile. "It reaches its peak brightness right before sunrise and right after sunset. It's the planet Venus, also known as the morning star. It's brighter than the brightest stars in the sky."

A shiver of pleasure runs through me at this information. "I can see a planet? I am actually looking at a planet right now. Liam! How did you do this to me? I never dreamed I'd be able to see so much."

"I used to be obsessed with stargazing when I was a kid," Liam says. "I never wanted to be a doctor—I wanted to be an astronaut. But we were very poor, and that seemed like a stupid and ridiculous dream to my parents. They didn't consider anything to do with space a *real* career. They wanted me to be reasonable, and reliable, and grow up to be a doctor like my grandfather who died in the war. So they borrowed lots of biology books from the library, and forced me to read them over and over. We couldn't even afford a telescope, although I asked for one on every birthday and Christmas. It was all I ever wanted... a goddamn telescope." He laughs at this memory. "I suppose they were right in the end. Being a doctor is a reliable career."

"And if you weren't a doctor," I tell him softly, "I never would have met you."

462

"Then I guess it's a good thing I didn't follow through with my plan of quitting school and becoming a UFC fighter," Liam says with a grin.

"Really?" I ask him. "You really considered that?"

"I considered a lot of crazy things. I nearly joined the military once. Owen always talked me out of it, and reminded me that I had really good grades, and actually liked medicine. What I didn't like was being controlled. But now that I'm here, I really am glad I listened to them. I do love my job." He pauses for a moment. "I just like looking at the stars a little better."

"Thanks to your job, I can look at the stars, too," I tell him. "Well, one star—the sun. Along with the moon and Venus. But that's more than I ever would have had without you. Your job might have stolen the stars from you but it did the opposite for me."

"I'm sure that you'll be able to see even better soon," he tells me. "And it wasn't really me—almost any ophthalmologist could have done this for you."

"It was you," I tell him with a smile. "You gave me the stars."

He leans forward across the center console of the car to kiss me again. His kiss grows deeper, and he slips his hand below my jacket. He stays lip-locked with me for a few minutes before pulling away and clearing his throat. "I don't want you to miss the sunrise," he tells me.

I am a little dizzy from his kiss, but I nod and look back to the sky. "Whoa! Did all that happen while we were kissing?" The horizon has exploded in color. There are little wisps of clouds that have been tinted deep orange. I look down at my paint chips and try flipping through them frantically. I get to the variations of orange, and try to find the words to describe what I'm seeing. Amber, Pumpkin, Coral, Salmon? Nothing seems to fit quite right. It's a good thing I was born blind. If I could have seen all these divine colors, I might have become a painter instead of a writer.

"I want to step outside to see it better," I tell Liam as I open the car door.

"It's really cold out," he warns me, but he also opens his door and steps out to join me.

I move to the front of the car and lean against it, taking in the breathtaking view. I try to capture the sight in my mind, or paint it with words that I could use in a story, but I find that everything in my mind is completely inadequate compared to the cosmic proportions of this natural splendor.

It also tears my heart to pieces a little.

"Everyone gets to see this," I say, fighting back tears. "Every single day. Everyone gets to see the sunrise." I find myself feeling bitterly jealous of every day that has been stolen from me.

"Winter," Liam says gently as he moves to

my side. "Most people don't even look. They don't
have the time, or they've seen so many sunrises
that they don't care anymore. They're desensitized.
It happens every day, after all."

"Like this?" I demand angrily. "It's this
beautiful every day?"

"Yes. I mean, it's different every day.
Sometimes when you're in the city, it's blocked by
huge buildings. Or you're sleeping through it due
to your work hours. We can't always look at the
sunrise."

"That's a tragedy," I say softly. "Because
when I look at this, I feel like it's the beginning of
everything. I feel like my whole life has just
disappeared and I'm brand new. I feel like this is
going to be the best day I've ever lived."

"See?" he tells me gently, pulling me
close and kissing my temple. "It's not about the
colors; it's about what they mean. It's not about
what you see, and seeing clearly. It's about seeing
more deeply beneath and beyond that. That's true
clarity."

I stare for a few more minutes, ignoring
the cold wind that is nipping at us. I still do wish I
could dissect each color and find a way to capture
this moment forever. But even as I stare, each
color changes and each shape evolves, teasing me
with their ethereal nature. Liam is right. It's more
than any mere mortal can understand.

When I finally see the little ball of fire

peeking over the horizon, my eyes widen. It's unreal that anything could be that beautiful. It's unlike any color on the paint chips. It's a combination of marigold, tangerine, flamingo pink, and so much more... and the fiery glowing quality could never be replicated on paper.

I toss aside all my paint chips, letting them scatter on the beach. "Screw it," I mumble. "These are useless. Nothing can describe this. There aren't words in the English language. Or any language."

Liam laughs, and his breath tickles my neck. "I figured you might feel that way."

"You're amazing," I tell him, turning to gaze at his face. I can see more of him now, and he seems to be almost glowing in the light of dawn. "I'm completely in love with you."

He seems taken aback by my words. "Are you sure? I think you might be under the influence of the sunrise."

"The UV rays are loosening my inhibitions and my tongue, but what I feel is real. I think I've felt this way for a while." I look down shyly, feeling suddenly very vulnerable. "I love you, and I've never been this happy."

Of course, as soon as the words leave my mouth, I feel absolutely sure that something is going to go terribly wrong. Liam reaches out to pull me close until my body is pressed against his. He leans down to kiss my lips. Even though he is holding me tightly and reciprocating my affection,

I can't shake the feeling that I have just cursed myself and ruined everything.

"We should go back inside," he tells me. "It's getting really cold out here. Do you want to get into the backseat and cuddle a little while we watch the end of the sunrise?"

"Sure," I tell him with a mischievous smile. "We can 'cuddle.'"

"My first sunrise ever," I say teasingly as I re-arrange my clothing, "and you had to distract me."

"I think I enhanced the experience," he tells me with a grin. "You really seemed to like it. You made so much noise that you woke up all the seagulls!"

I laugh as a flock of birds actually does fly quite close to the car. "I'm sure they were waking up anyway."

"Let's move back to the front seats," he tells me as he buttons up his shirt. "We should try to get home before the traffic gets really heavy."

"Wait," I say as he opens the door. "Liam?" An idea suddenly strikes me as I stare at the empty beach. It's not only extremely early on a cold winter morning, but it's a weekday. It's perfect. "You know what would be even more amazing than having sex on the beach in the sunrise?"

"What?" he asks.

"If you taught me how to drive."

He looks at me in surprise. "But your eyes—and you don't have a permit."

"I can see quite well now that the sun is up. There's no one around for miles. I should be able to get a permit soon. Come on, please?"

"I'm not sure," he says, hesitating.

"Pleaseeee," I beg him, tugging on his sleeve. "I'll do anything."

"Anything?" he asks slyly.

"Well," I say nervously. "Almost anything. You're not going to ask for something Owen-y, are you? Because I really don't think I'm a back-door kind of girl."

"I can assure you that I'm much more sophisticated than that," he tells me. Then he grins at me. "Plus, I wouldn't use my one wish to ask for something that I'm pretty sure I could convince you to try under normal circumstances, anyway."

"Aren't you confident?" I say with a smirk. However, I'm pretty sure that he *could* convince me to do just about anything. Sometimes, I get so swept up in being with him that I could swear I've lost my mind.

"I will teach you to drive if you cash your dad's check and try to re-establish ties with him," Liam says. "Deal?"

I pause and wrinkle up my nose. "Just my dad? Not Carmen? And can I just do phone calls? I don't have do actually go to the house?"

"Just your dad, and phone calls are fine," Liam responds, "for now. But you have to think about visiting him sometime soon."

"Why do you want me to do this?" I ask him curiously. "What's in it for you?"

"Family is important, and I want what's best for you. I know you'd be happier if you reached out to him. Your dad never did anything wrong, and you can't let him suffer because of things that Grayson did."

"Fine," I say, climbing forward in the car to sit in the front seat. "I'll do it. Now, teach me how to drive!"

Chapter Eleven

Four weeks later...

My eyes scan over the pages as I viciously hit the 'down' arrow to read through my document. There are only three more chapters left in my book, and they are the most important chapters of all. I find myself anxiously wasting hours reading and rereading the beginning of the book to make sure I haven't missed anything or left any loose ends. I've never cared so much about making every single part of the story so perfect—I used to write only for myself, and mostly ignore the comments of others, but now, for the first time, I really want to hear what my readers have to say. I'm not so scared of disappointing them that I can't face them. And even if they hate the book and rip me apart, at least I have Liam to lean on for emotional support.

I continue reading rapidly, hardly closing my eyes to blink.

My vision goes a little blurry for a second, and the words all seem to melt together on the page and drip down into a little pool of ink. I press both of my hands over my eyes and wait for a moment to allow them to rest. Sometimes, after serious writing marathons of sitting at the computer for twenty-four hours or more, my vision will begin to grow dim and falter. Wearing my glasses or contact lenses doesn't seem to help. I haven't told Liam yet, although I'm sure he could fix it quite quickly. Frankly, I'm exhausted with having my eyes poked and prodded, and I just want to use them to do what I love. I don't have time to waste sitting in a hospital chair.

A ringing sound temporarily distracts me from my fuzzy vision. I reach out to pick up the phone, smiling at Liam's name on the display. I no longer find myself jumping out of my own skin whenever I receive a phone call. On top of that, my nightmares have stopped. Sleeping beside Liam every night has given me a lot of comfort and security, and I don't feel like the whole world is out to get me anymore. At least, not all the time. I have even grown to love the city again, and sometimes I can even muster the courage to go for walks by myself and do some light shopping. I feel like now that I have the ability to see, I am on more of an equal playing field with everyone else. I am less of a target. Keeping up with martial arts now and then has also bolstered my confidence.

"Hi doctor," I say into the phone upon answering. "How's work?"

"It's hectic as hell today," Liam says in an exhausted way. "I wanted to hear your voice and some good news. How's your book coming along?"

"Slowly," I tell him with a frown. "I feel like it's taking forever. I've re-written three chapters from scratch, and it still doesn't feel good enough."

"You just need to adjust to the new computer," he tells me. "Your typing speed has gone up a lot since you stopped writing your stories on your notetaker and started using a QWERTY keyboard. I'm sure that once you get used to it, you'll be writing many more books in far less time."

"I hope so," I tell him, but I don't feel like the problem is with my equipment.

"Winter," he says tiredly, "if you get a chance, can you check the mailbox to see if there's a letter about my research grant? Or about my publication in the journal?"

"Sure," I tell him, closing my laptop. "I need to check for my new driver's license anyway!"

"I hope you get it," he says. "Can you also

call that guy about the retail space we looked at the other day, and tell him we can't afford it? Owen's loan fell through—he has too many other debts."

"Sure thing," I tell him, "but you know I offered to help you guys out with the money. Most of my check is still sitting there."

"I would prefer not to take any of your money," Liam says quietly. "That's yours."

"I don't mind investing some of it in you," I tell him with a smile. "Interest free."

"I'll think about it," he tells me, "if everything else falls to pieces. Now onto more important subjects. Did you remember to call your dad?"

"Yes. We're going to go out for coffee once I finish this book."

"Great. And how's Snowball?"

I glance down under the table at the ball of fur curled up around my feet. "She's napping for once, and not bouncing all over the place."

Liam laughs. "I still think we should have called her Spring. It would have been so clever. I could have introduced people to my girls, Winter and Spring Rose."

"But she *loves* the name Snowball, and it suits her perfectly. Now you can introduce people to Winter and Snowball. It's just as clever." I gently stroke her fur with my toes as she naps.

Two weeks ago, Liam bought me a puppy. I can still remember the conversation like it was yesterday, when he first came home and pressed the little creature into my arms.

"I know that you never liked the idea of a guide dog," he'd said. *"You're far too self-sufficient for that—but this little puppy is a rebel, just like you. She flunked out of guide dog school because she refused to follow instructions for any amount of treats. She was also incredibly antisocial and wouldn't get along with any of the other dogs. Naturally, I felt that you two belonged together."*

"Liam, is our relationship really ready for a puppy? We only just started dating." Of course, I had already fallen in love with the lively bundle of fur from the moment I first held her, but I had to protest.

"You need someone to keep you company all day while you write! It's not healthy to be alone so much. I think we should call her Spring."

"Why?" I asked curiously, setting the puppy down and watching her run all around us in energetic circles.

"For a few reasons," Liam said, moving close to me and slipping his fingers under the straps of my dress. *"She is obviously bouncy like a little spring, but it is also the season after winter. She's like a warmer, more cuddly version of you."*

"Spring?" I asked, testing the sound on my tongue as I lifted my hands to undo Liam's tie. *"Wouldn't it be prettier to call her Summer or*

Autumn?"

"But someday," Liam said, slipping my
dress off my shoulders and letting it slide to the
ground, *"if we have daughters, we could name*
them *Summer and Autumn. I'd love to collect the
whole set."*

I must have stood there for a full minute,
staring at him speechlessly. Finally, I managed to
clear my throat and think of a witty response.
"What if we have sons?"

I've never been in a real, adult relationship
where everything goes perfectly smoothly all the
time. All I've ever known is how to run away. I'm
very skilled at finding a man's greatest flaws, and
blowing them out of proportion until he's forever
tainted in my mind. I can mentally cling to these
flaws as the reason that things could never work.

But with Liam, I can't even find a flaw.
Trust me, I've been looking.

Sometimes he works a little too hard, and
he is out for long hours. While this might bother
most women, I barely notice, and capitalize on the
time to write. I'm glad that he doesn't require more
attention. I find his work ethic endearing and
admirable.

When he is with me, he is with me
completely; he treats our time together as precious.

Sometimes, when he jokes about marriage
and kids, I can see a grain of truth behind his eyes.
I think that's the most powerful aspect of my new

vision. I can now look into a man's eyes and see what he's feeling; whether he's honest or insincere. I can't think of a single reason why a future with him wouldn't be a good idea. I find myself daydreaming about it very often. I think he'd make an excellent father.

After all, he always remembers to feed our puppy.

"Winter, did you hear my question? Are you still here?"

"What?" I say in surprise, realizing that he is still on the phone with me. "Sorry, I was distracted. Can you repeat that?"

"What do you feel like having for dinner?" he asks me. "Should I grab something on the way home, or do you want to go out?"

"I could try to cook for a change," I offer. "I'm getting the hang of how to use things in the kitchen."

"No wasting time until you finish that book," he orders me. "I'll bring home our usual Chinese."

"That works, too. Thanks, Liam. I hope your day gets better."

"I hope you can get that perfect ending to your book. Text me if there's something good in the mailbox. See you later, Winter."

"Bye." I carefully slip my feet out from underneath Snowball, and get up from my chair. Picking my purse off the counter, I sling it over my shoulder and drop my phone into it before heading for the door. I am pretty sure that my hair is a mess, but I don't really care. As soon as I turn the doorknob, Snowball wakes up with a start, and begins yipping with delight. Eager to accompany me, and afraid of being left behind, she manages to go sliding across the hardwood floors and diving headfirst into the door before it is even opened.

"Okay, sure," I tell her with a laugh. "You can come along."

I retrieve her leash and clip it onto her collar. She stares up at me with happy eyes as though she is sure that we are going to do something incredibly fun.

"We're just going to check the mailbox, Snowball. Nothing amazing. Fine, maybe a tiny walk around the block, but then I have to get back to work!" I lead her through the door with me, and she begins eagerly pulling me down the hallway. I begin moving along with her, but the sound of a door opening behind me causes me to turn around.

"Hey, blind bitch! I thought you said you wasn't the doctor's girlfriend."

I am so stunned by the woman's appearance that I immediately break into a smile of pity. I am in much too great of a mood to allow her rude salutation to bother me.

"I guess I was wrong," I say to her, trying not to stare at her extremely eclectic fashion. She looks like she has stepped out of the 70s, with hot pink pants that cling to her generous thighs. She is also wearing a tie-dyed flowery shirt, a small neon yellow band in her very frizzy hair, and large hoop earrings. For a moment, I swear that her outfit is so blindingly bright that I'm going to lose my vision again.

"So, how is he?" she asks, chewing loudly on her gum. "If you're going to keep him all to yourself, at least share the deets."

Snowball barks at the woman, annoyed that she has interrupted our little adventure.

My smile grows larger. "He's amazing," I tell the woman. "So amazing. He blows my mind." I turn to leave, but as I'm walking away, I swivel and look back at her. "By the way! I'm not blind anymore."

"Well, ain't that lucky for you!" she shouts down the hallway.

I try hard not to laugh as I take Snowball toward the elevators with me. I think I'll have the image of that woman seared into my brain for a long time. It's always a little surprising the first time I see someone I've met before and get to match their face and body to their voice. I always thought that voices told the whole story, but I never realized how much information I was actually missing.

Snowball nuzzles my leg as we ride down in the elevator, and I gaze at her happily. How did Liam know that I needed a dog? Even I didn't know, and I probably would have declined if he had asked me first; but Snowball really is perfect for me. I can no longer imagine a life without her—or him.

When the elevator doors open, we head out toward the mailboxes. I fish around in my purse for the key, and open up Liam's mailbox. There is a bundle of letters, and I begin flipping through them. I find some advertisements and flyers, and I toss those into the recycling bin. There are some bills for him, but I nearly squeal in delight when I see a letter for me from the DMV. Thanks to Liam's lessons, I was able to pass my test on the first try. I have been browsing through vehicles online, and I am thinking of buying myself a little car. I really love the feeling of driving. When I find another letter for me, I am surprised to see elegantly written handwriting covering the envelope.

I remember that my dad recently asked for my address so that he could send over a letter. Is this my father's handwriting? I have never received a handwritten letter before—at least not one that I didn't need to ask someone to read for me. I hook my finger under the flap of the envelope to tear it open hastily, excited to devour its contents.

> DEAR HELEN,
> YOU'VE RIPPED MY HEART TO
> PIECES, SWEET ANGEL.
> IT'S EATING ME ALIVE FROM
> THE INSIDE. I NEED YOU.

I feel like the world around me has gone very quiet. There is a kind of ringing in my ears as I stare at these sentences. I am not sure how long I remain standing there and looking at the letter. My stomach has tied itself into knots. I am so frozen that I find my eyes are locked to one sentence, and unable to continue reading. My fingers slightly quiver. I must not have blinked for a long time, because my eyes begin to ache and the letter grows blurry.

Shutting my eyes for a moment, I take a deep breath. It suddenly occurs to me that my dad must have given Grayson my new address. Grayson knows where I am.

"What the fuck," I whisper. "What the actual fuck..."

The letter flutters from my fingers, and Snowball chases it as it lands. She sniffs it to determine whether it is an item of interest, but seems to decide that she is not fond of its contents. She growls softly at the offensive piece of paper, as though she can sense my distress.

I lean against the mailboxes, suddenly feeling very tired. A few sentences are all it took to ruin my day and steal all my good energy. I don't know if I'll be able to get back to writing after this. Do I need to move again? Is Liam safe? Dozens of questions collide in my brain, and I feel the need to crawl under the blankets and escape in sleep.

"Miss Winter?" says the concierge from behind me. "Are you okay?"

"Yes," I say, straightening slightly. When the young man stoops to retrieve the letter, I flinch as he hands it back to me. "Thanks, Brian."

"What's the matter, Miss Winter? You look like you've seen a ghost."

I hesitate before speaking to him. "The person who sent this letter isn't supposed to know my address. I moved here to get away from him. He could be... dangerous."

"Don't worry," he assures me. "You know we have excellent round-the-clock security here. I'll make a note of it, and we'll screen guests to Dr. Larson's apartment more carefully."

"That's nice of you, Brian." I try to smile in gratitude, but my face doesn't seem to work. I glance toward the glass doors that lead outside, where Snowball is so eager to go for a walk. I also have a very strong desire for some fresh air, but the idea of being in public is suddenly far too much to bear. I hate this feeling of backsliding, and letting my fear resurface, but I need to be alone, behind closed doors, as soon as possible.

"Is it a bad ex?" Brian asks.

"Sorry?" I say, turning to him. I realize that I had been staring blankly into the distance. "Oh. Something like that."

"It will be fine, Miss Winter," he assures me before returning to his desk.

I frown, finally gathering the courage to look at the rest of the letter.

I NEED YOUR FORGIVENESS. I REALIZE THE GRAVITY OF WHAT I'VE DONE. I DON'T KNOW HOW TO LIVE WITH THIS GUILT. PLEASE SAY YOU'LL TRY TO FORGIVE ME OR I DON'T THINK I CAN CARRY ON.

Once again, I can't read very far before it grows too upsetting to continue. I stuff the letter back into its envelope, and put it into my purse, along with all the other mail. Snowball is growing restless in waiting for me to take her outside, but I ignore her when I notice the glint of my phone in my purse. Seized by anger, I grab the phone and hastily call my father. I move into a quiet corner of the lobby while the phone rings.

"Hello, darling!" my father answers. "How's your book coming along?"

"You gave Grayson my new address?"

There's a silence on the other end of the line. "No, of course not," he finally says. "I just sent the letter for him. He told me that it was just an apology, and that it wouldn't upset you."

"Dad," I say, gritting my teeth. "Why would you do this to me? Why would you put me at risk like this?"

"Sweetheart, I promise that he doesn't know your address! Grayson is not a bad person, and he would never really hurt you. You just happened to see him when he was very sick last month. But he's feeling better now, after spending several weeks in the hospital..."

"How stupid do you think I am?" I ask him angrily. "Grayson has always been this way to me. Why do you think I really left home all those years ago? Ask him. Ask him if he'd ever really hurt me."

"Helen, honey..."

"Fuck you!" I hiss, and I immediately regret the words as they leave my mouth. Just hearing my name spoken sends me over the edge, and suddenly my father is my enemy. I fight against my tears. "I'm sorry, Dad. I appreciate the money you gave me, but I didn't need money. I needed safety. I thought fathers were supposed to protect their daughters?"

"Helen, I don't understand..."

"Please stop, Dad. Five hundred thousand

dollars can't bring back the years that I lost. If Grayson comes to my door and hurts me again, five hundred thousand dollars isn't going to cover the cost of my sanity or my life. If he hurts Liam..." I shut my eyes tightly, horrified at this thought. "He already shot Liam once. What will he do next time?"

"Darling, you need to calm down. Please. Grayson has made some mistakes, but he's family now. I think you and Liam should come over on Friday night and join us for a family dinner. Just give him a chance. It would mean the world to your old man to have your company—to be together as a family."

"Are you serious?" I ask him in disbelief.

"Your sister is pregnant, sweetheart. It could be nice if she had another girl around to talk to now and then. Don't you want to be there for Carmen? She's been really depressed and I've been taking her to therapy. All this stress isn't good for the baby, you know?"

"Dad," I say quietly. "I just got my driver's license in the mail. A few nights ago, I was feeling restless and I just got in the car and drove. I just drove down the street in the middle of the night, and there was no one around. All the lights were green. I just drove and drove, and I didn't encounter a single red light." I look down at Snowball with a sad smile. "It felt like a sign of some sort. That I'm moving in the right direction."

"Darling, you sound just like your mother."

"I'm finally starting to be okay again, Dad. Better than okay. I'm finally starting to have all the things that every normal person has. You know what a struggle it's been for me. Please don't take that all away from me now."

"Helen, I want you to be happy. I want all these things for you more than anyone. I just don't want to lose you, dammit! I don't know how to do this. I don't know how to keep a family together, but I'm trying my damned hardest. Your sister has made some poor choices, but you can't turn your back on her now. She's family. Her baby is family. Grayson is family."

I shake my head in refusal, even though I know he can't see me. It's more for my personal resolve. "I'm sorry, Dad. I love you, but I need to protect myself. You just gave Grayson a method of contacting me and finding me. I was wrong to think that it was safe to talk to you on the phone. We can't communicate anymore."

"You can't be serious. Darling, I'm your father! You can't do this."

"Liam is my family now. He's the only person I can trust." With that, I hang up the phone and hit the buttons to block my father's number. I am filled with the familiar urge to get the hell away. If Grayson knows this address, then all of my worst nightmares could come true. I stand still for a moment, staring out into the street with a frown on my face.

My puppy barks at me in a disappointed way.

"And you, Snowball," I assure her gently, stooping to my knees to ruffle her fur. "I trust you most of all!"

Chapter Twelve

I turn the steering wheel to navigate through the hospital parking lot. Since receiving Grayson's letter, I haven't felt comfortable being home alone for extended periods of time. Snowball isn't very vicious looking or sounding, and I'm not sure she'd make the greatest protector. I bought a little used car, and I often go for drives by myself and try to discover various cafés to sit and work in all day. I find that watching people walk by through the windows helps my writing. I have missed an entire lifetime of watching people, and I never grow tired of examining every little detail of the way they move and interact.

Sometimes I think I am growing quite fond of people.

Today, it happens to be Liam's birthday. We were supposed to spend the day together, but he was called away to work. I decided to come to the hospital and surprise him with a present, and maybe spend his break with him. I turn a corner in the hospital parking lot, squinting to see better in the dim lighting. There don't seem to be any available spots, and I circle around impatiently. I have visited Liam at work a few times, and I always make sure to stop by the hospital café and hang out with Krista, the waitress. If I'm stuck on a chapter, talking to her always helps. It turns out she's a philosophy major, a few years younger than I am, and she hopes to be a writer too someday. She actually looks up to me.

It's a little weird being old enough for someone to look up to me. I am not even really that successful yet, and no one knows my name. Any of my names. But Krista seems to admire me anyway. She thinks it's cool that I dropped out of school to do what I love, and she wishes she had the courage to do the same. Of course, she doesn't know the whole story, but I almost prefer it that way. No one in my life has ever looked up to me— no one other than Snowball. When I see myself through Krista's eyes, I feel a little bit happier with who I am and what I've accomplished.

She's the closest thing to a friend that I've had in the longest time. I haven't been too affectionate or called her that officially, but I like her company now and then. Back when I was in college, I thought I had friends. Or almost-friends. We obviously weren't that close, because when the shit hit the fan, I was able to leave them all behind without a second thought. I guess I've always been scared of getting too close. But now that things are working out well with Liam, I feel like maybe I could be brave in other ways.

I'm tired of running away. I want to have people in my life that enjoy spending time with me—people that like me for who I am. People who will still be there tomorrow, even if something unspeakable happens. I am starting to feel like Liam will always be there.

A car finally begins pulling out of a really great parking spot, and I squeeze in nearly as soon as it exits. It is close to the elevators, so I don't have to walk very far with Liam's present. I turn off my car and exit to grab my computer bag from the back seat. After slinging it over my shoulder, I tug a long, gift-wrapped rectangular box out of the vehicle. It's heavier than I expected it would be. I kick the car door shut and begin moving toward the hospital elevators. After hearing Liam's story about how his parents never got him that telescope, I decided I should get him one for his upcoming birthday. I shopped around a little before finding the perfect portable device that we could take out of the city on romantic stargazing trips now and then. It's not very powerful or expensive, but I am sure it could be useful for looking at the moon and planets.

Liam is always planning nice surprises for me, and I thought that I would try to surprise him for a change. After hanging out on his break, I intend to write in the hospital café with Krista until he finishes work, and then maybe we can try using the telescope on the hospital rooftop.

Depending on how private it is up there, maybe I can even give him a different kind of present.

This thought puts a mischievous smirk on my face as I wait for the elevators to carry me upstairs. When we arrive at the lobby, I blink rapidly to allow my eyes to adjust to the bright light. My eyes have been bothering me a lot lately, but I've been trying to ignore it. Once I can see clearly, I make a beeline for the café, excited to see Krista and get some good coffee inside me.

When I enter the little eating area, she turns to see me and her face lights up. Krista looks adorable with her blonde hair styled in two messy braids, and her little red apron. She also has freckles spotting across her nose, giving her the appearance of being a country milkmaid. She looks far too innocent to be so wise and worldly; if I had seen her first, before hearing her speak, I might have never listened to a single word.

"Oh! You got the telescope?" she says, moving up to me with the coffee canister in her hand. She has been hard at work keeping everyone's mugs refilled. "He's going to love it!"

"I hope so," I tell her with a smile. "If not, I'll have to do something else to make his birthday special."

"Sit down and let me get you a cup of coffee," she orders me, moving back behind the counter to finish up a few chores.

I place the telescope box down, along with my computer bag, as I take my usual spot.

Krista returns almost instantly with a steaming cup of coffee. She sits down across from me and folds her arms on the table. The café is not very busy today and it seems like we have some time for girltalk. "You look much less miserable than usual today, Winter!"

"Thank you," I tell her with a grin. I did try to put a splash of makeup on for the special occasion. "I guess I'm excited about Liam's birthday. It's nice to do something special for someone."

"Did you say he was turning twenty-nine or thirty? Either way, you should do something epic that you'll both remember for the rest of your lives. You should go big."

"Go big?" I ask her quizzically.

"Yes! You should take him on a spontaneous vacation somewhere," Krista suggests. "Hasn't Liam been bugging you to go on a trip with him lately?"

"Yes, he has been," I muse. "We've been looking at brochures for all kinds of special landmarks—the 'things that I *should* see now that I *can* see.' He's been trying to convince me to do something crazy once he gets some time off. The pyramids, the Great Wall, Machu Picchu, an Alaskan cruise, or one of those Eurotrips. He seems to be a little burnt out from work and he's craving an adventure."

"What's stopping you, Winter? Don't you have all that money that your dad gave you?"

I lift my shoulders in an awkward shrug. "I'm not making that much. I should probably save that money until I start getting more income from writing."

Krista sighs. "You poor, poor blind woman."

"What?" I ask her, lifting a hand to touch my eyes subconsciously. My vision has grown somewhat unclear for a few minutes, and I wonder if Krista can somehow tell. "I'm not blind anymore."

"But you are!" she says. "Metaphorically. You have an amazing guy, an amazing life, and amazing potential. Yet you constantly choose to shelter yourself from everything wonderful due to your crippling fear. When are you going to get over it?"

"Krista, I don't know. I just..."

"Seize life by the balls, my friend!" she says, making a small fist to emphasize her strength and enthusiasm. "When I look at you, I see this quiet, reserved person by day, who is totally capable of being a superhero by night. You have the ability to fly, when most of us never will. Why would you choose to keep your feet on the ground when you could reach the stars?"

CLARITY

I stare at her for a moment. I wonder what I've done to make her think so highly of me. It makes my heart soar a little. "Maybe you're right," I tell her softly. There's something contagious about Krista's bright energy and sanguine nature. Every time I talk to her, I leave feeling renewed and ready to conquer the world. "I'll let him know tonight that I'm ready to go on a trip with him. Maybe an adventure could help my writing."

"And you'll have to take lots of pictures and tell me all about it," she says with excitement. "I need to live vicariously through you while I'm stuck working here and taking night classes. I need you to give me hope that I'll get to live a real life someday."

"You will," I assure her with a puzzled smile. She always seems so positive—except for when it comes to herself. "There's no way that someone with your attitude won't succeed."

"I hope so," she says with a sad smile. She reaches into her apron and pulls out her notepad, and quickly scribbles something down on it. "Here's my number. Feel free to text me anytime, day or night. I never seem to get a chance to sleep lately."

"I will," I tell her, taking the number happily. Another customer walks into the café and Krista excuses herself to take his order. I watch for a moment as she helps the extremely old man into his seat. Even if I didn't know her, I'd probably

493

grow to love her from watching her kindness as she takes care of all of her customers. She is one of those people who does absolutely everything with grace and care. She is never mindless or mundane.

She throws herself into life with her full being. She treasures each fleeting moment as a new blessing. I am so proud to call her my friend. I am honored that she might consider me hers.

I watch her for a moment longer as she elegantly moves about the café. She turns back toward me in the middle of a coffee run and sends me a secret smile. The word that comes to my mind to describe her is "angelic," but that word has been ruined for me. To wash this appalling thought from my mind, I take a large gulp of my coffee.

Did Grayson see a similar quality in me to what I see in Krista? Is that what he meant?

And if so, why would he ever want to hurt someone like that?

I look at Krista, and feel fear and dread blossom in my chest. The thought of someone hurting her makes my stomach turn over. I find myself praying silently that she will never go through the horrors that I've lived. She is so pure and light, and I don't want anyone to ever steal that away from her. I stare down into my coffee and consider the ridiculous idea of bargaining with devils. If anything horrible is ever going to happen to Krista, I would like for it to happen to me instead. I am already broken, and I would rather be a little more broken than see her damaged in any way.

The world needs people like Krista. I wish I could be her shield against fate. I would happily protect her from all the arrows life might toss her way. I don't mind if they get deeply embedded in me, along with the others that are already stuck there.

A single tear splashes down into my coffee, and I frown at it. I bring the coffee to my lips and drink deeply again before pulling out my phone and programming her number into my contacts. I move to my text message inbox and send a quick message to Liam, asking him to give me a call when he gets a break. He responds almost immediately saying that he's between patients at the moment, but that he needs to make a few other phone calls and doesn't think he'll have a chance. He also says that he won't be home from work until very late tonight. I look down at my telescope box with worry, wondering if I won't get a chance to give him his present on his birthday.

"What's going on?" Krista asks as she returns. "Do you need a refill, or are you going to go seduce your man with the gift of a phallic object that symbolizes his virility?"

I choke on my coffee. Glancing down at the telescope in surprise, I look at it in an entirely different way. I clear my throat to remove the coffee from my airways. "He said he's busy making phone calls," I tell her in disappointment.

"Who cares?" she tells me. "Go up there and surprise him! It's his birthday, and he sounds like a chronic workaholic. It is your duty to make him relax for five minutes."

"You're so smart," I tell her gratefully. I rise to my feet and begin to gather my things. I pull out my wallet and leave a single bill to cover the coffee and a tip.

"Winter!" she exclaims. "The coffee doesn't cost fifty bucks. Not unless it comes with a blowjob, and unfortunately, I don't serve those. Not even to a girl with a really long, hard telescope."

I try very hard to keep from laughing and maintain a straight face. "Krista, you need to stop staring at my telescope. It's making me uncomfortable. I know it's huge and you probably really want to touch it, but it's off limits. I'm saving it for someone else."

Krista dissolves into giggles. "Just hold on a sec so I can grab you some change."

"I'm blind!" I tell her innocently as I walk away backwards. "I have no idea what bill that is. Keep the change!" Even as I say this, the banknote actually does grow hazy and distorted in my vision, and so does Krista. I turn away and blink to try and refresh my eyes. This is happening too often lately. I'm too scared to mention it to Liam. I don't want to hear that there's a possibility that I could lose my sight. It has been such a gift, and the idea that my vision could be stolen from me is terrifying. There's so much that I still haven't seen.

As I move through the hospital, I begin fantasizing about taking a romantic vacation with Liam. Even if my vision does eventually deteriorate, there's so much I'd like to see and do first. I imagine the ambience of beautiful candlelit dinners and fine wine. Cozy hotel rooms in romantic cities, and breathtaking landscapes. Mountains and rivers, and majestic historic sites. I smile as I enter the elevator with the telescope box, leaning my shoulder against the wall. Krista is right. I should take advantage of my newfound ability to have these experiences; I have the money and I have the time. Best of all, I will have Liam beside me to share every lovely adventure.

I did some traveling when I was younger. My parents liked to drive all over the country to visit wineries, but sometimes we would also travel to France or Italy. I enjoyed the trips, but I think it would be completely different to actually *see* those places. Everything is already different; I feel like a tourist in my own city and in my own skin. I feel like a tourist of nature, architecture, and people. I suppose that we are all only visitors to this planet for a short time—the only thing we can do is soak up as much of the magic as possible.

The elevator opens to my floor, and I walk out with a new spring in my step. Imagining these amazing vacations has put me in a stellar mood. A funny thought suddenly occurs to me; I wonder if and how Liam will propose to me? The thought is a little scary and a lot premature, but I figure I will allow myself to entertain the idea. Do I want him to propose? Would I say yes? I think it might be a bit too soon. But maybe going on a trip together is the perfect way to get to know him better. You can learn a lot about a person from traveling with him, and seeing how he adapts to new and challenging circumstances.

But marriage? Part of me feels too young, but part of me feels like "too young" is just an excuse people use to make themselves feel better when they haven't found the right person. What if I *have* already found the right person? I certainly can't imagine anyone better.

I figure that I will leave these decisions in his hands. He has never moved too quickly for me before; he is sensitive and thoughtful, and I know that he plans his every move with utmost care. I've been alone for so long that it's nice to trust my life in someone else's hands and let him take the lead. If life were a dance, Liam would be my perfect partner.

When I round a corner in the hospital corridors, I nearly bump into a nurse. I see that her nametag reads *Melanie*, and I smirk a little as I remember the way she used to hit on Liam. She is very short, and wearing makeup that is a little too heavy—especially around the eyes.

"Sorry," she mumbles. "Oh, it's you! How is your vision?"

"It's great," I tell her. Then I hesitate. "Sometimes things go blurry or dark at random moments, but it's mostly excellent."

"You should tell the doctor," she informs me. "Would you like me to get Dr. Larson? He's on break, but I'm sure he'd be happy to help."

"I'm not here for my eyes," I tell her with a smile, gesturing down at my gift-wrapped box. "I have a present for the doctor—to thank him for all his hard work."

"Aww," she says. "That's so sweet. He *is* amazing, isn't he? You can just head over to that break room and give it to him. I'm sure he'll be thrilled!"

I thank her and head over to the door she indicated, feeling a little shy. Whenever I visit Liam at work, we usually meet down in the café. I hope that he won't be upset that I'm showing up out of the blue like this—I hope it won't seem creepy or like I'm crowding him. I just really wanted to give him some sort of surprise on his actual birthday. He would have done the same for me.

Feeling a little burst of confidence, I move to enter the break room. There is a small seating area that is littered with pop cans and coffee cups, and half-finished meals. There is another room adjacent to this one, and it looks like there is a small kitchenette. I can hear Liam's voice filtering through from the other room, and I am about to go over there and meet him when his words cause me to pause.

"No, you have to listen to me," Liam is saying angrily. "I can't keep lying to your daughter like this. Helen is smart, and she's going to figure things out."

I step back quietly, trying not to alert Liam to my presence.

"That's not fair, Mr. Winters. You promised you would use your influence to help me get this research grant. It's really critical to my career right now, and I've done everything you asked." Liam's voice grows suddenly drained and exhausted. "Can't you just call the pharmaceutical company and put in a good word for me? Is that really too much to ask?"

There is still a wall between us, and he probably thinks that it's only another doctor who's entered the break room. Actually, he's so immersed in his conversation with my father that he might not even have heard the sound of the door opening. I put my hand on the doorknob, knowing that I should leave before I hear anything more.

I wish I hadn't walked in at this moment. But I can't stop listening.

"Didn't I hunt Helen down like you wanted?" Liam is demanding. "Didn't I convince her to come back here with me? Didn't I convince her to stay here even when she wanted to leave? Didn't I perform the surgery like I promised I would? That was our deal. That's all. I have gone above and beyond, and risked my job to take care of your daughter—that was never part of our bargain."

A bargain. I was just a bargain. I twist the doorknob in a feeble effort to leave before the poison can seep into my ears. But I already know that it's too late. *The master key. That's why I was special.*

"Please, sir. I have tried to convince Helen to reestablish ties with you. I got her to talk to you, didn't I? Things were going well until she got that letter. That wasn't my fault. I'm sorry, but she's very stubborn. Once she sets her mind on something, it's hard to dissuade her. I have tried my best, but I can't control your daughter in every way."

At this point, I need to remove my hand from the doorknob and clamp it over my mouth to keep from making a sound of disgust or breaking out into hysterical laughter. *Control me? Control me in every way? Really, Liam?* I simply cannot believe what I'm hearing, but now it all makes sense. Why he was so nice to me. So attentive and caring. He was manipulating me.

"I know you gave her all that money, sir, and I appreciate that. It has helped us both a great deal, but..."

I nearly drop the telescope box that I'm holding, but I manage to clutch it against my chest and keep it from tumbling to the ground. Was that money a kind of dowry? Was I just, like... *sold?* I shut my eyes tightly, feeling nausea and pain spreading through my gut. Liam didn't come to find me because he wanted to help me. He was given incentives by my father. He probably only read my books to do homework on me. I feel like a fool.

"Are you serious, Mr. Winters?" Liam says quietly. There is a pause. "Yes, I'll do anything. I can't lose that grant money. I am just getting sick of these games. I can't keep doing this to her."

Games. He's been playing games. I'm the game, and he's been playing me this whole time.

"Wait a second. Let me get this straight," Liam says sharply. "You want me to kick her out? You really think that's going to solve your problem?" There is a pause. Liam gives a small laugh. "I see. So you want me to break up with her in the worst possible way, so that she'll need her father? So that she'll come running to you? You want me to be a jackass to her, is that what you're saying?"

I wait for a moment, placing my hand back on the doorknob. A muscle in my cheek twitches as I wait for Liam to refuse. I wait for him to say that he actually loves me and he refuses to lie to me or manipulate me anymore.

"Okay. And if I do this, you'll guarantee that I get my research grant?" he asks.

I quietly turn the doorknob and step out of the break room. However, I don't walk away just yet, and I don't let the door shut fully behind me. I stand there for a moment, breathing deeply and trying to gather my composure. Should I confront him? Or should I just try to get away? Should I run away before he can break up with me? People are walking by, but everything is spinning and distorted in my vision. My chest aches and I struggle against the onset of one of my familiar old panic attacks. I try to breathe.

I hear the muffled sounds of Liam finishing up his conversation with my father, and I hear him beginning to pace back and forth in the break room. It seems like he has made another phone call, because he begins speaking to someone else in a less respectful tone of voice.

"Hey, Owen? I'm screwed, man. Royally fucked. I never expected things to get this far, and I'm in too deep. This man can't make up his fucking mind. First he wants me to babysit his daughter, and I was doing a damn good job of that..."

My mouth falls open slightly in disbelief. I am so frozen in shock that I am unable to think clearly or listen to what else he's saying. *Babysit me? Babysit me!* My shock quickly dissolves into anger, and I am filled with the urge to throw the telescope box across the room, and break every piece of furniture in sight. I want to scream.

Instead, I just remain still, silently quaking with the rage that is building like a tidal wave inside of me. My fingers tighten around the telescope box, and I feel like I might crush it with this major rush of adrenaline.

"You know how hard I worked to get close to her, man. Helen is so hypersensitive and it wasn't easy. Dealing with her was like walking on thin ice. I had to be so careful to call her 'Winter' to pacify her and keep her from freaking out..."

Okay. That's the final straw. I really don't need to hear him utter another single word. Ever. I move away from the door rapidly, intending to exit the hospital as soon as possible—and to permanently exit Liam's life even faster than that. I move to the nearest trash can and stuff the telescope box down into the slot. It does not fit, and sticks out awkwardly, but I don't care.

I turn and walk briskly down the hallway, so fast that I might as well be jogging. Finally, I give up on this and break into a full run. I don't know how to feel. I don't know what to do. I just need to get away from here.

Everything I thought I had was a lie. Of course it was. I should have known. Doesn't this story make more sense when the handsome doctor *doesn't* love me? Why would he? I'm a mess. That first night when he didn't want to touch me—that was real.

I just want to get to my car and get away. I continue running through the hospital halls, and my vision becomes temporarily fuzzy and dark. I can't see for a moment, and I'm moving too fast to keep from slamming directly into someone.

I recognize his voice right before I go tumbling to the ground.

"Dude, just relax. You're not thinking..." Owen is on the phone when I crash into him, and he drops it to the ground and staggers back with the impact. When he sees who hit him, he quickly retrieves his phone. "Shit. I've got to go, man—I'll call you back." He hangs up before moving over to check on me. "Whoa, Winter! Are you okay? You came at me like a tank, sister." He moves to my side and begins to carefully help me to my feet.

I shove him away viciously. "Don't touch me. I don't need any more *babysitting*."

"Oh, fuck. You heard that?" Owen takes a deep breath. "Shit! Winter, he didn't mean it. God, Liam loves you. He really didn't mean any of that. You know he's been working twenty-hour shifts and he's barely slept. He's not himself right now."

"Right now? You have *both* been lying to me for *months!*"

"He's just having a really bad day. Please, just give him a chance to explain. It's a Jekyll and

Hyde thing, you know? Liam is usually Dr. Jekyll—but today he's Mr. Hyde. It's just today, I swear. 99% of the time he's Dr. Jekyll."

I reach out and shove Owen hard, causing him to stumble back to the ground. "You knew. This whole time, you knew. And you just went along with it and helped him. You let him *seduce* me into being his little puppet. He weaseled his way into my life like a common salesman. I bet you two joked about it a lot, huh? Liam dangling his cock in front of me like a carrot?"

"It wasn't like that," Owen says with a sigh. "Look, he gets really depressed on his birthdays. He's had a darker past than he lets you in on. He didn't grow up in the greatest home, and he was very poor. His parents were abusive drunks. He's worked his ass off to get out and build a life for himself. It was a huge struggle for him to become a doctor, and he's still struggling every day. Try to understand where he's coming from."

"And apparently I'm just collateral damage on his climb to the top, right?" I glare at Owen fiercely, narrowing my eyes. "He'll fuck me in order to control me so that he can use the influence of my wealthy father. I'm just a rung on the ladder of his greed?"

"No. You know that's not true," Owen says softly. "Winter, I have known Liam for a long time. Yes, he's *very* greedy and ambitious. There's

506

hardly *anything* he won't do for money—but he wouldn't do that. I swear to you, he wouldn't do that. He wouldn't hurt you for money. Don't you know him better after all this time?"

"Maybe you don't know him," I hiss. "He just said he was going to leave me if my dad guaranteed him the fucking grant. He was going to leave me in a ditch and break my heart for a bit of money." Saying this out loud is equivalent to stabbing myself in the chest. My anger is starting to give way to pain, and I need to get out of here before it cripples me.

Owen puts both of his hands on my shoulders. "Winter, listen to me. You're being emotional and ridiculous right now. You and I both know Liam, and there's no one more loyal or loving on this planet. Don't you think you should give him the benefit of the doubt and talk to him about this?"

I rise to my feet and smooth my clothing to maintain some dignity. "Owen, I know he's your best friend. Bros before hoes and all that—but will you please do me a favor and not tell him that I heard that? Please."

Owen hesitates. "I have to tell him."

"If you were ever really my friend, for even one minute, please do me this favor. Give me twenty-four hours' notice before telling him."

"Why?" Owen asks.

"That's all the time I'll need to wipe

myself off the face of the planet," I inform him with a smile. "Neither of you will ever see me again."

"You can't do that to him," Owen says. "It would destroy him."

"It's what he wants, isn't it? He can tell my dad that he broke up with me and get his grant money. And I'll get my freedom. It's a happy ending."

"Winter, he's never loved anyone the way he loves you. It's not fake. It might have started out being fake, but it became real. Will you please relax for a minute and talk to him?"

"No. Just give me twenty-four hours, Owen. You owe me this after helping him lie to me the whole time. I'm just asking for a bit of time."

"Fine," Owen says softly. He lets his eyes drift down to the ground, looking a bit defeated. "I'm sorry."

I turn away to exit the hospital, but I am hit with another wave of distorted vision. I shut my eyes tightly and hesitate, turning back to the doctor on the floor. "Wait, Owen? Tell me something— did any of the people you performed these surgeries on lose their vision?"

"Huh?" he looks up at me with concern. "Yes. A very small percentage of people experienced a complete reversal after a few months. Their bodies rejected the drug. Why do you ask?"

"I just..." I pull my lips together into a tight line. "I am beginning to... never mind. No reason."

"If there are any issues with your eyesight, you need to tell us now. Winter, this is serious. If you've started having problems, you can experience a very rapid deterioration of your vision. You shouldn't get behind the wheel of a car until we can get you checked out. Let us help..."

"Fuck you," I tell him, turning to walk away. "I would rather die than accept help from either of you again."

With that, I begin moving through the hospital again, intending to get back to my car. I am too fired up to wait for the elevator, so I move into the stairwell and race down the stairs. However, instead of going directly to the garage, I find myself bursting out of the building for fresh air. I breathe deeply, letting my chest heave and expand. I felt like the hospital was suffocating me with its ugly atmosphere of sickness and death. I stare up at the cloudy sky, noticing that it does not seem as bright as it did only a few days ago.

Am I losing both my vision and my boyfriend at the same time?

I move to lean against a wall as I stare up at the sky with my defective eyes. I remember how nice it was to watch the sunrise with Liam for the first time. Did he ever really love me? Or did I just seem like a good long-term plan due to my likely inheritance? How far was he going to take this ploy? I remember him agreeing to teach me to drive on the condition that I talk to my dad. Was I always just a pawn on their chessboard? I have tried to be my own person; I have tried to escape, but I still ended up being merely a plaything for the men in my life.

I feel so dead inside. I am angry at Liam, and furious at my father, but I can't seem to feel any of these emotions. Even my vision is seeping away quietly, without any pain. There is just the loss and lack of something wonderful that used to be there. I feel like my world is growing dark again to mirror my fading hope and blackening soul. I just want to feel something.

I notice an older doctor a few feet away, smoking a cigarette. He is looking out at the street with blank eyes. He looks as miserable and empty as I feel. I have an urge to move over to him.

"Hey," I tell him quietly. "Could I have a cigarette?"

"Sure," he says, handing me one from his pack. "Need a light?"

"Yes, please."

He stares at me for a moment as I hold the cigarette out, close to his lighter. "You haven't done this before, have you? You need to put it between your lips and suck while I hold the flame up to the end of the cigarette."

"Oh," I say dumbly. "That makes sense." I follow his instructions and allow him to help me light the cigarette. When I finally draw in the tainted air, I expect that it will burn my lungs in some delicious way. Instead, it is just mildly unpleasant. "That's not so special."

"Yeah," he agrees, taking a pull from his own cigarette. "Nothing really is."

I try to inhale more deeply, rebelliously sucking the toxins into my body. I like the idea that it's harming me. I'm already losing my ability to see, so what does it matter if I do more damage to my body? I glance at the older man, carefully studying his expressionless face.

"Isn't it a bit strange for a doctor to be smoking?" I ask him.

He shrugs nonchalantly. "I lost three patients this week. They were all non-smokers. I'll smoke if I feel like it." He turns to give me an appraising look. "What's your problem?"

"I just found out that someone has been lying to me for my money," I explain as I drag more air through the cigarette.

"You have money?" he says with interest, raising his brow. "I can lie to you next, if you want. Or lie with you."

I shift uncomfortably as the sleazy doctor lets his eyes roam over my body.

"I bet he enjoyed lying to you," the doctor says as he moves closer. "I'd lie all over you for money. Or for free."

I wince in revulsion and take a step back. The doctor breathes on my face, and his breath smells sickening; like rotting flesh. I grit my teeth together angrily. For a moment, I consider sleeping with this random jerk just to be wild and reckless. To try to wipe Liam from my brain. I consider taking him home to Liam's apartment and I get a rush of pleasure as I imagine sleeping with him in Liam's bed. But the thought makes me even more disgusted.

I just decided that I don't like doctors very much.

"No, thanks," I tell him, dropping the cigarette to the ground and putting it out with my shoe. I turn around and head back to the garage to get in my car and get the fuck out of here. I am so done with this city.

It's time to disappear.

Chapter Thirteen

"It's just me and you now, Snowball," I tell her as she sits in my passenger seat whimpering softly. She can tell that something is wrong. "We don't need him anymore. We're going to be fine. You're going to get a lot more room to run around and play, and you can even chase the squirrels and birds. That will be fun, won't it?"

I was going to leave her behind because I didn't want to take any reminders of Liam along with me, but she looked up at me with such big sad eyes while I packed my suitcase. When I said goodbye and left the apartment, she cried and scratched the door as it closed behind me. I had almost left the building before I realized I couldn't stand the pain of leaving her behind.

I shouldn't have to lose everything good in my life just because Liam is a prick.

"Turn right in two miles."

It's hard to focus on the voice of my GPS

513

when there is so much chaos in my head. I am feeling really emotionally numb, but my mind is racing. I can't stop thinking about the fact that I never got to say goodbye to Krista. I was so upset and in such a rush to leave the hospital that I didn't even think of stopping by the café one last time. I can still text her later once I'm settled, but it would have been nice to see her one last time and say a formal farewell. Maybe even give her a hug. There's no time to do that anymore, but there is one thing that I feel I must do before leaving this time.

I want to apologize to my sister.

When she told me that she accepted Grayson, even with all his issues, I refused to understand. I didn't even try. I acted superior, high and mighty, like I knew everything about everything. I can still hear her words echoing in my brain: *"Believe it or not, I've had worse boyfriends. Yes, I'm sad and pathetic. But Grayson is the best guy I've ever met. He's the best guy I've ever been with, even with his flaws. And I'm marrying him!"*

Carmen is older than me and she has had a lot more experience with men than I have. I should have deferred to her wisdom. Maybe marrying a rapist is slightly less terrible than marrying a liar. At least she knows who he is. After discovering Liam's duplicity, everything Grayson did no longer seems so odious. It's not like I know any

514

better than Carmen.

Maybe everyone is a monster to some degree. Maybe all we can manage to do is find a partner with lesser degree of evil, or a type of evil that we can tolerate. I didn't know this. I saw the world entirely in black and white. I have never really lived; I have only lived in stories.

The thing about fairytales is that they always end before the real story begins. I have now lived long enough to watch my knight in shining armor become the villain, and it's left me wishing I'd never lived the fairytale at all.

At any rate, I should not have abandoned my sister the way I did. If she loves Grayson and accepts his flaws, there is a certain beauty in that. I understand it now. It's her life and she deserves to make her own choices. She deserves a chance at her mild sort of happiness. Maybe it's enough. She chose to settle for a less-than-perfect life to avoid being alone forever. That seems like a very mature decision to me. I could never do such a thing; I am too prideful. I would rather be alone than lied to or disrespected—but not everyone can live their life completely alone like I can. That is why I have set my GPS for my dad's so that I can see my sister for the first time. And for the last time.

"In 300 feet, bear left. Then continue straight for 5 miles."

I follow the instructions, squinting to better see the road. I glance up with worry, observing the ominous storm clouds. I really hope it doesn't get any darker out or begin to rain. My vision is too poor to drive in bad lighting. My phone rings, and I see that it is my realtor returning my call from earlier. I press the button on my steering wheel to answer.

"Did you find a place for me?" I ask her.

"I think I have two properties that might suit your needs," she responds. "Both are fully furnished and available immediately. They're in very remote and scenic areas within five hours from New York City. We can do a small one-bedroom cabin in the mountains in Pennsylvania for $75K. It's only three hours away. Or we could go a little nicer and get a two-bedroom cottage in West Virginia for $100K. That one is a little farther away, but it's close to a lovely small town with a library and..."

"Pennsylvania," I tell her. I am worried that my eyes won't be able to handle a longer drive. "Go ahead and do the paperwork to get it for me. I can transfer you the money in full. Text me the address, and I will start driving there now. I want to move in by tonight."

"Sure, Miss Rose. I'll do that right away. What about your old place in New Hampshire?"

"Sell it," I tell her. "Take your time. I don't need it anymore."

"Great!" she says. "I'll text you soon."

I hang up the phone and keep driving. I

need to move fast, because I realize that Owen probably won't be able to keep silent for the full twenty-four hours. Even if he can hold out for the rest of the day, once Liam goes home and finds me missing, I am sure that he will begin calling me in order to figure out where I am. I am also sure that he will call Owen, and that Owen will cave and tell him everything. He loves Liam too much, and the moment he sees his friend getting upset, he will do anything to help him. Owen really is a softie.

I need to hit the brakes as I encounter a red light. If Liam walked over to me now, as I'm sitting at this intersection, and apologized, I'd probably cave too. I would take him back in an instant. Even though he's a slimy son of a bitch, I still love him. Being angry doesn't automatically wipe away all my good memories and how I feel about him. That's why I need to get away. I don't trust myself to be near him ever again. The light turns green and I keep moving forward.

"In one mile, you have reached your destination."

When I pull up to the driveway of my childhood home, I am a little stunned by the size of the mansion. I always knew that it was an impressive house, but seeing it for the first time is a little overwhelming. I peer through my windshield in awe, with my mouth slightly agape.

"Wow," I whisper to myself. "I can see why someone would pretend to like me if it meant getting a piece of that." I immediately wrinkle my nose at how awful this sounds as I park the car near the fountain in our front yard. I lean over and ruffle Snowball's hair gently. "I'll be back in just a minute," I tell her. "You won't even notice that I'm gone."

She yips at me with encouragement.

I exit the vehicle and take a deep breath before marching up to the intimidating house. When I am standing before the giant stained glass double doors, I ring the doorbell. I am not sure what I'll say if I encounter Grayson or my father, but I don't really care anymore. I just want to see my sister. I am feeling crazy and invulnerable. I also have Grayson's gun tucked away in my purse, and the knowledge of judo beneath my belt.

I frown when I remember the intimacy of our judo lessons. Why would Liam have gone to such lengths to do so much for me? Every beautiful moment is now so unbearably painful to think about. It was all fake. Every touch, every kiss, every word. It was all just an act. I try to push it from my mind so I can get through this day. Once I'm safely in my new home, hundreds of miles away, I can deal with this in the security of nature. I can think about this far too much and overanalyze how stupid I've been. I can cry for hours or days, and drink myself silly.

How many years will it take to get over this? When a figure comes to the door, I observe their shadow through the foggy stained glass. When the door cracks open, I see a plain-looking man standing there. A young man with a cleanly shaven face.

"Helen," he whispers in awe. "You came home."

"Grayson?" I ask in disbelief. I recognize his voice well, but I find myself staring at his face, body, and clothes in amazement. He has shiny, jet black hair that is combed off to one side. He has kind eyes and freshly-ironed clothes. "You look— you look like a normal person."

"What do you mean?" he asks.

I shrug and scowl. "In my head, I always imagined you'd look different. Tentacles, sharp teeth, blood dripping down your face. Giant warts, claws, and bulging hairy eyeballs. Like some kind of hideous, grotesque beast."

"Sorry to disappoint you," he responds softly.

We stand there staring at each other for a moment before I clear my throat. "I'm here to see my sister."

"She's at a doctor's appointment with Dad," Grayson tells me.

It makes me a little uncomfortable to hear him calling my father Dad. At the same time, I'm so angry with my father that I really don't care what anyone calls him. "When will they be back?" I ask him.

"It might be a while. They only just left, and you know how Carmen likes to go shopping for hours on the way home from everything. It's worse now that she needs new maternity clothes."

"Oh," I say in disappointment. "I guess... I'll just... go."

"Wait, please." There is a desperate look on his face. "Didn't you get any of my letters, Helen? I started writing them as soon as I could move my arm again."

"Look, Grayson. I'm not in the mood to do this right now."

"Please," he says gently. "I'm not the same person I was before. I've changed. I would never hurt you, your sister, or anyone. I've confessed my sins, and I've found God. I'm trying my best to repent every day. I just need to know if you can forgive me." He looks at me with the same big sad eyes that Snowball had earlier. "Please, Helen?"

I stand on the doorstep of my childhood home, staring at this pathetic excuse for a man who has caused such a huge impact in my life. I spent so many years being afraid of everything because of him. I spent so many nights replaying his act of violence over and over in my mind, and keeping these horrors alive. I perpetuated my own pain and multiplied his cruelty exponentially.

But now, I can see clearly for the first time; it doesn't even matter anymore.

CLARITY

Grayson is not worth it. He's not worth my suffering. He's plain and forgettable. He's just a mindless brute that isn't even that brutish anymore. Now that he's a bit older and doesn't play college football, he has lost a lot of the fearsome bulk he once used against me. He's not even that intimidating to look at—Liam has a lot more muscle. Grayson has even begun to grow a bit of a potbelly. But even if he were still a hulking giant, what would it matter? Even if he tried to hit me or force himself on me in this moment, why would I care?

The worst pain isn't caused by some random stranger. The worst pain isn't physical.

When the person you love most in the world rips your heart out, the bruises from a brutal attack seem petty and insignificant. For a moment, I even wish that Grayson would hurt me again so that I could feel something. Would it hurt? If he forced me down and raped me, would I even be able to care? I want to use him as an instrument of self-harm like I used that cigarette earlier. I am tempted to taunt him and egg him on until he snaps and repeats his normal depraved behavior. I want to feel his hands around my neck again.

These thoughts are deeply disturbing to me. Besides, if he actually is getting better from some sort of illness, it would be downright despicable of me to dig up his issues. It would be like giving a recovering addict who has been clean for some time one more hit of crystal meth or crack cocaine. (Both of which I would probably be eager to try right now, given my current state of mind.) If he weren't married to my sister, and if she wouldn't be the one to suffer, I wouldn't care. I would love nothing more than to be the tornado that takes Grayson down. I would love to watch him spiral out of control and crash and burn. I would love to take out all of my anger at Liam on him.

"Helen?" he says again. "Please. Do you ever think you can forgive me?"

That question always seemed so ridiculous to me. How could I ever forgive him? But now, I feel a bit different.

There is no such thing as forgiveness. There is only someone hurting you more, so that you care about the initial hurt a lot less. It fades into the background, dominating your life less, and thereby creating the illusion of forgiveness.

This has finally happened to me. Liam has overridden Grayson. His carefully calculated manipulation, and his months of conniving and conning me have taken precedence in my mind as the greatest injury of my life. I have never been so methodically and meticulously betrayed. He should win a medal.

Thanks to Liam, I am now standing in front of my rapist and feeling absolutely no fear. I am actually rather bored and wishing he would physically attack me to cause me some superficial pain to distract from my deeper, more devastating wounds. I never could have imagined this moment in a million years.

I find myself beginning to laugh a bit hysterically. Grayson sends me a puzzled look.

"My dog is waiting in the car," I tell him. "I should probably get going."

"Why don't you stay?" he asks me. "This is your home. Bring your dog inside, and move back in. Your dad and sister miss you and talk about you every day."

"I can't," I tell him. "My dad has been a major asshole, it seems. I'm leaving for good. None of you will ever see me again."

"Then will you please stay for a minute?" he begs. "I can show you around the house—you could grab a bite to eat."

For the first time, I do look inside the house. A sharp pain shoots through my chest, and I find that even when I have reached my maximum pain threshold and ultimate numbness, it can still get a little worse.

"Mom?" I whisper as I walk forward, stepping past Grayson as though he is not even there. There is a large, magnificent painting hanging on the wall. It depicts a beautiful woman sitting in a dignified pose. She has sandy brown hair tied up in stylish bun, along with sophisticated pearl earrings. I move forward until I am standing directly below the painting. I stare at it for a moment as my eyes fill with tears. There is a man standing behind her with his hand resting on her shoulder. He has a bright smile that is mostly concealed by his dark beard. There are also two little girls wearing polka-dotted summer dresses and standing on either side of the woman. The older girl is standing confidently, as though she knows that she's beautiful. But the younger girl looks shy. As if to reassure her, the seated woman is affectionately holding the hand of the younger girl.

It's me.

I remember posing for those photos when I was eight years old. I remember how stiff and scratchy the dress was, and how I just wanted to put on normal clothes as soon as the photo was over. I can almost remember the feeling of my mom's hand in mine. I wasn't ready to lose her. If only she was still around, all our lives would be so much better. None of this would have happened. She loved us so much that she kept us all safe and strong.

I lift my fingers to touch my quivering lips.

I feel Grayson's hand on my shoulder, and it gives me a little shudder of déjà vu. And now we've come full circle. Here I am, in the same position as I was all those years ago when he found me on the stairs. Broken down, at my weakest moment. Exposed and vulnerable. Isn't that what gets him off?

My head snaps around to glare at him viciously. "Do it," I tell him. "I don't give a fuck. Do whatever you want. Hurt me. Come on! Fucking hurt me."

He reaches out to embrace me, and I cringe at his touch. For a moment, I grow dizzy as I flinch and instinctively lift my hands to protect my face, expecting some sort of violent impact. My whole body grows tense and stiff. When he pulls me against him, he is gentle and there is no pain. He does not try to hurt me. He just holds me close for a moment.

"I'm sorry," Grayson tells me. "I'm so sorry. I'll never hurt you again."

I try to breathe as I wrap my head around these confusing events. Today, I have been deceived by my lover and comforted by my enemy. And somehow, as ironic and twisted as it is, there is almost no one who could comfort me better than Grayson in this moment. As I gaze up at the painting, I feel myself really letting go of her for the first time. How could I really have grieved for my mother when I had never even seen her? Now, at least, I have been given the final piece of the puzzle. Now I feel like I can finally close her book in my mind. Every page has been given the colors of her complexion and the contours of her smile. Every memory I have of her has become more vivid, precious, and complete.

"That's exactly how I imagined she would look," I tell him softly. "She was so beautiful."

"She loved you," Grayson says as he touches my hair tenderly. "Your whole family loves you so much, Helen. You should come home."

"I can't," I tell him, turning away from the photo to keep my tears from spilling over. I try to fixate on anything else in the majestic room, and I easily find a focal point. "Wow. That's an amazing chandelier," I comment trivially.

"Yes. I have always loved that chandelier," Grayson tells me. He hesitates and his voice grows heavy. "Your dad has been bugging me to replace some of the light bulbs. I should probably do that before they get back."

The concept of Grayson doing such a domestic chore for my dad surprises me. Maybe my sister really was right to see something good in him. Maybe he really never was the monster that I believed he was. Maybe everything I have ever believed is wrong.

"I'm really glad that your doctor was able to help you see," Grayson says with downcast eyes. "I'm so sorry about... what I did to him. I don't know what came over me. I'm glad that you found someone. I never meant to hurt either of you. I just..."

"It's okay," I tell him softly. "He gave me

the ability to see, but he pulled the wool over my eyes in a lot of other ways. He didn't give a fuck about me."

"He took a bullet for you," Grayson reminds me.

"He took a bullet for money," I say bitterly.

Grayson frowns. "Helen, that man broke both of my arms and gave me a black eye. He would do anything to protect you. Trust me, I could feel how much he loved you in how hard he hit me. If you can't see that he really cares, then you really are blind."

I smile sarcastically at this. Who knew that my rapist had such a strong sense of honor? "I can't believe I'm having this conversation with you," I tell him, "or any conversation. You seem... different."

"I don't know if I'm different," he says softly, "but I'm aware." Grayson steps away from me abruptly, moving over to the staircase. He sits down with an exhausted expression on his face as he stares up at the chandelier. "There was so much that I didn't know; very basic things about how to treat people. I don't know why I couldn't learn. It didn't make sense to me. Helen, I don't know if you believe this—but I can't even look at myself in the mirror. I see the same beast that you imagined. I can't believe the horrible things I've done."

Wrapping my arms around my stomach, I stare down at him with a mild curiosity and a deep pity. Now that I can see the sad and remorseful look on his face, it is so much harder to hate him. I can see that he feels the full impact of his actions. It feels over. I believe that he will never hurt me again. It is clear to see that he is so downtrodden and defeated that has been rendered harmless and incapable of violence ever again.

"They've been giving me medication," he tells me. "I've been taking it, but—I don't think my actions can be explained away as some sort of illness. It's deeper than that. It's a fundamental flaw in who I am. It's some sort of incurable ignorance. It will always be a part of me. I'm hopeless."

Against my better judgment, I find myself moving over to sit beside him on the stairs. I reach out hesitantly to place my hand on his shoulder. "You're not hopeless," I tell him softly. "You're going to have a baby. A fresh start with a whole new person, who will love you unconditionally. You might have made mistakes, but you can change everything from now on."

He shakes his head. "You don't understand how terrified I am. I'm going to fuck it up. What if the kid is better off never meeting me? I'm just a fuck up. I've always been a fuck up, no matter how hard I tried."

"Grayson..." I begin to say, trying to think

528

of a way to soothe him.

"No," he says, cutting me off. "You don't even understand, Helen. How could you understand? Everything I said and did to you— even the worst things—it was all because I loved you. I know that it doesn't make sense, and that you'll never believe me. But it's true. I loved you so much, so uncontrollably. I loved you with such a violent obsession that it drowned all common sense."

His hands are clenched and there is a muscle twitching in his jaw as he speaks. There is a strange cloudiness of turmoil in the irises of his eyes. "I needed you so furiously and forcefully that it consumed my every thought. That maddening passion just soaked every rotten, disgusting cell of my body. I loved you, and *that* is how I expressed it. I know you'll never believe me." He lets his head fall forward into his hands.

I find myself swallowing down a gulp of saliva. "I think I do believe you," I tell him quietly. Yes, it's twisted and outrageous. But Liam treated me so well, and it turns out that I was just a chore to him; he didn't love me in the least. So it might as well make sense that Grayson treated me like shit and he actually did love me. Maybe love is that fucked up.

"That's what scares me most," Grayson tells me. "If it is true, then how can I ever let myself love someone again? How can I be a father? How can I love a newborn child who is completely innocent? My love is a perverse and warped thing that no one should have to suffer. My love is a curse."

My heart is filled with involuntary compassion as I stare at the broken man. "You can learn," I promise him as I run my hand over his back. "You still have time to figure things out. It isn't too late. You have already made progress..."

Grayson's shoulders begin to shake. "It's too late for me, Helen," he says with a sob. "You and I both know that it's too late. I'm too far gone. I can never forgive myself."

"Shhh," I say, reaching out to wrap my arms around him. I am not sure why his anguish gives me pain instead of pleasure. "You have Carmen," I whisper. "She loves and accepts you. She will take care of you."

Grayson's sobs grow in magnitude as his pain tears his body apart from the inside. "I'm killing her," he tells me. "She can't stand me. I'm hurting her more every day. I've destroyed everything. I've torn apart your family."

"No," I tell him, speechless in the face of his remorse. "No. Grayson, it's going to be okay. Things are going to get better."

"Please," he says with eyes that are tortured and bloodshot. "Please forgive me."

I pull my lips into a grim line as I consider this. "It turns out that there are worse people in the

530

world than you," I tell him begrudgingly as I think of Liam. "I don't think you're the biggest monster I've ever met. So, yeah. I forgive you."

I am startled when he falls against me, burying his face into my chest and sobbing wildly. He holds onto me tightly, as though I can offer him some sort of salvation. His fingers dig painfully into my side, and I can feel his torment and grief in the way his body trembles. For a moment, I am frozen, but then I hesitantly lift my hands to hold him against me. I press my fingers soothingly against the back of his head, gently caressing his hair. My own actions are both shocking and troubling to me. I spent so much time imagining hurting this man, and wishing and praying for an opportunity to do so.

But now that he is here, I just see a confused and lost human being. Nothing that he's done seems to matter any longer. A torrent of his penitent tears begins sliding down between my breasts, soaking my skin and the front of my shirt. I look up at my mother's solemn face in our family painting. She was not a religious woman, but she firmly believed that there was good in all of us. I can hear her voice echoing inside my mind.

Love your enemies.

I think I finally understand the wisdom in these cryptic and seemingly impossible words.

"I'm sorry," Grayson says, suddenly pulling away and wiping his face on his sleeve.

"You don't need this. I bet you want to get going."

"Yes," I tell him softly. "I need to head out."

"Okay," he says with a decisive nod. "Before you go—I think your dad left some photo albums up in your bedroom. He wanted to give them to you in person, but you refused to meet with him."

"Thanks," I tell him, rising to my feet. "I'll definitely grab those."

"I should change those light bulbs," Grayson says, getting up and staring up at the chandelier. "If I can remember where we keep the spares..."

"They're in a drawer in the kitchen," I tell him as I begin moving up the stairs. "The third one down from the forks and knives."

"That's right," he says in a hushed voice. "Helen? Please say it again. Do you really forgive me?"

I frown as I turn around to look down at him. "Yes. I do forgive you."

"Thank you," he tells me, smiling through his tears as he gazes up at me. "I have needed to hear those words for so long. Now, maybe I can finally have some peace. Thank you, my angel."

I find myself making an amused face at these words. "I'm hardly an angel," I inform him lightly.

Grayson moves up the steps until he's

standing on the one directly below me. He looks into my eyes with a strange intensity, and reaches up to slide his hand against my jaw and cup my cheek. I find myself growing tense again, and flinching slightly at his touch.

"May I kiss you?" he whispers.

I lift an eyebrow. "It's not like you to ask permission," I tell him dryly.

"I'm never going to see you again," he says. "Please, Helen. Just one kiss. I'm begging you."

"If I say no, are you going to do it anyway?" I ask him mockingly, but I can see how devastated he is. Maybe I shouldn't be making fun of him in this moment.

"Helen," he says in a hushed voice. "Will you have mercy on my poor, damned soul and kiss me one last time?"

Perhaps it's just like the cigarette. Perhaps it's just my damaged state of mind after Liam's betrayal. Perhaps it's due to the fact that I'm about to permanently isolate myself from humanity, and I might never touch a man again for as long as I live. Perhaps I just don't give a fuck anymore. Or perhaps it does seem like the perfect ending to my story with Grayson; a small act to signify that we're putting all this behind us for good.

I am appalled at myself as I lean down and place a kiss against his lips. For a moment, I almost expect that my skin will sizzle and melt at the contact, like I've kissed some kind of demon. But nothing happens. I feel absolutely nothing. I don't even feel disgust.

He is just a man. All along, he was just a man.

The tears sliding down his cheeks moisten mine, and for a moment, I do feel like an angel. I can feel his hands on my back, and I almost feel like he is caressing my wings. I didn't know it was possible to put all of my compassion into a kiss, but that is what this is. Now, it's really over.

I pull away and step backward, moving up the stairs a little shakily. "There," I say bitterly. I'm feeling a little disturbed by all of this emotion. "I'm going to go grab those photo albums and leave. Goodbye, Grayson."

"Goodbye, sweet girl," he says softly. "Thank you for setting me free."

There's a strange madness in his face, and I can't look at him any longer. I turn and head up the staircase, feeling dizzy and dazed. I am a bit overwhelmed by the confrontation, but I am also satisfied with the sense of completion and closure. I think that maybe we both needed this to move on with our lives.

I think that now, I can finally find peace, too.

Moving swiftly through the hallway to my bedroom, I open the door and try not to get distracted by the gorgeous furnishings and décor. I move directly to the albums that are sitting on my dresser. I flip a page open just to make sure that they are the correct albums, meant for me. Seeing the smiling faces is instantly too much to bear. It hits me like a punch in the stomach as I see the love of my mother and father covering the pages. I can also see the old, familiar closeness that my sister and I used to share. We're tangled up in some sort of brawl in most of these photos, with our expensive dresses covered in mud.

A nostalgic smile touches my lips. It's almost enough to convince me to stay. All the memories I've lost, like sand slipping through my fingers, are crystallized here in photographic form. I almost can't believe that all these precious moments in time have been frozen in images that I have never been able to see. Looking through these albums will be like reliving my entire childhood through new eyes.

For a moment, I fantasize about sitting by the roaring fireplace with my father and sister, and flipping through these albums as we laugh and reminisce. Maybe we could all be a family again. I don't think I even mind if Grayson is there. I think that maybe we could be cool. Maybe I could be there for the new photographs and memories. It's been years since we've made any. Maybe, I could be part of the childhood of Carmen's baby and watch him or her grow up. I could see all the new smiles and new joys that we always dreamed of when we were little girls. Maybe there is still hope for all of us.

A loud crash startles me from my thoughts. I close the albums and gather them up in my arms as I exit my room and head back to the center of the house where I can see the light from the chandelier illuminating the staircase. As I approach the landing, I turn and gaze down into the foyer.

My heart skips a beat.

The scene before me is too horrible to be real. I am sure that it is only my faulty eyes playing tricks on me. It's impossible.

"Grayson?" I whisper, as I stand rooted to the spot. I fight against my paralysis to begin moving down the staircase. I hug the albums tightly against my chest. There is a small ladder lying on the ground, as though it has been kicked over.

A few feet above the fallen ladder, a pair of legs are swaying back and forth.

I want to shut my eyes to keep from seeing this, but I find myself looking up to take in the rest of the man's body. His arms are lying limply at his sides, and his head is tilted to the side at an odd angle. There is a rope around his neck, and it is tied to the gorgeous chandelier in the center of our foyer.

I have to hold onto the railing of the staircase to help me descend. I am feeling a bit faint, and I am worried that I might collapse. I feel as though all the blood has drained from my body. I manage to get to the final stair before I fall forward, collapsing to my knees. I drop the photo albums and bring my hands to cover my face. I find that my breathing is erratic and strained.

"Grayson!" I call out, half-expecting him to respond. *"Grayson!"*

I place both of my hands flat on the ground as a sob shakes my chest.

I had only just started to see the goodness in him.

"You're not a monster," I tell his swaying body. "Grayson, why? I forgive you. I forgive you. I promise. Please don't be gone." Pain shoots through the back of my eyes as I experience a few seconds of distorted vision. I welcome this, almost wishing that I could never see again. I know that this is my fault. I must have said or done something that led him to do this.

I find that tears are pouring down my cheeks and I am unable to stop crying. My head begins to ache, pounding worse than the worst hangover possible. My heart hurts so badly that I feel that it might stop. I don't know why I feel so much pain for the loss of a man that I cared so little for. What does it matter now? He was a man. A few minutes ago, he was a living, breathing man.

Even he deserved to live.

Looking around, it occurs to me that he never even brought the light bulbs. He never intended to change them. This was his plan all along. "You bastard!" I scream as I stare at his shoes, which are swaying back and forth in front of my eyes. "How could you do this? You have a baby on the way. My sister is having your baby."

I clutch at my chest, digging my fingers into my ribcage to try and claw out my traitorous, senseless heart. My stomach constricts with pain and nausea, and all my insides explode with agony. A wail of misery leaves my throat as I gasp and cry. I sob until I cannot breathe.

"Grayson," I whisper. "It's not too late. Please. You can be better. You can still be a good person." I fall forward until my face is resting against the cool floor, and my tears begin to pool beneath my cheek. "It's not too late. I forgive you."

My eyes close for a second, and when they open, my vision is hazy and imperfect. I see the fallen photo albums lying a few feet away, and I reach out and place my hand on their leather covers. "Carmen," I whisper to the thousands of photographs of a joyful young girl. What have I done? My sister. My big sister that I loved more than anything in the world.

Have I ruined her life forever?

I continue to lie on the ground and cry until the pain is too intense to bear. I place my hand on the ground and try to push myself up into a seated position.

The worst part is that I have the strongest desire to run home to Liam. I want to throw myself at him and feel his arms around me. Liam was my hero and he could have made anything better. Even this. He would have found the words to heal my heart; he would have touched me in a way that mended my soul. He would have made me feel safe.

But he isn't mine anymore. He isn't my home anymore. This isn't my home anymore, either. For the first time, it really hits me how alone I am.

Everything is falling apart.

I have to get away.

Reaching out, I try to pick up the photo albums. It takes me a minute as my arms are suddenly very weak. I stumble as I try to stand up, and I run out of the house. I trip toward my little car, and yank open the driver's door to collapse into the front seat. I let my head fall back against the headrest as I continue to sob brokenly. When Snowball nudges her wet nose against my arm, I look down at her with love and desperation. She's all I have left. I put the photo albums down in the passenger seat and gather Snowball up into my arms. I hold her close and press my face down into her small body to cry into her fur.

Snowball licks my cheek affectionately.

She nuzzles me with concern, as though she's trying to figure out what's wrong with me. I pull away and look down at her wretchedly, petting her soft head with both sorrow and adoration.

"Let's get away from here," I tell her with a sniffle. "Let's find a place to call home."

Chapter Fourteen

I have been driving and crying profusely for almost two hours when the phone calls start coming at more frequent and frantic intervals. It is clear to me that Liam now knows that something is wrong. He is barely letting a minute pass between his phone calls. I don't care. I intend to ignore them all.

It has been becoming increasingly difficult to see the road due to the darkening sky and my declining vision. It is only mid-afternoon, but there is a menacing thunderstorm brewing. I think that the nonstop crying has only escalated the regression of my eyesight. There is a great pain behind my eyes, and my head is throbbing. Sometimes, the road will become completely obscured for several seconds, and I'll have to slow down and drive forward tentatively, trying to remember where the guardrails were. Now that I am far from the city, it is becoming more dangerous to drive on these remote, winding mountain roads. I have never driven on highways like these before, with such high speed limits and insane elevation changes and curves.

I am afraid.

As the heavy gray clouds gather above, I can see that they are preparing to dump oceans of tears down on my windshield. I am sure that the sky knows what has happened, and is grieving along with me. I can already hear the angry rumbling and see the flashes of lightning. It's the perfect weather to be the soundtrack for this unbearably dreadful day. After getting the new address from my real estate agent, I programmed it into my GPS and have been driving to Pennsylvania ever since. I wish I could enjoy the scenery of the new landscape, but I am in no condition to appreciate this. The lightning is periodically illuminating the mountains on either side of the road, creating ominous dark silhouettes.

It is so terrifying to be alone out here.

Well, I am not, strictly speaking, alone. Snowball is curled up on the photo albums and shaking in terror at the sound of the thunder. She also seems rather upset at me for refusing to answer Liam's phone calls. When his name first began to flash on my dashboard, it was a little comforting to see the letters. It was somewhat nice to know that he was trying to reach me at all— even if he was only calling to preserve all the dollar signs I represent. I know that I should turn off my phone so that I don't have to listen to the loud, repetitive ringing as I ignore each excruciating phone call—but I want to listen. The ringing is a relic of what we used to have. It's a small reminder of how he used to care—or how I used to believe that he cared. I almost wish I could have remained blissfully innocent and let him continue this farce.

Was it so awful that he was being kind to me for the wrong reasons? At least someone was being kind to me at all. Maybe it was nice of my dad to try and purchase a man for me. Maybe it was a realistic approach to the situation. He did choose well; Liam was a wonderful boyfriend. Besides, it's not like anyone in their right mind would ever love a sick girl without some kind of real motivation. My dad was really just looking out for my best interests.

Snowball barks at me, growing very frustrated that I am letting the phone ring and not picking up Liam's call. I think she wants to hear his voice.

"Trust me, we're better off without him," I tell her, wiping my nose on my sleeve. "He didn't really love either of us. I know that you liked our little family—and I did too—but it turns out that he was just a con artist. It was all a fraud."

Snowball barks again, as though she disagrees with me.

"Look," I tell her firmly, "I'm the human! I know these things better than you. He might have seemed nice, but things are a lot more complex than you can understand. I'm the daughter of a rich man, and you're just a device to mollify me. Do you hear that, Snowball? You were just there to make me more trusting and easier to control. He was just toying with both of us. We were nothing to him. Nothing!"

Saying this causes a new onslaught of tears to cascade down my face. The rain starts pounding down on my car at the same time, and I reach out to flip on my windshield wipers. Even this tiny flick of my fingers manages to make my heart ache a little more, because I can remember Liam's hand on mine as he taught me how to do that. Everything about driving reminds me of him, and it's agonizing even to be using the skills that he taught me. Even in this way, I am proving that I needed him.

"Nothing at all," I repeat miserably. "We're nothing."

Growling softly in disagreement, Snowball turns away from me. I could almost swear that she's performing the canine equivalent of pouting.

I glance over at her in annoyance. "We were just temporary installments for him. Don't you understand that? Even if he stuck with this scam for a couple years, he would have gotten bored. He was going to find a better girl someday—and a better dog. You should be thanking me for saving us from him."

Snowball refuses to respond. The silent treatment is the worst thing she could possibly do to me, for once I am no longer talking, I can think about everything far too clearly and quickly. The ringing of the phone calls and the pounding of the rain on the car all begin to fade into the background as my mind begins to fixate on the one thought I'm desperately trying to avoid.

I can still see Grayson's body swaying back and forth as he hangs from the chandelier.

All the mountains and trees and road signs disappear, and all I can see are his shoes drifting a few inches to the right—and then a few inches to the left.

A horn blares at me and car behind me flashes its high beams. I gasp and recoil; the bright glare in my rearview mirror causes my eyes to completely malfunction for a few seconds. I can see nothing, but I can hear the sound of tires squealing as the car that has been tailgating me begins to pass me in the opposite lane. When I can finally see, I am startled to find that a large SUV is inches away from my driver's door. The other car passes by so close that if his passenger side mirror weren't far above mine, it would have ripped my mirror off. He drives in front of me and slams on his breaks, causing me to nearly crash into the back of his car. I have to hit my own brakes forcefully, and I'm worried for a moment that I won't be able to stop as my car skids on the slippery roads. I try to turn right hastily to drive into the shoulder, but I need to hold onto the steering wheel tightly and wiggle it around to try and help my tires catch their grip on the road again.

I narrowly miss hitting the car in front of me as it drives off, disappearing down the mountain road. I gasp as I pull into the shoulder and put my car in park, hitting my emergency lights so that other drivers can see me. I let my head roll back against my headrest as I try to catch my breath. My heart is pounding. This has to be one of the worst days I have ever lived. I only have about an hour left to arrive at my new home, but I don't know how I can possibly make it. I don't know if I can even manage to travel one more mile without falling apart. I gaze at the guard rail that leads to a significant tumble down a steep cliff, and I seriously consider just removing my seatbelt and hitting the gas pedal to launch my car down that cliff.

The idea causes me to cry harder. I don't want to be having these thoughts. Plus, I have Snowball with me. She doesn't deserve that. I turn the key in the ignition to shut off the vehicle to deter myself from doing anything crazy. I have to live, at least to take care of my dog. I'm also in the middle of writing a book! I need to finish the story that my readers have been waiting for. But do any of them really care? So what if I never finish? There are thousands of other great books out there for them to read. I run my hands over the steering wheel, feeling like my reasons to live are pathetic and unconvincing.

I shouldn't have taken Snowball along with me. If she weren't sitting in my passenger seat, I don't think I would have any qualms about driving my car headfirst down the side of this mountain. It would put an end to all of my pain. It would erase all the despicable images from my mind. I wouldn't have to struggle to make it across the state with eyes that aren't capable of the task.

The sound of ringing causes my eyelids to flutter open, and only then do I discover that they have been closed. This scares me, because the world looks almost the same when my eyes are closed and open. I can't even see Liam's name flashing on the dashboard, but I know that he is the one calling. More tears slide down my cheeks, and for a moment, I wish that I could answer the phone and ask him to come and save me.

He probably would. My dad could cut him a check to make it worth his time.

A vehicle drives by at a high speed, and the wind causes my car to shake. I realize that I'm in danger by even just sitting here on the side of the road. This is not a safe place to stop. If I got out of my car and tried to walk, that would be even more dangerous. I'm screwed. I'm stranded. The best I could manage to do is call for help, but I am too prideful to get a tow truck when there is nothing wrong with my car—and I worry that the police might give me a ticket for getting behind the wheel at all when there was something wrong with my eyes. I don't want to talk to any strangers.

The only voice I want to hear is the one belonging to the man who is currently calling me. I want to hear his voice so desperately. I begin trying to rationalize it to myself. What if I died now? What if I died here on these slippery mountain roads? What if I died without ever getting to hear Liam's voice one last time?

Before I can talk sense into myself, I reach out and press the button on my steering wheel to answer his call. I don't say anything. I just sit there with tears pouring down my face, and I listen to the silence on the line. The silence is deafening. It is the loudest silence I have ever heard.

"Winter?" Liam says into the phone. "Hello? Are you there? God, Winter, please—say something. I'm going out of my mind. What the hell is going on? Where are you?"

I shut my eyes tightly, letting my head fall forward to rest against my steering wheel. I grab the sides of the steering wheel and grip it tightly in my fists, trying to prevent myself from letting Liam hear how hard I am crying. I don't want him to know how much he has destroyed me. I try to control my gasping breaths to keep from betraying myself.

"Please," Liam begs into the phone, as his own voice breaks. "Winter, I love you so much. Please talk to me. I—I don't know what to do. I've been calling for hours. Please. I need you. I need you so badly. I just need to hear your voice." I can hear that he is crying, and the sound of his pain amplifies my own. "Winter, please..."

The idea that he might actually love me causes my shoulders to shake violently as I am unable to repress my brutal sobs. I want to believe this so much, but I know it can't be true. I try to muffle my tears by pressing my face against my steering wheel.

A little yipping sound alerts me to the fact that Snowball is excited to hear Liam's voice. She sits up and moves back and forth in the passenger seat, with her little tail wagging. She has no idea that he has betrayed us.

"Snowball?" Liam says softly. "Oh god, Snowball. Are you okay? Is Winter okay? Please, I just need to know that you're both safe. I've been calling and calling..."

I reach up to run my fingers through my hair as I take a ragged breath. I hear a small whimper, and I am startled to find that it is coming from my own throat and not Snowball's. Hearing Liam's voice is shredding my insides apart. Every syllable he speaks causes my anger to be replaced by the awareness of my love and need for him. I just want to throw my arms around him and beg him to make this day disappear and tell me it's all going to be okay. I just want to be close to him again.

"Winter," Liam says shakily. "I'm freaking the fuck out here. Please just say that you're okay. Say anything."

"Grayson just killed himself in front of me."

There is a pause on the line. "Jesus, Winter," Liam says, and his voice is hoarse. "Are you serious? What happened? Are you okay? Talk to me."

"He hung himself."

"God. Did he hurt you? Winter, are you safe? Where are you?"

I drag my forehead back and forth against the steering wheel in a feeble effort to ease the pounding in my head. I still love Liam. I love him so much that it feels like it's physically destroying my body. I can't believe this is happening. Why is this happening to me? Why couldn't it just be real?

"Winter? What's going on?" There is panic in Liam's voice. "Please talk to me. Where are you? Where is Grayson?"

"He asked me for forgiveness. He asked me for a kiss. Then he hung himself."

"He kissed you?" Liam asks, and he seems

suddenly jealous and possessive. "That motherfucker. If he wasn't dead, I'd see to it myself. Who the fuck does he think he is? How dare he touch you?"

It sounds like he cares. He's still pretending; I can hear it in his voice. He sounds so angry and aggressive. He sounds zealous and passionately in love with me. It's all bogus. Maybe, after all this time, it's become so habitual to pretend to be my boyfriend that he can do it in his sleep.

"Winter, just tell me where you are. I'm coming to get you. Whatever's happened, we'll get through it together. Just tell me that you're safe. I love you so much. Where are you? Please."

I can hear that Liam is crying. He sounds so broken up. Is it real? Is there a chance that even one percent of his love is genuine? And if he does have even a morsel of true attachment to me, am I actually going to hurt him by leaving? Am I hurting him right now? The idea causes a sob to rip from my chest. I hate the idea of causing him any harm. Even now. He has only been good to me. I can't stand to hear him suffering.

After what I've done to Grayson, I can't bear to cause another man any pain.

"Liam," I whisper as my body shakes with weeping. I reach out to touch the speakers of my car, from which his voice has been emanating. I imagine that I might be touching his lips. I just

551

want to touch his face and kiss him. I want him to make love to me and make this all go away.

"Winter, I need you. I need to see you now," Liam begs. "I'm sorry—I know that was cruel, what I said about Grayson. I just—I'm not myself right now and I can't think clearly. I can't seem to give a fuck that he's dead. I only care about you, Winter. You mean everything to me. I'm imagining the worst right now. I'm imagining that something bad happened to you. Please. Please, just tell me that you're okay."

"Something bad did happen to me," I say softly.

"Winter? Winter, I can't hear you." Liam exhales unevenly. "You're scaring the shit out of me. Are you hurt? Are you injured? If you can't speak to me clearly, I'm going to call the cops. Where are you?"

"I'm not injured." Taking a deep breath, I press my both of my palms against my eyes. I hold them there for a moment, hoping that the heat from my hands will somehow revive my vision. "I'm fine."

Snowball barks softly, as if to interject in disagreement. She does not think I'm fine.

"Thank god," Liam says with a sigh. "To be honest, I'm glad that you're only upset over something Grayson did. For a moment there, I thought you were angry with me."

I remove my palms from my eyes and

stare down at the dashboard in astonishment. Does he really not know?

"I'm so relieved," Liam says. "Melanie said you stopped by the hospital and mentioned that you were having trouble with your eyes? Why didn't you tell me sooner? She also said you brought me a gift, and we found the box in the trash—Winter! You got me a telescope? That's the sweetest thing anyone has ever done for me. I called and texted, but when I couldn't reach you, I started freaking out. I spoke to Krista and she didn't know where you were. When I came home and saw that you and Snowball were gone, and I started imagining the worst. I thought you had been taken. Then I saw that your stuff was gone and I started thinking that you might have left me..."

"Liam. I have left you."

There is a pause on the other end of the line. "What?" he finally asks in shock. "Why?"

"Why?" I repeat, looking down at my dashboard with my mouth slightly ajar. I burst out laughing. "Are you serious right now? *Why*? Owen didn't tell you?"

"Tell me what?" he asks in a fearful voice.

"Liam, I know. I know everything."

There's another silence on the other end of the line. "Winter..."

"And yes, my vision is failing. It's nearly gone. I can't see anything." I smile sardonically through my tears. "I guess you're a better actor than you are a doctor. I actually did believe that you gave a shit about me. I thought you loved me this whole time. You really fooled me."

There is a long pause. Finally, I hear him take a shuddering breath. "Winter," he says tearfully. "You're the best thing that ever happened to me. You're my whole world. I'm sorry. I know I didn't tell you the whole story at first—you started out being just a job, but it became real. I fell for you really hard and fast. Why does it matter now, how we met? We belong together. You know that we belong together."

"You lied to me," I say through gritted teeth. "You've been lying to me this whole time."

I hear a loud clatter on the other end of the line, and it sounds as though Liam has smashed something. This is immediately followed by a roar as he yells my name in anger. "Winter!" he screams so loudly that it reverberates through the speakers of my car. "I fucking love you to pieces. It was so hard! It's such a mess. I wanted to tell you, but I didn't know how—I just couldn't risk losing you. Please believe me. Please come home. I just want to hold you. I need you. I need to know that you're safe—and that you're mine."

A loud peal of thunder echoes across the mountains. Snowball whimpers and covers her eyes with her paws. I wait for the booming to subside before I speak.

"But I'm not yours," I tell him softly. "Maybe it was all a game to you, but I really grew to love you, Liam. It isn't fair.... what you did to me. I trusted you. You were the only person I trusted."

"I fucked up," he says. "Please punish me all you want. Punish me forever. Just don't leave me."

"I have to."

"Winter, I didn't know where this was going when we first met. I didn't know I was going to fall in love with you. It was supposed to be all business, but you're not like any girl I've ever met. You're special. We've been through so much, in such a short period of time. I've never been this close to anyone."

"These are all just more lies," I murmur to myself. When the sky is illuminated by lightning, I am grateful that I can see this. For a moment, it's as bright as day. I can see the curves of the landscape in the distance, and I think that if I turn on my high beams, I might actually be able to make it through the night...

"Just come home, Winter—let's talk about this. I'll never lie to you again. Anything you want to know, I'll tell you." Liam sounds frantic. "Remember that first night, when I stopped? It was because of all this. I had this huge secret, and I wasn't sure. I could see how much it meant to you, and I didn't want to be with you unless it was real—unless I was ready to commit to you completely. I waited until I knew for sure. Once I was one hundred percent sure, I told you that I would stop holding back. Remember? I haven't held back since then."

"You told my dad that you were going to break up with me for money."

"Winter," Liam says in an agitated voice. It is strange to hear his lack of composure; he is usually so calm and self-possessed. "Your dad can go fuck himself. I would never do such a thing to you. Sorry—that was an awful thing to say. I have great respect for your old man; he was just desperate to be close to you again, at any cost. I think I would have probably done the same thing. You have no idea how much he loves you. I wish my dad ever cared that much. The only reason there is a cure for LCA is because your dad loved you; he's spent years convincing influential people in the pharmaceutical companies that curing this form of blindness could be profitable. They would have tossed the drug aside and focused on more popular diseases. But your dad has been spearheading the research here, and even traveling to Europe to supervise clinical trials there..."

"After my surgery," I mumble in realization. "You were talking to him on the phone."

"Yes," Liam says. "Winter, he did all this to try and bring you home. He did all this to try to give you a better life; the life he always wanted for you."

"I guess every father dreams of their daughter getting fucked by a doctor," I say scornfully. "Or was that part of the deal? Maybe he just wanted you to fuck me—"

A loud wave of thunder begins to boom and echo across the mountains, and it is a few seconds before I can finish my sentence. "—over?"

"Winter..." Liam pauses and waits. "Jesus fuck, Winter. I just realized that there is thunder where you are, and there isn't any here. You're really far away, aren't you? Where the hell you?"

"I'm long gone," I tell him softly as I put my hand on the gearshift. "You'll never see me again."

"You can't be driving right now if you're having problems with your eyes," Liam says with concern. "Especially not in the rain."

I sigh as I stare out of the car windows at the obscured path before me. "I can't see the road. It's so dark."

"Tell me where you are," he demands. "Don't move. I'm coming to get you."

"Liam. Did I ever tell you that my mom died in a car crash?" I cock my head to the side thoughtfully. "Maybe it would be poetic if I died in the same way. I wonder how my dad would feel about that? It'd be difficult to control me then."

"You need to stop talking like this. I'm

557

not going to let anything happen to you."

I gaze down the mountainside, and all I see is freedom. "You couldn't control me anymore, either. Control me in every way."

"Listen, Winter. I didn't mean those things. Can you just forgive me so we can move past this?"

I start laughing lightly. "The last time I forgave a man, he hung himself a few minutes later. So I think it's safe to say that I'm never going to forgive you."

"Stop comparing me to that sack of shit," Liam says angrily. "I only lied to you, Winter. Really small lies. I concealed some information. You're not allowed to do this. You can't act like what we have isn't real—our whole relationship isn't invalidated by a few lies."

"Our whole relationship has been built on lies," I point out.

Liam groans loudly. "Jesus, you're acting like I'm the one who fucking raped you. Just because you have been victimized by one cuntbag doesn't mean that all men are like him. Stop confusing me with Grayson. I'm not him."

My eyebrows lift in surprise.

"I have been really good to you," he says. "I have been trying my best. Can't I make one mistake?"

"*One* mistake? Fuck you, Liam. What you've done is far worse than anything Grayson ever did to me. He was sick, or disturbed, or messed up in some way. He couldn't control himself. But you. You are a sensible, intelligent man. You did this intentionally. It wasn't a fleeting moment where things got out of hand—it was every minute of every day, for months. It wasn't one thing; it was *everything*."

"I never hurt you, physically or emotionally. I took care of you..."

"Oh, that's right. You babysat me. And you did a damn good job of it."

"Jesus," Liam says with a groan. "Sometimes you can be so oversensitive!"

"Don't worry. You don't have to be careful anymore." I turn the key to start my car again. "I'm already in a different state, hundreds of miles away. I'm not your problem anymore."

"Winter, please. This is only our first fight, and we can get past it. Please don't do anything reckless. Are you heading back to New Hampshire?"

I narrow my eyes. "Yes," I say softly, lying to him for the first time. "I'm going home."

"I'm coming after you," Liam says adamantly. "I know I screwed up, but I'm not letting you go without fighting for us. I'm not losing you."

"You can save yourself the trouble," I tell him. "You don't need to act like you give a damn anymore. Please leave me alone." When I realize that these are the words that I wrote on the inside of his book when we first met, I feel my tears begin again. It feels like that was years ago, in another lifetime. "Just leave me alone," I tell him brokenly. I flip my high beams on and put my car into gear, driving aggressively back onto the road.

"Helen—Winter!"

I hang up the call and focus on the road ahead of me, trying desperately to see the yellow lines. The high beams are helping slightly, but it is still a struggle. "See?" I whisper to Snowball. "I told you. He's a worse bastard than I thought he was."

To be perfectly honest, I was almost hoping he'd say something to give me a reason to turn around. I was praying that there might be some kind of explanation. Some reason for all this that made sense. Maybe it was all a practical joke. But it's not. It's real.

"He doesn't even think what he did was that bad," I tell Snowball. "That means he'd probably lie to me again in the future, you know? If I let him. If I gave him a second chance. Which I would never do." I tighten my grip on the steering wheel. "I need to be strong. I can't be a pushover like my sister."

Snowball barks at me softly, in confusion.

I shake my head angrily. It upsets me that Snowball's love for Liam is so unconditional. She can't even understand the situation enough to give me a sympathetic ear. All she remembers is that his voice was attached to a hand which gave her lots of treats. Well, his hands gave me lots of treats, too. And so did his filthy, lying mouth. But I'm too strong to let myself be controlled by his falsely affectionate handouts. I never want to see his revolting face again. Maybe if I changed my name, it would help to give me a completely fresh start. The great thing about being a writer is that when being who you are gets too difficult, you can just change your identity and rewrite yourself.

Breathing deeply, I try my best to calm down. At least I sent him clear in the opposite direction. Now he'll never be able to find me.

Chapter Fifteen

The GPS says that I am only thirty minutes away from my new home. That's all. Thirty minutes, and I can finally rest. I blink frantically to try and clear my fuzzy vision. I alternate between mashing my eyelids tightly shut and ripping them open, trying to create a windshield-wiper-effect over my eyes. The storm outside the car has not begun to subside, but it is the strengthening storm inside me that is creating far more difficulty.

I can't stop my thoughts from spiraling out of control. I can't stop seeing Liam's face and hearing his voice. Almost everything beautiful he has ever said or done is replaying in my mind, with a new taint of dishonesty. I can still feel his touch lingering on my skin, and the memory of his body pressed against mine. I can still feel him moving inside me, and it makes me sick. But it makes me even more sick to think that I will never feel him that close again. I let him in completely, so deeply in my mind, body, and heart. It feels like he is still with me now. I feel like I am still breathing him with every breath. He has somehow become a part of me, and I want to rip that part out. I don't care how critical it is to my survival; I need to escape and leave that part far behind.

With each passing mile, I should feel a little closer to freedom. I should feel a little more healed and protected by the distance. That is how I felt last time, when I ran away after Grayson hurt me. But I don't feel any of these things. I just feel more and more betrayed. I thought that our love was a heavy chain around my soul, strangling the life out of me. I thought those chains would fall away. But now I realize that it's too deep-seated; too ingrained in my being.

My love for Liam is a cancer that is quickly disintegrating every vital organ of my body.

It's starting with my eyes.

I am now passing through a small town, and while I can't read the numbers on the street signs, I am vaguely aware that I probably need to slow down. I ignore this and continue to grind my foot down on the gas. Snowball whimpers with concern, and I can't bear the pathetic sound. I bite my lip to suppress the emotion.

"We don't need him, Snowball. We

don't."

I can't tell if the stoplights are red or green. I don't even care anymore. I have to keep driving. I have to get away from here.

My mascara feels heavy and disgusting as it clings to my eyelashes in clumps, crumbling under the corrosive torrent of my tears. It was once waterproof; waterproof like a canoe meant for small streams, trying to take on the ocean. It feels like my lashes are getting stuck together with toxic glue. I lift my hand from the steering wheel to wipe the gunk out of my eyes. I try to massage them roughly, coaxing my eyes to work in the way one might abuse a malfunctioning piece of technology. I fail to notice that my car has begun drifting into the opposite lane until a deafening horn assaults my ears. My heart leaps into my throat. I am driving headfirst into a pickup truck.

With a sharp intake of breath, I correct my steering and jerk my vehicle back into my own lane—or what I believe is my own lane. I can't exactly make out the confines of my designated space on the road. I take a deep breath. I should really stop driving. I am in no condition to be out here.

But I can't stop.

I need this more than I need water. After crying for hours, I am very dehydrated, but I don't even care. I drink up every drop of distance thirstily, and it sustains me, giving me hope for renewed life. There is nothing else; I need to feel the sensation of getting away. I need to feel weightless and free as the car is hurled forward, slicing through the air. I need to feel like I am going somewhere safe.

But there are no safe places. Not anymore.

A blaring horn is heard as I blast through an intersection, and another car brakes and swerves to avoid me. My heart skips a beat at the sound of screeching tires, and I look into my rearview mirror to assess the damage I've caused. Of course, I can see nothing. My rearview mirror looks hazy and unclear. All I see is darkness. My world is going black.

Snowball barks fretfully, and I begin to breathe far too quickly.

"Come on, eyes," I whisper, "don't fail me now."

I stare forward into the distance, and I am barely able to make out the streetlights. There are large halos of light around each lamp, creating nebulous phantoms that hover before me and block every part of my vision. I know that's not the way it's supposed to look, but I can't blink or squint the bleary lights away. The world looks comical and distorted.

If I keep this up, someone is going to get hurt. I hope that someone is me.

"Turn left in 300 feet. Continue straight for fifteen miles."

I breathe erratically as I make the awkward left turn into what I think might be a road. I am semi-grateful that we are leaving the populated area and driving out into the wilderness again. Unfortunately, this also means that the streetlights are all gone. All I have are my high beams, which are doing very little to illuminate the dark night.

All my concentration is focused on the road ahead, and each mile feels like an eternity. I just want to get to my new home. I want to put my head down on my soft new pillow. Just a few more miles. A ringing is heard, coming from my vehicle, and it distracts me from the road briefly. I frown as I try to make out the letters of the caller's name flashing across the dashboard. I squint, but can only see four blurry blobs of light. I should not answer. I will not answer. I cannot answer. But staring at the darkness ahead of me makes me feel so miserable and alone that my heart grows heavy like a stone, sinking in my chest.

I think that even in this blackest of nights, I can find a fragment of wisdom.

I know I need to answer the call. My thumb sinks into the button on the steering wheel. When his voice filters through the speakers, it surrounds me like a blanket and envelops me in warmth. I understand everything in this moment.

"Winter, I'm so sorry."

He is the one who tore my soul into chaos,

but he is also the only one who can make it calm. He is the one who hurled me into turmoil, but with a single whisper, he can give me serenity again.

"It's okay," I tell him as I drive forward into what is starting to look more and more like oblivion. I am starting to realize that I'm never going to make it home. And even if I do, nothing will ever feel like home again without Liam beside me. "I'm sorry, too."

"What are you sorry for?" he asks. "You've done nothing wrong."

"You're right about me," I tell him. "I'm oversensitive. I'm needy, desperate, clingy. I don't know how to be in a relationship. I've never done this before; not like this. I didn't realize that life isn't a perfect fairytale and you need to make concessions. I was never willing to make concessions."

"You shouldn't need to," he tells me angrily. "I should have treated you better. I should have been more honest. I disrespected you."

"Don't worry, Liam," I tell him softly. "It's over now. You'll move on and find someone better. You'll find someone healthy, in both mind and body. Someone more fun."

"Winter, I don't want anyone else. I only want you. I love you."

"Maybe," I say, closing my eyes for a second. I can't tell whether my eyes are closed or open. I push my foot down harder on the gas pedal anyway. "It doesn't matter anymore. Just know that I'm glad that I met you. You changed my life, Liam. You gave me so much, and I'll always be grateful. I'm not just talking about the physical ability to see—but everything else that you helped me see. I love you. I'll always love you."

"Winter, you're scaring me. I just called to let you know that I'm driving now and I'm coming after you..."

I shake my head in refusal, and it causes my brain to ache. Crying has given me an agonizing, throbbing headache. "Don't come after me," I tell him softly as I try to focus on the road ahead. "I love you, Liam. Goodbye."

Hanging up the phone, I release a pent up sob from deep in my chest. Talking to him hurts, but the silence in the car from not talking to him hurts just as much. Possibly more. Looking up at the murky path ahead of me, I try to make out any recognizable shapes. I think that I can see the branches of a tree to my left. What I wouldn't give for just a sliver of moonlight in this darkness! I start to feel the road becoming rough and I realize I have drifted too far to the right. I just want to go home. I just want to be safely sheltered indoors, away from the storm. A flash of lightning illuminates the road for a second, and my eyes widen in surprise.

There is a sharp curve directly ahead of me, but I was too late to notice this. I try to turn, but I am going too fast. I lose control of the vehicle, and it spins out of my hands on the slippery roads. I gasp as the car breaks through the guardrail and begins to plummet down into a valley. I can feel the sensation of falling, and my stomach shrinks in fear.

Liam.

His name is my final thought as I shut my eyes tightly. I'm not sure if it's a plea, a prayer, or lament. For a moment, nothing happens. My body and the car feel frozen in suspension. I hold my breath. Finally, the impact. My car slams into a tree, and a sickening crunching sound is heard. My body jerks forward before the car closes in around me. It feels like I am being flattened. There is a blinding pain in my head, and a piercing ringing in my ears.

The world goes pitch black.

A bit of sticky moisture irritates my cheek.

My face twitches and I try to pull away from the odd sensation. When moving even an inch causes my entire body to explode in pain, I groan loudly. I open my eyes, and I see a white pillow. I lift my hand to touch it, and all my muscles feel stiff. When my fingers sink into the thin fabric of the pillow, I realize that it is not a pillow at all.

Air bag.

The word manages to jog some of my memories. I realize that the funny feeling on my cheek is Snowball licking me in a frenzied attempt to wake me up. I must have been out for hours. I look toward her, and once my vision is able to focus, I can see a few droplets of blood hanging on her white fur. I am immediately filled with worry, and I reach out to touch her to check for injuries. Somehow, she seems perfectly intact. A bit of liquid sliding down the side of my face alerts me to the fact that the blood must be mine.

My head is pounding like a bitch, so I am not surprised. There is so much pain from the impact that I feel like my skull has been cracked open. I am also very cold. My chest hurts so much when I breathe that I am beginning to grow certain that these are my final breaths. I reach up and touch the tender spot where the seatbelt dug into my collarbone. I wince at the burning sensation in my skin. I am sure that there's a nasty bruise there, but that's the least of my worries. I press both of my hands against my chest, feeling like my lungs are ablaze. I cough softly, and this tiny movement sends a ripple of fire through my chest. I begin wheezing painfully for several seconds, before I can finally be still again. But the stillness does not ease my agony.

I manage to turn my head a little, and I can see that the sky has gotten a bit clearer and the sun is beginning to rise. Tears touch my eyes.

It looks like I might get to see the sunrise one last time.

I am suddenly overwhelmed by the desire to find a better place to die than in this cramped, semi-crushed car. I reach down to unlatch my seatbelt to give myself some freedom. Putting my hands to my side, I try to open my driver's door. For a moment, it refuses to budge as it has become slightly sandwiched, but I push as hard as I can until the door finally swings open. I go tumbling forward with the door, as I needed to use my entire body weight to make it move. I collapse roughly onto the ground, and for a few seconds, I am so lightheaded that I think I might pass out. Snowball quickly crawls over me to freedom and begins running around in excited circles in the thin layer of snow that covers the ground.

When did it start snowing?

After hanging halfway out of the car for a moment, I take a deep breath and manage to use my weak arms to pull the rest of my body onto the ground. Once my legs flop outside, I become aware of all the injuries in my pelvis and lower body. I wince, but it becomes a bit easier to drag myself across the wet, slushy ground by using my bruised knees. I move inch by inch, panting and gasping for breath as I crawl forward. I notice that I am leaving a glittering trail of blood on the fresh snow, just visible in the dim light of dawn. I manage to get a few feet away from the car until I am lying in a position with a good view of the sunset. I turn over to lie flat on my back for a moment, looking up with my arms spread wide. I smile as snowflakes drift down around me, falling gently on my cheek and forehead. I feel peaceful.

Turning my head ever so slightly, I gaze at the touches of color on the horizon.

All my pain seems to dissipate into those pastel clouds, and I know that it's over for me. As the hues become more vivid and striking, my heart soars with them. I can imagine no better way to die. No better sight to see the last time I close my eyes. The beauty is so sublime that it stings my weary eyes with almost too much joy. I am so fulfilled and content in this moment that I have no more room for any more emotion; I am finished. When Snowball moves over to nestle against my side, I hug her gently.

"It's not quite home," I whisper to her, "but it's close enough."

She lets out a tiny woof of agreement.

I inhale deeply and let my lungs get filled up, thinking about how wonderful it feels to simply breathe. The air is clear and fresh, and it tastes delightful. I should have appreciated each breath a little more—but if this breath is all I have left, I am satiated.

When I let my eyes flutter closed, I know that they will never open again.

I feel myself drifting away.

"It looks like someone is in need of a doctor."

There is a deep silence throughout the valley now; the kind that is common in the hours of early morning. It's almost too silent. I find myself quirking one eye open in surprise.

Seeing Liam crouching over me, I am almost certain that I am hallucinating. I didn't even hear his footsteps approach. But Snowball seems cheerful and excited as she barks in greeting. Does she see him too? Is he really here? I am confused and disoriented.

"You're going to be okay," Liam assures me as he brushes a few strands of hair from my cheeks. "Just stay with me, Winter."

"But," I manage to croak out. "You can't be here—you were going to New Hampshire."

"Yes," he says tenderly as he examines the cut on my forehead. "I started driving up north before I remembered that you are way too smart and stubborn to make it easy for me to find you. Luckily, we got that GPS tracker for Snowball's dog collar."

"Oh my god," I whisper in horror. I glance over at Snowball's little blue collar, completely ashamed that I forgot this critical piece of information. "Now you've betrayed me, too," I accuse the adorable puppy, and she responds with a tongue-wagging grin. I groan and reach up to touch my throbbing head. The pain is now so severe that I can't think straight, when a few seconds ago it had nearly faded away. "Couldn't you just let me die in peace?" I ask Liam in annoyance.

"Absolutely not," he responds. "It was a decent attempt; you've wrapped your car around that tree quite nicely. But I'm not going to let you die without knowing how much I love you. I won't allow it."

I smile at this, and my eyes close again. I almost feel obligated to try my best to die now, simply to be rebellious. For a moment, I am positive I will be successful. I have stepped halfway through the door when his voice begins tugging me back.

"Winter!" he says, shaking me gently. "Stay with me. Dammit. Didn't you hear me? I love you. You're going to live so that I can fucking prove it to you. Every single day from now on, you'll know that this is real. I'll do everything I can to show you that this is real."

"Just let me go," I whisper. The idea of escaping this harsh and painful existence is becoming more and more alluring. Maybe it's what I needed all along. No matter how far away I drove, or ran, I couldn't seem to get far enough. Maybe my true home is a special place in the distant void beyond this life. I am filled with the desire to explore onward and discover something new. Something better.

"Come back to me, Winter. Dammit! Fuck. Winter!" Liam holds me in a way that is both fierce and delicate at the same way. "I am fucking serious right now. I am not going to let you die. You can't. Not here and not now. Not like this. You can die when I give you permission; in at least seventy years, when you're a wrinkly old woman who can't remember her name or achieve orgasms."

I can't believe he's making a joke at a time like this. I don't have the energy to laugh, but I move my fingers to grasp his hand. He feels warm. He feels real. It hurts to speak, but I squeeze his fingers and try to whisper. "I don't think any of your fancy medicine can save me now, doctor."

"Forget medicine, Winter. I've got something more effective than that. I love you. That's the true magic of life, isn't it? My love is more powerful than anything science can ever conceive; and I'm going to make you see that. We just need time. Just hang on—give me a little more time."

The pain in my skull is so piercing that when I try to look at him, he dissolves into a hazy cloud of whiteness. Is he a just ghost or a vision?

An apparition of the thing I want most to see? The idea breaks me. "You're not real," I say in a dry rasp. "I'm delirious."

"Come on," Liam says, slipping his hands under my body and lifting me off the ground. "We need to get you to a hospital."

The sensation of weightlessness startles me. I see the stark, ugly halls of a hospital, and I am immediately filled with terror. "No," I say in panic, grabbing the collar of his jacket. "No, please. I don't want to go to a hospital. Please just let me die here, in the sunrise?"

"Unfortunately, that's not an option," he tells me. Then he frowns. "Where the heck were you going, anyway? What's in Pennsylvania?"

I press my cheek against his leather jacket, trying to remember. I see a pretty little cabin inside my head, surrounded by snowy mountains and trees. I begin using my fingers to draw the shape of a house on his chest, trying feebly to communicate before I am able to speak. "Home. I got a new home."

"We'll go there, then. I'll nurse you back to health. What's the address?"

I can't seem to remember the address. My mind is fuzzy for a moment, and I struggle to remember where I wrote the information down. "My phone," I whisper. After a second, I feel myself being carried back over to my car where Liam grabs my purse. I feel that he is carrying me away from the car when I open my eyes in alarm. I remember the thick leather-covered books with the precious photographs I never got to see. "There are photo albums... in the passenger seat. Can you return them to my dad and sister?"

"It's okay," he tells me. "Your dad has copies."

"Please get them for me," I whisper. I try desperately to remember everything I need to remember. It's time for tying up loose ends. If I had a priceless artifact or a map to buried treasure hidden somewhere, now would be the time to tell him. Images of dollar signs and zeros dance across my brain, and I am struck by an idea. "Put me down and hand me my phone?"

He kneels to gently lower me to the ground. I find myself being placed into a seated position with my back pressed against my car. He reaches into my purse to get my phone, and hands it to me before leaning forward to dig the photo albums out of the wreckage.

I feel tremendously scatterbrained as I lift the phone close to my eyes so that I can see the screen. I have to fight very hard against the pounding in my head in order to do what I need. I feel Snowball nudging my legs as she moves around the landscape curiously, but I can't see her. My eyes close several times and my head droops forward in the middle of performing a very basic function. But it's the last thing I really need to do, and I know that I must.

"What are you doing?" Liam asks. "Is that your banking app?"

"I just transferred the rest of my money to your account," I tell him as I let my hand fall to the ground and my eyes close again. "Maybe that will help you and make you happy," I say as I let my body slide down to rest beside the mangled wreck of my vehicle. "It's the last thing I can give you."

"Winter. Winter!" he grabs my shoulders and pulls me upright, as though yanking me from the very grasp of death. "Jesus. Do you think I drove all the way out here for your money? Is that what you think of me?"

"Maybe," I say softly as my head rolls to the side. I feel so woozy. "You can go now, Liam."

"It's worthless," he whispers. He crouches down next to me and pulls me into his arms. He cradles me gently against his chest, and places a warm kiss on my cold cheek. He touches me with such infinite tenderness; the kind that is used only in the first few moments of a person's life, and again in their final moments. "I've never realized how worthless money is more than I do in this moment. I spent my whole life chasing it, but that's only because I had nothing else. Now I have you, and all the love you've given me. I'd chase you to the ends of the earth. Don't you understand, Winter? It's just like you said about your writing. I didn't know how to be anything else or do anything else until I met you. I didn't know anything about love. You've become my family. You're my reason. Just stay with me."

"It hurts too much. Everything hurts." I press my face against his neck, trying to get closer to his warmth. "I was so happy—then it all crashed and burned. I lost you."

"Winter, I'm right here," he insists. He runs his fingers over my neck, examining my seatbelt-bruise. "You're pretty banged up, but I know how tough you are. There is no reason you should die from these injuries unless you decide to lie out here in the cold and just surrender. Don't you dare. Don't even think about it. Just hang on. The body is tied to the mind, and if you give up, your body will give up, too. Let me be your strength. I can take care of you, if you just let me. I can help you fight."

"Why should I let you?" I ask him, sliding my hand across his stomach.

"Because I'm blackmailing you," Liam tells me with a growl. "If you give up on me now, I'm going to take that gun out of your purse and pull a Grayson. I'm going to die here with you."

I frown at this, and my hand pauses just below his ribcage. "No way," I whisper. My fingers inch upward to feel his heartbeat. "You wouldn't."

"Wanna bet?" he says angrily. "How do you think I feel right now, Winter? I know I'm responsible for doing this to you. If you die, it will be entirely my fault. And I'll be condemned to live in a world without you. I think I have a lot of motivation for joining you."

"You have everything going for you," I tell him. "You have a great job. You have great friends. You have a great apartment, and all the money I gave you. You have a bright future ahead of you."

"Without you, I have nothing," he says softly. He presses his lips against mine forcefully. "Please stay with me." He kisses me again and again, growing more desperate. He holds me so tightly against him that it makes my injured bones ache. "I need you." His hot tears spill over my eyes as he puts his forehead against mine and lets his breath drift over my lips. "God, Winter. I love you so much."

"Liam," I murmur in astonishment. I have never seen him like this.

"I would give anything for you," he tells me. "I would burn everything I own for one more kiss."

I gaze up at him drowsily, wondering if this can be real. His hazel eyes are filled with sincerity and longing. I lift my fingers to trace the trail of tears on his chiseled cheek. It's hard to think that anyone could really ever feel this way about me, but when he is holding me like this and looking at me in this way, it is hard not to believe him. His outrageous words are sinking into my skin and infecting me with faith. It feels like he is wholly here with me, tightly wound together in the insanity of love.

"Will you stay?" he asks, tightening his grip on me. "I don't know what kind of vast cosmic paradise lies on the other side; but will you choose me over infinity?"

I smile at this question. Now that we have come to this point, our problems don't seem to mean much anymore. Money really doesn't matter when faced with questions of life or death. I can feel his love. I can see it etched in every line of his face, and staining the warm circles of his irises. I run my fingertips along his lower eyelashes, as though trying to read tiny sentences painted on each strand of hair.

"Okay," I whisper in agreement. "I'll stay with you. Take me home."

Liam sighs in relief as his body moves into action. When he places the photo albums in my lap, my arms move to hug them weakly against me. He grabs my purse before gently lifting me off the ground, and begins carefully walking up the slippery hillside that my car went plummeting down. As he climbs the steep incline, the sashaying motion lulls me to sleep. The world begins to drift farther and farther away from me, until I can't feel Liam's arms around me anymore. I hear Snowball barking in concern, but she sounds like she is miles away.

"Winter," Liam says in a demanding voice. "Winter. Come back. Stay awake."

I try to follow his voice, but there is only pain. I can't help trying to run away somewhere dark and quiet, where the pain can't reach me. In all that darkness, I think I see my mother. She looks more beautiful than she did in the painting. She is wearing a radiant white dress that shines with some kind of ethereal light. She looks young, and strong. She looks happy. She holds her arms out to me, beckoning me forward into her embrace. I want to go to her. I miss her so much, and I just want to be with her again. But I feel like there is a rope around me that won't let me go. A masculine voice tugs me back, over and over. I can't fight against it; and even if I could, I don't think I would want to.

"Look," Liam is saying as he kisses my eyelids gently. "The sunrise is breathtaking. Can you see it?"

Even the tiny motion of lifting my eyelids feels like a struggle. Now that it is getting brighter out, it is a little easier to make out the landscape. I realize that we are standing at the side of the road, near to Liam's car. He's right. The sunrise is more beautiful than before. I wish that I could live to see a thousand more sunrises by his side, but the considerable pain makes me unsure.

"I don't think I'm going to make it," I tell

him in warning. I don't want to disappoint him by dying after I've said that I would stay.

"You are," he tells me. "People live through worse every day. It may feel like the end of the world now, but you'll come out of this stronger than ever. You're a survivor, Winter. You're going to survive so that you can marry me."

My lips pull into a smile without my permission. "What makes you so sure?"

"I'm a betting man, and I'd bet everything on it," he tells me with conviction as he looks out at the horizon. "I'll spend every day trying to be a better man until I can win your trust back. And I'll never lose it again. Every day is going to be better; starting with today. We can begin again."

The sunbeams are falling gently on his face, and he looks as though he is being enlightened by them in an impossibly profound way. Every spectacular color is reflected in his eyes, and the rosy shadows of dawn dance across his olive skin. I was wrong. The sunrise wasn't the best sight I could possibly behold before closing my eyes for the last time—he is. He is a far more wondrous creation of nature, and I could stare at him forever. His eyes are filled with a genuine awe that is almost childlike, but they also hold the true appreciation of a grown man in their amber depths.

"Life is filled with pain," he tells me softly, "but you have to hang on. You need to endure the pain to earn the pleasure. Someday, you will give birth to a baby, and it's going to hurt even worse than this. But the pain doesn't last forever, and once it's over, you'll know that it was worth all the misery and heartache. Pain is the price of life."

He smiles down at me with such hope in his face that it brings tears to my eyes. I don't want to leave him now; I never wanted to leave him. Now that I know that he feels the same about me, I can't bear the thought of not being able to stay. But the pain still floods my head, even though he has lifted the agony from my heart.

"Just in case," I whisper, "you had better kiss me goodbye."

He shakes his head in refusal, tightening his grip on my limp body. He carries me around his car, and struggles to opens the passenger door while holding me. Once he manages this, he carefully places me inside and stacks the photo albums on the ground near my feet. Snowball barks cheerfully and jumps into my lap, happy that we have a shiny, new, undestroyed car to ride in. Her weight causes pain in my legs, but I don't care. I reach out to put my hand in her fur lovingly.

Liam pulls out the passenger seatbelt and leans over to firmly strap me in. I wince as it digs into the lower part of my bruise from the earlier seatbelt that crossed in the other direction. He looks down at me, staring silently for a moment.

CLARITY

His eyes are a delicious drizzle of honey within a warm glass of cognac. Finally, when he leans down to place his lips against mine, I discover that he tastes far sweeter than this. He kisses me in a manner that is both savage and sensitive. He kisses me with a thousand unspoken promises. The gentle pressure brings healing warmth to the cold and frazzled parts of my soul. He lets his lips linger there, as if we have all the time in the world. When he removes his mouth, he does so slowly, letting his warm breath drift over me.

"Just in case you couldn't tell," he says firmly, "that wasn't a goodbye kiss."

He slams the car door and begins moving around the vehicle.

I sink back into the seat with a dazed sort of satisfaction. I feel peaceful again. Somehow, his lips managed to steal away all of my pain. All I can feel is the phantom tingle of his touch, still comforting me. It's a little terrifying how much power he has over me. Did he somehow manage to give me the antidote for death? Or is this only a deceiving sort of numbness to make my last moments a bit more pleasant? Either way, it was excellent. Even if he didn't intend for that to be a goodbye kiss, I am quite positive that it must have ranked within the top five best goodbye kisses in history.

I hear him climbing into the driver's seat

as I let my head fall to rest against the cool glass of the window. "I'm sorry I never got to use the telescope with you," I tell him softly.

"Silly girl," he says in a teasing voice as he turns his key in the ignition. "Once you get better, I'm going to be using my telescope with you all night."

I remain still for a moment, but then the corner of my lips twitch slightly. This man! It's simply impossible to die around him when he's giving me so many reasons to smile. He really is some kind of genius; not everyone understands that next to love, laughter is the best medicine.

"Liam," I say in a tone of mock disapproval.

"I'll give you all the telescoping you can handle," he promises in a low voice. He reaches over to clasp my hand in his. "And I'll make sure that you see stars."

A Note from the Author

Thank you for reading *Clarity*! I really hope you enjoyed the story.

This was my first real attempt at writing contemporary romance, as I am used to writing fantasy/paranormal romance. More importantly, this was my first attempt at actually finishing a story. I have a lot of trouble letting go, and I usually write extremely long series that sweep through several generations. (If you would like to check out some of my other books, I also write as Nadia Scrieva.) I have been a bit more private than usual lately; writing under a new pen name was sort of like a fresh start for me, much the same way that Helen needed to change her name. I always put a lot of myself and my life into my stories, and the writing process gets far too emotional sometimes.

The ending of this book actually came from a story I wrote when I was fourteen years old. It was not a car crash, but a shipwreck, a very long swim, and a battle with sharks that caused my main character to be injured. As she lay on the beach, all bruised and bloody, she looked out at the sunrise as she was dying. She had this overwhelmingly beautiful moment—not only due to the development and affirmation of her love with the hero, but due to the peace and strength she seemed to find in herself. It was a really poignant depiction of love conquering death, and it meant a lot to me.

I wrote that scene twelve years ago, and I still think it was one of the best things I have ever written. Halfway through writing Clarity, I realized that I could not think of a better ending, and I really wanted a chance to revisit that beautiful scene in the sunrise, and rewrite it as an adult—with these new characters I have grown to love so much. I hoped that if it had the power to stay with me for all these years, maybe it could stay with you as well. Most of that old story is very juvenile and terribly written, but I put so much effort into writing that one chapter that it completely drained me. I actually didn't touch that story again for five years after writing that scene in the sunrise, and I later told people that I needed to "grow up a little more" in order to finish writing the story. I felt like my character had been through this life-altering event, and I didn't understand her anymore.

My writing is the most important part of my life, and my strategy has always been to constantly put myself into dangerous new situations as research. When I was younger, I used to walk around without my glasses or contacts in bad neighborhoods at night, to experience the fear that comes with having a complete lack of vision. I did this because I used to be heavily into martial arts, and I wanted to become more confident in myself and my skill, and toughen myself up. Even though it was a long time ago, I think those experiences might have impacted a lot of the scenes in *Clarity*. Sometimes I seek out these situations intentionally, and sometimes they happen by accident and it only becomes clear later on how they are important and can be used. Either way, I very grateful for the memories, and I love the mysterious way that they weave together to make something new when I write.

Back when I first wrote the original shipwreck-sunrise scene, I actually swam across a wide river with a strong current so that I could better describe how tired my limbs were and how scary it was to be alone in the middle of a body of water. Similarly, this time, the scenes where Winter is crying and driving through the mountains of Pennsylvania were taken almost directly from some of my experiences last year. Even down to the lightning storm illuminating the mountains. After being deeply betrayed and disrespected by *two* of my closest guy friends, I was in a terrible condition as I tried to get home to Canada. I actually had to stop at a little motel in Pennsylvania because I couldn't seem to stay on the road. When my friend followed me there to randomly *propose* to me, it only made things worse. Luckily, I escaped that whole situation with only a speeding ticket and some bad memories of beautiful landscapes experienced in a very emotional way.

I believe that imagination is the most important factor in writing, but I also think it's important to seek out crazy experiences to cultivate and train the imagination. I try to follow the advice to "write what you know," but I also write what I would like to know, and would like to become.

Again, thank you so much for reading my work!

I would love to hear your thoughts on the book, so please feel free to shoot me a message if there is absolutely anything you'd like to say. You can find all the methods of contacting me at the end of each book. Of course, reviews are also very welcome.

If you haven't already joined my mailing list, please be sure to sign up so that you can hear about my next book.

All the best,

Loretta Lost

Connect with the author:

Facebook: facebook.com/LorettaLost
Twitter: @LorettaLost
Website: www.LorettaLost.com
Email: Loretta.lost@hotmail.com

Made in the USA
San Bernardino, CA
22 December 2018